REVOLT AMERICAN STYLE

Fresh Start SeriesBook 1

DICK DOGGETT

REVOLT AMERICAN STYLE

ISBN 978 – 1 – 947664 – 00 – 5 (paperback)

This is a work of fiction. Names, characters, places, and incidents are products of the author's imagination or are used fictitiously and are not to be construed as real. Any resemblance to actual events, locales, organizations, or persons, living or dead, is entirely coincidental.

Prologue

The Criminal & His Daughter

Jet Taylor, age 62, is no ordinary criminal. Although still plying his trade, in his illicit career he has earned more bent nose money than all USA criminals combined. Add up all the money ever stolen, robbed or obtained by fraud in the United States of America since its founding in 1789. That's chump change, exceeded by Jet years ago.

Jet did not intentionally enter the criminal world. He did not seek out a life of crime. The criminal world sought him out. That world recruited Jet Taylor primarily because he possesses two crucial character traits: (i) intellect; and (ii) honesty. The criminals who recruited him venerate intellect and honesty among thieves.

Every man has a price. Two top tier capos determined Jet's price; offered Jet his price; then accorded Jet the opportunity to perform his magic, relying totally upon his allegiance. It worked for the thieves and it worked for Jet, beyond all expectations.

Ambivalently, along with a majority of his fellow American citizens, true blue expatriate Jet Taylor is convinced that the United States is totally fucked up, excoriated beyond repair. For several decades the Republic has been run by traitors, criminals, perjurers and thieves and is now morally, fiscally and militarily dysfunctional.

Pick a reason why. Yours is as good as mine. Jet's reason is the greed, dishonesty and gross incompetence of government officials. Jet is not willing to take it anymore. He intends to return America to its long-lost glory, the most important nation in history; more important than historical giants Greece, Rome, Great Britain and China, combined.

Since 1789, Jet Taylor is the only person with the intellect, the desire and more importantly, the wherewithal, to overthrow the government of the United States of America, by force. He has a dream; to bend America to his will for the good of all. Jet will prevail, come hell or high water.

*

Natalie Taylor is her name; catching criminals is her game. She is Jet Taylor's 39-year-old daughter, the number two guy in the FBI, America's Federal Bureau of Investigation. Under no circumstances will Natalie allow the government of the United States of America to be overthrown. It won't happen on her watch; she will die first.

Natalie is director and head knocker of a special joint task force charged with the responsibility of thwarting nuclear weapons criminal activity by an unknown treasonist.

With access to an unlimited budget, she uses every means available to the FBI and the CIA to search worldwide for the perpetrator, a wanted man subject to arrest. Natalie is unaware she is tracking her father. Policewoman she is, she will apprehend Jet Taylor; dead or alive.

Jet's federal moles inform him that Natalie is on his tail, tenaciously hunting him down. If Natalie catches Jet, there's a good chance she will kill him. If Natalie doesn't catch Jet, there's a good chance he will overthrow the United States government. The irresistible force versus the immovable object; perplexing for participants but delightful for everyone else.

1

WASHINGTON, DC
Colombian Drug Runners

On Sunday, September 9, 1990 Norlando Herrera and partner Octavio Benitez departed José María Córdova International Airport, near Medellin, Colombia, arriving at Baltimore - Washington International Airport (BWI) in the midafternoon. After clearing customs and immigration Norlando and Octavio rented a mid-sized Ford sedan and booked into a modest hotel on the eastern outskirts of the capital city of what was then the United States of America.

Early Monday morning the pair of successful drug dealers made a scheduled visit to the DC office of a small law firm specializing in international law. They departed the law office at 10:30 am, arriving thirty minutes later at 1819 H Street in downtown Washington, DC, a medium rise office building accommodating Taylor Aircraft Brokerage, Inc.

James Edward Taylor ('Jet' to his friends) anxiously awaited the pair of Colombians. They might be moving their business to another aircraft broker. That would revert Jet to square one, an economic disaster.

"Amigo, great to see you looking so good," said Norlando, amicably opening his pitch to Jet in first-class English, a mere hint of Spanish accent. A masculine European hug by both visitors preceded Jet's polite offer of refreshments.

Both Latinos opted for bottled water, 'con gas.' The three men shared a large bottle of Pellegrino. Jet was curious about two backpacks the criminal duo brought to the meeting. The bags rested inconspicuously in a corner of the spacious office, one small and one extra-large.

"May we have privacy, Señor Jet?" asked Norlando.

"Yes, of course, Norlando. Lucy, close my door and hold all calls regardless of ID."

"Yes, sir," replied Jet's secretary. Four visiting eyeballs locked on to the posterior view of an appealing feminine torso as it gracefully exited the office. *Have mercy on me.*

"Norlando, what's on your mind today? How can I help you?" asked Jet.

"Jet, I'm sure you know how Octavio and I make our living," said Norlando.

A quick study, Jet sensed conflict, "Norlando, I run a straight business. I provide quality aircraft brokerage services to buyers and sellers of used commercial aircraft throughout the world. Even though I lost my business partner in an automobile accident four years ago, I have been fortunate. My company has done reasonably well, perhaps because of me; perhaps because of the business climate; perhaps a little of both. At any rate, my brokerage business is 'ahead of the power curve.' Not bad for a 32-year-old."

"Norlando. we have known each other for over five years. Directly answering your question and in all fairness, respectfully, I could care less what you do for a living." Jet continued, on edge and uncomfortable, "I have no concern about activities of my customers, vocationally, avocationally, socially, whatever. As long as they don't violate any laws, rules, regulations or ordinances, for my purposes they are golden. Hopefully that's an adequate answer."

"Yes, Jet. Yes, it is. Bear with me, Señor. Let me share a melancholy story with you. For one thing, I am sure you know Octavio and I are partners in the drug business, operating out of South America."

Jet frowned, but said nothing. *Yes, I know; but no, until now I didn't believe you two criminals were aware of my knowledge. Damn, this is going to be tricky.*

"Amigo, we are successors to the original Medellin Cartel. We are legitimate experts in our business; successful beyond our wildest dreams. The old Medellin drug cartel is small potatoes compared to us. In gringo lingo, 'We make more money than Carter makes little liver pills.' I always liked that one."

"We are big time operators. So what? Collateral problems, that's what. Our bottom line has never been consistent with our gross income. We sell our products at a handsome profit but don't have much to show for it, the profit, that is. Never did, never have, and apparently, never will have much to show for our hard work. We intend to change that, right now. Work with us, Señor Jet."

Jet grimaced, gritting his teeth and cursing under his breath. *Work with us? What the hell does that mean, Work with us? I'm in over my head.*

"Octavio and I learned the hard way that we are the worst businessmen who ever walked the face of the earth. We make big money but we blow almost all of it away. Practically every financial decision we ever made turned to shit."

"My partner and I cannot handle money the way you can. We know nothing of sophisticated fiscal management; we know nothing of accounting, finance, investments, hedging, arbitrage, barter, present values, future values, and the like. We are muy stupido when it comes to handling money. That's where you come in, Jet."

Jet is now more than uncomfortable. He has visions not of sugar plums, but rather of FBI agents and Federal penitentiaries.

"We carefully screen everybody we deal with. One requirement is mandatory, no exceptions; competence with a capital 'C.' Truthfulness too, but that's hard to come by. Every which way we turn, we encounter liars, tricksters, blackguards, masters of the half-truth, and even downright thieves, con-men with slick tongues, all worthless."

"We have learned the hard way to deal exclusively with reliable, competent associates who know what they're doing. Sadly, few if any candidates we cross paths with have world class fiscal management skills, like you. Some have paid a heavy price for their infidelity, but frankly, dishing out punishment wastes time and money. Unfortunately, as I am sure you know, some of the bad guys, the worst ones, are no longer with us."

Jet is well aware of the mortality risk associated with crossing international drug dealers. Instant death is the norm. Their rule number one is 'Shoot first, ask questions later.' "Enough, Norlando. No more, please."

Norlando seized the moment, "I was certain you would cut me off, Jet." In Spanish, "Octavio, el pequeno bolso, por favor." (The small bag, please.)

Octavio retrieved the small backpack, carried it to Jet's oversized desk, opened it and casually emptied the contents of the bag onto Jet's desk.

Jet gasped. One million dollars in crisp new one hundred dollar bills bound in White Kraft Currency Bands manufactured and color-coded to Federal Reserve and ABA Standards, packed a thousand to the bundle. $100,000 per bundle; ten bundles in all. End on end the cash bundles equaled Jet's height, 6'3" tall, seventy-five inches. *Hells Bells, one million dollars, that's impressive!*

Jet was dumbfounded. Considering expenses and after paying his deceased partner's widow her share, in 1989 Jet took home $50,000 pre-tax. He knew it would take a good 20 years at current rate of income to accumulate one million after tax dollars. By then Jet will be over 50 years old, retirement rearing its ugly head. *Damn, Doubledamn.*

Jet leaned toward Norlando and smiled wryly, pain in his voice, "I can't do it, Norlando. I'm law abiding. I'm straight." Reluctantly declining the offer of one million dollars, Jet continued, "I have always been straight and always will be straight. Thank you, but damn it all to hell, I just cannot accept your money."

"You misunderstood, my friend. You already earned the money in front of you, and more. The creative aircraft financing devices you introduced to us is the envy of every non-scheduled commercial aircraft owner in the world. Every aircraft you sold to us performed as advertised."

"During our five-year relationship, your aftermarket service, your maintenance and your performance monitoring has been invaluable. In our dealings, you have always been upfront with us, candid I believe is your English word. We know we could not have achieved our success without your help."

"For instance, you took a financial hit when the Constellation, when the Lockheed 'Super Connie,' you sold to us turned up lame, one bad engine and severe hydraulic problems. You took the lemon back and refunded us the full purchase price towards a replacement aircraft. You ate your loss with dignity and honesty. We were sold on you from then on."

"Jet. you are important to our financial well-being. The bottom line is we want to double down on a good thing. For us, you are a good thing. We know we can trust you. Please listen to me, Jet. The money is yours. With your help Octavio and I know we can do better. We sure as hell can't do any worse."

Norlando could feel it slipping away, losing Jet's attention and boring him with details, drivel. *This is a greed sale. Get on it, Norlando,* he thought to himself. "Jet, my sad story would be mucho mas (much more) eloquent if I could speak to you in Spanish. It is hard to master your language. I am doing my best. All you have to do is listen and the money on the desk is yours. Fair enough?"

"Fair enough. It never hurts to listen," reasoned Jet, still amazed at what was going down in his modest office in downtown Washington, DC. *Will wonders never cease?*

"Thank you, amigo. The way we see it, we do all the dirty work. Your job is squeaky clean. We send you money and you manage it. The most important thing about our relationship is trust. Trust is everything."

"Here's the deal. Octavio and I continue our successful business. We retain and maintain a working capital reserve. We send you investment cash. You and you alone determine where to commit our funds. All stocks, bonds, derivatives, real property, commodities, whatever, are bought and sold in your name at your sole discretion. Financial decisions regarding investment identity, time of purchase and price, along with capital gains holding period and investment selling date and selling price are exclusively in your domain. You call the investment shots."

"Most important of all, you earn an immediate upfront cash commission of 5% of the gross (not the net that we convey to you) sales price of all drugs we sell. The 5% is yours to keep, to use as you so desire. Spend the money any way you want to, any time you want to, anywhere you want to."

"Understand that Octavio and I, along with our closely aligned compatriots, control over one half of the drug business in the western hemisphere, North, Central and South America combined. Depending upon who you talk to, 20% to 30% of the population of the United States routinely uses what is euphemistically referred to as 'recreational drugs.' Half of that business is ours."

"I won't dig too deep into it except to say that in the not too distant future your income before expenses will be in the range of one hundred million dollars per month, not per year, per month. This includes your 5% share of the gross, plus your share of profits from four or so new businesses, plus your aircraft brokerage business. Anticipate your immediate net income with us to be about five million dollars a month tax free. That commences at day one, today, right now."

"We have thought about this for some time. We suggest you consider creation of four new and different entities in whatever business form you desire, corporation, partnership, trust, what have you, for instance: (i) a non-profit international charity, perhaps a foundation;

(ii) an offshore bank, perhaps in the Caribbean; (iii) an international casualty insurance company, and last but not least; (iv) a for-profit private investment company, a holding company perhaps, domiciled in a Caribbean country, perhaps the Bahamas.

"All income in your companies will be termed 'non-domestic' and therefore not taxable by the foreign tax havens where you domicile your businesses. You will never again pay any income tax on any income you generate. I repeat, no tax, ever! We never pay taxes."

"Now, back to your share. In addition to receiving a 5% gross commission on all business, you may pay yourself whatever salary you believe is appropriate for running the four companies we suggest. We understand you will most probably continue to own and operate your aircraft brokerage company for your own account."

"For what you Anglos call 'exit strategy,' liquidation of the companies at a future date, you will receive one half of the net sales proceeds on the sale of the charity, the bank and the insurance company; 50/50, half for us, half for you. Our side will receive 90% of investment company liquidation proceeds, with 10% for you."

"Jet, to help you get started, we offer your aircraft brokerage business a five-year interest free loan of up to 20 million dollars. Straight away, as early as tomorrow, you have the economic ability to establish a used aircraft inventory to buy and sell commercial aircraft for your own account."

"We meet face up once a year. No paperwork, no balance sheet; no income statements. No audit trails. You trust us and we trust you. That's the deal, Jet."

"I can't do it, Norlando. I just can't do it," doom and gloom enveloping Jet's entire body. *How in the hell is this happening to me? Why me, Lord? Why me?*

"I understand, Jet. I anticipated you might turn us down." Norlando nodded toward his partner, "Octavio?"

In response Octavio toted the larger backpack over to Jet's desk, opened it and spilled 40 more bundles of 100 dollar bills on the desk, a few bundles falling to the floor. Smiling, while looking Jet straight in the eye, Norlando said, "There's your signing bonus; four million dollars; altogether five million, tax free. Not bad for a morning at the office, eh Amigo?"

Grimacing visibly, Jet's body, by itself and on its own, commenced a series of involuntary up and down, back and forth, head nods which he was unable to control. Orlando acknowledged with a smile and a hand wave. Never one to stick around after making a sale, he and Octavio departed Jet's office without delay, encouraging Midas to count his gold.

Jet salted away the currency. A boatload of desk files were relocated to make room for the cash. The Taylor Hierarchy was born in Washington, DC on September 10, 1990. The world was never the same thereafter.

2

JET TAYLOR
In the Chips

Regaining composure within the hour, Jet said, "Lucy, book me a round trip charter jet from Baltimore Washington International Airport (BWI) to Gibraltar International Airport (GIB) for tonight, departing at 8:00 pm; estimated time of arrival (ETA) in Gibraltar at 3:30 am Eastern Standard Time (EST), which is 9:30 hours Central European Time there."

"Ground time of six hours with a same day departure from Gibraltar for arrival back home to BWI early Wednesday morning at about 7:00 am local time."

"Wilco, Jet. (Aviation lingo for 'will comply') Confirmation in less than an hour. How do we pay?"

"American Express. Do we have $20,000 credit available?"

"Barely. To be precise, $21,644 with AmEx; five grand and change with Visa."

'AmEx it is. Press on."

*

Tuesday afternoon Jet Taylor bought a virgin Gibraltar 'shelf corporation' from a local attorney. Naming the corporation World Aircraft Brokerage, Ltd., Jet opened two new Gibraltar bank accounts for the one-day-old corporation, depositing $2,300,000 in one bank and $2,000,000 in another bank, both cash deposits.

Pursuant to traditional offshore banking customs, a non-related trustee provided by the attorney became the nominee 'owner' of the new corporation, with Jet as the only signatory on the bank accounts. Except for the bankers and lawyers, nobody knows or suspects that Jet owns World Aircraft Brokerage, Ltd., and has access to money in Gibraltar bank accounts.

Upon return to Washington, DC, Jet bought out his partner's widow with a half million dollar cash payment. No paper work. She was elated, pleased for herself and proud of Jet for keeping his hand-shake promise to her.

Later that day, Jet telephoned an acquaintance with whom he has done business for more than 10 years. Sam Bishop runs a one-man aircraft brokerage shop in Los Angeles, California.

"Sam, do you still have control of those nine Lockheed L-1011 airliners?"

"Is this Jet Taylor, a voice from the past?"

"It sure is, Sam."

"What's doin', my man?"

"I have a cash buyer for one of your birds, and might option the other eight."

"Cash, for an L-1011? Is he crazy?"

"Probably. The bid is 10% of asking price, and confidentially, negotiable up to 20%. You and I split the difference over 10%. My buyer is ok with that. A confidential closing statement will reflect that my buyer paid you and paid me a commission of 5% each, making this a 50% commission deal, half for you, half for me. My buyer pays 20% of asking price in cash. Your seller gets 10%; you and I split the other 10%."

"Like I said, Jet, I have control. Done on the cash offer for one bird. How about the options?"

"I want to clean you out. 15% offer on the other eight aircraft, closing one aircraft monthly for the next eight months. You and I each earn a 2.5% commission on each option purchase and sale. Same as before, except for the lower commissions; buyer pays 15% of asking price, all cash - 10% to the seller. You and I split the remaining 5%, half-and-half."

"Done."

Jet bought the nine used Lockheed L-1011 commercial jet aircraft. During the next year he sold each of the aircraft on credit to emerging African nations which had no scheduled airlines. Jet's average capital gain was 400% on aircraft purchase price; with no risk. African down payments in total exceeded Jet's cost of goods sold.

Interest rates well below market motivated the African buyers. The Africans were happy; they are now scheduled airline owners. Jet was happy. He is now a major international player in the purchase and sale of used commercial airliners.

All transactions closed in African nations. No taxes were incurred in Africa or in Gibraltar. Sales proceeds were deposited in a Gibraltar bank.

Jet's new casualty insurance company, All Risk Insurance Company, Ltd., insured each aircraft against physical harm, hull insurance. All Risk re-insured 95% of the hull risk through a Lloyd's of London syndicate.

Jet funded his new international bank, All Word Commercial Bank, NA with $4,200,000; $2 million of his own cash, plus nine secured aircraft purchase and sales promissory notes from the African nations, a market value of over $2,200,000.

3
JET TAYLOR
Bermuda – December, 2018

Nearly three decades later, Jet Taylor is de facto owner and CEO of the criminal 'Taylor Hierarchy.' He sits comfortably at an oversized mahogany executive desk in his elegant office, mulling how to spring his latest brainstorm on two senior executives.

"Imogene, page Harvey Pryor and Mike Hill. Tell them both to drop everything and report to my office post haste."

"Right away, Mr. Pennington," replied private secretary Imogene Harrelson.

Within five minutes Harvey Pryor and Frederick Stone ('Stony') Randolph, alias Mike Hill, knocked on the usually closed door to Jet's private office at the charity owned mansion/office.

"Come in, Gentlemen, come in," poker faced Jet nondescriptly greeting the crooked hierarchy's number two and number three executives.

Harvey Pryor, age 63, hired on 24 years ago in 1995, is a retired USAF fighter pilot. He graduated from the Air Force Academy in Colorado Springs, Colorado, class of 1974. An expert in business administration, Harvey is responsible for all aspects of hierarchy logistics and support. He is Jet's overall second-in-command, his most trusted, most valuable associate.

Stony Randolph, age 31, is a Canadian national with an electrical engineering degree from Syracuse University. He has worked six years for Jet. He rose through the ranks faster than any of the 561 employees in the hierarchy. Stony is the equivalent of Executive Vice President. He resolves all day to day business problems other than finance. Stony is Mr. Black Ops for the hierarchy.

Harvey and Stony are the only executives in the Taylor Hierarchy on a first name basis with Jet. Only Harvey and Stony know Jet's real name and the name of his alias for the charity, the bank and the insurance company, William Pennington. Only Jet knows Mike Hill's real name is Stony Randolph.

Harvey's tax free income for calendar year 2018 was ten million dollars. Stony's tax free income was three million dollars. Both men enjoy free room and board. They belong to a good union. Neither Jet, Harvey nor Stony own an automobile.

Harvey is married. His wife lives in Seattle. They enjoy conjugal holidays six to eight times a year at luxurious vacation locations throughout the world, Easter Island, Bali, Bangkok, Taj Mahal, Rio de Janeiro, Buenos Aires, London, Paris, Venice, St. Petersburg. You name it, the Pryors have been there.

Jet's appearance is stern, more severe than ever. Both executives sense something important on the horizon. Neither man knows Jet Taylor is poised to undertake a mission which has never before in the history of the United States of America been attempted. Many pretenders broached the challenge. None had substance. All hopefuls promoted futile ambition with superficial rhetoric. Jet is the real McCoy.

"Guys, listen closely and carefully. Because the Taylor Hierarchy is successful, I have the financial wherewithal to do damn near anything I want to do."

"Since I have the intellect, the ability and a burning desire, I intend to overthrow the government of the United States of America," pausing for effect, "by force." Harvey's internal organs cartwheeled. Stony took the proclamation in stride.

"I have a plan. No part of my plan has been implemented or reduced to writing. No one outside this room knows anything about my plan."

"Harvey, Mike, tell me whether you are in or out. Since this is a volunteer outfit, a show of hands is appropriate. Harvey, in or out?"

If I say out, I'm all the way out. If I say in, I'll be living a lie; working against America. I can't do it. If I say out, he'll kill me.

"In," said Harvey.

"In," echoed the young Canadian. He knows where his bread is buttered.

"Target date is April, 2021, two years and four months hence. I'll keep you advised of our progress. 'Fresh Start' is the name of the project. Are there any questions?" Jet asked the two criminals.

"There being no questions, that's all I have for now."

If Jet is successful, he will be recognized throughout the realm as the savior of America. Should he fail, he will doubtless be executed as a common criminal and buried in a pauper's grave, a Hitler, ToJo, Jefferson Davis or Rommel example of high stakes loser.

Harvey and Stony departed the office without formality. No goodbyes, no handshakes, no nothing; except concern as to whether they will be dead or alive two years from now. If alive, will they be incarcerated? If in jail, will it be pursuant to a life sentence?

*

Jet Taylor lives and works in Windsor, the capital city of Bermuda. He is engaged in the lucrative business of money laundering and investment of 'Clean Funds' created thereby. Although he is not a drug dealer, he manages half of the profits of illegal drug sales in the western hemisphere. His customer pool is 860 million strong, 370 million in North America, 45 million in Central America and 445 million in South America.

Jet earns 5% of the gross sales price of one half of every dollar paid for drugs in the western hemisphere. In December, 2018, his gross drug income was $280 million, netting him $240 million tax free, for the month.

His four offshore business activities: (i) a charity; (ii) a commercial bank; (iii) a casualty insurance company; and (iv) an aircraft brokerage firm, net a shade over 60 million dollars each year, including salary and capital gains. His yearly discretionary income is two billion eight hundred eighty million ($2,880,000,000) dollars.

Over 30 years have passed since Jet threw in with South American drug runners as their money-launderer and investment advisor in chief. Eight years ago, he reached a milestone, becoming the richest man in the world.

Jet's net worth as of December 31, 2018 was just over two hundred forty three billion ($243,000,000,000) US dollars. Jeff Bezos of Amazon is closest, with a net worth of over one hundred ten billion ($110,000,000,000) US dollars. Bill Gates is third at ninety-five billion ($95,000,000,000) US dollars.

He owns a 100% interest in the Aircraft Brokerage Business; along with a 50% interest in the Charity, the Bank and the Insurance Company. He owns a 10% interest in an Investment Company, which is otherwise unrelated to the other businesses. For descriptions:

THE CHARITY - One New World, Ltd., a Liechtenstein trust with home office in Hamilton, Bermuda and offices throughout the industrialized world, is the largest international charity in the world. The charity is primary cover for Jet Taylor's illicit money laundering operations. Gross assets: 300 billion dollars; Net Worth: 70 billion dollars; 21 offices; 356 Employees. Although diverse, the charity specializes in the health and welfare of females, young and old.

The charity accepts deposits every day from sources throughout the world, some of which is 'Clean Money' (actual charitable contributions) and some of which is 'Dirty Money' (drug sale proceeds), to be laundered. 'Clean Money' is ledgered into a charity 'operating account' in the hierarchy bank. 'Dirty Money' hits a charity 'transition account' in the bank.

THE BANK - All World Commercial Bank, NA, a Cayman Islands Corporation with home office in George Town, Cayman Islands and branches in Zurich, Switzerland; London, England; Hong Kong, China; Nassau, Bahama Islands; and Hamilton, Bermuda. Gross Assets: 135 billion dollars. Net Worth: 24 billion dollars; 6 offices; 38 Employees. The bank emphasizes commercial loans, letters of credit and foreign currency brokerage.

The bank wires 'transition account' money is to a third-party Bahamas Investment Account "owned" by Jet Taylor. Thereby 'Dirty Money' in the bank becomes 'Clean Money' in the Bahamas. On a regular basis, bank books and records are adjusted to 'erase' any evidence of 'Dirty Money' deposits and 'transition account' conveyances. Two sets of bank books are maintained, one for the house and one for bank examiners.

All parties at all levels of the drug related financial transactions are fastidiously mindful of exposure to risk of harm, of outsiders learning about the money-laundering scheme. Chicanery at its best. Recall Balzac's quotation, 'Behind every great fortune there is a crime.' Ask the Kennedy family about bootlegging.

THE INSURANCE COMPANY - All Risk Insurance Company, Ltd.; a Turks & Caicos corporation with home office in Hamilton, Bermuda and other offices in London and Hong Kong. Gross Assets: 100 billion dollars. Net Worth: 20 billion dollars; 4 offices; 63 Employees. The insurance company is straight, lending credence to the charity and bank.

THE AIRCRAFT BROKERAGE COMPANY - World Aircraft Brokerage, Ltd, a Gibraltar Corporation with home office in Turks & Caicos and branch offices in London, Paris and Hong Kong. Gross Assets: 122 billion dollars; Net worth 36 billion dollars; 5 offices; 45 Employees. The aircraft brokerage company is Jet Taylor's original straight business and has remained straight over the years.

THE INVESTMENT COMPANY - Caribbean Traders, Ltd,

a Cook Islands trust with home office in St John's, Antigua. Gross Assets: 1.57 trillion dollars; Net worth 1.5 trillion dollars; 2 offices; 35 Employees. Jet parks drug money profits in various "Investment Company" accounts throughout the world. He manages all the accounts and once a year advises Colombia of the status of the accounts., in full but not individually.

Jet's net worth as of December 31, 2018 is presented below in amounts of millions of dollars, i.e. overall the charity is worth 70 billion dollars. Jet's 50% share is worth 35 billion dollars, which is represented on the chart as $35,000 (thirty five thousand million dollars).

Charity	$ 35,000
Bank	$ 12,000
Insurance	$ 10,000
Aircraft Brokerage	$ 36,000
Investment Company	$150,000
JET'S TOTAL NET WORTH (243 billion dollars)	$243,000

*

A 'true blue' military veteran, over the years Jet Taylor watched America slowly but surely deteriorate. In the beginning, he was certain American leaders would eventually 'right the ship' and revert government practices, policies and procedures to the 1950 – 1960 era of greatness and prosperity. Not a chance; it never happened.

Instead, the fiscal debt spiral which commenced to entrap the USA in the 1950's intensified geometrically over the years, interfering with the ability of the United States to function normally. As of 2018, the amount of American government debt exceeded the

America gross domestic product (GDP, the value of all goods and services consumed in 2018). This is not a good sign, not good at all. Downright dangerous, as a trend. Alarming as a fact.

Although Jet is an expatriate he remembers with nostalgia and melancholy the days and times when America was at its zenith. He despises the socialistic welfare state which the United States has become. He loathes political correctness and everything former Presidents Johnson, Nixon, Carter, Bush I, Bush II, Clinton and Obama, among others, fostered upon the American public, the American taxpayers.

Regarding the methods by which the Government of the United States administers the laws of the land, Jet cannot understand and does not accept, without limitation:

1. Quantitative Easing, the watering down of the value of the US dollar;
2. Unwillingness to control US national borders;
3. Unwillingness to enforce federal laws on the books.
4. Unwillingness to balance the budget and pay down the national debt;
5. Unwillingness to deport all illegal aliens, forthwith;
6. Obamacare and its progeny;
7. United Nations membership.
8. Favoritism (coddling) of Islamists in general and tolerance of Islamic terrorists;
9. X-fer of 158 billion dollars to Iran in return for a worthless 'no–nuke' promise;
10. Trading five enemy generals (equivalent) for an enlisted private, a deserter;
11. Political correctness in any form;
12. Affirmative action;

13. Unearned welfare payments, i.e. food stamps, earned income credits;

14. Queers and lesbians in general, especially homosexuals in the armed forces;

15. Same sex marriages and transgender preferential treatment;

16. Unwillingness to require photo ID to vote in national elections.

*

Jet will resolve every USA problem; political, economic, immigration, military, legal, health, banking, manufacturing, human rights, foreign relations, education, you name it. He will resolve those problems by force. He knows the only way America is going to change is 'out with the old and in with the new.' Jet has a strong broomstick.

Politicians must be driven from their posts by muskets; on the business end of pitchforks. There is no other way. Every logical, objective thinker knows there is no other way. If this does not happen, the USA will continue for a few more decades to die a slow death, each year more miserable than the last. Deep down, every reader of this book knows that something is wrong with the United States of America and that the American government caused or allowed the wrong to occur and to fester out of control.

Since Jet has the ability and the wherewithal to do so, he has taken it upon himself to assemble and supervise a group of latter day patriots to overthrow the government of the United States of America, to become undisclosed CEO of an interim martial law government, and to transition the new nation ('America') to the former glory of its heyday, circa 1945–1965.

In 2018 Jet devised a plan to use his vast fortune in an effort to overthrow the government of the United States of America within the next two years, by and through the use and application of militia forces, in being and under his de facto control.

Major loose ends are selection of an American target site and acquisition of a nuclear weapon. According to plan, within two years Jet's team of over 200,000 experienced, paid patriots will be combat ready, on one-week alert for T-Day, (Target Day, atom bomb delivery day).

To a man the troops are anxious to deploy; anxious to revolt, anxious to destroy the feckless government of the United States of America, anxious to engage in project 'Fresh Start.' Small minded, weak politicians in charge of the American government fail to detect and realize there is a tremendous amount of unrest in America. Jet is cashing in on that unrest.

He has committed more than ten billion dollars to acquire and posture conventional weapons, ordnance, vehicles, technical equipment, supplies and personnel in amounts and quantities necessary to reasonably ensure success of the revolt. His budget envisions expenditure of an additional thirty billion dollars during the next two years. He is ready, willing and able to commit his entire fortune, even his life, to the cause of restoring America to glory.

Jet opposes the strongest force ever assembled, the United States military. He knows it is oblivion for either him or them. He intends to neutralize and eliminate Democrats, Republicans, the Establishment, naysayers, constitution violators, treason committers, federal lawbreakers, criminals, mainstream media and the like.

Jet is on the side of right. He knows the white collar, modern times, self-styled Robin Hood rapists who pillaged and destroyed the American way of life have had their day in the sun, their 15 minutes of fame, and shall be banished from the face of the earth.

He is optimistic he can overthrow the government of the United States by force. The odds against him are long. In 250 years not only has the United States government never been overthrown; more importantly, no one has tried to overthrow the government by force, successfully or unsuccessfully. Jet's attempt will be the first. Will he succeed? Or is he Guy Fawkes incarnate?

The time to strike is ripe. A sizable number of Americans recently polled believe military dictatorship in the form of martial law is preferable to democracy as practiced by Democrats and Republicans who control the government of the United States of America.

Will Jet prevail where no one else has ever toed the line, on a mission no one else has ever attempted? Money and military assets will not be enough. Guile and chutzpa of the highest order are required. Jet is blessed with guile and plenty of chutzpa. Either he lives in fame or goes down in flame. Which? Who knows? Time will tell.

4
ESTILL BARNES
Bermuda – October, 2020

Thirty five years ago, Estill Barnes and Jet Taylor were First Lieutenants, young officers in a tactical fighter Wing in the United States Air Force (USAF). Jet was a rookie fighter pilot in a Tactical Fighter Squadron and Estill was a junior Wing maintenance officer, in charge of keeping fighter aircraft combat-ready, providing maintenance, repair and parts. Estill 'kept 'em flying,' good days and bad. The pair became drinking buddies, lifetime fast friends.

Neither officer was an Air Force careerist, a 'lifer.' Estill returned to civilian life after four years in the service. Jet remained on active duty in the Air Force for seven years, plus an additional seven more years as a part-time pilot in the Air National Guard.

T-Day is six months down the road. Estill Barnes is the main man in Jet's 'Fresh Start' personnel chart. He is responsible for recruitment of militia personnel, for management of and expenditure of funds associated with ginning up the 200,000 man militia force and for acquisition and servicing of various and sundry military equipment required by the militia to do their job as they overthrow the American government.

Of critical interest is the mindset and posture of senior military commanders after martial law is declared, on or about April 5, 2021. What will the Army do when the government experiences an overthrow attempt?

Estill is responsible to forecast opponent's responses and respond to same on the fly, in real time. No small feat. Estill's performance is critically essential to 'Fresh Start.' As Estill goes, so goes 'Fresh Start.'

He has an MBA from the Wharton school of business and is a retired senior executive of Delta Air Lines, a maintenance and repair expert. Estill is from Missouri; a no nonsense; opinionated, rough around the edges, brilliant logistician. He is 63 years old. Jet trusts Estill with his money and with his life.

*

"Welcome to Bermuda, Estill. I don't expect another office visit from you in the near future."

"Suits me, Jet. Been here two hours. I already have island fever."

"Reminder, my name is Bill Pennington around here."

"Sorry."

"No problem. Comes with the territory. Let's get down to business. In the next few minutes we meet with Wayne Spenser, our head banker. Wayne has been fully briefed. He is reliable, experienced and knowledgeable. He becomes your direct subordinate as of one month prior to T-Day, relocating to the contiguous United States at a location selected by you, to work for you as required, for as long as necessary. By the way, for tenure, can you handle T-Day plus two years with my option for another year?"

"Yes, I'm good for two years, plus a one-year option."

"Perfect. Remember, Wayne knows me as Bill Pennington."

"I won't forget," said Estill as he removed two documents from his oversized briefcase and handed one of them to Jet.

"These 300 page T-Day 'Schedule of Events' planning documents are identical. The one in your hand is yours to keep. The document contains day-by-day duties, responsibilities and instructions for each of our military line commanders and management/technical specialists, addressing the first 90 days of American Martial Law."

"Instructions are essentially mandates, subject to change during the heat of battle. Instructions apply to platoon commanders, all the way up to Generals. Duties addressed are operational, support, supply, communications and intelligence, among others."

"It's all there, an itemization of all tasks, assignments, obligations and responsibilities for each and every important party and unit involved in 'Fresh Start.' If our Army executes as anticipated, we will control a majority of American society no later than April 12, 2021."

"That's promising, Estill," said Jet.

"You did not ID your two generals. T-Day is only six months down the road."

"True. I will ID both generals no later than two weeks prior to T-Day, along with respective command post locations."

"Is that cutting it close?"

"Perhaps. The dates are estimated. I'll come in early."

"Fair enough."

"Estill, tell me the initial 'Fresh Start' activity out of the blocks. What comes first?"

"Swear in the successor President."

"Who does that and where?"

"At Minneapolis, by Judge Sam Williston, swearing in Secretary of Labor Brewster Ganley as successor president of the United States of America."

"And after that?"

"Up to you. First, new President Ganley anoints your chosen general as commander of American Martial Law forces. Second, depends upon whether or not you immediately nuke the bad guys that we will claim destroyed an American target city."

"If we do not execute a first day retaliatory nuclear strike, a number of agenda items compete for first event out of the starting gate, including but not limited to bank closures, national curfew, Islamic restrictions, UN withdrawal, IRS closure, termination of personal income taxes, etc. The ball's in your court, Bill," said Estill as he shared a coy smile with Jet.

Jet smiled back, "You always were a smart ass, Estill," then admiringly, "Great job as usual."

"Estill, one of my generals asked me about the legitimacy of his command-and-control over state militias as of T-day. He didn't like my response. In retrospect, I didn't like my response either. Please review with me your understanding of federal law as relates to the legitimacy of our personnel exerting hegemony over the militia of each state on T-day, along with the resulting organized and united national militia exercising control over the United States of America."

"Sure. Listen closely, you dumb ass," smiled Estill, the only man in the world who can talk like that to Jet Taylor and get away with it. With a closed lip smile, Jet conceded the podium.

"Any problem with the history of the Militia of the United States of America, from pre-revolutionary times until today?"

"Nope; that history bullshit is not important to me. I'm concerned about the legitimacy of our militia in taking control of the country."

"OK, then, a brief review, very brief. Originally, the militia, 1776. Two kinds of soldiers, the regulars and the militia. Highest number of American soldiers under foot at any one time during the revolutionary war was 90,000."

"Yeah, yeah, I get all that shit, Estill, cut to the chase."

"Antsy pants, that's for sure. Tally ho, the fox, to the chase, milord." Jet smiled.

"Two kinds of soldiers in 1776; three kinds of soldiers now: (i) regulars, including extended active duty reservists; (ii) inactive duty reservists (that includes all national guardsmen); and (iii) the militia of each state.

"Federal law regarding militia nomenclature and militia

responsibilities has evolved; has changed. The term militia is anti-quated and hardly ever used anymore; the term 'militia' is totally avoided by the media and the congress. The new term for the militia is State Defense Forces (SDF)."

"To some extent SDF's are regulated by the National Guard Bureau. SDF's are commanded by governors of states, 23 of which states have active SDF's. The other states are authorized to create and maintain SDF's, but have elected not to do so. Those states are carried on the rolls as inactive."

"32 United States Code section 109 recognizes SDF's. Subsection (e) gives us a hiccough. It mandates that 'A person may not become a member of a defense force******if he is a member of a reserve component of the Armed Forces.' We disregard that obscure limitation by our self-determination that SDF personnel are not reserve component members of the Armed Forces."

"Another problem is that the governor of each of the 23 SDF's is in control of his state's SDF. Governors of 17 states have agreed in writing that our man, the state SDF ranking general officer, may assume command and control over his state's SDF in the event of an emergency. We own those generals. On T–Day we shall declare an emergency and assume command of each of those 17 state SDF's. Regarding the six other states, we shall incapacitate each of the six governors and timely assume command of those six SDF's."

"Hopefully that's a sufficient review, Jet."

"Yes, it is. Nobody could have done it better, Estill. Don't die on me, man. I need you more than you need me. Should I croak today, you could press on. If you croak today, I'm in deep shit."

I've known that for some time, Jet. "One final question, compadre."

"Have at it, Estill."

"Out of curiosity, what if you're wrong? If you are wrong, it appears to me that the collateral cost of your error will be two to three million dead and maimed Americans. By my reasoning, that's a hell of a risk. I know you, Jet. I know you're a serious man; you don't speculate; you don't fuck around; you're not a jokester, a trickster or a hail fellow well met. Why are you willing to kill millions of Americans on the if-come? I don't get it."

"That's the $64,000 question, Estill. I'm doing what I'm doing because it's a sure thing, a sure bet, the only variable is when, not if."

"Take a look at world affairs. Ten countries are now armed with delivery capable nuclear weapons. From all indications, more and more nations will come on board, countries which over time will become armed with nuclear weapons capable of long-range delivery to any target, anywhere in the world, day or night, 24/7."

"With that in mind, I ask you, Estill, what country in the world is the most hated?"

"Easy, us; the United States of America. Obviously, because almost all the other countries are have-nots and we are the ultimate 'have' country, the richest country in the history of the world, 5% of the world's population consuming 30% of the world's energy, for instance. Everybody hates us. If they don't hate us, they envy us to the extent of hatred."

It clicked for Estill, "I get it. You don't need to explain anything else to me. I see that the first chance they get, the fucking Islamists will nuke New York City. For sure, within five years the Muslims will destroy Manhattan, just as soon as they get their bastard hands on an atomic weapon. Hell, it could happen as early as tomorrow. You're beating the SOB's to the punch."

"I see it clear as hell. Imagine New York City being obliterated tomorrow. What would socialist ignoramuses like the governor and mayor of New York do? Even if they could do something, the dumb ass bastards would sit on their asses, suck their thumbs, lamenting and cursing the fate that dealt them a losing hand, and pontificate. Oh, boy, would they pontificate. Press releases, one and all: 'Hold fast, America,' plus 'We will prevail, America,' and 'We won't let them get away with this, America,' worthless pontification, trash talk by trash politicians."

"With rare exception, American government leaders at all levels are hopeless pacifists. There's no way in hell our leaders will do anything other than verbally malign unknown Islamist assailants who destroy New York City, urging citizens to passively resist, knowing full well the only acceptable opposition is to kill them before they kill us."

"Long-term, defenders always lose. If you don't go on offense; in time, your nation is doomed, dead meat, a target practice bulls-eye. Look at Europe. Essentially Muslim. Hardly a shot fired. Oral resistance limited to encouraging citizens to 'keep an upper lip' while continuing to volunteer them as soft targets for random Islamic terrorist attacks."

"Germany, Belgium, France, Sweden, all pacifist losers; all surrendering hegemony to Goddamn sharia law loving, mother fucking Islamists. If you see an Islamic terrorist, you damn well better cut his head off before he cuts yours off. You want to reason with him, talk with him; he wants to kill you, kill you dead. Think about that, America."

"I see what you're doing, Jet. I understand why you have a lot of money in the bank; you're bright; you have foresight, knowledge, instinct and a willingness to engage the enemy. What you're planning is well worth the risk. I'm all in, as you very well know."

"By destroying an American city now, rather than waiting for the Islamists to destroy it, you control post-attack casualty assistance and effectively posture America to defend itself, simultaneously garnering volunteer assistance of citizens, soldiers and even the media. Genius, pure genius."

Jet acknowledged with a nod, reassured that Estill is the right man for the job.

*

"Mr. Pennington, Wayne Spenser is here to see you," sounded the intercom.

"Send him in, Imogene."

"Wayne, please meet Estill Barnes, soon to be your new boss."

"I am pleased to meet you, Mr. Barnes."

"It's my understanding you selected a new US currency design, said Estill.

"Yes, sir. The new bills are in denominations of Five, Ten, Twenty, Fifty, One Hundred and One Thousand Dollars. No one dollar bills. They are extinct. One dollar and two dollar coins are being minted as we speak; they will be in circulation within two to three months."

"The country is to be divided into six regions. Each region will have a bank. Each regional bank will receive an initial shipment of new US currency the day following T-Day, totaling in all, three trillion new American dollars."

"That much?" questioned Estill.

"Yes, sir. Continuing on, we scheduled a Bank Holiday for one week, commencing with T-Day. On T-Day plus eight days, selected banks will reopen. Since ATM's will not close, they will be continuously restocked during week number one with old dollars."

"Old US Currency will be honored for 90 days. Old US Currency is eligible for exchange in person only, in the United States and its possessions exclusively, by individuals only, for a period of 90 days after T–Day. No money exchange is authorized by corporations, partnerships, associations, etc.; only for individuals, only in person, only in the USA, and only at a federal bank controlled by us. As of T-day +1, our militia will be in control of all banks in the United States."

"After 90 days, old US dollars will be worthless; good for wallpaper, little else. Conversion is limited to 250,000 old dollars per person, exchanged at a rate of one new dollar for one old dollar. Of course, all this depends to a certain extent upon the deactivation and closing of the Federal Reserve Banking System," said Wayne Spenser.

"The Federal Reserve Bank and its branches will close on T–Day, gentlemen," said Jet. "Estill, gotta go. This is October. Our next meeting will be near you in the continental US no later than early February. Imogene will arrange for your transportation to the airport. It's been good hosting you."

"I'll see you then, Bill. Take care," said Estill as he departed Jet's office.

"What say you, Wayne?" asked Jet.

"I'm impressed, Mr. Pennington."

"In what city do you want to establish our national Bank, specifically home office whereabouts and under what name?"

"Our new 'American Bank' opens in Charlotte, North Carolina, in facilities now occupied by the current Bank of America."

"Why?"

"That's my hometown, Mr. Pennington."

"Okay by me."

5
NASSAU
the Target – January, 2021

On Monday, January 4, 2021, a Gulfstream G650 jet aircraft, Bermuda registration number VQ-BRB, was number one for takeoff, a brand spanking new commercial jet aircraft featuring entrepreneur Jet Taylor at the controls from the left seat of General Dynamic's most recent 'lead the fleet' offering.

Eleven days ago, VQ-BRB rolled off the assembly line at Savannah, Georgia. She was processed under Bermuda registration protocol with minimum delay, lawyers working overtime. The owner of the Gulfstream G650 is a charity, One New World, Ltd.

Gulfstream's latest model goes by two names, the Gulfstream G650 or the Gulfstream VI. A rare beauty, our bird has a total of 12 flying hours entered in her log book, with an MSRP of a cool 75 million dollars, paid in cash on the barrel head.

The airplane is capable of hauling eight people a distance of 7,000 nautical miles one way. Representative non-stop journeys feature New York to Tokyo; Los Angeles to New Zealand or London to the Philippine Islands, among others.

Gulfstream VI flight controls respond to touch like a friendly kitten. When her twin Rolls-Royce BR725 engines whine and roar, she resembles a wild mustang aching to romp playfully over hill and dale, hither and dither, power to burn, all bases covered, not a care in the world, dusk to dawn. Quite a machine, the Gulfstream VI.

If you believe the journey is the destination, the Gulfstream G650 is your baby. She transforms a pilot's vocation into an avocation. When work is play, arguably one has maxed out Maslow's hierarchy of needs, attaining that ever elusive commodity, self-actualization. Such is life for a Gulfstream G650 pilot. Maxed out.

Jet Taylor loves the Gulfstream G650, loves the air she flies in and loves the ground she returns to. A lifelong love affair with airplanes, validated by knowledge, planning, training, experience and performance, many times over.

Aviation is not entirely risk free; hours and hours of boredom interrupted by moments of sheer, stark terror. Pilot's adage of the ages: 'There are old pilots and there are bold pilots; but there are no old, bold pilots.'

Jet was the number one graduate of his USAF (United States Air Force) pilot training class and the number one academic graduate of his USAF advanced fighter pilot training class. He managed to survive one in-flight seat ejection and a separate mid-air collision. He has a reputation as an outstanding "stick," the ultimate pilot tribute.

As is Jet's custom, perhaps even habit, prior to every takeoff he muses internally regarding the subject of death. Today he thought to himself. I *wonder if this is the day I shall die. Perhaps so, perhaps not. If so, I shall die with my boots on, doing what I want to be doing. The loss to the world will be no more than a bucket of water bailed from the ocean.*

Let's see, about 93 per cent of all the people who ever trod the surface of the earth are dead. The 7 billion or so souls living today represent only seven per cent of all the men and women who ever lived, an estimated 93 billion graves and counting.

160,000 deaths per day, 357,000 births per day; 60 million deaths per year, 130 million births per year. Malthus was correct. We are fornicating ourselves into oblivion. Soon we shall run out of food, unable to sustain unbridled instinct to replicate. Alas.

The weather is almost always perfect in the Bahamas. At noon on this early January Monday the temperature is 75 degrees Fahrenheit with relative humidity of 85%. The sky condition is CAVU, clear and visibility unlimited, with the exception of a few cotton ball cumulus clouds at 1,500 feet above New Providence Island's primary aerodrome, Lynden Pindling International Airport, 18 miles west of Nassau.

Although he is flying shotgun from the copilot right seat, charity Chief Pilot Bubba Jasper signed the International Civil Aviation Organization (ICAO) instrument flight plan as pilot in command. Bubba is always relegated to de-facto copilot status when his boss flies Bubba's aircraft 'hands on.' Bubba cannot recall the last time he manned the controls for even an instant when he was on board a flight with Jet. Bubba is a retired U.S. Navy Commander and a former fighter pilot.

On Very High Frequency (VHF) 118.3 megahertz, Bubba transmitted, "Roger, VQ-BRB cleared to Havana, radar vectors to flight level 310," as he acknowledged receipt from Nassau Departure Control of clearance for the Gulfstream G650's intended flight from Nassau, Bahamas, to Havana, Cuba at 31,000 feet altitude. Jet is on his way to attend a conference where the only subject on the table is purchase and sale of nuclear weapons.

By policy the charity does not fly directly from Bermuda to Cuba. Today's first flight leg departed Bermuda in the mid-morning, with interim landing at Nassau International Airport; followed by this leg, departing Nassau for Havana at noon.

Jet carries two passports, William Pennington from Bermuda to Nassau, then on to Havana. Jet will clear Cuban immigration as Enrique Echeverria, his nuclear weapons acquisition alias.

Señor Echeverria will depart Havana tomorrow in the early evening and will emerge in the Bahamas as William Pennington. Mr. Pennington will continue on from Nassau to Bermuda. Bubba knows Jet

33

as William Pennington. He refers to Mr. Pennington as 'boss.' Bubba has never heard of Enrique Echeverria. International intrigue as usual.

*

Having completed pre take-off checklist items, Bubba and Jet are holding short of active runway 32 pursuant to Nassau Tower instructions. Two triple spool turbojet engines idle at slightly over 7,000 RPM each. Both pilots bask in the 'new car' smell of the Gulfstream dream machine.

"VQ-BRB, taxi into position and hold," barked Nassau Tower on VHF 119.5.

"VQ-BRB, Roger," responded Jet, whose right hand cradled both center mounted paired throttles, easing the throttles gently forward, coaxing the Gulfstream G650 toward the active runway from its 'hold short' position.

The Gulfstream taxied into takeoff position, stopping precisely at dead center of the downwind end of active runway 32, ready for takeoff to the northwest into the prevailing wind. Ten seconds later Nassau tower handed the Gulfstream off to Departure control and authorized takeoff, "VQ-BRB, change to frequency 125.3. Cleared for takeoff runway 32, winds north at 10 knots; altimeter 30.05."

"VQ-BRB, Roger, Nassau, 125.3, VQ-BRB cleared for takeoff," responses repeated by Jet a thousand times over during his past 35 odd years in professional aviation.

Acting copilot Bubba Jasper switched the VHF channel to frequency 125.3 as Jet simultaneously eased both throttles full forward to maximum engine rotation speed of over 16,000 RPM, causing the 80,000 pound behemoth to slowly commence acceleration down runway 32.

At 30 seconds after 17:00 GMT (noon local Bahamian time, same as EST) and at rotation speed of 120 knots, Jet exerted mild back pressure on the active control sidestick and observed the aircraft take itself off. Takeoffs are easy. Landings are a different story.

Destiny looms - sooner rather than later.

6
NASSAU
the Kill

Earlier that day a charter jet from Cancun, Mexico made a 9:00 am touchdown at Lynden Pindling International Airport. After clearing Bahamian customs and immigration, Angel Lopez and companion Enrique Martinez rented a full-size Nissan sedan under the alias Angel used to clear immigration.

On the airport's eastern perimeter road Angel drove north and slightly east for about four miles, where the Nissan intercepted West Bay Street, the east-west arterial road parallel to the Atlantic Ocean on the north coast of New Providence Island. Driving on the left side of the road was unfamiliar but not as uncomfortable as one might think.

From the point on West Bay Street where Love Beach becomes Cable Beach, Angel drove east precisely four miles, stopped the Nissan on the left (north) side of the road and waited for his contact.

While waiting, Angel mused, *Amazing. Shades of 9/11. At this rate, we can destroy everybody's economy, just missile the hell out of them at ten thousand dollars per launch until they run out of money to build more multimillion-dollar airplanes, much less feed themselves. Economics 101, Mexican-style.*

Send every fertile Mexican Latina to California, Arizona, New Mexico and Texas, all presumably illegal aliens. Fornicate day and night, pursuant to and supported by, without limitation, food stamps, free medical, earned income credit and other typically Democrat benefits.

Continue fornicating day and night until American born anchorbaby Mexicans reach voting age in an amount sufficient to bloodlessly 'overthrow' the existing United States government by majority vote; legal in its entirety, absent a single ounce of force. We are going to fuck you to death, America, on your nickel. Te Amo, America, I love you America.

Brown power! Brown power! Brown power! Screw you, you old white bastards. We are going to take your God damn country away from you and jam it up your ass.

*

At 10:15 am a swarthy mixed-race Bahamian in his mid-40s appeared out of thin air on the north side of West Bay Street, cryptically emerging from a stand of indigenous Bahamian bushes. Consistent with the Assassination Plan, Swarthy wore a red baseball cap. Angel held his ground and awaited developments.

A minute later a 15-year-old ramshackle green Dodge pickup truck appeared from the east, drove past the Nissan, made a U-turn and after backtracking parked five feet in front of the Nissan. The truck payload consisted of a large cardboard box, seven feet in length; three feet in width; and two feet in depth, more or less.

Angel and Enrique approached the contact. Angel did all the talking. He opened the conversation in perfect English, "Born Yesterday."

"Dead Tomorrow," replied Swarthy in a heavy Bahamian accent.

Removing the cash payoff envelope from his knapsack and

clutching it in his left hand, he asked the contact, "Is the merchandise in working order?"

"Yes," said Swarthy.

Angel handed over the sealed envelope. Obviously anxious, Swarthy opened the envelope with care. Spotting the contents, he expertly shuffled crisp new C-Notes quicker than a casino dealer, confirming payment in full within ten seconds. A sinister smile replaced an otherwise stoic demeanor. A minor criminal coup d'état nearing completion.

Beckoning toward the cardboard box, Swarthy offered to close and finalize the transaction. Angel nodded acceptance. Pursuant to a second nod from Swarthy, the driver of the Dodge pickup unloaded the cardboard box, assisted Enrique in moving and loading the box into the back seat of the Nissan, then departed the exchange point, driving east in the direction from which he arrived.

Absent even an adios, Swarthy disappeared alone into contemporary Bahamian society with the cash, high stepping east through the bushes along Cable Beach in top gear, never to be seen or heard from again.

During the six-mile drive west to the weapon launch site general area, Enrique rode sidesaddle, uncomfortably sandwiched between the cardboard box and the right rear door of the Nissan. They passed Orange Hill Point and Northwest Point, stopping near the western terminus of Love Beach, where Angel selected a missile launch site. Angel helped Enrique carry the cardboard box containing the missile to the site, near Old Fort Point, a position about three miles west northwest of the takeoff end of Runway 32 at Nassau International Airport.

At 11:20 am Angel commenced weapon assembly. He opened the cardboard box with a box cutter. Inside was a Russian surface to air missile system, including a battery and one live projectile. There is no second chance today. One and done, hit or miss, a career in crime extended in fame or terminated in shame.

During weapon assembly Enrique queried Angel about the

mission, "Angel, why in the world are we doing this? Must be somebody or something real important aboard the airplane we are going to shoot down."

Angel replied, "Enrique, the only thing I can tell you is, one of the men on the target Gulfstream has done so many bad things to El Jefe that he needs to be offed. We were hand-picked for the job. No more discussion. Dispose of the cardboard box. If you can't find a place, bury the box in the sand. Now, pronto! Get busy! Fifteen minutes maximum."

Angel completed weapon assembly in less than half an hour. The last item in the checklist was firing sequence continuity, which tested A-OK. *Bueno. Bueno, Good, Good. Muy Bueno. Very Good.*

Satisfied with the functional status of his weapon, Angel carefully inserted the payload projectile into the firing tube, completing all requirements precedent to posture Angel to kill two men and destroy an expensive airplane with one missile projectile, professionally, effectively and mercilessly. A ten thousand dollar missile with the realistic ability to destroy a brand new aircraft worth 75 million dollars represents a serious return on investment!

Angel knows the stage III MANPAD heat seeking missile is accurate and nominally effective within a missile to target range of slightly less than four miles, a distance of about 20,000 feet. The missile is a 'fire and forget' weapon. Once fired, the missile will inexorably and efficiently 'on its own' attack and destroy the Gulfstream VI.

Today's launch shot is from the left and slightly from the rear of the target. Angel is holding off, waiting for the target to fly into his weapon's lethal kill envelope, within four miles; waiting to fire his infra-red technology heat seeking missile; waiting to kill Jet Taylor and Bubba Jasper.

With Enrique's assistance, at precisely one minute before noon Angel stood and hoisted the weapon upon his shoulders, turning to face the presumed Gulfstream flight path. Angel pre-aimed the weapon, east and slightly north, awaiting an unsuspecting target, the Gulfstream G650 carrying Jet and Bubba.

A Boeing 737 operated by American Airlines came and went, aircrew and passengers escaping certain death. Queasy and nervous, Angel caught the first glimpse of the next aircraft climbing out at about 1,500 feet above sea level, emerging from behind trees and brushes inhibiting a direct view of the airport. "This must be it," Angel muttered to Enrique.

"Yes, yes, this has to be it. It's time, it's past time," replied Enrique in a near falsetto high pitch voice, weak but excited.

"Yes, yes, one thousand times yes," stuttered Angel in steady rhythm. "I will kill those bastard gringos, this very Goddamn minute," Angel raving, more to himself than anyone.

"Yes, kill the bastards. Shoot them out of the sky. Don't miss. We have only one shot, Angel. Kill them, and let's get the hell out of here," Enrique rambled on, eager for blood.

First, Angel identified the bogey as a Gulfstream G650, confirming that the profile of the aircraft matched the photographs he studied and memorized during missile training in Colombia last week. Next, he inhaled a deep breath and held the breath for the duration of the firing sequence, a trait of professional marksmen.

Angel refined his aim by estimating the optimum azimuth lead angle for a successful kill, drawing lead on the target by aiming and pointing his weapon slightly above and in front of the climbing, accelerating Gulfstream G650. Since the target was flying from Angel's right to his left, Angel pulled lead by aiming a bit to the left and a bit above the streamlined G650 aircraft. Kentucky windage, used by all marksmen.

One and done. One shot and one shot only. It has to be perfect. So much on the line, money, prestige and survival.

BAM, SWOOSH, missile away! Five seconds from initial target sighting to missile launch, epitome of a professional missile kill.

Angel's estimate of range was perfect; his estimate of lead angle was perfect; his estimate the target was within range was valid. A kill for sure.

One last glance. Angel eyed the G650 as the aircraft sustained missile impact in the right wingtip area. Angel saw sparks fly, saw vestiges of metal debris and observed the aircraft lurch clumsily into a roll to the right, the commencement of a descending death spiral.

Angel knows the Gulfstream G650 is fatally wounded. It is falling from the sky, out of control, and will crash into unfriendly Atlantic Ocean waters within a minute or so, beyond Angel's view. The Mexican assassins buried the missile launching tube, vacated the kill site and boarded the next available commercial flight from Nassau to Cancun, anticipating a warm return and sizeable bonus. Maybe so, maybe not. Time will tell.

*

The best pilots are active, alert, attentive, observant, vigilant and cautious. Jet is one of the best pilots in the world. While airborne, his head is ever on a swivel, vigilantly observing the horizon from port to starboard, from fore to aft, from ground to the heavens; all the while constantly observing active and static read-outs of vitally important cockpit instruments, those dials and gadgets displaying real time data pertaining to aircraft performance, navigation, communication and safety.

Today is no exception. While initiating a visual scan from left to right Jet detected and instantly recognized a puff of white smoke at eight o'clock low, on the sands of Love Beach. The smoke was slightly behind the Gulfstream on the aircraft's left side.

'Eight o'clock' is pilot's description for location 120 degrees counter-clockwise from the nose. The nose is 12 o'clock. The right (starboard) wing is 3 o'clock. The tail is 6 o'clock and the left (port) wing is 9 o'clock.

Alarm, not terror, flooded every one of Jet's physical receptors; sight, sound, feel, taste and smell. All aspects of Jet's body functioned simultaneously and cooperatively, with one and only one objective; to instantly and optimally posture Jet for survival. MISSILE AWAY!!! Jet knew it.

There's no way anyone in the past could have taught Jet how to counter an in-range missile attack on his unarmed, relatively non-maneuverable private passenger jet aircraft. The moment an aircraft like Jet's Gulfstream G650 wanders into firing range of a surface, hand-held, man launched, aircraft attack missile, the aircraft and everyone in it is as good as gone. On balance Jet and his airplane were dead meat the instant the missile was launched.

A pilot who reveres longevity does not attempt to avoid a launched missile by flying away from the missile. Rather, the pilot turns into and towards the fast moving missile so as to create the optimum possibility of missile avoidance. The objective is to establish a deflection scenario (wrong aiming angle) and not a tracking scenario. Much easier said than done, emphasizing 'much.'

Jet is traveling at 300 knots (400 feet per second). The missile is traveling at about 600-800 knots (900-1200 feet per second). In less than a nominal 10 seconds the missile will impact. Jet has only ten seconds to maneuver his relatively sluggish passenger jet aircraft away from the tracking missile's kill envelope, an almost impossible task. Jet is driving a Mack truck. He needs to be driving a NASCAR coupe.

Two seconds elapsed. He who hesitates is lost. Get on it if you want to live! Instinctively, simultaneous with the white puff evidence of missile launch, Jet reacted like the virtuoso he is.

On intercom, Jet spoke calmly, "Bubba, go guard (emergency) frequency. State our call sign and advise 'missile attack;' do it now. Get on the controls with me. I need help. Full throttle, hold it full! Full left aileron! Full left rudder! Maximum turn bordering on high speed stall, 135 degree left roll, nose down 60 degrees. Hold it there and pray. Help me out here, Bubba!"

Without delay, Jet smoothly, firmly and positively positioned the active control stick full left and near full aft, while simultaneously feeding in left full rudder, thereby commencing a maneuver you will never find in a Gulfstream pilot's handbook, a hard 5G (centrifugal force equal to five times gravity) descending, rolling, left turn into and toward the missile, attempting to confuse the aiming device in the missile responsible for making in-flight lead (aiming) corrections.

Initially, the missile pulled normal lead on the Gulfstream G650, heading toward a point in space where the missile and the G650 will collide. As the Gulfstream executed its descending maximum hard left turn, the missile realized it had to turn right and decrease pitch angle so as to establish new and proper lead parameters.

While attempting to do so, the missile's lead angle calculation was disrupted. Jet's severe diving, turning maneuver had the desired effect of causing the missile to recalculate lead parameters under close tolerance conditions.

The missile's newly calculated lead angle was ever so slightly off. The missile did not optimally perform a mandatory right descending hard turn. In layman's terms, the missile could not turn and dive down and to the right quickly enough to establish a destructive intercept with the Gulfstream G650. Close but no cigar.

The missile impacted the Gulfstream G650 near the tip of the right wing, blowing off four to five feet of wingtip and inflicting incidental damage to the fuselage. The engines and flight controls were unharmed. A fuselage strike would no doubt have terminated airworthiness, resulting in a crash at sea, more than likely killing all on board.

The most important checklist item for any airborne emergency is to 'maintain aircraft control.' Aircraft checklists are designed primarily to protect weak pilots from themselves. The best pilots indelibly embed all checklist items in their subconscious, especially emergency checklist items.

When the uncontrollable, descending right wing roll commenced, Jet concentrated exclusively on maintaining aircraft control, with the ultimate objective of performing a safe crash landing at sea within the next few minutes. All other considerations were irrelevant. He did not notice Bubba's injury.

In a flash, Jet determined it was impossible to maintain aircraft control because wing lift on the good left wing was substantially

greater than wing lift on the damaged right wing. For the scant duration of flight time remaining, the G650 will sustain a continuous
uncontrolled roll to the right, even though full left aileron and full
left rudder will be applied from now until just prior to an emergency
crash landing at sea.

*Hot diggety damn. Not dead yet. Still alive and flying. So far so
good. Good enough? Too soon to tell. The Grim Reaper wants to mow
us down. Screw him.*

Jet timed the roll rate of his out-of-control aircraft, which he
determined to be twelve seconds per full wing roll. That is, in the
next 45 seconds Jet and Bubba's aircraft will complete slightly less
than four full uncontrollable wing rolls to the right and then impact
the ocean. That's a heavy duty problem.

Jet needs to maneuver his broken aircraft to hopefully arrive at a
point in space and time at the surface of the ocean, with wings level,
5 degrees nose up, traveling at 120 knots air speed, enabling Jet to
perform an 'at sea,' pancake crash landing. Even a small deviation
portends certain death.

Eerily, as if spellbound, Jet perceived his situation to be synony-
mous with synchronized dancing or synchronized ice skating. Subconsciously, Jet's mind and body harmonized with the right-wing
roll rate of the aircraft. Everything is in sync, his body, his mind,
the aircraft, the altitude of the aircraft, the nose down pitch of the
aircraft, the right roll of the wings, the aircraft speed, and the loom-
ing horizon, where the Bahamian blue sky merges in a straight line
with the beautiful azure ocean offshore from the north coast of New
Providence Island. In the entire world, no better place to die; but
not today.

Bubba lost consciousness one minute ago.

Jet is preoccupied; dueling with death, the most dangerous of
human activities. Somewhere in the computerized cortex of his
mind, neurons and axons are continuously and cooperatively grind-
ing, so as to provide cognitive understanding of a primal nature,
enabling Jet to observe, comprehend, and respond by operating

flight controls and throttles so as to posture the Gulfstream G650 to safely pair bond with calm ocean waters.

Roll rate synchronization almost perfect! *Ease off on both left aileron and left rudder, NOW. Throttles idle! Control Stick neutral! Take what you have; that'll do it.* The aircraft touched down slightly nose up, with the left wing ten degrees off horizontal. Imprecise but not fatal, for Jet that is. Close enough for government work. An almost perfect pancake crash landing at sea at 120 knots airspeed. Hallelujah!

During the brief period of time devoted to the emergency, Jet determined within reasonable probability; (i) the identity of the mole in his organization who fingered the assassination attempt from the inside; (ii) the identity of the party who ordered the hit on Jet and Bubba; (iii) the identity of the party responsible for implementing the hit; and (iv) his employee, the man who fired the missile. Multitasking at its finest. *They are all going to pay through the nose. It's time to don my life jacket and escape through the emergency egress door.*

7

NASSAU

The Rescue

Revered employee and friend Bubba Jasper, age 52, was killed by what pilots call the 'golden BB,' a shard of shrapnel which pierced the co-pilot right window side panel and struck Bubba in the right temple. Death occurred within two minutes. Bubba never experienced substantial pain.

Jet did not realize Bubba was dead until the Gulfstream coasted to a rough, full stop crash landing in the Atlantic Ocean a few miles northwest of Love Beach. Jet and Bubba were both restrained by shoulder harness. Both were leaning forward when the aircraft shuddered to a full stop.

Jet recovered. Bubba did not recover. He was dead, sitting in the copilot's seat, slumped forward, waiting to be buried at sea in his coffin of choice.

Jet felt for a pulse. Nothing. What followed was the most poignant, pitiful sound the human ear is ever exposed to, a death wail. There exists on earth no sound more wretched than a professional death wail.

The sound both defines and defies death. Jet's death wail for

Bubba was from the heart; boding revenge, sweet revenge, fateful revenge, absolute revenge.

Death, oh yes, death, the condition which philosophers and theologians down through the ages have pontificated upon in great detail, to no avail of course. The people who most clearly understand death are combat soldiers, since they are the ones who sustain death in great numbers in the ordinary course of their profession. Next closest are beat police patrolmen and patrolwomen.

"Bubba, the bastard who did this to you will burn in hell. I swear it on my mother's grave," sobbed Jet uncontrollably. No one was listening as the burial at sea commenced.

The aircraft sank beneath the surface in no time at all. Sea water flowed ever faster through fuselage structural cracks as external water pressure steadily increased proportional to the depth of the sinking, mortally wounded Gulfstream G650.

Jet nearly drowned escaping from the bent and broken aircraft hull. After he located and donned his life preserver, he pried open the jammed passenger entry door. Then he inhaled the deepest breath possible, abandoned the sinking aircraft and commenced to half swim, half pray his way to the surface, up through 80 feet of hostile saltwater. Once outside the aircraft Jet inflated his life preserver, saving his life by increasing ascension rate toward choppy waves atop the Atlantic Ocean.

Jet thanked his lucky stars as he surfaced. With some difficulty, he located his waterproof international cell phone and with a less than steady index finger pressed speed dial eight and selected speaker function. On the second ring, the line answered "May I help you, sir?"

"Damn right," gasped Jet. "Get your ass over here. I am in the water in a life preserver at a position approximately four nautical miles north northwest of the Nassau runway, about one mile offshore. Pick me up now, on the double!"

Sam Turner has been on emergency standby duty for every takeoff and landing at Nassau International Airport by Jet Taylor during the past five years. One can hardly imagine the surprise experienced by Sam when he realized he was talking face-to-face with the old man, arguably the richest and most important person in the world, to Sam's limited understanding. At any rate, that was the word making the rounds.

Sam does not gossip. Idle chatter does not matter to Sam. Every month for the last five years the old man's paychecks cleared. Sam knows he can depend upon the old man to provide for himself and his family for the rest of his life.

That's good enough for Sam. He put his ass in gear, roused his other crew member, revved up the inflatable boat's twin Toyota outboard engines and hightailed at maximum speed toward the position provided to him by the old man. Within five minutes Sam spotted an orange life preserver. Within eight minutes Jet was safely aboard the inflatable. Within 15 minutes Jet was safely deposited on dry land on New Providence Island, saluting Sam as he sped out to sea. A bonus is in order.

*

Revenge, Shakespeare's favorite topic, is Jet's number one interest. The lost aircraft is a chattel. Chattels come and go. Chattels don't matter. To Jet's way of thinking, people matter; little else ever matters. Every asset other than personnel is expendable. Sadly, most personnel are expendable.

The 75 million dollar aircraft at the bottom of the Atlantic Ocean a few miles north of New Providence Island is out of sight and out of mind. It exists only as a ledger entry on a charity balance sheet, soon to be written off in the same manner as paper towels and hand soap.

Back on terra firma, Jet took advantage of his new lease on life. First, he lapsed into reflective mode; serious decisional considerations in process. Five minutes later he speed dialed nine on his cell phone. "Customer service," answered the cell phone in Spanish. "How may we help you today, sir?"

Jet replied in almost perfect accent Spanish, "This is Beaver 1. Implement plan CXL 4, read back."

"Roger, Beaver 1, we have instructions to implement plan CXL 4, numero Quattro. Please provide the password."

"La contraseña es Tortuga Verde. (The password is Green Turtle) replied Jet, muttering 'green turtle' to himself in English.

"Roger, Tortuga Verde. Muchas gracias, Señor," stoically replied the death squad employee. "Estado informe manana." (Status report tomorrow).

"Thank you, customer service. Looking forward to initial report," replied an exhausted Jet. Revenge round one has commenced.

Jet speed dialed 6. Answer was prompt, "Travel here, how may we help you?"

"Travel, this is Cadillac 1. My plans have changed. I need travel accommodations for one person right away, from my last known departure point to my intended destination. Satisfy my requirements without delay. Cadillac 1 over," said Jet.

"Right away, Cadillac 1. We will notify you via this venue when travel arrangements are confirmed," stammered the astonished agent. He knew he just terminated a private conversation with the most important man he had ever communicated with in his life.

The agent ended the cell phone call and activated a direct secure telephone land line to his supervisor. "Steve, beats me, but for some reason Cadillac 1 just notified me out of the blue via unsecure cell phone that his flight in the Gulfstream from Nassau to Havana, noon local departure, was aborted."

"Cadillac 1 requests alternate travel to Havana from Nassau for only one person, himself, right now. What should we do?" implored the nervous agent. "I realize how important this is."

"Calm down, calm down," soothed the supervisor. "I told you many times that emotional considerations can detract from one's ability to function professionally. This situation is relatively simple."

"Hire a high-end Nassau private aircraft taxi. Provide pickup instructions, ID and location; allowing up to three days in Havana, Cuba, with return to Bermuda via Nassau."

"Price is no object. Identity of the passenger is William Pennington, a British citizen and Bermuda resident. Do this without delay. Call me after you have made arrangements with the air taxi."

"On second thought, let's make the call to the air taxi a three-way call, to avoid confusion and ambiguity. We have to get this absolutely right. The old man is easy going, but never forgives a mistake by a professional," droned the supervisor.

Within 15 minutes Travel called the old man, "Cadillac 1, this is Travel, over."

"Roger, Travel, what do you have for me?"

"Your air taxi in Nassau is named Lyons Air Service. Lyons Air will pick you up at a location of your choice, sir."

"Have Lyons Air meet me at Lighthouse Creek, just off Western Road. I have no luggage. I require a complete set of new clothing and shoes for Havana. Don't forget toothbrush, toothpaste and disposable razors. Thank you. Cadillac 1 out."

Ten minutes later a limousine picked up Jet and delivered him to the Lyons Air Service facility at the general aviation complex on Nassau International Airport. One hour later Jet was enroute to Havana, Cuba in a Learjet charter aircraft.

The first thought is the best thought. I was right. The Colombians had something to do with the loss of my airplane. It had to be an inside job. Yep, inside job, and I know the names of all the parties who had access to my itinerary. Somebody is sweating blood just about now.

8
CUBA
Nuke Purchase

A t 3:30 pm Enrique Echeverria (Jet's nuclear acquisition alias) was met at Havana airport's relatively private terminal number five by his personal squire, the fifth ranking official of the Cuban government, a four-star general whose sole responsibility is to keep 24/7 tabs on Jet during his nuclear weapons acquisition visit to Cuba.

Dapper Jet was decked out in a Cuban guayabera, a light blue linen shirt distinguished by two vertical rows of closely sewn pleats running the length of the front and back of the shirt; paired with dark blue wool and polyester blend trousers. Accessories included Allen Edmonds black oxford shoes and belt, black socks and Jockey shorts and T-Shirt. Jet's blue eyes match the color of his guayabera. His aura, carriage and demeanor reek of success, money and power.

Clothing was purchased on short notice from a Nassau high end men's store. No problem with shoe size. No problem with shirt and pants sizes. A Dopp kit fully stocked. Good work.

Bypassing Cuban customs and immigration, Jet and his squire were chauffeured via a well maintained, vintage 16-year-old 2005

Mercedes-Benz black government limousine; driven to the Hotel Nacionale, one of the oldest and most well-known Havana hotels. Today's nuclear negotiation meeting was postponed until tomorrow, Tuesday. Jet respectfully declined the offer of all night feminine companionship at the hotel. He never mixes business with pleasure; on that score, he has a full plate.

Lyons Air personnel were provided overnight accommodations at Havana's Hotel Colina. Jet arranged with the Lyons Air captain for a Tuesday 5:00 pm Havana departure, with a stopover in Nassau on the way to final destination, Hamilton, Bermuda.

Tuesday's four hour meeting was held at a confidential, secure location in the exclusive Miramar section of Havana city. On the limousine trip from Hotel Nacionale to the meeting, Jet observed that most of the buildings fronting the Caribbean Sea on the north, ocean side of Havana were architecturally sound but sadly in need of repair. *This town needs a WD-40 bath.*

The flag rank squire chaired the meeting. Attending with Jet were envoys from the governments of North Korea, Pakistan, and Iran, along with an entourage of administrative support personnel, 14 people in all, plus interpreters. Because the meeting was conducted in Spanish, four interpreters were required for translation of communications to Spanish and from Spanish; the languages were Korean, Urdu, Farsi, and English.

Jet captured the essence of the meeting and mesmerized the attendees with his closing summary, delivered in Spanish, "Gentlemen, as I understand it, today we reached an oral agreement in principle whereby Pakistan will within the next month provide four nuclear warheads, atomic weapons in working order, FOB Matanzas, Cuba, to a Cayman Islands Corporation to be formed, payment, delivery parameters and warhead size to be negotiated within two weeks."

"Cuba will hold cash payment in escrow at All World Commercial Bank pending compliance with conditions precedent by weapon sellers. Payment shall be made in American Dollars. The

Corporation is responsible to pay Cuba a 10% commission upon completion of the transaction contemplated here today. I personally guarantee all performances agreed to by the Corporation."

Enrique Echeverria just promised to pay one billion dollars to Pakistan. I can't believe it, thought the squire.

The Pakistani negotiator replied, "Agreed, unconditionally. Upon your arrival in Islamabad, we will provide to you a proposed formal agreement for your consideration. The language of the document shall be English."

"Thank you, sir," said Jet in English. "I'll provide my travel plans to you within the week. Good day, Gentlemen.

The 10% Cuban commission augments the handsome amount of money paid to Cuba by the Taylor Hierarchy over the years in return for Cuban drug smuggling support. Continuously, for the past three decades Cuba aided and abetted Jet's Colombian partners in their distribution of illegal drugs within the United States. Cuba continues to do so. It's good business. Americans have a healthy appetite for illicit recreational drugs.

*

On Tuesday night at 9:00 pm Jet arrived home to his Bermuda mansion. He surprised Helen and Amanda. Jointly the young ladies prepared a light dinner, filet mignon, boiled potatoes and broccoli, along with a glass of Argentinian Malbec for Jet, his favorite red wine.

Small talk over dinner addressed accounting and advertising. Helen has a shot at Madison Avenue. Amanda wanted to talk about accounting, of all things. She was all ears.

Half an hour later Amanda accompanied Jet to his bedroom. During the past three months, Helen explained, over and over again, to Amanda the funded binding agreement which Jet is willing to enter into with Amanda. She got the message. Amanda came to an axiomatic conclusion; if she cozies up to Jet she has it made for life.

Three months and one week into her scholarship and for the first time, the 18-year-old turned Jet every which way but loose. Amanda relinquished her virginity to Jet on January 5, 2021. He could not believe how satisfying she was. Life is good, for Jet and Amanda, that is. Life will soon be bad for others. Tomorrow a death warrant shall issue.

9
STONY RANDOLPH
Promotion

After the Mansion Security supervisor cleared his office, Jet said, "Stoney, we have a problem. Harvey deserted us."

"Jet, I've been on board for eight years. Early on it was made crystal clear to me that whenever I departed the premises, I was to check out with mansion security, providing date, time of departure and destination, along with estimated time of return to the premises."

"If Harvey failed to follow protocol he is AWOL, absent without leave; to my understanding essentially a capital offense."

"True. Bear with me on this. Hear me out. First, I want to address an important topic on a different subject. Stony, one of the things you must do if you are to be a successful manager, in addition to planning your flight and flying your plan, is to know your people and to treat them hard but fair. Hard and fair. Those traits are absolutely essential. I say this to help you deal with responsibilities you are soon to assume."

Although Stony is a veteran employee who has worked for Jet

for nearly eight years, he has no idea what Jet is talking about. *This is going to be really good or really bad.*

Jet said, "Harvey is AWOL. His absence is consistent with me being shot down on Monday. Only five people knew my first flight leg terminated at Nassau, and also knew my estimated ground time and estimated departure time from Nassau. The five are myself, Imogene, Bubba, Harvey and you."

"Bubba is stone dead. Harvey is AWOL. I trust you and my secretary implicitly. Our two-week old, 75 million dollar Gulfstream is at the bottom of the Atlantic Ocean. You and Imogene are here with me. Ipso facto, Harvey is the Goddamned mole who informed the missile shooter and his boss the exact date and time our G650 would take off from Nassau two days ago."

"I know Harvey well. His motivation was twofold. He is a bleeding heart liberal. He didn't want me to take down the government of the United States. More importantly, had I been killed at sea with Bubba, Harvey stood to assume control and ownership of the hierarchy, along with my extensive financial holdings. Arguably Harvey tried to kill me for my money."

Jet never tells anyone exactly how much money he has, "I'm worth well over a hundred billion dollars, Stony."

"Wow, that's big bucks."

"Yes, that's big bucks. It surely is. Be that as it may, I am more than satisfied turncoat mole Harvey committed treason against the Taylor Hierarchy. Bubba is dead. Thereby Harvey's sentence is death. An eye for an eye. Death to Harvey and death to his family. Stony, you're commissioned to carry out the sentence."

"Just a moment," Jet hit speed dial nine on his cell phone.

"How may we help you, sir?"

"This is Beaver 1. Report results regarding implementation of plan CXL 4. Read back."

"Roger, Beaver 1, you request results regarding implementation of plan CXL 4, numero quattro. Please provide the password."

"The password is Mujer Bonita. (Pretty Woman)

"Beaver 1, Plan CXL 4 successfully completed today. 45 Units, all accounted for."

"Thank you, Beaver 1 out."

"Stony, be advised the missile launch shooter, his boss, the 'soldiers' of his boss and their families were taken out this morning by one of my death squads; 45 persons in all, men, women and children. They operated out of Matamoros, Mexico."

"Nobody in Matamoros is sophisticated enough to plan and execute a missile attack on our Gulfstream. Only my two partners in Colombia could have pulled it off, and only with Harvey's help. Wealth does not always equate to reason. I haven't decided yet how to handle Colombia."

"I'm changing gears now. Stay with me. Pay close attention. During wartime in the Army Air Corps, and after 1947 the United States Air Force, whenever a pilot went missing or was killed, especially a high ranking pilot, everybody moved up one notch. Expediency reigns. He who prevails has a shot at the big time. Precipitous death deprives the best of us of an opportunity to participate in the game of life."

"Stony, Harvey is gone. You are moving up one notch. For better or worse, I'm promoting you today. As of right now, you are the hierarchy's head knocker, in command and control, top dog, CEO. I relinquish sole authority to you, over the charity, the bank, the insurance company and the aircraft brokerage company. This is no temporary promotion; all things considered, you're the most qualified."

"Today I resign from all four steering committees and appoint you as sole member of each committee. Stony, your salary is increased to 12 million dollars yearly, that's one million dollars a month, backdated to January 1, 2021."

"Damn, you always said things move fast in the fast lane, I believe it. Thank you, boss."

"Thank yourself, Stony. You earned it. I don't expect you to fill Harvey Pryor's shoes. Harvey's authority, his span of control, covered everything in our business except day to day operations. Harvey was Mr. Support Officer for the charity, the bank and the insurance company."

"Promote the most qualified Support Officer in our organization to Harvey's position, at a salary of three million dollars per year. Unless you have good reason, take no action regarding the aircraft brokerage company. They are doing just fine."

"While you're at it, promote Ewe Schweglewski to chief pilot @$25,000 per month. Ian Thomas becomes #2 pilot @$20,000 per month. Hire a third and fourth pilot from the waiting list maintained by personnel, @$15,000 per month for the new pilots. Schedule Ian Thomas and the new hires for Gulfstream G650 ground school and flight simulator check-out. The new hires must be experienced fighter pilots, no exceptions."

"Our number two guy at the bank is moving up to bank president to replace Wayne Spencer, who transfers to 'Fresh Start' within two months. His replacement is named Wainscot. I don't remember his first name. He's ok, though."

"Stony, on a grander scale, take whatever action you deem appropriate and necessary to run our railroad. Don't be afraid to make mistakes. Learn from your mistakes. For the next month consult with me every day at the close of business. I repeat, do not refrain from taking actions because you might be wrong. You will be wrong, hopefully less than 50% of the time. Cut your losses and ride with your winners."

"I anticipate your departure from Bermuda no later than noon tomorrow, Thursday, on your manhunt to track down and terminate the Pryor family. Harvey has no children. Stiff him and his wife. This is your last termination assignment. You are finished with that line of work. We need you upstairs, not in the field. Hire your terminator successor within a week."

"Will do, Jet."

"All our aircraft, except the short range Sabreliner, are committed or buried at sea. Your travel options to track down Harvey are private contract air taxi or commercial airline service or a combination of the two. It's up to you. Spare no expense. You can use the Sabre-liner to fly to JFK this afternoon."

"Introduce yourself to two books located on the desk in your living quarters: *Money & Banking*, a college text for business majors, and *Introduction to Casualty Insurance*, a college text for students taking a survey course in insurance. The books are standard fare for offspring of the gnomes of Zürich."

"With a twinkle in his eye, Jet said, "Oh, yes, I almost forgot; a small but important administrative detail of interest to you, Stony. Harvey has on deposit in various accounts at our bank a little over 158 million dollars. He wired the money from our bank to an account in Panama, but he didn't know I established a three day hold on all wire transfers outbound from the bank by certain account holders. Harvey lost his money."

Jet stared Stony down, looking him directly in the eye, "His loss is your gain."

Stony cannot believe his ears, "What does that have to do with me, boss?"

"Everything. Tomorrow, Harvey's deposits in total will be trans-ferred to a separate and different account in our bank, owned by you as beneficiary. The money will be conveyed to you in ten equal yearly installments, principal and interest. You receive the first ben-eficiary payment tomorrow, 15.8 million dollars, tax free."

"No, boss, that's not right. I don't deserve Harvey's money. I just don't deserve it."

"Not your call, Stony. My call. You're a rich man. Get over it. That's that."

"One trait most rich people have in common is to refrain from talking with others about money, absolutely refrain. Think long and hard about my unsolicited advice, young man. While I'm on the sub-ject, if and when somebody, stranger or otherwise, asks you about your money or your net worth, or your annual earnings, always reply with the comment: 'I am comfortable.' Never discuss your personal financial circumstances with nobody, and I mean NEVER with NOBODY."

"One last instruction, for now and until further notice, put half of your money in gold and the other half in investments not denominated in US dollars. Get out of American stocks, bonds and commodities, now. For example, buy Volkswagen stocks or Canadian Bonds. Demand delivery. Do not let a broker hold your certificates. Keep $100,000 or so laying around in cash, Canadian dollars or Euros, for emergencies. Possess no US dollar denominated assets until further notice."

"We purchased the 'awaiting-delivery' position of an existing Gulfstream G650 customer. Their aircraft is now ours. Tomorrow it will be ferried from Savannah to Bermuda by Ewe and a Gulfstream company pilot. We paid a premium through the nose, a million bucks. The expense couldn't be avoided. We need the bird."

"Carefully monitor charity cash receipts on a daily basis. I want to know when and if Colombia stops remitting drug profits for investment, in fear of my reprisal."

"Yes, boss." Stony shook his head in awe, in disbelief of the remarkable turn of events within the hierarchy. His life will never be the same.

10

HARVEY PRYOR
Turncoat's Reward

In the late afternoon of Wednesday, January 6, 2021 Stony sent a DHL overnight packet to Tony Preston, a top drawer licensed private investigator. Afterwards he commandeered the charity Sabreliner for a two hour hop from Bermuda to JFK, arriving in New York City at 7:14 pm EST.

Thursday morning at 10:00 am in his Miami office on Biscayne Boulevard, Tony Preston opened a DHL packet marked personal. His secretarial staff is well trained. No messing with the boss's personal mail.

Enclosed was a bank check to Preston & Associates for $50,000, drawn on a local Miami 'Edge Act' Bank. A photograph and resume of both Harvey & Alice Pryor were the only other items in the packet, with the exception of the address, telephone number and one-time alias cover for Stony at the Ramada Inn servicing JFK International Airport.

New York is a closer staging city than Bermuda. Stony will depart New York for mission destination when he is provided Harvey's last known location by Preston & Associates. Tony Preston has never failed Stony.

At 4:13 pm EST on Thursday, January 7, the Miami skip tracer par excellence located the whereabouts of Harvey Pryor and wife Alice. They are settled into visiting officers' quarters at Malstrom AFB, Great Falls, Montana.

Harvey used a military 'Star' credit card to purchase gasoline for his rental Cadillac at Malstrom AFB. Harvey believed no one could access his military credit records. How wrong Harvey was. A $5000 bribe turned up Harvey's point of sale location within ten minutes after gasoline was purchased via the Star card.

Stony received the following text message at 4:45 pm on Thursday:

Destination: Great Falls, Montana

Reservation: Delta Flight 1067, Friday, January 8, 2021 @ 7:00 am

Friday morning Stony boarded Delta first class flight 1067 from New York City to Great Falls, Montana under a one–time alias, Nelson Abrams, departing JFK at 7:00 am and arriving at Great Falls International Airport at 12:23 pm Mountain Standard Time (MST). Direct flights were not available; one stopover. Great Falls is two hours behind New York City.

Stony deplaned at 12:35 pm MST. The first person he saw at the Great Falls arrival gate was a meeter-greeter holding a good sized poster bearing the name Nelson Abrams.

The meeter-greeter committed to meet every Friday commercial flight originating in New York and arriving in Great Falls. Fortune smiled on him. His client was the third passenger deplaning from the first flight of the day.

As the pair walked toward temporary airport parking, Buzz Thompson said, "Mr. Abrams, you have reservations at Malstrom AFB under the name Thomas Martin, Major, USAF. You will travel with one wheeled, carry-on suitcase."

"Your Class A officer's uniform is in the back seat of this Toyota SUV, along with black service shoes and a leather billed hat. Military decorations and rank are attached to the blue officer blouse. We will stop at the first available gas station where you can change into the uniform. Place your civilian clothing and shoes in the wheeled suitcase after changing clothes."

"You look great in your uniform, Major Martin," complimented Buzz as he handed papers and such to Stony. "Here's documentation necessary for you to penetrate Air Force Base security and proceed to Malstrom Inns and Suites, a travel accommodation building with military overnight facilities for visiting officers."

"The documents include a USAF active-duty photo ID card, a Maryland photo ID driver's license, a vehicle registration document, a vehicle insurance document, and an untraceable MasterCard."

"After dropping me off, you will drive straight ahead on 2nd Avenue North to Malstrom AFB in this SUV, approaching the security perimeter fence for the base. The visitor control center is located just outside the main gate. The control center is open Monday through Friday from 7:00 am to 5:00 pm and is concerned primarily with entry onto the Air Force Base. The center usually has no interest in personnel exiting the Air Force Base."

"All visitors require a visitor pass. You will provide the documents I just gave you, to the on-duty enlisted air policeman. Roll down your window. You will be saluted. Salute back like this." Buzz showed Stony how to salute. "After a look-see at the documents, the Air Cop will issue you a visitor pass valid for three days."

"The Malstrom Inn building has 83 rooms, including 6 distinguished visitor suites, 25 visiting officer quarters (VOQ) suites, and various enlisted and transient quarters. The address of the Inn is 7228 Fourth Avenue North, building 1680."

"The Air Cop will either give you a map of Malstrom AFB or will provide you with driving directions to the Inn, or both. The document I am handing you is a sketch of the room layout of the Malstrom Inn building, including room numbers."

"Park outside the Inn. Proceed to check-in with your wheeled suitcase and your documents. Tell the clerk at the check-in counter you have a reservation and are checking in. The clerk will examine your AF Identification Card and ask for your credit card."

"I suggest you tell the clerk you are having a reunion with Colonel Harvey Pryor, USAF, Retired, and you wonder if he is in one of the six distinguished visitor units or in regular Visiting Officer Quarters. This might reduce search parameters considerably."

"It is 1:45 pm. Arrangements have been made for you to depart Great Falls International Airport via Learjet. Provide a 45 minute departure notice to the Lear pilot by calling the number pre-set on this throw-away telephone."

"If you have difficulties, call me on the second throw-away burner phone I am providing to you, which is also pre-set. I'll monitor your progress and assist your egress, as required or as requested."

"Do you have any questions, Major Martin?"

"Only three," said Stony. "Where and when do you exit the Toyota, where is my weapon and does the egress pilot know my destination is DC?"

"The weapon is in the glove compartment, a Glock 19 with silencer and one extra clip. I will exit your SUV on foot once we are on 2nd Avenue North and within one mile of the AFB entry gate. Your weapon was test fired today. The chamber is empty."

"I suggest when your mission is complete and after you exit the base, you proceed south about ten blocks to US 87, west on US 87 and follow the signs to Great Falls International Airport. Your GPI selected destination is Great Falls International Airport. I'll inform the Lear pilot of your ultimate destination, Washington, DC. Leave the keys to the unlocked SUV in the ashtray or in the glove compartment. Park the SUV in airport 'temporary parking.' Good luck, which DC Airport?"

"Reagan National, thank you," said Stony. *Preston & Associates have their ducks in order. Hell of a good job on short notice. A sizable bonus is appropriate.*

Less than 15 minutes after Stony arrived at the main gate of Malstrom Air Force Base, he opened the locked door to his visiting officers' quarters room at the Malstrom Inn & Suites building. A visitor's pass hung from the rear view mirror of the SUV parked outside the Malstrom Inn. Buzz's instructions and suggestions were winners, first class.

No problems so far. Good start. Harvey is bedded down in one of the six distinguished visitor suites. I lucked out there.

Stony reviewed his plan while changing into quick getaway civilian clothing. His disguise was limited to clear glasses, a false moustache and goatee, along with a Seattle Seahawks baseball cap pulled down over his face.

At 2:30 pm Stony commenced knocking at the first of six doors, behind one of which in all likelihood is Harvey Pryor and his wife. Stony's subterfuge is simplicity. In the event an officer guest other than Harvey answers the door, Stony's remark will be, 'Sorry, wrong suite.'

Door number one, nobody home. Doors number two and three, 'wrong suite.' Door number four, Bingo. Harvey answered the door. Stony shot him dead with three silencer rounds to the heart. Alice Pryor exited the bedroom to determine what caused the commotion in the suite's living room. Stony shot her dead with three more silencer rounds to her upper abdomen.

Stony calmly closed and locked the door to the Pryor suite, stowed the Glock under his belt and deliberately walked to his quarters. After wrapping the semi-automatic pistol with a bathroom towel, he stowed it in the wheeled suitcase along with the military uniform, shirt, necktie, belt, shoes and billed hat.

After policing his quarters for prints and any other evidence of room occupancy, Stony called the Learjet pilot via burner cell phone, providing a 45 minute notice of departure. He stowed the used telephone in the suitcase and calmly exited the military quarters, locking the door behind him.

After departing the AFB perimeter in the Toyota, Stony located a supermarket and paid cash for a few throw-away items. Back in the

SUV, he transferred the contents of the wheeled suitcase, except for the Glock, into a large brown paper bag he obtained with the super-market purchase.

He disposed of the paper bag in a dumpster behind one of the stores in a strip mall, about two blocks from the super market. He trashed the now empty wheeled suitcase in a second dumpster, three blocks from the first dumpster.

On his way to the airport via US 87, Stony detoured to the 1st Street bridge over the Missouri River. He parked on the east side of the river, walked to the shore and tossed the Glock, the silencer and the extra clip far out into the running water of the Missouri, the longest river in the United States. Competent assassin that he is, prior to dis-posal of the Glock, Stony wiped down the weapon and accessories to remove fingerprints.

One hour after clearing the gate and departing Malstrom AFB, Stony broke ground at Great Falls International Airport, snug as a bug in a rug in his chartered Learjet, headed for Reagan National Airport. Down in Montana at 12:35 pm. Up again at 4:00 pm, more than effi-cient by any standards. Stony knows he has not lost a step; he still has the assassin's killing touch. *It's a shame I'm retiring from this vocation.*

Completely relaxed, Stoney popped the cap on a bottle of Samuel Adams lager after the Learjet reached cruising altitude. Another day, another 158 million dollars.

Apparently, Harvey forgot everything he learned about Escape and Evasion when he attended Air Force crew member survival training for three weeks at Fairchild AFB, Spokane, Washington. Harvey is a dead man only three days after taking a hike from the mansion. Not much of a retirement. Then again, Harvey was not much of a man.

It is a five hour flight via Learjet 60 from Montana to DC, some-what less than 2,100 miles. By 1:00 am local time Stony will be tucked in at the Hampton Inn serving Reagan National Airport. Tomorrow he returns to Bermuda via Delta Air Lines.

11
BERMUDA
A Patriot's Viewpoint

The charity's 28,000 ft.² two story granite mansion in Hamilton, Bermuda is home and workplace for 104 managers and employees, comprised of 85 foreign nationals and 19 indigenous blue-collar upkeep, maintenance and supply personnel.

Essentially an enclave, the imposing fenced mansion is located in the northern portion of Bermuda on a slightly elevated promontory, inaccessible and relatively impregnable. Formerly three Taylor Hierarchy executives, Jet Taylor, Harvey Pryor and Stony Randolph, resided permanently at the mansion. With Harvey's demise, the number has been reduced to two, Jet and Stony.

Today is Monday, January 11, 2021. The occasion is the hierarchy's first joint management breakfast since Harvey's death four days ago. President elect William Wilson will be inaugurated as the 46th president of the United States on January 20, 2021.

Cups and crystal glasses have been refreshed with coffee and effervescent Perrier water by impeccably dressed food servers. Bus boys removed bone china breakfast plates previously graced by pork chops, Canadian bacon, tomatoes, home fries, eggs over and scrambled (Jet prefers scrambled, Stony over easy), whole wheat and rye bread (Jet prefers rye, Stony prefers whole wheat), along with in-season fresh fruit. Jet and Stony live 'high on the hog.'

Over coffee Stony said, "There has been no interruption or diminution in Colombian drug money deposits."

"That's interesting. Our response to Bubba's death and the aircraft loss remain open items for now. Loose ends; on the back burner, but not all the way back."

Stony replied carefully, "Boss, please don't dock me for the query I'm about to lay on you, but I've been thinking; I know, I know; it's dangerous for me to think."

Jet frowned, curious but concerned.

"Accepting that as gospel, I'm no Einstein or Newton but it beats the hell out of me why a wealthy man postured like you would be interested for even a millisecond in the possibility of losing it all, including your life, in a 'Fresh Start' rebellion against the strongest military of all time; especially since last Monday you managed to get your ass shot down. For all I know you were no more than a hang-nail away from death."

"Jet, did the Colombians shoot you down a week ago today? Was it the American Feds? Should we strengthen our security perimeters? Should we retire? From my vantage point, a lot of weird and crazy things are happening and there's a bunch of things to be concerned about."

"Mind you, I'm not suggesting passivity, just examining options and trying to learn something. If it's okay with you, please share with this 'grunt' the direction we are headed, and the reasons for same."

After briefly thinking about the question, Jet responded, "Stony, since you are now running our show on a day to day basis, I owe you a response. You asked about more than one subject. Here goes."

"For openers, Stony, be aware that the USA has already 'gone to hell in a handbasket.' Are you familiar with that American phrase?"

"Yes, I am, boss; but it's not one of ours."

Jet nodded understandingly, "Not going to hell, but gone;

already gone to hell, Stony. I watched America go to hell in a hand-basket, all the way to Hades; I smelled it; I tasted it; I heard it; I felt it; Most important of all, I lived it. School's out. Class is over. Everybody failed. Pink slips are in the mail. Damn, this is hard to admit."

"So be it. Before I answer your 'Fresh Start' query, please understand one thing. But for the government of the United States of America, you and I would not be enjoying our God-awful abundance of wealth and the freedom to use that wealth to fund whatever pursuit whets our appetite."

"From the first day I interned as an orphan in Louisville, Kentucky at age eight and continuing until I was 35 years old, I was subsidized by both state and federal earned and unearned welfare services and programs. I wouldn't be in this mansion today if it weren't for those subsidies."

"From age eight to age 17, I was destitute. Because I was an orphan, the state of Kentucky absorbed my living expenses during that ten year growing up period. During the next four years I was an AFROTC student/cadet at the University of Louisville, Kentucky, working my way through college. After university graduation, I served seven years on active duty as a fighter pilot with the United States Air Force and another seven years in the Virginia Air National Guard, working aircraft brokerage full time."

"So far this is news to me, Jet," said Stony.

"Throughout those times I loved the government and the people of the United States of America as much if not more than any man, woman or child in America ever did. That was circa 1960 – 1995. I still love the people; but the government, that's another story."

"I would never have thought that."

"I reckon not. During my lifetime, American-born and raised citizens of the United States of America have changed a lot. Regrettably the United States government has also changed, much more than a lot, and practically all for the worst. I do not recognize, respect or have any allegiance to the present government of the United States of America. I hate, loathe and despise the present government of the United States of America."

"So much for the introduction. Here's the knitty–gritty, motive; my reasons for creating and promoting our 'Fresh Start' revolt are factual. I am hardly ever emotional, if at all. However the sad condition of the United States has generated a hell of a lot of internal toil for me; misery, strong feelings, and that sort of thing; all foreign to me."

The emotion part surprises me. I have never known you to be emotional."

"Nobody ever gets close enough to me to observe anything like that. You're an exception. As regards emotion, whenever the US government crosses my mind I become sick to my stomach. I become violently ill inside because the collective combination of a worthless triad: (i) the president: (ii) the Congress; and (iii) the Supreme Court, and their collective predecessors, has essentially destroyed everything my country once stood for."

"President Trump offered a slim ray of hope, which was mercilessly snuffed out by established media, businessmen, bureaucrats, Democrats and Rinos (Republicans in Name Only). Trump was castrated pursuant to the Schwarzenegger syndrome, which featured, among other things, a complex mass of lies and half-truths circulated by: (i) illegal government leaks: (ii) false claims by elected and nonelected high-ranking Democrats; (iii) media lies, half-truths and out of context 'news' releases, articles, magazines, newspapers, and emails, all conspiratorially implemented to perfection by the combined effort of the deballers."

"Arnold Schwarzenegger, a renowned American bodybuilder and movie star, was born and raised in Germany. After moving to America as a young adult, he ultimately parleyed his Hollywood movie career into election to the governorship of an important liberal state, California."

"Jet, I remember his Terminator movies. Didn't he follow-on, succeeding Trump as emcee in a reality TV show, or something like that?'

"Yes, and finishing up on Schwarzenegger, he attempted to change California government from socialistic tax and spend, to middle of the road conservativism."

"He failed, since the California state legislature controlled California purse strings. Sadly, Arnold was not able to accomplish much of anything in the way of conservative change in California during his two terms (eight years) as California governor. No California money to speak of was ever appropriated to fund any meaningful Schwarzenegger attempt to improve the lives of California citizens and residents."

"That's a hell of a note, Jet."

"It is and it gets worse. During his presidential tenure, unlike Schwarzenegger, Trump had majority control over both the US House of Representatives and the US Senate. Even so, Trump suffered the same political impairment as Schwarzenegger, but at the Federal level. As I said, Trump was ganged up on by the media, the establishment (bureaucracy and business), the legislature and his own party (the Rinos). Unfavorable polls and high level, important, damaging classified information leaks; along with shootings and other violence by Democrat minions, didn't help either. Everywhere Trump turned, he was sabotaged; the most severe reverse whitewash in American government history; a good man victimized and ruined by the system. So be it."

"President Donald Trump accomplished nothing to speak of, except for ObamaCare '2,' which he euphemistically referred to as repeal and replacement of ObamaCare. Pitiful. Well, maybe he improved international relations, but not much. What can a man do when his 'allies' won't pony up their share of expenses and have to spend time at home in their own country defending against domestic terror attacks by the damned Arabs?"

"We have some strange allies. US treasury bonds held by Germany and Japan roughly equal the value of our defense expenditures on their behalf from 1945 to 2021. We totally pay their way and our reward is we owe them money. Go figger."

"As for facts, Stony, I didn't read what I am about to tell you from newspapers or books. I didn't hear about it on the radio or on TV, I experienced everything firsthand from the trenches of life."

"All of it, boss, every last despicable piece of information?"

"OK, you're calling me out. Not everything, not each and every dinky ass piece of information, but damn near everything. For certain, I saw and heard with my own eyes and ears very nearly everything I am saying to you. Miserable though it may be, this is my personal story, first hand, true as hell."

"I would never have mistaken you for a political philosopher, Jet."

"I just got started, young man. For the purpose of this foray into political philosophy, facts are divided into two parts, money and politics."

"Before we address the subject of money, one thing is clear to the casual observer. From the 1930s up to now, and on into the foreseeable future, practically every MFWIC (motherfucker who's in charge) running the US government, the administration, the congress and the supreme court, has now, has always had and always will have, an overall agenda which is diametrically opposed to reason and common sense. Exceptions to this statement are few and far between."

"Short answer, they don't know what the fuck they're doing. If they do know what they're doing, it's treasonous. Either way, the country is screwed by its own management."

"Cutting to the chase, money. The most important commodity in the world, the United States Dollar, depreciates in purchasing power as we speak, primarily because of deficit spending and increased money supply, M1 and M2. That is America's biggest problem. Hardly anyone in the country agrees that deficit spending is a critical problem."

"Here's the scoop. From about 1950 to 2021, the United States of America: (i) lost five wars; (ii) ran up over \$25 trillion in debt; and (iii) committed the US Treasury to assume debt of approximately

$190 trillion (the present value of obligations which come due in the future) to pay for Social Security and Medicare.

"Every country needs an effective monetary system. Ours is as nearly ineffective as it could possibly be. The United States is on death's door because we are strangling ourselves by and through continuous, intentional mismanagement of our fiscal system. It's tricky to explain. Simplistically, our currency is weak and failing as we speak because there are too many dollars chasing a fixed number of goods and services."

"On a regular basis, we intentionally devalue our currency by creating fiat money, currency and demand deposits (bank deposits) backed only by the worthless promise of the US government that the money is valuable. When fiat money (money not backed by hard assets, not backed by gold) enters the fiscal marketplace, existing United States currency is 'watered down,' decreasing the purchasing power of money in circulation. Trump could not halt this fiscal tsunami."

"A hypothetical describes how it works. A high school educated clerk is told by her supervisor to sit at her cubicle, turn on her desktop computer, select wire transfer outbound, type in the amount of 80 billion ($80,000,000,000) dollars; identify the recipient as Riggs Bank (an important DC bank) for deposit to the Account of the Treasurer of the United States of America. Then hit send."

"Unfortunately for us all, Riggs Bank treats the incoming wire transfer of funds as real money ($ 80 billion dollars in this hypothetical), which real money is immediately spent on guns and butter by our worthless treasonist (towards its citizens) Federal Goddamn government."

"Favorite butter projects include unearned welfare such as food stamps and earned income credit IRS cash payments. Favorite guns projects include unnecessary or overpriced weapons sold to the federal government by greedy weapons manufacturers, represented by slick talking conmen, snake-oil registered federal lobby agents."

"The name of the transaction is QE (quantitative easing, the creation of funny money, fiat money), the most despicable euphemism to ever be coined by Washington, DC. The effect of QE over time is to permanently water down the value of hard earned cash in the possession of workers, especially in their pension funds. The Federal Reserve Bank is but a tool used by the United States government to water down the value of American money, nothing more."

"In our hypothetical, the clerk works for the Fed, the Federal Reserve Bank of the United States of America. The Fed has no money. Nevertheless, the Fed claims that it is owed north of five trillion dollars by the United States of America. Unbelievably the media identifies the Fed as the biggest public debt creditor of the United States; they claim the Fed is owed more money than either China, Germany or Japan. That's pure bullshit because the Fed never at any time in the past advanced even one dollar of cleared funds to the United States government, all funny money."

"This is ridiculous, Jet. I don't believe it."

"Believe it, my man, it gets worse. On a slightly different vein, the majority of nations which have failed in recent history (last 100 - 200 years) have failed because both national debt and money supply expanded until unsustainable levels were exceeded. In layman's terms, the money became worthless."

"When the money supply is increased, more dollars than before compete to purchase the same fixed number of goods and services; thereby the prices of those goods and services increase to maintain a new and higher equilibrium."

"Politicians (Democrats and Republicans) share joint responsibility for creating this dismal state of affairs. Commencing in the 1930's the US government initiated a deficit funding policy, spending more US government money than raised through taxes and fees. That draconian policy caused the US treasury to now be 25 trillion dollars in the red, deep down in a bottomless debt hole we will never climb out of. As I said earlier, fiscally, the United States of America is doomed, is bankrupt."

"Continuing on, a distinct majority of political leaders, actively and interactively, directly and indirectly, promote the appetite of the masses for unearned entitlement wealth transfer ('Free Stuff'). Unfortunately, the masses will never get enough and will never have enough Free Stuff, regardless of how much and how many things the government 'gives' the masses. Democracy at its worst."

"The masses have already taken the United States down. Our country is bankrupt, going deeper and deeper into the Black Pit of Calcutta 'monetary chasm of desperation and despair,' every day. The definition of bankruptcy is 'the inability to service debt in the ordinary course of business.' That's us; that describes the fiscal condition of the United States of America to a 'T.' Our government can pay its bills only by borrowing money or by printing worthless money, no other way. We are dead broke and have been for decades. Half of Americans pay no federal income tax. The other half pays their way, 100%. The IRS is no longer exclusively a tax collector. By and through the magic of earned income credits, the IRS is now a welfare agency.

"I don't know what to think, Jet. I'm confused."

"Don't feel bad, Stony, you're not by yourself. Moving along to politics, one of my all-time favorite subjects. My last shot at money is to share with you the fact that by and through intense pressure, the Federal Reserve Bank for the past ten years or so has lowered and maintained national interest rates at well below historic norms. When interest rates return to normalcy, as they are certain to do, the problems I brought to your attention will geometrically exacerbate, accelerating America's impending fiscal collapse."

"Stony, like I said before, US government activities and programs eviscerate my gut, tear my heart out and torture my soul. There's no end in sight. Democrats are hopeless tax and spend, big government socialists. Democrats routinely trade entitlement 'Free Stuff' for votes as a matter of pride and principal. Republicans are no better, perhaps even worse, because Republicans routinely spout half-truth lip service to the effect that 'We are going to reduce government spending; we are going to reduce big government; we are going to build a southern border wall; we are going to strengthen our military; we are going to reduce taxes.' One false platitude after another, ad infinitum, ad nausea. All lies or half-truths."

"Among other things, Democrats support open borders, including amnesty and welfare for illegal immigrants, along with abundant unearned entitlements for immigrants in the form of food stamps, free medical care and generous earned income credits. Often these unearned benefits are bestowed upon able-bodied illegal immigrants and refugees, in return for anticipated future Democrat support at the voting booth."

"Our veterans slave and do without to make ends meet, while we invite the itinerant world into our backyards and pay their way, apparently in perpetuity. The present value of the obligation to support one political refugee throughout his/her lifetime in the United States is in the hundreds of thousands of dollars. Multiply that number of dollars by the number of refugees the Obama administration forced upon America, and you can see one major reason why our government is dead broke. We need to send those people back home."

"For the last 90 or so years we have provided free goods and services to the masses in excess of our ability to pay for the goods and services. We borrow from the Chinese and give to the American poor, and as well, provide foreign aid to Third World foreigners in need of aid, among others. On a regular basis, we borrow money to pay for milk for babies in Africa while denying our veterans precious medical care. Scandalous.

"Our government systematically courts theoretical 'good will' from mostly itinerant, ignorant, unskilled voters who are anticipated to vote Democrat in future elections. 'Good will' is the only return for taxpayer money lavished on an ever-increasing population of poor and sometimes fraudulent unearned entitlement recipients, all clamoring to vote Democrat so that even more Free Stuff will enter the death-spiral fiscal pipeline of everlasting, unending, infinite federal waste."

"The federal government will never get a penny's worth of return on money given away. Economics 101. Free means free to the rest of the world. In the USA, free means death, sooner rather than later. It's simple, our grandchildren are going to die because our government leaders are mishandling today's nickels and dimes."

Stony said, "Nothing could be simpler than that, Jet."

"Republicans, the loyal opposition. Ahhh---the loyal idiots is more like it. Republicans respond with empty rhetoric, never with substance, never with an alternate, viable plan. Republicans are complicit as relates to the destruction of America. Stony, I just told you that fellow Republicans refer to themselves as the loyal opposition. In reality, contemporary Republican loyalty is to the agenda of the Democrat Party. Get along, go along is their creed. The typical Republican politician is a person who pontificates but fails to produce. After eight years of Republican preaching against ObamaCare, in 2017, the senate, with a Republican majority, refused to repeal and replace ObamaCare; Republicans argued against each other, essentially voting Democrat by and through their refusal to repeal and replace ObamaCare. Republicans, piss-heads, one and all."

"The dynamic duo of Democrats and Rinos have adopted a creed which goes like this, almost word for word: 'We shall subvert the rights and expectations of a majority of US citizens and taxpayers in favor of the unsavory appetite of an ever increasing, greedy, shortsighted, sub-optimization postured, relatively ignorant electorate consisting of the masses, the blacks, the Latinos, the Islamists, the refugees, the poor, the uneducated, the ignorant and the unentitled; the unfortunate among us.' Collectively and under Democrat leadership, minorities are calling the shots, with valuable assistance from Democrat appointed Federal Judges. The tail is wagging the dog. The insane inmates are running the asylum, Stony."

"Damn," said Stony, continuing to be confused by Jet's revelations and knowledge about the state of American affairs. *Who would have thunk it?* "What you describe is weird, Jet. Let me stop you right here. I know you. I know you're bright, educated, erudite, astute, and a whole lot of other similarly descriptive adjectives. To me, the things you have just told me are true. How in hell can that be? Do you mean to tell me that the majority of American federal politicians, the majority of the American media and the majority of voting Americans don't understand the importance of the simple truths you just described? Help me out here, Jet. Why doesn't everybody agree with you? Closer to the truth, why does nobody believe you, why does everybody disbelieve you?"

"Stony, I'll I get back to you on that question," Said Jet.

Jet continued, "In closing, the leaders of the United States of America are chicken shit. Because of political correctness and fascination with polls, our leaders are afraid of their own shadow. In the last 13 short years, the USA frittered away its reputation as a world leader. Allies do not trust the USA. Enemies ridicule and laugh at the USA."

"Our leaders are afraid to make decisions, afraid of the threat of re-election lost, afraid of criticism. Most importantly of all, our leaders are afraid of bringing themselves to the negative attention of the major media, national TV and major newspapers, by engaging in behavior opposed by the major media."

"I'll answer your question about why nobody believes me by using a metaphor, addressing the five stages a cancer patient experiences when informed that he or she has contracted terminal cancer. The five stages, from diagnosis to death, are: Denial, Anger, Fear, Grief and Acceptance."

"Deep down, everybody knows the $25 trillion debt is never going to be paid off. They know they have to pay their own debts but, en masse, Americans do not believe that something really bad will happen if the government doesn't pay its debts. That's denial."

"Stony, a majority of Americans are already at the tail end of Anger, approaching Fear. They accepted the fact that we have a money problem; reacting first with anger, then by being afraid of the debt."

"Many Americans have transitioned past Fear and are now in

the Grief stage, extremely sad that the United States has a serious money problem. A very few citizens are already in the Acceptance stage, having emigrated from the United States. Recall the rich man, a co-founder of Facebook. He denounced his citizenship and moved to, New Zealand, I think it was. An example of Acceptance."

"To me it is bizarre that high-ranking Democrats and Republicans, to a man, appear to be neither angry or afraid. Obviously, those nitwits are deluded. It's clear to me that, with rare exception, essentially every politician in America is suffering from a form of economic delusion."

"Regardless, our country's fiscal system has failed; whether or not its leaders and constituents believe the system has failed is irrelevant. If you have cancer, you have cancer, whether or not you believe you have cancer. That's us, we have a fiscal problem. Those responsible either do not believe the problem exists, or are not willing to admit the problem in public. Figure it out for yourself, Stony. I already did."

"You can't work with dumb people. Neither can you work with delusional people. Dialogue is useless. The only tool available is force. Otherwise our country will fail and inexorably transition from respected and feared super-power to the equivalent of modern-day western European pretenders such as France, Spain and Italy; all once great nations, now reduced essentially to footnote status as relates to world importance."

"Damn, Jet, that's dismal, man."

"You bet your sweet ass it's dismal, and you can bet your bottom dollar it's true."

"As to the Colombians shooting down our Gulfstream, the Feds, and increased perimeter security, I'll discuss those matters with you at a later date."

"Boss, your diatribe was far out; bizarre, even heartbreaking. I never heard anything like it in my life. You should've been a politician. I'd vote for you."

12

NATALIE TAYLOR
Super Cop

Natalie Taylor was raised by her mother in Louisville, Kentucky. She graduated from Louisville Male High School in 1999. A cum laude graduate of Vanderbilt University in 2003, she majored in government and politics with minors in history and philosophy. She earned her 2006 law degree at Duke University, on the Dean's list all six semesters, emphasizing money law; consisting of corporate law, real property law, insurance law and securities law. Natalie's IQ is 157, higher than 99.982 % of the general population. Natalie is not only smart; she's a genius.

After law school graduation Natalie clerked for Supreme Court Justice Andrew Thompson for two years, followed by employment with the FBI in 2007 as an agent recruit. Thereafter she embarked on a meteoric rise up through the ranks, from boot FBI agent to Deputy Director of the FBI in 13 years; a remarkable accomplishment, the first and only of its kind.

Natalie Taylor, a knockout if there ever was one; 5' 8" tall, weighing in at 125 pounds. She is a cross between Nephrodite, Sophia Loren, Carrie Nation, Margaret Thatcher and for good measure,

Isaac Newton. Natalie has black hair and cold blue eyes; a beautiful face, perfect profile, lovely body and great legs. Dress size 6, shoe size 8. She holds a karate black belt and is in pro athlete physical condition. She works out at the J Edgar Hoover FBI Building three times a week, one hour per session, primarily cardio and free weights.

Her flawless employment record is studded with signal achievements, including single handedly stalking and killing two fugitives in a cross-border kidnapping incident which led to the solving of a multistate, multi-nation, money-laundering scheme. She headed a successful computer/email investigation related to a combination of domestic and international wire fraud, and RICO (racketeering) violations.

Natalie is apolitical. Notwithstanding, over the years she observed with interest the creation of a quasi-partnership of elected Democrats and Rinos, legislators who in lock step consistently vote to spend copious amounts of money in excess of revenue and increase the national debt year-after-year to unsustainable levels.

Natalie met husband Pete Branson, MD (after marriage Natalie retained her maiden name) while she was an undergraduate student at Vanderbilt University. Pete is a native of Nashville, Tennessee. The Branson family traces its roots from the Mayflower down through Andrew Jackson to a Branson who was an esteemed Tennessee politician, serving as Lieutenant Governor for eight years. The Bransons made their money in real estate.

After Natalie graduated from Vanderbilt and was accepted by Duke University Law School in Durham, North Carolina, Pete relocated his cardiology medical practice to nearby Raleigh, North Carolina, 25 miles southeast of Durham. The couple rented a gated community home for three years, located half way between Raleigh and Durham.

After Natalie's graduation from law school in North Carolina and subsequent appointment as a clerk at the United States Supreme Court, the couple settled down in West Springfield, Virginia, a

Washington, DC suburb. Husband Pete Branson hired on with a group of cardiology physicians practicing in Arlington, Virginia.

Pete is seven years older than Natalie. He always wanted to be a doctor. He was enamored with medicine. Tragically, four years ago Pete sustained a cervical spine injury in a three car rollover accident on the Washington, DC Beltway. Cause of the accident was the gross negligence of a drunken, uninsured Central American illegal alien, a man whose rap sheet contained 17 entries. As a result of the accident, Pete will be a quadriplegic for the rest of his life.

Donald Branson, Natalie's 16 year old only child, experiments with recreational drugs. He is an addict. He regularly abuses cocaine, heroin and methamphetamine, the hard stuff, along with a lot of pot and hashish.

Natalie's plate is full. She has no fuel in her tank; she is running on tapped out fumes. Natalie is out of juice. She wonders when the momentum of her youth will desert her, leave her high and dry. Then she will surely die.

13
WASHINGTON, DC
The Oval Office

It is Tuesday, January 26, 2021. Novice and newly elected president Bill Wilson has been in office for six days. You can hear a pin drop. The oval office is almost full. Dignitaries attending include President of the United States, Vice President, Speaker of the House, Senate Majority Leader, Chairman and Vice Chairman of the Joint Chiefs of Staff, Military Service Chiefs from the Army, Navy, Air Force and Marine Corps and the Chief of the National Guard Bureau.

Also in attendance are holdover Directors of the FBI, CIA and NSA, along with two holdover cabinet members, Secretary of Defense and Secretary of Homeland Security.

Animation, exuberance and positivity describe White House Chief of Staff Thomas Redding as he opened the meeting, "Mr. President, distinguished guests, it gives me no great pleasure to reaffirm that our known enemies continue aggressive nuclear related activities against the contiguous United States."

"Today is the first meeting of our administration on this subject, so let me bring you up to snuff. Since the final meeting of the previous administration on this subject six weeks ago, alarming events have occurred, unthinkable events, immoral events, events incompatible with the health, safety and welfare of any nation in the world, much less the United States. Individually and collectively, these developments warrant immediate pro-active response."

A Goddamned bullshit false alarm by nitwit Chief of Staff Tom Redding, an idiot if there ever was one. What a waste of time, thought each of the seven generals in his own vernacular.

"We acknowledge receipt of solid evidence that certain enemy attempts to conduct a nuclear strike on a US city are well past the planning stage and are anticipated to be implemented sooner rather than later."

"Intelligence sources believe a nuclear strike will occur upon an as of yet unidentified US city no earlier than two months at the inside and no later than five months at the outside. Inside, mid-March. Outside, mid-June. We have as few as two months' notice, only two months."

"These people mean business. This is no half-assed lone wolf, shoe bomber scenario. We are at war. We don't know who we are at war with, but we are at war."

Same old Tom Redding, a piss poor introduction to an important military problem, thought President Bill Wilson, a functional illiterate as recent presidents go, only slightly weaker than Bush II, the initial 21st century functionally illiterate president.

"Mr. President, I recommend that we immediately, today, form a special project joint task force comprised of CIA and FBI operatives, equal manning; only the most qualified operatives of the CIA and the FBI."

We are screwed, thought CIA Director Jack Fleming; because Tom Reading blessed the CIA with top billing one sentence ago, the CIA gets the short end of the stick on this one. The FBI will have the lead on this project. *Our turn next time.*

"Tell it like it is, Tom. Tell it like it is. No embellishment, pure vanilla. Let the chips fall where they may," interrupted President Bill Wilson.

"There are ten known nuclear powers. USA, UK, France, Israel, Russia, China, India, Pakistan, North Korea and Iran."

"We don't know for sure, but best estimates indicate there are about 16,300 nuclear warheads in existence. Russia has 8,000. We have 7,300. Of special interest is Pakistan with 120 weapons and North Korea with 10 weapons. We don't know how many nuclear weapons Iran has."

Chief of Staff Tom Redding droned on for 30 more minutes, boring his audience with platitudes, metaphors and outright errors of fact. He embarrassed the president and offended every official present at the first staff meeting of the Wilson Administration when he nominated an inexperienced, barely qualified female to head a new joint task force charged with the responsibility of seeking out and eliminating a nuclear poacher, with the existence of the United States at risk.

After the presentation was completed, the President said, "Gentlemen, you're all excused except for Tom Redding and FBI director Jim Burns. Thank you for your time. I anticipate moving on this subject promptly."

"I know I can count on you all, individually and collectively, to give preference to this matter over everything else on your plate, regardless of importance. I trust you to cooperate with me and with each other in communications, recommendations, and so on, regarding anything of importance, factual, theory, hunch, whatever. I'm satisfied the wellbeing, the existence, of this nation is at stake. Good day, gentlemen."

Tom Redding whispered to no one in particular, "Gentlemen, no questions and answers today."

This is an all time low, thought Senate Majority Leader Benjamin P. Worthington.

Not one Goddamn NSA appointee. SOB Redding has lost his

mind, thought NSA director Seth Bennison. *Maybe he has no mind. Stranger things have happened.*

After attendees departed, the president turned his attention to Chief of Staff Tom Redding, silently confirming the presence of Director Jim Burns, the FBI holdover. Rubbing his chin as is his habit, after a brief pause President Wilson said, "Tom, how is it you can come in here half-cocked, presumably from out of nowhere, drop a bombshell about nuclear weapons on my desk and suggest a Goddamn split tail, a presumably sorry ass, emotion burdened, narcissistic bitch for all I know, should run this important show?"

"A woman, for God's sake, to be appointed by the president of these United States, to be totally responsible for the defense of America against the presumed salacious activities of three independent rogue states, North Korea, Pakistan and Iran. Perhaps even Russia, China, and India. Yes, I know you didn't mention Russia, China and India. I'm not a total nitwit, Tom. I didn't get elected to this thankless job because of my good looks, goodwill or bribery."

"I'll tell you one thing. I'm out of my element. I didn't sign on for this kind of thing. On the other hand, the buck stops here. Goddamn it all to hell, and against my better judgment I might add, this time, perhaps for the last time, I'm going ahead with your Goddamn recommendation and pray to hell you've put us on the right track, gotten us off on the right foot."

"Now, tell me once again, who in the hell is this Goddamned Natalie Taylor and why in the hell is she qualified for such an important job? I never heard of her. I know you, Jim Burns, the top policeman in the entire world, are doing a journeyman's job," nodding deferentially to the aspiring J. Edgar Hoover clone. "I have complete confidence in you, Jim."

Jim Burns blinked. He was daydreaming. *Son of a bitch, I'm losing Natalie for I don't know how long. My piece on the side is not going to like this at all. No more Wednesday afternoons. Damn.*

"I don't anticipate problems with Jim or anybody else in the FBI under Jim's tutelage. But otherwise, why have I never heard of

Natalie Taylor? Talk to me, Tom," the President implored. "Are you fucking Natalie Taylor, Tom?"

Disregarding the question, Tom Redding boomeranged, "Mr. President, trust me on this one. She's the best man for the job, even if she is a Goddamn woman."

Reluctantly saith the President, "Approved, contingent upon an interview, a private powwow between yours truly and this Natalie Taylor in my office at 1:00 pm tomorrow. And if I find out you have been fucking Natalie Taylor, I will nail your ass to a cross with your own hammer. Capiche?"

A tired, reluctant nod beckoned acknowledgment.

*

Tom Redding's secretary was busy with a priority assignment. She got around to calling Natalie Taylor's office at 4:25 pm Tuesday afternoon. Dina Watters, Natalie's secretary the past five years, acknowledged notification of Natalie's appointment with the President in the oval office for tomorrow, Wednesday, January 27, 2021 at 1:00 pm.

Commencing at 4:30 pm, Dina rang Natalie's cell phone unsuccessfully every half hour on the half hour until 6:00 pm. Dina then closed the FBI Deputy Director's office for the day. Natalie's voicemail was not full because Dina's four messages were accepted for recording. Dina was uncomfortable, but not overly so. She will attend to this matter first thing tomorrow, Wednesday morning.

14

WEST SPRINGFIELD
the Druggie

Traffic in the city was heavy, even heavier on the up to 16 lane beltway which encircles most of the Washington DC metropolitan area. Normally it's over an hour's drive from downtown DC's Wilsonian Preparatory School to the Branson home, a three story townhome in West Springfield, Virginia, located in a small subdivision named RyeGate, about 19 miles west southwest of the town center of Washington, DC.

This January Tuesday is dreary and overcast, temperature 48 degrees Fahrenheit, electric wiper blades self-actuated in response to a light drizzle. Clicking the door opener as she turned into her driveway, Natalie drove her five year old 2016 Audi down and into the basement garage. The red brick townhome has four levels: basement (garage); 1st floor (ground floor); 2nd floor (2 bedrooms); and 3rd floor (2 bedrooms).

Exhausted from traversing rainy DC traffic and confronting her drug ridden only son's problems, Natalie arrived home just prior to 2:00 pm. Don usually gets home from school a little after 4:00 pm.

Natalie has two hours to visit with husband Pete and to provide daily instructions to her live-in nurse/housekeeper, Betsy Ann Mathers.

Although days at home for Natalie are bad enough, today is worse than usual. Today is Natalie's day to confront her only child, 16 year old high school junior Don Branson, with her knowledge of Don's illicit drug use. The worst of it is the remedy which Natalie intends to impose upon Don as punishment for Don's experimentation with hard drugs. Don is in for it.

"Hello, darling."

"Hello yourself, Miss Priss," Pete, the quadriplegic, making small talk.

The visit with Pete went as well as could be expected, considering it was the continuation of a four-year serial discourse between a cripple and his wife, a 39 year old highly intelligent, active female with one of the best jobs in America, a woman imbued with more virility than most men. Try that on for size.

The first 13 years of Natalie's marriage to Pete were the most wonderful years of her life. Pete was bright, competent, sensitive, productive, and irrevocably committed to Natalie's best interests. Seven years older than Natalie, he provided more than a modicum of stability, which contributed significantly to her near instant transition from a novice new hire to an experienced, journeyman FBI agent.

Natalie's learning curve is incredible. Because, among other things, she is brilliant, active and curious, she knows more about the internal functions of the FBI than anyone inside or outside the Bureau, past or present. She is confident she can handle any task related to any aspect of the Federal Bureau of Investigation, anywhere, anytime, anyhow, regardless of complexity. It's true. She can.

Genuinely humble, Natalie credits Pete as the primary factor contributing to her instant success as an FBI agent, the only job Natalie has ever had, full or part time. Pete taught Natalie how to function as an adult. He treated her as an equal. She loved it. In those formative days, she could not have imagined life without Pete Branson.

Time marches on. Four years ago, Pete was incapacitated for life in that horrible automobile accident. Four lost, wretched years. Except for her job, every aspect of her life is despicable, miserable. Politics, political correctness, sub-optimization; those things and more contribute to Natalie's disenchantment and vocational malaise.

Even so, Natalie is postured for promotion, in better career shape than practically any American professional female within ten years of her age. She is situated perfectly for a productive career in the upper echelons of government; Cabinet member, Senator, Representative, Governor, all realistically attainable goals in the reasonably near future. With rare exception only a government stair climber postured as Natalie can realistically aspire to attain high political office.

The bad news: her personal life is a disaster and she knows it. Pick a day, any day; she stumbles through it. Nothing motivates her. She gets by on the momentum of her youth, little else. *I wonder when the momentum of my youth will desert me, leave me high and dry. On that day I will surely die. Without Pete, I am nothing. I expose only a false façade. Inside, my body and soul are dead, and have been for four years.*

"Betsy Ann, I'm stressed out. If anyone calls, I'm not here. I have an important business meeting tonight which may continue until as late as early in the morning. Please don't stay up for me," said Natalie.

Betsy Ann Mathers replied softly, "I won't Ms. Taylor. Thank you for letting me know."

During the past two years the 56-year-old live-in licensed practical nurse and experienced caregiver for hire, endured that song and dance every month, to the day. Betsy Ann knows Natalie has a lover. *It's just as well. Mr. Branson, the poor thing.*

"What kind of day did Pete have? asked Natalie."

"Uneventful, but his mood was better than most days, sees as how for the past few months mentally he hasn't been up to much of anything."

Absentmindedly, Natalie replied, "A small blessing," as she shuffled from Pete's modified 'hospital room' into the townhome's kitchen.

*

One ding a ling. The unarmed home alarm system rings when anyone opens or closes any venue of ingress/egress, i.e., doors or windows. Don is home from school.

"Don, please take your books to your room and come back down here right away. I want to talk to you for a few minutes," said Natalie, standing in the center of the family room on the first floor of the townhome.

"Aw, Mom, can't it wait?" pleaded Don.

"Not for a minute, young man. A subject of international importance, it appears. You and I against the world, Don," spoofed Natalie, as was their habit of jocularly dealing with one another.

Five minutes later Don walked down the stairs from his bedroom on the third floor, regally appearing in the family room. Before the accident Natalie and Pete shared the master bedroom on the second floor. After the accident, Natalie contracted out a remodeling job, converting the main dining room on the first floor into a permanent hospital-like bedroom for Pete.

Floors two and three each have two bedrooms. The second floor comprises Natalie's private bedroom and Betsy Ann's private bedroom. The third floor contains two bedrooms, Don's bedroom and another bedroom used for storage.

Teenager Donald Branson violated all rules of posture as he slithered his body into the overstuffed living room chair. He looks like and moves like a salamander. "OK, Mom. What's the big deal?" asked Don innocently.

"This is the big deal," responded Natalie, as she walked over to the chair in which the contorted salamander was comfortably resting. Facing her son at close range, she moved her right hand from behind her back to the front of her body at waist level and opened the palm of her hand so as to provide Don an unimpeded view of the packet of cocaine which three days earlier Don had hidden between his mattress and box springs in the center of his bed.

You should have seen the look on Don's face. 'This is bad, really bad,' is what the face would have said to you if the face could talk. Really bad.

Natalie's rebuke commenced, "Don, unless you so desire, I'm not going to delve into particulars such as who, what, where, when, why and how. You know very well who, what, where, when, why and how. Unless you tell me different, right now, the only thing you and I are going to discuss is my course of action and your course of action as a result of your possession of cocaine in my house. Do you understand me?"

No response from a shell-shocked Donald Branson. The slithering salamander is in a fetal position, scrambling for defensible turf, none of which is available.

"Do you really understand me, Don? I wonder if you really do understand me."

"Yes, ma'am, I really do understand you. I really do, mom," responded a now repentant Donald Branson, a high school first semester junior who is burning up $28,000 of household cash annually for tuition, not including fees and supplies, at Wilsonian Preparatory School.

"Good. Now, listen carefully young man," calmly and forcefully demanded Natalie.

Don knows from Natalie's body language and tone of voice that this confrontation is going to be worse than really bad. He made no reply, because he has no reply.

Continuing, Natalie pronounced the sentence, "Donald Branson, as of here and now your family is placing you on permanent probation. I anticipate you will be on probation for a minimum of 1½ years and a maximum of 5½ years. Conditions follow."

"Number one: you were disenrolled from Wilsonian Prep today. Your books and materials will be sent to you within a week. You will never set foot on the Wilsonian campus again, never. That's final."

Don grimaced noticeably. Natalie continued, "Number two: you may, and I repeat may, I didn't say will, have an opportunity to save your credits from the first semester at Wilsonian. I'll let you know within the next two weeks."

"Number three: you will recommence high school as a boarding student second semester junior at Millersburg Military Institute, located in a small town in Kentucky by the same name, Millersburg. The school is referred to as MMI. You will attend MMI as a second semester junior, as a first semester senior and as a second semester senior, with one summer off between junior and senior years. I will determine this summer's schedule of events within the next month."

Don noticeably shook his head in disbelief. Natalie disregarded the headshaking. "Number four: no final determination has been made on where you will go to college. I'm contemplating VMI, Virginia Military Institute, and the Citadel, a military oriented college in the state of South Carolina. Both VMI and the Citadel are military style boarding schools, just like MMI."

Don clammed up and stopped listening.

"Unless you demonstrate to my satisfaction that I am wrong, your major in college will be accounting. Accounting requires the least investment of college time to posture a student for a chance, an opportunity, to become a successful executive in one of the most important professions in the world. Senior partners in nationally recognized accounting firms can earn seven figures a year." Natalie closed by saying, "You have the floor, if you have anything to say, Don."

"No, ma'am, not now," disconsolation apparent. Don remained in shock. Nothing has sunk in yet.

"Regarding housekeeping and ground rules during the time you live in this house before leaving for Kentucky, for openers, give me your cell phone. Give me your car keys. Detach your computer from the internet. Make no personal phone calls to anyone, from our land lines, from any cell phone, from any Skype location; receive no personal visits in this house from anyone."

Visibly disturbed, Don handed over his cell phone and both sets of keys to his still new, three months old RAV4. He had both sets of keys in his pocket because he intended to pawn the RAV4 for drug money.

"Do not leave this house without permission from me. I may sometimes be forced to provide permission through Betsy Ann. If you have an emergency, tell Betsy Ann to call me and say it's an emergency."

"Do not occupy the interior of any automobile, sedan, SUV or other vehicle absent my personal permission. Do not make any personal expenditure or commit yourself to make any personal expenditure absent my express permission. Do not drive my car. Do not drive anyone's car. Do not ride in anyone's car."

"Don, do you understand the conditions of family probation as I just explained them to you?" queried Natalie.

"Yes, Ma'am, I do," Don still disconsolate. Still in shock.

"One last thing. Your father knows nothing of your drug use and will never know anything unless you tell him. You have a chance, a very small chance, of redemption. Recidivism rates for serious drug users such as yourself are high. Do you know the definition of recidivism?"

"No, ma'am, I don't."

"To be recidivistic is to repeat something at least once. In so far as the drug culture is concerned, recidivistic behavior, and the term recidivism refers to the fact that a very large number, probably a lot more than 50%, of drug users who swear off drugs and try to quit using drugs, those people at some time in the future resume the use of illegal drugs. Did you understand my definition?"

"Yes, ma'am. I understand the definition of recidivist and recidivism. Thank you, mother."

"I suspect you are experiencing pangs of drug withdrawal as we speak. You have your work cut out for you, Don. Good luck. In the event you fail, this house will disown you for life and remove you from any contact with your father. Have I said enough? Have I made myself clear enough, Don?" the warden's final touch.

"Yes, ma'am, you have," Don totally destroyed.

"Remember, the TV, internet and telephones are all off-limits effective right now. You're free to visit my personal library and select any volumes which attract your attention. Unfortunately, I must attend a long and important meeting this evening. I may be home late. Good luck to you, my only son," the last sentence almost a whisper.

Don left the room sobbing. Natalie hates to see grown men cry. Donald Branson is not yet grown. Perhaps he never will be grown. Regardless, today is 'the day.' *Tonight is tryst night; trysting time is here.*

Although Don Branson is only 16 years old, he knows his mother is fucking a stranger. *How can I get mileage out of that?* queried the teenage drug addict to himself as he trudged up the stairs to his third floor bedroom, now a personal prison cell.

15
THE TRYST
Preparation

Both Natalie Taylor and only child Don Branson skipped dinner. Natalie, anticipation; Don, disconsolation. Natalie was not hungry. The last thing in the world Don was interested in was food.

The young druggie was holed up in his bedroom contemplating the difference between his perfect life in Washington DC and banishment to military secondary school in rural Kentucky. *Ugh, double Ugh, triple Ugh; all the Ughs in the world.*

Since Don is sexually active and has been since age 15, he is certain his mother has been screwing a strange man for over a year, one bang a month. He knows the FBI does not engage in long, drawn out, post-midnight government meetings. He is satisfied that his mother's 'fucking' behavior is worse than his drug use, much worse.

Don encountered the first pangs of drug withdrawal. He hates himself. He hates his mother. He hates God. He hates everything and everybody in existence, including himself. He hates everything that existed in the past, that exists now, and that might ever exist in the future. Once again, contemplation of suicide.

Natalie is not one bit sorry for Don. "As ye sew, so shall ye reap," her grandmother might have said. Serious drug users normally have no moral fiber, no work ethic, no interest in the future. Most serious drug users have no life outside of drugs. Don is a serious drug user. *He brought all his troubles on himself. Let's see if he has any mettle.*

At 6:30 pm Natalie shared domestic small talk with Betsy Ann, then climbed the stairs to her second-floor bedroom to dress for the evening's 'business.' Betsy Ann attended to chores. Quadriplegic husband Pete was fast asleep. Don continued contemplation of suicide.

Closing the door to her second-floor private bedroom, Natalie reflected. *Don didn't handle the drug confrontation well. That's too damn bad. My house has zero tolerance for drug use. No drugs. Nada. No Way, No Chance. No drugs in this townhome. How did this happen to us?*

*

In the final stage of masturbation; almost there, three minutes of strong, fast, near painful fondling. WOW!! Down below is hot as a pistol. *No, not now.* Natalie abruptly abandoned the precipice. *It's time to hit the shower; save the real thing for later.*

She closed her eyes and licked her lips passionately, hungrily. Natalie can taste it, see it, hear it, smell it, but she cannot touch it, any of it, at least not for a few more hours.

As she often does after masturbation, Natalie pondered, wondering if she is possessed by a female sex drive disorder. According to a recent US study 8% of males and 3% of females are cursed (blessed?) with an oversexed malady of one kind or another.

One out of 33, that ain't bad. How much longer can I keep this up without discovery by Pete, Don, or the FBI? I'm juggling, that's for sure. Not exactly professional behavior. On the other hand, I admittedly love it so. What a shameless melancholy bitch I have morphed into. Tragic. Okay honey, let's get it on. Showtime.

Natalie has no interest in the 'pretty girl' hairstyles prevalent and popular on CNN and FOX NEWS. During the past 13 years at the

FBI, she presented daily with a single hairstyle, alternating chignon variations, always up, chic and elegant.

She visits her favorite hairdresser once a week. Otherwise, she styles her own beautiful black hair, which is a bit wavy with a hint of curl, embellished by minute random specs of salt, the only indication she is much older than a teenybopper.

Black is Natalie's business color, her favorite color and her trolling color. Beautiful black. Black dress, black slip, black brassiere, black hose, black shoes, black purse, black man? No, she hasn't tried that yet.

Natalie is remarkably adept in all aspects of feminine appearance. She knows the latest styles. She knows the latest designers. She knows which materials are popular. Hardly anything about contemporary ladies' fashion goes unnoticed by Natalie.

She is a superlative dresser who never presents on the south side of glamorous. One of a kind; a gorgeous woman; a beauty to behold; everything to every man; the envy of every woman. The ideal man is tall, dark and handsome; the ideal woman is tall, bright and beautiful. That's Natalie; tall, bright and beautiful.

Natalie resembles a Mrs. America contest winner this early January evening. She is spruced up in a knock-off high end designer black dress, slim fit with knee length hem. Three-inch black heels top her out at near six feet even. Having abandoned the chignon for tonight, the combination of mid length black hair and clear, creamy complexion exudes the epitome of consummate elegance and femininity.

Cosmetics enhance Natalie's movie-star appearance. She is prettied up in all the right places, powder, facial and neck moisturizer, eyeliner, mascara for eyelashes and eyebrows, and inviting red lipstick, accentuated by a hint of Versace cologne.

She prefers gold accessories but for trolling always chooses silver. Natalie cannot in good conscience troll while wearing the gold Rolex watch gifted to her by husband Pete on the occasion of her graduation from law school in 2006.

For tonight, silver dress watch, five thin, fashionable silver bracelets on the right arm, silver clip-on earrings featuring opals and a stylish silver necklace gracing a respectable bodice.

After a final glance at the svelte reflection staring back at her from the full-length wall mirror, Natalie donned a lightweight, becoming, polyester/wool blend, black, knee length winter coat, selected from the five winter coats in her bedroom closet.

She carefully negotiated the bedroom stairs down to the first floor and checked on the cripple, her comfortably sleeping quadriplegic husband. After a moment of silent observation featuring an empathetic half smile, Natalie silently descended the stairs to the basement garage; all the while shaking her head left and right in disbelief of how the last four years have played out.

With one click of the garage door opener at 7:55 pm on a cold and dreary January Tuesday night, Natalie is on her way to commit an intentional moral crime against her marriage and against society.

*

The Deputy Director of the FBI self-parked her Audi in the well illuminated, exclusive parking lot of the Pentagon City Metro Hotel in Arlington, Virginia, a short distance west of the Washington Mall, just across the Potomac River from the Lincoln Memorial. She selected the hotel because it is near the Metro subway, perfect access for out-of-town businessmen to both the Pentagon and downtown Washington, DC.

In winter, the hotel's clientele consists primarily of such businessmen, typically salesmen attempting to garner a lucrative US government contract by promoting their wares, inventions and gimmicks. All represent corporations, foreign and domestic, large and small. The corporations attempt to score, to sell something to the Pentagon for future delivery to an Armed Forces end user.

Tonight's target, a corporate salesman (they all say they are in 'marketing'). For Natalie's purposes, all salesmen are the same. With rare exception, all are solo and lonesome. Many qualify as a candidate to service Natalie in the manner to which she has become accustomed. From Natalie's point of view, if you have seen one you have seen them all.

The weather is typical for a DC January, high of 60 and low of 35; 40 degrees right now. She manually locked the Audi, donned her winter coat and commenced the one and a half block walk from the hotel parking lot to the hotel. Her clutch contains a lipstick, $200 cash, a miniature bottle of unbranded petroleum jelly and an emergency key to the Audi, nothing more. She left her cell phone at home, having turned it off at noon.

In the Audi's locked glove compartment are Natalie's driver's license, FBI identification card, automobile registration and insurance documents. Natalie carries on her person no government issued identification documents. Small footprint.

Natalie approached the hotel in patented full troll mode; aloof, but 'perhaps' available. Stand offish, with a coaxing, friendly hint of 'Here I am, come and get it.'

Natalie mused:

Do you want some of me?

How much of me do you want?

If you want it, come and get it.

Don't scratch for it like a dog; ask for it like a man.

If you're up to it, do me, do me now.

Right now, Mister Man, right now, this minute, right here, right now. On the bar, on a barstool, in a booth, in the loo. Right now. Time's a wasting, sucker, do me right now, right here where I stand; nail me, you sorry ass son of a bitch.

Listen closely, you bastard, I'm the one who is hungry. What do you have for me? What do you offer me? How will you placate me? How can you satisfy me? I'm insatiable, how about you?

Fat chance you can even get it up. Fat chance if you get it up, it stays up. Chances are, if it stays up, it's shorter than my little finger, with the girth of an Office Depot ball point pen. Girth means how big around, you dumb ass.

I've been there, buddy boy, I've done that. My experience tells me you have the lasting power of wax paper, if that.

At this juncture in her life Natalie does not harbor an elevated opinion of the male gender.

Opening the manual side entrance door to the hotel, Natalie headed straight for the body exchange watering hole. Slim pickings tonight. Entering the smokeless, sterile bar through a frosted glass threshold, Natalie could barely distinguish a group of four or five stags together at a table in the back of the bar on the left side.

The bar entranceway continues 30 feet or so through to the end of the room, separating patrons at the bar from patrons in booths and at tables. The Fire Marshal authorizes a maximum of 120 patrons in the room at any one time. Not a Five Star establishment, but more than adequate for business travelers; more than adequate for Natalie's purposes.

Older bartender, dapper dress; black jacket, white shirt, black bow tie, "Good evening, missy, please sit wherever you like. The server is in the back. May I take your order?"

"No, thank you," replied Natalie, as she reconnoitered the dim room. Her nocturnal vision has not yet transitioned. In the subdued light of the bar, Natalie's daytime vision cannot discern shapes with any degree of definitiveness. Her nighttime vision is not yet functional, has not yet completed its adjustment to the minimum light available in the bar. In another minute or so, unhampered nighttime vision will be available.

Natalie addressed the bartender, "I'm from Wichita, Kansas; here on business. Is there anything happening in DC this week?" She recognized the bartender from a previous visit to the bar. Obviously he did not recognize her. *Good.*

The bartender replied, "Nothing special. Mostly business people staying here overnight. Action for the tourists is at and around the Capitol Mall, just a short distance across the Potomac River, over there," the bartender pointing toward the east northeast.

"Besides the Washington Monument and the Lincoln Memorial,

there are lots of tourist traps around the mall, the Smithsonian, the Bureau of Engraving and Printing, and those kinds of things. Lots of good restaurants all over the DC area. A few places in Georgetown and some of the suburbs light up at night. That's about it."

"Thanks for the tip," answered Natalie, as she locked her antennas onto a man about 20 feet further into the room, sitting on a barstool near the midpoint of the bar and nursing a highball. She reckoned scotch and soda.

Careful not to overplay, with perfect posture Natalie strode daintily forward on her three-inch black heels. Positioned optimally, in a fluid motion she pirouetted to the right and, with refined athleticism, eased onto a barstool three seats upwind from Jethro Armstrong, much like a Marine Corps helicopter pilot making a perfect three-point landing at Camp David with the President on board.

16
THE TRYST
In Progress

Natalie Taylor's objective	Have Sex with a Strange Man
Jethro Armstrong's objective	Kill a Female Prostitute

Natalie Taylor is trolling tonight for a male sex partner, which man she intends to engage in fornication with when she finds him.

Jethro Armstrong is trolling tonight for a female prostitute, which woman he intends to sexually abuse and then murder. Jethro is the DC serial killer. In the last three years, he murdered 34 female prostitutes. His theme is Christian Cleansing.

It is 8:40 pm. Jethro is preoccupied with introspective rumination as to how the evening will play out. Turning toward the bartender, he observed the final stage of a pirouette and agile mounting of a bar stool by an exceptionally attractive woman.

So as not to show undue interest, Jethro gazed at his highball glass; melted ice. The room temperature club soda has no fizz; it tastes like battery acid. Jethro summoned the bartender, who commenced a 15 foot walk toward Jethro from the end of the bar.

Unperturbed, Natalie made the first move, "May I buy you a drink, cowboy?"

"Ma'am, I thank you very much for the offer but I must respectfully decline. I'm not saying I don't want you to buy me a drink. I'm saying the way I was brought up, my money only goes one way where women are concerned, from me to you. If I was to accept a drink from you, I wouldn't be able to live with myself for the rest of my life. That's just the way it is for this Virginia boy, born and bred. However, and to the contrary, please let me reciprocate. Name your poison, ma'am."

This one is a real down homer, can't be far removed from the farm. On the other hand, he's not a redneck, clean-cut, conservative haircut, six feet one, maybe 195 pounds, Brooks Brothers blue suit, silk tie, Italian shoes, quasi handsome, good teeth, square chin, big hands, big feet and no ring. Not necessarily optimum, but passable. Big feet – that's an interesting feature.

"Let it be white wine, California Chablis. Do you have a name, cowboy?"

Jethro addressed the bartender, "California Chablis white wine for the lady and a refill on the club soda for me. Bill room number 318."

"Yes, sir."

"Ma'am, my name is William Samuel Marlette. My friends call me Sammy; my really close friends call me Sambo."

"Sammy it is. Jane Phillips here, Wichita, Kansas; in town on what was to be a pre-engagement gala. Turned out to be a bummer. I caught the son of a bitch swapping spit and sweet nothings with my best girlfriend. He got his walking papers last night. I'm going home alone tomorrow. Tonight I'm going to teach the bastard a lesson and you're going to help me, aren't you, cowboy?"

"Jane, I may not be Sir Walter Raleigh, but I sure as the dickens know how to help a lady in distress and you seem to fit the bill. How may I be of service, Ma'am?"

"I didn't just get off the Mayflower, Sambo. This is your lucky night; all you have to do is bed down, keep it up and enjoy the ride. I'll take care of everything. You have a room in this flea bag hotel, or was your order to the bartender for show?"

Jethro nodded his head yes, ambiguously answering both questions. *This one is definitely not a quick study.* "Are you in or out, cowboy? Yea or nay?

"Yea, I'm in, what's the tab?"

"Tab? There's no tab," thinking quickly, Natalie realized Jethro thought she was a pro. "Your only tab is the bar tab. I'm not a hooker, Sambo. This is not for love and is not for money. I'm going to fuck you for spite. I'm rid of Goddamn Jack Thompson for life and I'm celebrating my first anniversary a year in advance."

Jethro was confused. *Adultery is a mortal sin. Depending upon the dogma of your specific faith, unmarried couples who engage in fornication are not necessarily guilty of a mortal sin. In some Christian faiths fornication is not a sin. If it is a sin, fornication is seldom treated as a sin.*

Jethro made a snap decision; he knew God would approve, "Jane, as I just said, I'm in. Your place or mine, name the tune, little lady."

"Your place right now, Sambo," responded Natalie, as she eased her untouched glass of wine away from its resting place on the bar. She vacated the barstool with élan, turned left, retrieved her coat at the self-check rack, then exited the bar through the frosted glass door, Jethro in close trail.

The pickup took seven minutes, a record low. The previous low was 32 minutes. The record high remains at one hour and 29 minutes.

Shaking his head side to side, Jethro thought *The Lord works in wondrous ways.*

"We can't tell a player without a program, Sambo. Pick a number, any number. Let me know what it is. Hopefully it's a room number," prodded Natalie, recalling Jethro had told the bartender to bill room 318.

Jethro did not mind Jane's caustic wit. *A small price to pay. This one is courtesan material and I'm getting a 100% discount. You can't beat that with a stick.*

"Jane, turn right. The elevator bank is just around the corner on your left. We're headed for room 381. Turn left exiting the elevator, about 50 feet on the right, room 381."

"Good, Cowboy. Very good instructions. E for effort and P for performance, maximum performance, which I presume you are capable of, big man." Natalie wondered what kind of scheme or scam Sambo had cooked up with the bartender. She recalled with specificity Sambo telling the bartender he was to bill room 318, not 381. *Strike one, Sambo.*

Jethro sustained a rock-hard erection as the couple walked from the third floor elevator toward room 381. Natalie noticed a prominent bulge extending nearly half way to Jethro's right knee. *Damn, it's huge. It couldn't be that long,* Natalie nearly choked as she contemplated the possibility of penetration by such a whopping love dart. *Second thoughts already. Maybe I'm up to it, maybe not.*

Meanwhile Jethro amateurishly fumbled the plastic key card. Natalie expropriated the card and dexterously opened the hotel room door on first try. She entered the room and switched on the overhead light, Jethro close behind. After Natalie hung her coat in the closet, Jethro initiated an attempt to undress her. Natalie cut him short, "I'll handle mine in the bathroom. Get undressed and meet me in bed in two minutes. Don't be late."

"Yes, ma'am," meekly.

"Rendezvous in two minutes, Sambo. Last one in bed is a wooden nickel." Natalie couldn't remember how the quotation went, but wooden nickel sounded okay. Within a minute of entering the bathroom Natalie was down to her birthday suit, sans clothing, jewelry, and accessories. The only thing she had on was cosmetics and perfume.

She neatly stacked her clothing and clutch on the left side of the less than generous counter top, placed her pumps on the bathroom floor away from the commode and shower stall and stashed her watch, necklace, bracelet and earrings in the closed clutch. They barely fit.

When Natalie exited the bathroom with the jar of petroleum jelly in hand, room 381's bedroom was as dark as the Ace of Spades. Not an issue. Natalie had cased the hotel room within fifteen seconds of entry.

Jethro turned off the lights; bless his heart, the little darling. He is probably good for the missionary position, at midnight, lights out, under the covers, wearing a nightshirt; an 18th century Casanova at best. You can't win 'em all, Natalie Taylor, you can't win 'em all.

"Sambo, Sambo, where are you Sambo? Come out, come out, wherever you are; all-ee, all-ee in free." She remembered the lines to Hide and Go Seek. Adult playtime.

"Sambo, Sambo, I'm going to turn the lights on, Sambo. Don't be shy. I'll show you mine, you'll show me yours, I'll play with yours, and you'll play with mine. And then we'll play house together. I promise you will like it, Sambo. You will like it a lot, Sambo, a whole lot." Meanwhile Natalie searched in darkness for the location of the entry door near which the light switch was located, on the right side if entering, left side if departing the hotel room.

Half a minute later she switched on the overhead light, surprising a buck naked middle-aged male, "Cowboy, tell me your real name. You'll feel much better leveling with me rather than holding things back. What's your name, my man?"

Completely surprised, Jethro responded straight off, "My real name is Jethro Armstrong and I'm from Norton, Virginia." Jethro did not know why he said he was from Norton, Virginia, because he escaped the Appalachian Mountains of Southwest Virginia when he was 17 years old. It seemed like a proper response, the right thing to say. Jethro knows God is proud of Jethro for having told Jane his real name. He knows in his heart Jane's name really is Jane.

Jethro stared at Natalie. Through a different lens he saw Natalie for the first time, really saw her. She looked so God-awful lovely Jethro's breath was taken away. How could Jethro spoil, defile, ravage, or manhandle such a beautiful thing? It's like ruining a wedding cake with a first bite; it's like driving a new car through a mud puddle. Verboten. Off-limits. No entry. Maiden territory. Hands off.

Bewildered, Natalie gazed upon a nude male immobilized in space/time. In penile repose, Jethro was otherwise so stiff she thought rigor mortis had set in. More likely than not Jethro was experiencing emotionally induced total body muscle spasms.

He was sitting amidships in the king size bed, his back to the oversized pillows placed against the bed's headboard, knees at his chin with arms wrapped firmly around his legs. The position of his two arms and two legs almost completely concealed his privates, as Jethro had learned in Appalachian Virginia to refer to his groin area. He was shy, smitten, in a trance.

Abandoning her oral interrogation, a completely nude Natalie inched into bed alongside naked Jethro, who was 'frozen' in a comically bizarre, knees bent sitting position. Natalie was on her back, parallel to Jethro. From his vantage point, Jethro glanced down to his left. A carnal view revealed Natalie's perfect 34C breasts, with taut prominent nipples.

Jethro's mind and body automatically shifted into a higher erotic gear. He sensed a hoard of endless delights beckoning from a generous dapple of black hair covering the Fertile Crescent, about eight inches below Natalie's belly button. Jethro could almost hear her calling out to him. *Come to me, Jethro. Come to me, big man. I need you, Jethro.*

Jethro was sitting on the bed and Natalie was lying on her back beside him. Jethro's legs were clamped together. Viewed from the foot of the bed, Jethro was on the left and Natalie was on the right. Natalie turned toward Jethro, both hands coaxing Jethro into a position where he was lying flat on his back next to her; parallel, almost nose to nose and toes to toes, a mere three inches apart.

Natalie was amazed at the site of it. Jethro has the most immense phallus Natalie has ever seen, at least 10 inches in length by seven inches in girth. *This evening's piece of work is going to take some doing, but I feel up to it, or down to it as the case may be.*

Regardless, let's get started. First things first. Slow and easy, almost imperceptibly, Natalie's left hand crossed the Rubicon, alit on the skin of Jethro's left pelvis, lingering and gently finger-nail scratching there, teasingly heating Jethro up.

A minute later the fingertips of her left hand sauntered up and over to the mid-belly, searching on the way for any belly button fuzz in Jethro's naval. The next brief interval of teasing was comprised of activity by Roman hands and Russian fingers slowly but surely inching their way down to the masculine pot of gold at the end of the rainbow.

Pay dirt! A huge, engorged, virile male extremity. Quivering, throbbing, begging to be touched, to be fondled, to be stroked, to be titillated, NOW, right now.

Jethro doesn't know whether to fish or cut bait. He has never experienced anything like this in his entire life. It scares the hell out of him but he loves it. The muscle spasms are gone, replaced by involuntary tremors and lustful hot flashes.

Natalie is poised like a hungry frog, ready to feast upon unsuspecting prey. Moving into position she slowly, proficiently and firmly grasped Jethro's phallus with her left hand. After applying a judicious amount of petroleum jelly to the head and to the shaft, she simultaneously commenced to ever so gently and positively stroke Jethro's lavender glans penis with the fingertips and fingernails of her right hand while gently masturbating Jethro with her left hand. Double Dipping. Jethro's groans were barely discernable.

Continuing with firm but gentle right-hand finger fondling, with her left hand Natalie encircled the imploring phallus, squeezing in and out while simultaneously stroking her left hand (now an encircling fist) vertically up and down, in an exclusive male masturbation technique perfected by Natalie. Jethro commenced involuntary pelvic flinching.

Left hand gently squeezing, gliding phallic skin up and down on the shaft, creating erotic friction between the fixed shaft and the movable penile skin; simultaneously right hand fingers and finger-nails played Rachmaninoff's piano concerto number two on the head of Jethro's cock, a now finely tuned piano. Jethro was blown away, figuratively of course.

Thirty seconds later Natalie initiated the second most fabulous act of prurient activity known to mankind, Natalie's patented version of fellatio. An ingenious array of harmonious moves by mouth, lips, tongue and teeth blew Jethro away, with literal ease.

Jethro lasted one minute, not a second more. He gasped, he groaned, he moaned; he was closer to God than he had ever been.

"Do you have any water, Sambo?"

"Cold, in the mini-fridge."

Natalie arose, selected one of two sealed bottles of cold water from the mini-fridge and proceeded to the bathroom. Opening the seal with fingernails, Natalie took a medium drink of water directly from the bottle, pouring the remaining water down the sink.

She turned on the hot water which she had let run earlier and dampened a white hotel washcloth until it was comfortably warm to the touch but not hot. Within the minute she was back in bed, hand-washing Jethro's body, emphasizing the groin area; afterwards toweling down the emotionally stricken big man everywhere.

He continued to shake and tremble, savoring the aftereffects of the most wonderful climax he had ever experienced. *Where have you been all my life, sweet woman?*

Jethro possesses a socially redeeming feature, persistent virility. Post ejaculation he does not lapse into repose. Consistent performance on demand; hard to come by.

Like the battery of the same name, Jethro is ever ready. Ever ready for round two, for round three and finally for round four. Never flaccid, never soft, never limp. First the missionary position, next the doggie position, and finally Jethro's favorite, the female superior reverse position, sometimes referred to as the cowgirl reverse position.

The female superior reverse position was a first for Natalie. She believes it has been a bad day when she has not learned something. Her favorite adage, 'A person should learn something new every day,' right up there with 'She who hesitates is lost,' her anti-misogynist motto.

Natalie learned she could accommodate a huge man, on the condition he be delicate and careful. Surprisingly, Jethro was delicate and careful. Even though Natalie was tight, Jethro fit well, really well. She had two orgasms to Jethro's three orgasms. She was satisfied. Jethro was delighted.

At 9:45 pm Natalie's metamorphosis commenced. Jethro had no clue. He was in a trance, basking in delightful reflection. Jethro reckoned he might, stressing might, have been in love with his ex-wife, whatever her name was. Nevertheless, he knew he was in love with Jane. He knew God delivered Jane to Jethro in Jethro's time of need, delivered her to Jethro at a time when Jethro was diligently working on his mission for God, Christian Cleansing.

Having donned scanties and bra in preparation for departure, Natalie commenced fidgeting into her tight black dress.

"Jane, what are you doing? Don't go, Jane. We just got to know each other. I love you, Jane. You're such a wonderful woman. You taught me things about life I never knew existed. As sure as I love the Lord Jesus Christ, I'm smitten with your charms, Jane Murray," Jethro forgot Natalie's alias. "Come over here; let me hug you, Jane."

Earlier, Jethro had carefully opened both sealed water bottles, laced each of them with the date rape drug known by the street name "Ruffies" and resealed the bottles like new. Only an expert with a microscope could have determined the seal of either bottle of water had been tampered with.

Feeling a bit lightheaded, Natalie made a peace offering, "Like I said, Jethro, I'm from Wichita and I have a flight early tomorrow morning. I have to get some rest tonight so I can make the flight."

Annoyed because he revealed his real name to essentially a stranger, Jethro said, "You're not going anywhere tonight, Jane."

Trying to get the rest of the way into her dress, balancing on one foot and more than a smidgeon lightheaded, Natalie said "Jethro, you're a good man. We had a great time. You taught me. You showed me things I've never seen or done before. But, I'm telling you I must make my flight to Kansas tomorrow. I'm a professional woman, responsible for an important project requiring my presence in Wichita."

Natalie didn't see it coming. Jethro walked toward Natalie, all the while exuding calmness and friendliness. Without warning, Jethro sucker punched, coldcocked Natalie with a vicious right hook, his closed fist swiftly striking Natalie's left cheekbone. Natalie lost consciousness instantly.

Jethro fully undressed Natalie and put her back into bed. He turned out the lights and joined Natalie, hugging her in the spoon position, stroking her nipples ever so gently for a minute or two before falling asleep. Necrophilia comes to mind. Natalie is unconscious and alive, for now. Later, perhaps not. Her fate is in the hands of the DC serial killer. Is she victim number 35? Time will tell.

17

THE TRYST

Finale

Rohypnol is a prescription only sedative. The drug is illegal under the 1996 Drug-Induced Rape Prevention and Punishment Act. When used with intent to commit certain crimes, including rape, a 20-year rap in Leavenworth is appropriate. The drug has many street names. One of those names is 'Roofie.'

Roofies are 10 times more powerful than Valium. Among other effects, the drug causes amnesia and muscle relaxation as well as affecting psychomotor responses. Amnesia and unconsciousness are the big deals. Amnesia is probably the main reason sexual predators prefer Roofies. A close second reason is that a Roofie pill has no odor, color or taste and dissolves easily in liquids.

Roofies normally take effect 10 to 30 minutes after ingestion. Behavior limitations last from 8 to 24 hours; 10 to 12 hours is usual. A Roofie victim can be wide awake at the time she/he is being raped, and not remember anything about the rape.

*

Natalie regained consciousness at 4:50 am Wednesday morning, seven hours after Jethro punched her out. She was rendered unconscious partly because of concussion and partly because of ingestion of two ounces of bottled water laced with Roofies. A mere ten ounces of bottled water stood between Natalie and near certain death – the ten laced ounces of bottled water she did not imbibe.

Natalie knew she had been punched out. She also knew that a simple concussion does not normally induce the type of dizziness and haziness she was experiencing. *I'm under the influence of drugs. Jethro doped me. He put me down with some kind of poison. It had to be the water. I'm God awful lucky I drank only a single glurp. Why in the world would Jethro drug me? Why didn't I notice that the seal on the bottled water had been tampered with? A damn fine policewoman I am; no better than an amateur. Dreadful.*

I have it. The son of a bitch asked me how much I intended to charge him for sexual favors, 'The tab,' he said, 'what's the tab?' I told him nothing, nil. I told Jethro that I was splitting with Tom, my persona non-grata boyfriend.

The DC serial killer restricts his targets exclusively to ladies of the night, prostitutes and hookers. Shortly after we met downstairs, Jethro came to the conclusion, at least momentarily, that I was a hooker.

Jethro drugged me tonight using the same MO as the DC serial killer. There's a good chance Jethro is the DC serial killer. 32 of the 34 victims of the DC serial killer tested positive for Roofies. Damn! That's it, Roofies, the date rape drug. Jethro doped me with Roofies!

I remember now. As usual, I quickly depart the scene once I get my rocks off. I started dressing after we finished our last round of sex. Yes, now I remember. Jethro was unhappy that I was leaving. He wanted me to stay with him for the night, wanted that in a big way. Wanted it so much that he sucker punched me.

Natalie moved her left hand toward a sore area in the vicinity of her left temple and jaw. Surprise! Her left hand is attached to her right hand at the wrist by plastic handcuffs. *Damn, Doubledamn.*

At least she isn't handcuffed with her hands behind her back. Even so, the incapacity of both hands and arms portends with near absolute certainty that Natalie is going to die in the immediate future, sooner rather than later.

God, I know now why there are no atheists in foxholes. If I get out of this fiasco it will be only because of your help. God, I promise you if I do get out of this alive. I will live on the straight and narrow the rest of my life, no exceptions. I make this promise on the life of my son, Donald. I'm serious, God, I need help. I am really serious, God. I really do need help.

Jethro rises at the same time every day, 6:30 am. Today is no exception. It was dark outside the hotel and inside the room as well. He rolled out of the sack, walked to the bathroom, relieved himself and returned to the bedroom. On the way back, he turned on the overhead light. Natalie appears to still be conked out, and has been for the past eight hours, presumably under the influence of Roofies. Jethro knows the drug is effective for at least ten to twelve hours. He figures she will be under for another two to four hours. He needs to get busy.

Jethro's plan is to stuff an unconscious Natalie and her personal effects into a large cardboard box, place the box on the luggage carrier he snitched from downstairs and roll the carrier containing Natalie and her personal effects to Jethro's car; there to transfer the box into Jethro's automobile trunk, with the assistance of forward folding back seats; thence to drive to his favorite wooded area 25 miles south, southwest of DC; there to strangle and bury Natalie in a shallow grave; successfully completing episode number 35 of Jethro's Christian Cleansing project.

Jethro assembled the new, flat cardboard box and taped it so the box will retain its functional form. He left one end of the box open so he can stuff Natalie into that end, later to close it off with tape. Natalie will be trapped inside the cardboard box after Jethro tapes the open end of the box closed.

An excellent plan if Natalie had ingested enough of the drugged liquid in the sealed water bottle. She didn't. Natalie is wide-awake, poised and waiting silently like a coiled cobra, puffed up angry hood and all. The cobra has major handicaps; it is handcuffed and almost out of venom. Natalie will have to make do.

A vulnerability opportunity presented itself when Jethro reached down and over the bed to grasp Natalie's body so as to maneuver her into the cardboard box lying on the bed. Jethro was unconcerned because he knew Natalie was unconscious and was anticipated at a minimum to be unconscious for another two hours.

Wrong, dead wrong!! Expectational interests in the behavior of others can be downright dangerous, even fatal. With the speed of a praying mantis, a lightning fast, powerful, leg hooking kick drove the ball of Natalie's right foot deep into the front of Jethro's throat, crushing his larynx; fatally shattering and dismantling both Jethro's cervical neck bones and his spinal cord. God was kind. Jethro did not suffer. A short time later he died on the hotel room bed, unconscious all the while.

The female praying mantis is dangerous. Do not mate with a female praying mantis. After fornication she is apt to bite your head off and bolt it down for dinner. Mate with a female praying mantis at your own risk. You may die. Jethro died. Jethro fucked with the wrong cowgirl, literally and figuratively.

Cautious and conservative policewoman she is, Natalie has no concern with such 'feel good – do good' niceties as rules of engagement and political correctness. She up-righted herself on the bed and with a strong right foot stomp jammed dead Jethro's nasal bones deep into his brain. *That ought to do it. Goose and gander and all that jazz.*

*

Natalie smiled wryly to herself. *I, Natalie Taylor, number two guy in the FBI, just killed the DC strangler with my bare hands, correction, bare feet. I'm sitting stark naked in the strangler's rented hotel room in a prominent Arlington, Virginia hotel at 6:45 am. Check out time is 1:00 pm. I have six hours and 15 minutes to move the body and sanitize this hotel room. I'm naked and handcuffed. What to do? What not to do? Well, let's get it on. Time's a wasting.*

Prior to egressing the crime scene Natalie commenced to sterilize the hotel room, to eliminate all evidence of skirmish with Jethro. It wasn't easy, since her nude body was restrained by a functional pair of plastic bracelets immobilizing both wrists and arms.

Bound by the handcuffs, Natalie walked to the bathroom and retrieved two large white bath towels and her clutch. She placed both bath towels under Jethro's head to prevent bed linen stains in the event Jethro's fatal wound bleeds out.

The clutch has an emergency cache containing a miniature flashlight, a matchbook, a small pair of scissors, six feet of plastic twine and most important of all, a serviceable small file.

After 55 minutes of Neanderthal style sawing and the demolition of four elegant fingernails, the left wristband succumbed. Since time is of the essence a functional handcuff will remain on her right wrist for now, mangled left bracelet dangling in the breeze for all to see.

Shaking down Jethro's clothing and personal effects, Natalie confiscated his car keys and wallet. All other personal effects were wiped clean of fingerprints and enclosed in a small towel, then inserted into the improvised crypt, to be disposed of along with Jethro's dead body.

At 8:05 am the nude beauty addressed her need for clothing. Designer black dress and high heels for breakfast; the best she can do. She considered donning Jethro's suit, but no dice, wrong size. She wiggled into the black dress. *It's past time to vacate the premises.*

It took Natalie ten minutes to tamp Jethro into his cardboard crypt and maneuver the crypt onto the luggage cart at an angle. At 8:15 am, Jethro's dead body was wheeled via the luggage carrier from room 381 to the guest elevator.

During the 60 seconds Natalie was in the down elevator she ascertained that neither her face nor her profile was in view of the camera mounted in the elevator cabin. The only recorded feature was the back of her head and the back of her body, never her face and never her profile.

Natalie exited the elevator on the first floor, casually rolling the luggage carrier past a few people in the lobby, then departed the hotel through the main entrance way, the one with automatic double doors. She politely rejected an offer by a young man to push the carrier for her, preferring to maintain a respectable distance between herself and potential witnesses. She managed more or less to conceal the handcuffs from the eyesight of bystanders.

Despite the handicap of high heels, Natalie doggedly wheeled the coffin-laden luggage carrier over irregular surfaces for the one and a half blocks to her car, ever on the look-out for security personnel and policemen. None in sight. The crypt would not fit into her trunk. Her only option was to position Jethro in the backseat, again at an angle.

She returned to room 381 using the side door and stairs rather than the elevator. God answered Natalie's prayers by providing Natalie with documentary confirmation of room 381 checkout by Jethro. On the hotel room floor near the entry door was a standard hotel computer printout, a final bill dunned to a guest named William Marlette. *Jethro does not have to check out, a blessing.*

Natalie policed the room for evidence of blood residue and physical encounter. She once again wiped down the entire surface of every fixture and chattel which could possibly contain fingerprint evidence, a critical element of every murder scene investigation. She checked her clutch. It contained all the items she started with last night, including the petroleum jelly bottle and the used file.

One last look-see at the premises. The Roofie bottles! She poured out the contents of the second bottle, poured running water into the bottle and flushed the water down the toilet. After wiping down both bottles and disposing of them in the bathroom wastebasket, Natalie made one final inspection of room 381.

Jethro's clothing. In the bedroom on the chair. Natalie stuffed Jethro's suit, shirt, necktie, socks, underwear and shoes into a plastic hotel laundry bag, along with his toiletry items.

At 8:45 am Natalie departed the hotel room, laundry bag and clutch in hand, traversing the stairs to the first floor, hence out the side door to her Audi. The reliable automobile, now her erstwhile partner in actual crime, knows the way home from any location in the Washington, DC area. This fateful morning the Audi urged Natalie to turn to the south southwest and cruise amid heavy traffic for 14 miles. Natalie complied, still minimally under the effects of the date rape drug.

Daydreaming during the ride home, Natalie realized today is the first day in her 13 years of work for the FBI that she is late or absent from her assigned post. She feels pangs of guilt.

She cannot call her secretary because she left her cell phone at home. Returning to RyeGate to dress for work presents a major problem. She has a cadaver in the rear seat, a black eye, handcuffs on one hand and is decked out in evening attire; eye openers one and all, subject to observation by Betsy Ann, Don, and perhaps even Pete.

Natalie complied with speed limits as she traversed I-395, major arterials and local roads. A pullover for speeding or improper lane change could be troubling, even fatal to her career. A cop with a naked cadaver in the back seat. Indeed!

Upon arrival at RyeGate, she backed the Audi into the garage, decreasing the probability Betsy Ann or Don would notice the cardboard box in the back seat. The position of the Audi in the garage somewhat denied light to the Audi's back seat, partially concealing the crypt.

At 9:30 am she switched off the ignition, locked the vehicle manually and tiptoed up the basement stairs as quietly as a second story burglar. Fortunately, Pete was asleep, Betsy Ann was in the laundry room and Don was exiled to his bedroom. Thank God.

With a turkey tendon cutter from the kitchen she severed the plastic handcuff on her right hand. Upstairs, Natalie slipped out of the scuffed black heels and hid the mangled plastic handcuffs, Jethro's wallet and his car keys beneath her underwear in the bedroom dresser, to be disposed of later.

She crashed on her bed while speed dialing her private office number. Observing caller ID, Secretary Dina Watters answered, "Woman, where are you? I've been frantically attempting to contact you since 4:00 pm yesterday. No response, of course."

"Natalie, on most days it doesn't matter one way or the other whether you are present for duty. Not today, Boss. This is a bad day for you to be absent. I have news, both good and bad; first the bad."

"You, Natalie Taylor, Deputy Director of the FBI, have a personal interview with the president of the USA in the oval office at 1:00 pm today, which is three hours and 20 minutes from right now." Natalie cringed.

"The good news; it's my understanding and the scuttlebutt around here, President Bill Wilson is interviewing you for a high mucky muck, super top secret new job. You are the first woman in the history of the FBI to compete for such an important position. Great going, girl. Great."

"In your absence, I arranged for limousine service from FBI headquarters to the White House. Since we're cutting it close, and with your approval, I'm going to cancel the FBI to White House travel itinerary and have you picked up at your home for further transport to the White House, to stand by until your meeting is terminated; then to transport you from the White House to FBI headquarters. Is that acceptable, Natalie?"

The drugs have not totally cleared my system. I'm still hazy. Let's see, it's 9:40 right now and the appointment is at 1 o'clock. Like Dina said, I have three hours and 20 minutes to attend to my black eye, dress and travel to the White House. I need to give myself at least one hour for the drive from RyeGate to the White House, considering ID check-in delay at the white house perimeter.

Dina knows it is Natalie's habit to internally reason with herself when important decisions are on the table. She remained quiet as a mouse.

Natalie figured it out, "Dina, that's fine. Have the limousine pick me up at noon. On second thought there might be some extra traffic over the lunch hour, make it 11:45. Yes, have the limousine pick me up here at home at 11:45 am for transport to the White House, stand by for me at the White House and transport me to FBI headquarters when my White House business has been wrapped up. Are you with me, Dina?"

"Yes, boss, I understand. I will call you back if plans change. Otherwise, under pain of death, tornadoes, hurricanes, and the plague, there will be a government limousine outside your house in RyeGate at 11:45 am, precisely two hours from right now, boss."

Dina hung up without comment, as was Natalie's and Dina's custom. Identify the subject matter; state your observations or conclusions, request input as required, and get off the phone. Short and sweet. No embellishment. It worked for the two of them.

Natalie spent the next couple of hours not dolling up, but applying Hollywood style camouflage cosmetics to minimize, to the extent possible, the derogatory effect the black eye had on her personal appearance. Normally she looked luscious in business attire. Today, even considering the oversized black sunglasses, she is devoid of appeal and would not qualify as even an also-ran in a beauty contest featuring secondhand Rose's.

Natalie was out the door 15 minutes before noon, attired in a tasteful black pantsuit, chignon hairdo, dark sunglasses and her gold Rolex watch. She gave fast asleep Pete a brief goodbye kiss, conveyed household instructions to Betsy Ann and strode quickly to the street fronting her townhouse. No goodbye to the druggie.

The engine of the black US government stretch limousine idled smoothly at 600 RPM. Next stop, the oval office of President Bill Wilson, the trust baby.

18

WASHINGTON, DC

Inner Sanctum

T he chauffeur meticulously cross checked the photograph and information on Natalie's FBI identification card against her Virginia driver's license. Determining Natalie was not an Islamic terrorist, he confirmed her destination to be the White House, specifically the Oval Office.

Natalie knows it will be difficult if not impossible to emerge from this melee with her body parts intact. As the limousine traversed I-395 she mused. *I don't know what I'm interviewing for. Regardless of the question the president asks, I'm going to say something to the effect that 'I understand the question completely; the answer is difficult to provide because of changing circumstances or some other dumb reason; and with the proper assistance in terms of logistics and funding, I should be able to resolve the problem in one month, hopefully two weeks.'*

That should do it. The behavior most successful in this town is to do nothing, say nothing and claim victory for everything. Obama established the validity of that proposition beyond reasonable doubt.

Like I said, I'm tired; limping along on the momentum of my youth. I remember when I was invincible. I could do anything for any-body, at any place, at any time, regardless of difficulty index. I can beat you at any game you can name for any stake you can make. And I could, then; not anymore. My heart's not in it.

If I had stayed in the legal system, I would've been a judge by now. The only thing judges have to do is listen to lawyer's bullshit and make decisions. No real work at all. Why didn't I become a judge? Only the Shadow knows.

Pete, I'm not spending enough time with Pete. I can tell. Why me, Lord? Why us, Lord? I know the Lord helps them that helps them-selves, and blessed be the name of the Lord. Lot was tested and ulti-mately prevailed. But I am not Lot and this is not Judea, or Canaan, or Samaria, or whatever.

Another thing. Nowhere in the Bible is there a scenario regarding a situation wherein a woman with a quadriplegic husband assumes head of household status. In biblical times, quadriplegics died early on. Back then, a brother in law inherited legitimate conjugal control over a dead brother's widow, his strange new piece of ass. Pray for my dead brother while fucking his widow. Isn't that a crock of shit?

I'm not trying to be trite and not trying to be irreligious. I'm just saying, for a professional working woman there's not much guidance available on how to negotiate the troubled waters I'm treading in.

The trip from RyeGate to the White House consumed slightly more than 45 minutes. As the limousine approached the White House perimeter it stopped behind a queue of eight vehicles. Ten minutes later Blackie cleared the queue. A few minutes later, subsequent to a second ID check, Natalie approached the White House on foot. She relinquished her sidearm at the 2nd ID checkpoint in exchange for a receipt.

At 12:50 pm an escort assigned to Natalie flagged her down, "Ms. Taylor, I'm from the Secret Service. My name is Benjamin Santiago. It's my job to accompany you to the oval office for your appointment with the president."

"Well, Mr. Benjamin Santiago, thank you very much. I am in

your care, custody and control, sir," smiled Natalie at the young kid, a fresh-faced, wet behind the ears 30-year-old Latino who appeared to be working his first day at the job of protecting the president from all enemies, foreign and domestic. The kid seemed thankful for Natalie's easy-going demeanor. Natalie figured she must have been preceded by some mean bastard guests.

As Natalie approached the Oval Office, she recalled she had killed a man about eight hours ago. His body is perched at an odd angle in the back seat of her car in her basement garage. *I wonder if this is a famous first for an Oval Office visitor, a murderer within the past eight hours jawboning with the president. Perhaps Ripley's Believe It or Not will reserve a spot for me.*

*

The oval office is located in the west wing of the White House. Three large south facing windows are located just behind the president's desk. Seated at the desk, the president looks north. Some presidents remain seated behind the desk when receiving visitors. Other presidents randomly mingle with visitors.

A fireplace is ensconced on the north end of the oval office. There is a spacious sitting area in the middle of the room, tables in the center and upholstered chairs on each side of the tables. A large rug features the presidential seal. President Wilson's favorite color is red but he selected medium blue as his oval office floor color.

Natalie was summoned into inner sanctum at 1:10 pm. A smiling President Bill Wilson greeted her with an offered handshake. She respectfully accepted. The handshake was firm but not overbearing. He didn't squeeze her hand.

"Ms. Natalie Taylor, Deputy Director of the FBI, please be seated," friendly manner belying an ulterior misogynistic bent. The president nodded and pointed his hand toward the chairs on either side of the table where visitors to the office sit and listen to the president pontificate.

Surprisingly, Bill Wilson parked his imposing 6'5" 250 pound body directly across the long table from Natalie. Right away, the pair of cautious antagonists embarked upon a tête-à-tête, face to face, less than four feet separation. They could feel and smell each other. *Bill Wilson is a smoker; cheap cologne. One-on-one with the president of the United States in the oval office. I have arrived.*

"Natalie, may I call you Natalie?" asked the president.

"Of course, Mr. President, of course."

Succinctly, the experienced interrogator pounced, "Natalie, no small talk. Tell me why you're here in the oval office today," in a friendly and inoffensive tone of voice.

Natalie parried, "Mr. President, I'm here today because you're creating a new government position and you're considering me for the job. The reason you're considering me is I was recommended to you by my superiors because I'm experienced and competent in the area of expertise the new job requires."

"Right answer, young lady. You attended the best PR seminar money can buy; either that or you're a born schmoozer, perhaps both."

"Tell me right now, how you got your black eye. Level with me."

The blunt inquiry took Natalie by surprise; she countered with the fastest retort on record, "Mr. President, I don't lie, cheat or steal. I have never lied, cheated or stolen. I will never lie, cheat or steal in the future. That's not me."

"I know you're a busy man. I know you have a reputation for being misogynistic. Sir, as we both know, I'm a woman. My definition of a woman is a mind trapped in a female body. Regardless of this bullshit about women being from Mars and men being from Venus, or vice-versa, whichever way it is, both of our minds, the minds of each of us, are essentially the same. When either you or I add one plus one, both of us come up with the same answer, the number two." Unnoticed, mild Presidential chin rubbing commences.

"Since you might agree with me the body is the temple of the soul, the only significant difference between the two of us other than age is the fact that guys like you have one third more upper body strength than girls like me; and as well your plumbing is external while my plumbing is internal."

"I have to live out my life as a woman and you have to live out your life as a man. Because of your upper body strength, among other things, I maintain, from the standpoint of power and control, the English language is prejudicially canted in favor of males."

"Males wrote the language; males created the words; males assigned meaning to the words. The late Professor Hayakawa of the University of San Francisco maintained we are trapped by the language, unable to adequately express ourselves because of limitations inherent in the language. That may very well be true."

Noticing President Wilson rub his chin with moderately hard strokes, paired with mild, squirmy body motions, Natalie said, "Mr. President, you're annoyed. Please bear with me, sir. Do you mind?"

"Have at it, Natalie, you have the floor for now," the perplexed and annoyed president answered.

"Thank you, sir. Back to my script. There are at least 50 sexually oriented words in the misogynistic English language which confirm unequivocally or at least imply unequivocally that females are inevitably and innately inferior to males, and will always be inferior to males."

"The offensive female oriented words include but are not limited to: whore, cunt, bitch, slut - I could go on but I won't bore you. Like I said, there are at least 50 such words. The most recent such offensive word was coined by your black brothers, the word 'Ho.'"

"There are only two such male words, both of which words refer to bad females. The two words are 'bastard,' an illegitimate child of a bad woman, and 'son of a bitch,' child of a bad woman."

"For a long time, the distaff side of American society has struggled not only in the vocational sense but also in the avocational sense, mostly wives I'm talking about, just to keep their heads above water, much less to progress forward pursuant to the American Dream. Over the years, both language and severe ancient customs have more than handicapped feminine efforts to achieve a modicum of equality, vis-à-vis the male gender."

"Much has changed, not significantly, but changed nevertheless. I'm a product of that change. It took women like Carrie Nation, Helen Keller, Mother Teresa, and more recently Golda Meir and Margaret Thatcher to effect change. I don't presume to travel in their company. However, among my aspirations is an objective to emulate those remarkable overachievers to the extent of my ability."

"Thank you for bearing with me. Mr. President. Directly to the point, if I were a man visiting with you for the first time, and if I told you my black eye was sustained in a fist fight over the love of a woman, you would almost certainly admire my willingness to engage in fisticuffs to fulfill mating obligations of an adult male. A guy thing."

Natalie lowered her sunglasses and provided the president a clear view of her less than 24 hour old black eye. Gazing at the black eye longer than necessary, Bill Wilson finally nodded his head slightly, apparently in approval; no concurrent chin rubbing.

Natalie said, "An unmarried sexually active man in our society is a stud. An unmarried sexually active woman in our society is a whore. That's just the way it is." Another approving head nod, stronger than the first.

"I'm not sitting in front of you this morning, telling you I'm a whore. I'm telling you I will never lie to you. You will never get a half-truth out of me. I will never cheat you and I will never steal from you. I'm a female. You're a male. Males and females in society are worlds apart. Nobody's going to change that." A third approval nod, this one very slight.

"I'm suggesting that we don't have to be worlds apart. We are on a pedestal. You and I are at the top of our food chain. We are exceptional. We are special. I believe that the time has come, regarding the vocational level at which you and I function, that it does not now and will never in the future, matter a tinker's damn whether or not we are male or female." Disapproving head shakes, left and right.

"Like you say, cutting to the chase, leveling with you, I got this black eye 15 hours ago in a major, very major dispute with a lover. He didn't get the best of me; I got the best of him. Believe me, you wouldn't want to see what the other guy looks like." The president grins.

"Mr. President, I prefer to leave it at that. On the other hand, you are the chief executive of our wonderful nation and I and everybody else in my circumstances owe it to you to be faithful to you, to work diligently for you day and night, and to trust you to make those decisions which hopefully will ensure the continued health, safety and welfare of American citizens and residents." A series of approving head nods, stronger than the others.

The jury is out. This could go either way. "President Wilson, what say you, sir?"

Thirty seconds of silence. "To be brutally frank, Natalie, I don't know what to say, except you have the silveriest tongue I ever listened to, man or woman, then or now. I'm thankful November's election is over and done with; I would certainly hate to be running against you. You're hired, Natalie. You're hired. I reserve the right to fire you at the drop of a hat, but I cannot envision firing you while I'm holding this office, ever."

"Now, tell me what you've done for the FBI, how you came to be promoted as quickly as you did. So far as I can tell you are the Douglas MacArthur of the FBI, the man who made the best academic scores as a cadet in the history of West Point, a record which still stands."

"Mr. President, I'm highly qualified as an organized crime fighter, both domestic and foreign, in a number of complex technological areas, including but not limited to human intelligence, banking, computer hacking, code and algorithms, ISP skipping and tracing, electronic breaking and entering, identity theft, and the like."

"What does ISP mean?"

"ISP is short for Internet Service Provider. When tracing Email messages, you have to trace trails from one ISP to another because a sender of an Email may not want you to know where he lives. Therefore, he will initiate an Email in say India, send it to, for instance, Indonesia, Brazil, Mexico, Japan, Southern California, and from there on to final destination, your computer here in the District."

"At first glance, it appears your new Email was sent from and initiated in Southern California but that's not true, it originated in India in our hypothetical. We are quite good at tracing trails and detecting initiation sites."

"Like I said, I would sure hate to be running against you. Now, get out of here and get to work. I'm sure you've been told you're relocating to Norfolk tomorrow."

Shock, intense internal shock, "Yes, sir, I'm aware of my Norfolk relocation."

"Chief of Staff Tom Redding is waiting outside. Tom will bring you up to snuff on everything you need to know to run the show for us, personnel, funding, logistics, etc. You need it, you got it. If you're not satisfied with the support provided to you, at any time, for any reason, call this number, day or night, rain or shine. My secretary will patch your call to me. Do you understand?" asked the President as he handed Natalie a professionally engraved business card containing a single telephone number, nothing else.

Do you understand? The same question I asked Don yesterday. What goes around really does come around.

"Yes, sir, I do understand," said Natalie as she rose from her oval office chair and accompanied the president of the United States to the appropriate exit. *I will live to fight another day; a miracle. Rain did not fall on my snow job.*

19
REDDING & DONAHUE
Snake Oil & Treachery

Although Natalie's oval office interview was docketed for 30 minutes; it lasted only 17 minutes. Tom Redding was as surprised as anybody Natalie made it this far, considering President Wilson's penchant for misogyny. Tom had a gut feeling the President would reject Natalie. He had three names in reserve as replacement nominees.

Tom approached Natalie as she emerged from the oval office, turning his right thumb alternately up and down, asking her by body language whether or not she got the job. Natalie stoically flashed thumbs up.

"That's great, Natalie, just great," remarked the snake oil salesmen, now in high gear, noting facial discolored skin trailing down and away from the rim of Natalie's left tinted eyeglass. *I'll be damned. Natalie was mugged last night.*

"Tom, don't you think it was a bit much to allow me to interview without a hint of what I was interviewing for, not even a job title?"

"Natalie, your project is so sensitive the security clearance is classified higher than TOP SECRET–SAP. The mission of your task force is the most highly secret non-wartime mission ever engaged in by the United States of America. A new and distinct name was created for clearance to information related to your mission: TOP SECRET–IAR. The acronym stands for individual access required."

"TOP SECRET-IAR applies to each and every item of information exposed to anyone and everyone who is associated in any way with your task force. Be advised the new task force has an official name, USTF-18. That acronym stands for 'Ultra Special Task Force.' The number 18 was picked at random, to fend off intelligence hackers. You will receive a full task force briefing tomorrow."

"By the way, the job of the task force is to find and neutralize a person or persons who are attempting to purchase nuclear weapons from others, presumably weapons to be used against USA targets. We have one lead and only one lead. The lead was obtained by a CIA operative. You now know as much as I know. This is no small job. I don't envy you."

"You have no doubt heard through the grapevine there exists one or more moles buried deep in the bowels of our administration. Even though he has been on the job only a week, President Wilson is paranoid. He believes classified information regarding national matters is treasonously conveyed by enemy moles to the bad guys within hours, sometimes within minutes."

"Our president believes a copy or accurate detailed synopsis of every existing federal government contingency plan has been revealed to our enemies. He believes one of the moles is a cabinet level executive or perhaps a highly placed first or second-tier assistant. President Wilson doesn't trust anybody."

"He strolls around the White House muttering things to himself such as 'Seems like it all gets disseminated to the bad guys, if not overnight, then on the same day,' or words to that effect. He's mildly delusional, perhaps even medically paranoid. The Secret Service has been on it since he took office, but nothing actionable yet."

"The surgeon general opines, within reasonable medical probability, that as of now the 'delusions' are not severe enough to interfere with President Wilson's competency and ability to perform his governmental duties."

Why is Tom Redding telling me this? Definitely out of character for a Presidential Chief of Staff.

Natalie recognized the 'Government Speak' deluge of dialogue emanating from Tom Redding's lips: TS-IAR, SECNAV, moles, synopsis, scenario, on balance, hyperbole, etc. Big, unusual words, one after another, syntax meaning nothing to anybody, including nothing to Tom. Government acronyms, also known as 'alphabet gobbledygook,' the worst offenders. Who would ever have thought the president is a 'United States pot,' à la POTUS.

Washington, DC is inundated with Government Speak at every level. There appears to be no permanent rite of passage to the federal fraternity unless the apprentice is fluent in 'Government Speak.'

"Natalie, you're the boss of USTF-18, our new special task force. Your title is Director, USTF-18. I was told an hour ago that your task force Deputy Director, nominated by the Director of the CIA and approved by the President, is the CIA Deputy Director, Mitch Donahue," said Tom Redding.

Boom! Could've been a round fired from a howitzer. Natalie's de minimus wince was detected instantly by Tom Redding, a bona fide expert in body language. "I understand you know Mitch personally," smooth snake oil peddler that Redding is. Observing Natalie flinch when Mitch Donahue's name was mentioned, Redding awaited Natalie's reply with baited breath. She didn't disappoint him.

"You bastards! You may be new guys on the block, but every Goddamn one of you, probably including the President, knows that for the past three years Donahue has tried to cut my balls off, promoting a fabricated, trumped up claim I exceeded FBI jurisdictional authority and overlapped his CIA jurisdictional authority in the international money-laundering case I solved almost single-handedly."

"Ever since then, that son of a bitch Donahue and I have had no use for one-another. I know there is a way I can bury that bastard six feet under. I just haven't found it yet. The dipshit is going to work for me? You can tell that sorry miscreant his ass is grass and I'm the lawnmower. Tom, this is a boiling mess of bat entrails."

Tom Redding and not CIA director Jack Fleming recommended Mitch Donahue. The President met Donahue for the first time today. Donahue presented as a dominant male with a good track record; not exemplary, but good.

Mitch is not promotable. He will retire no higher than number two at the CIA, if that. Nonetheless he is faithful and reliable. Mitch Donahue will dutifully take a bullet for the president, and as far as it goes, for Tom Redding also.

Tom knows a storm of his own making is brewing. He has his reasons, "Natalie, suck it up. The problem is bigger than you, Mitch Donahue, myself and the president combined. You're running the show. I am confident that by and through tolerance and restraint you'll establish dominant control over Donahue. Eventually you'll feed him the poison pill both you and I know he deserves, at the right time and at the right place."

Reluctantly Natalie responded, "If you say so, Tom. If you say so. But if Donahue steps out of line I'll grind him into sawdust so fast he won't remember he was once a tree. I'm going to nail Mitch Donahue. Changing the subject, what is this BS about me relocating to Norfolk today? Is that right, today?"

"That's right, Nat," he knows she detests the nickname Nat. "Today. Take this, please," said Tom as he handed Natalie a sealed envelope. "The enclosed $10,000 in cash is an advance for expenses you are certain to incur. Please keep a record of each individual expenditure over $100."

"You and Mitch Donahue each owe me the names of five task force members, each member to be an experienced expert in a different, but related, field. Exchange names and CV's with each other. Either of you can strike any name, no recourse. If you need more than five worker bees, check with me. No one outside of you two has authority to nominate or fire anyone assigned to the task force. Do you have your five names on the tip of your tongue?" Tom asked as he showed her Donahue's five nominees, along with their resumes.

Natalie concluded that the only condition under which Mitch Donahue could have provided his five names to Tom Redding today was for Mitch Donahue to have been selected to serve on the new joint task force prior to today. *Those three sorry bastards, the President, Redding and that son of a bitch Donahue.*

"Yes and no, I have seven people in mind. Maybe I can pare that list down to five. I'll be back to you before close of business today."

"Okay, but no later than 5:00 pm. We are already playing catch up. We have to run, not walk. Of course, a requirement for instant response is no excuse for negligent mistakes. That's why we picked you and Donahue. You're both bright, competent shakers and movers."

Natalie knows Tom Redding was in on Mitch Donahue's selection. *I'll be Goddamned, Tom Redding is a two-faced, lying, master of the half-truth, a con artist. Perfect oval office material, perfect. Nixon the criminal, Clinton the perjurer and Obama the treasonist have nothing on Tom Redding.*

*

The number two guy at the CIA interviewed next. Mitch Donahue's meeting with President Wilson lasted 20 minutes. He was approved. Later, at a Redding/Donahue meeting, Mitch learned his job within a job is to shadow Natalie Taylor as a personal tail. He is to arrange for others to intercept and record all her telephone messages and email messages, as well as to have a tail personally observe her off-duty activities, 24/7. Beginning immediately, Mitch is to establish a 24 hour watch on both her West Springfield home and her temporary quarters in the Norfolk area, as well as monitoring audio and video bugs planted in both her home and temporary quarters in Norfolk.

Five Secret Service agents authorized; no limit on expenditures. Do the job, whatever it costs. Daily reporting by way of secure communications to Tom Redding. The president wasn't taking any chances. He didn't like the black eye.

Mitch Donahue was impressed. He spent the remainder of the day devising a scheme to destroy the career of Natalie Taylor.

20
NATALIE
the Young Widow

That afternoon at 4:00 pm Dina said on intercom, "Natalie, you have two parties holding, Tom Redding and Betsy Ann. Both say their calls are important."

"Hold Betsy Ann, put Redding through."

"Tom, please hold for 15 seconds. I need to terminate another call." Natalie clicked her dial tone button and the connection switched to her home telephone line, "Betsy Ann, Natalie here, sweetheart. What can I do for you?"

Natalie clinched her teeth at the tone of the first words out of Betsy Ann's mouth. "Oh, Natalie, Natalie, I don't know how to say this, darling lady. Pete died fifteen minutes ago. I feel so bad. I'm so sorry."

Natalie was not unfamiliar with death. In her job as a line special agent in her early years with the FBI she had been shot at on a few occasions and had killed two perpetrators in a firefight. On a percentage basis very few FBI agents are killed in any given time period, perhaps because only the most qualified FBI agent applicants are accepted.

The FBI ceased publishing FBI casualty statistics in 2013. As of then, the FBI had been in existence for 103 years and only 57 agents had been killed, 36 in adversarial situations, and 21 in conditions related to adversarial situations. Amazingly positive statistics considering the extremely dangerous conditions an FBI agent is exposed to in the ordinary course of employment.

Natalie calmly soothed Betsy Ann. "Darling, I'm in a really important meeting. I'll call you back within 15 minutes." She clicked her dial button again, hanging up on a nonfunctional and distraught Betsy Ann Mathers.

"Tom, can you possibly spare me two days? My husband just died."

Nonplussed, Tom responded, "Take two days plus the weekend. Today is Wednesday; you have bereavement leave of absence for Thursday and Friday. Report to my office at 8:00 am Monday morning. My sincere regrets, Natalie. I'll pick five out of your seven. I'll cover for you during the two days. On Monday morning, I'll give you a complete briefing on your task force mission and the support available for you to successfully complete your mission."

Be prepared to depart DC no later than Monday noon for your new assignment in Norfolk as Director of USTF-18. I'll arrange for temporary quarters for you, either on Langley Air Force Base proper or in the Norfolk vicinity."

"I almost forgot. In addition to you, Mitch, and your 10 upper-level supervisors, you are initially authorized to staff USTF-18 with an additional 20 worker bees, 10 FBI and 10 CIA. I'll nominate your 10. Gotta go, another call."

A dead husband, a drug ridden child and a cadaver in my basement; what do I give a damn about right now? Nothing, certainly not my additional ten at USTF–18.

For Natalie, Pete didn't die today. Pete died the day the Central American illegal alien's gross negligence struck him down, irrevocably sentencing Pete to a lifetime of quadriplegic bedriddance.

Natalie learned early on that the illegal alien was intentionally set free by the San Francisco, California police just prior to Pete's roll-over automobile accident, even though wants and warrants were properly filed against the illegal alien in other jurisdictions. San Francisco is a sanctuary city. Salt on Natalie's wound.

Natalie's life was never again the same. She loved the old Pete. She wouldn't admit it, but she felt nothing other than compassion and sympathy for the crippled Pete; No love; only pity, compassion and sympathy. The new Pete could never fit into the shoes of the old Pete.

God knows I loved that man. He made me what I am today. I know that as time passes I will remember only the good years and suppress the bad. The years 2016 to 2020 will vaporize, relegated a day at time, then a week at a time, a month at a time, and finally a year at a time, relegated to inassessable crooks & crannies within my subconsciousness, never again to emerge.

Assuming there's a heaven, I'm sure the old Pete is standing at the left hand of God, maybe even the right hand. He is that kind of guy, a great guy. I have to think about using 'was' instead of 'is,' don't I?

*

Natalie arrived home at 6:15 pm. "Oh, Natalie, what do we do?" asked Betsy Ann.

Natalie didn't know whether Betsy Ann was more distraught over Pete's death or over losing her job, since she was no longer a necessity for the Branson household. It doesn't matter because Betsy Ann earned her salt. She's a good, honest person.

"We shall get through it, Betsy Ann, we shall get through it. I contacted Thomas & Boswell, funeral home operators here in West Springfield. Please give them a call and ask them to retrieve the body. They might be closed. It's after 5:00 pm. Did you cover Don's body with a blanket?" Natalie asked, as she realized for the first time that she is a widow.

"Yes ma'am."

"I think there's a requirement for a death certificate, so the coroner's office may have to be notified. On your phone call, ask the funeral home representative about that, will you please? Oh, I almost forgot, the body is to be cremated. I know I have to sign some papers. Set an appointment, earliest, for me to visit the funeral parlor."

"Yes, Natalie. Right away, right now. Is there anything else I should be doing; anything that's really, really important?" Betsy Ann was amazed at Natalie's composure.

"No, not now. Where's Don, does he know?"

"He's upstairs in his room. Yes, he knows. I told him. He started crying and went to his room. I haven't heard as much as a peep from him since."

Yesterday afternoon, the last time she saw Don, Natalie laid down the law to him. *A lot of things happened in the last 24 hours; a lot of things, mostly bad. When it rains it sometimes doesn't simply pour, it floods.*

First things first. Up the stairs to the third floor, first door on the right. Knock on the door, two quiet raps, "Don, it's your mother, may I come in?" No response, "Don, I'm opening the door."

Donald Branson, Natalie's only son, and more likely than not fated to be her only child (menopause is around the corner), was postured in a starkly familiar position, decedent Jethro Armstrong's pre-coital pose. Déjà vu, all over again.

Don was sitting on the floor in the only empty corner of his room, his back against both walls, knees under his chin, arms clasping his legs, shielding his groin area from onlookers, of which there were none. The coincidence of the two positions was an uncomfortable reminder of last night. *Never mind.*

"Don, I am so sorry your father died; you and your father are the loves of my life. Although you disappointed me, I'm sure you know I still love you more than anything. I stopped in to see if you're all right. It appears you are. How's about you and I going out for pizza in a couple of hours?"

"I need to contact various people regarding your father's death and funeral. I don't want to bother you with the details. I must call your three grandparents."

No reply from Don. No movement by Don. He might as well be dead, too.

Natalie departed Don's bedroom, down but not out. *Don is no longer my son. He's a druggie. He belongs to the world of drugs. He does not belong to me. A pity, but nevertheless a bleak reality. Alas.*

*

Pete's mother picked up on the third ring, "Mrs. Branson, this is Natalie. I have really bad news, Mrs. Branson. Pete died in his sleep two hours ago. He didn't suffer. He was such a good man, I feel so very sad and I know that you do too."

"Please don't take this the wrong way. I know not from personal experience but from sharing the experience of others, it's a cruel anomaly when a child predeceases a parent. As for me, I feel inadequate; I'm filled to the brim with sorrow and grief; it seems that everything I do right now is either futile or inappropriate, perhaps even useless."

"Pete didn't deserve what happened to him; you and Mr. Branson didn't deserve what happened to Pete; Don and I didn't deserve what happened to Pete. I suppose that's the way it is sometimes. We did the best we could."

"Again, I'm so sorry that I had to give you this bad news by way of a telephone call. I encourage Mr. Branson to call if he wants to talk with me. I'll probably stay up until midnight or so and be at it again early tomorrow morning. I've arranged to have Thursday and Friday off to handle all affairs associated with Pete's death. I believe the funeral will be the middle of next week."

"Oh, dear, please forgive me. I am so thoughtless, so rude. I have rattled on and not let you say a word. I call you and tell you your son is no longer with us and I heartlessly dominate the conversation without even thinking of your feelings. Please forgive me, Mrs.

Branson. Do you have any questions or anything you want to say, Mrs. Branson?"

Two quiet minutes. Not a word; not even a sound. Frances Branson despised Natalie from the first day the two women met. The Bransons are 'old money.'

Young Natalie is obviously a plebian social climbing opportunist attempting to speed-dial her ambitious agenda of transcending social status, all on the back of Pete Branson, MD, the distinguished Branson family and our family ancestors. To top it off the bitch embarrassed the entire family by refusing to go by her proper married surname, Branson.

Pete Branson always was 'too good' for Natalie, regardless of the compliments Pete showered on Natalie over the years. The fact that my grandson is on track for acceptance by an Ivy League University, perhaps Dartmouth or Cornell, won't change things. Natalie is not 'one of us' and never will be. My son is dead. I won't be saddled with Natalie Taylor anymore. I must influence Donald to transfer his affections from the bitch to his grandparents.

Before hanging up Natalie said, "I understand your silence, Mrs. Branson. You and Mr. Branson will be hearing from me tomorrow at the latest. Mrs. Branson, Pete loved you and I love you. Good night for now."

As Natalie hung up, teardrops gathered in both eyes. She acknowledged that providing notice of death to close relatives is not her strong suit. *A chore to be avoided in the future if at all possible.*

At 7:30 pm the second telephone call answered on the fourth ring, a local call transferred automatically to an international telephone land line, "Daddy, it's Natalie. You gave me this telephone number to call you in the event I ever had an emergency."

At 8:30 pm local time, Jet Taylor, alias William Pennington, answering from his charity's main office, a mansion in Hamilton, Bermuda, responded "So I did, pretty girl. So I did. What's troubling you?" Natalie is unaware the charity exists, much less that her father owns it.

"Daddy, this is the worst day of my life. Pete died four hours ago. That's incredibly depressing but more or less expected considering the recent deterioration of his health. I'm home from work and have off until Monday morning," Natalie answered, composed and businesslike in a heartbeat, an executive attribute.

'Don't let the bastards get you down,' her father had lectured to her over the years. 'This too shall pass,' was another good one he conditioned her with. The one she liked best was Chinese. 'Too soon old; too late smart,' brilliant in its simplicity and relevance.

"I know you travel a lot and I don't know where you are right now, but Daddy; I have a problem I cannot talk to you about on the telephone. All I want to say is it concerns your grandson, Don. It concerns Don's future."

"The problem needs immediate attention. I cannot resolve it by myself. If you can see your way through to it, could you please manage your schedule so you can visit me for two or three hours tomorrow, face to face, at my home in West Springfield? If you're flying, I could pick you up anywhere in the area. Can you help me, Daddy? I'm begging; it's that bad," implored the number two guy responsible for the FBI's 35,000 employees.

Jet is 62 years old, soon to be 63. His daughter, his only adult child, is 39 years old. She is just like him; Ever since she was a little girl, she never asked Jet for as much as a thin dime, or for that matter, for any favor whatsoever, big or small. Both mother and daughter were home town girls, Louisville, Kentucky, both Southern Belles. In their time, both cute as a doll; Natalie still is.

Susan Taylor, Natalie's mother, was a quality Air Force wife during Jet's one year of Air Force pilot training and six months of advanced fighter pilot training. Jet and Susan lived together for only four years. Long term, Susan refused to tolerate the possibility of Jet being killed on the next fighter aircraft training sortie, much less the possibility Jet might be ordered to fly actual combat missions in the event a cold war somewhere became a hot war overnight.

What made it worse was facing the five to eight permanent

home location changes within the next 18 years if Jet made the US Air Force his career. Susan was a homebody at heart. She wasn't willing to commit for the next two decades to regularly uproot her family every three years or so, sometimes on short notice.

Susan and Jet amicably agreed to a divorce after Jet completed advanced fighter pilot training, with Jet providing child support. Susan never remarried. She died ten years ago. She was a good woman, a good mother.

Jet mused: *Natalie, independent woman with a mind of her own. Prouder than a prancing peacock. No help from nobody, no time, no way. Just like me. Yes, just like me, only a girl. What a waste of a uniquely competent mind, trapped in a beautiful woman's body.* Misogynistic observation by an otherwise fair-minded man. Normal.

The father and daughter were close but not exceptionally close. He keeps an eye out for her. She always remembers him on his birthday and major holidays. They see each other every two or three years. Perhaps the best way to describe their relationship is it transcends love. Love comes and goes. The divorce rate in the USA is over 50%. For second and third marriages, the percentage of failure is even higher.

Husbands and wives come and go; blood is permanent. That's how Jet and Natalie view their relationship. They are blood, of the same blood; father and daughter, the closest possible blood. Their relationship is as strong as iron and steel, joined and welded together forever, a solid, unbreakable, indestructible lifetime relationship created pursuant to human instincts older than Methuselah.

The last occasion father and daughter broke bread together was over three years ago. Natalie's FBI job demanded more and more of her time and attention. Pete's quadriplegic condition did not help.

Clicking away like a teen-aged digital pro, Jet opened an app on his cell phone which displays his schedule for the next 30 days. Two important meetings are booked; one tomorrow and one Friday. Outcome determinative decisions regarding both the charity and the drug business are on the horizon.

The lay of the land bodes hostility. The natives are restless in South America. Jet's federal moles report the US is ramping up anti money-laundering activities. 'Fresh Start' has rounded the final turn and is on the home stretch.

Be that as it may, Jet disconnected his speaker, picked up his hard line telephone and said, "Daughter, I'll be there by way of private jet no later than tomorrow at twelve noon. I don't know which airport yet. I'll let you know by telephone tomorrow morning. See you then."

Jet hung up, then called his secretary on her home telephone number, "Imogene, cancel all my appointments for two days, Thursday and Friday. Reschedule as required, minimum delay. Alert Ewe and Mike Hill for Sabreliner travel tomorrow, Round Robin flight, out and back, Washington, DC and return, 7:00 am departure from Bermuda."

"Yes, Sir, Mr. Pennington."

Natalie emitted a sigh of relief. Her father is something else. Her love for him is unequivocal. Jet doesn't know it but Natalie patterns her work habits and her work ethic exclusively after Jet. She will ask Jet for advice on how to dispose of the cadaver. She isn't certain how she is going to level with him. It won't be easy.

The comment about Don was diversionary. She does not want an NSA snooper, if any, to be exposed to even a hint that Jethro's body and clothing is resting quietly in her basement garage. God forbid.

Natalie is wary and cautious like a fox. Be ever both wary and cautious; otherwise be the subject of a premature obituary. Take your choice. The two are incompatible. Wary and cautious, or dead. Experienced police officers know this sage advice is valid.

I hope and pray daddy can help me. I'm in serious trouble. I know hope is not an option. Daddy is a businessman, not a criminal with knowledge of how to dispose of criminal evidence. What am I thinking? I know more about how to resolve my problem than daddy does, and I'm asking him for help. Idiot such as I am, I do need help.

*

Mitch Donahue, temporarily assigned as a subordinate to Natalie Taylor; moonlighting as ordered by Tom Redding, to maintain 24/7 bugs and tails on Natalie Taylor. Mitch Donahue, a professional, US government employee, with the personal objective of destroying the career of Natalie Taylor. Your tax dollars at work.

Mitch doesn't give a damn one way or another whether Natalie is involved in some crazy ass hanky-panky. If it takes lies, half-truths, planted evidence, whatever, Mitch Donahue will bury Natalie Taylor dead or alive, a solemn pledge. In Mitch's clouded mind, Natalie's days are numbered. He thanked the heavens for this assignment, able to look Natalie Taylor directly in the eye while measuring her for a shroud.

Mitch dialed a DC phone number. "What progress on the Taylor surveillance job?"

"Well, a minor problem. Recall a couple of months ago you had me place an unauthorized, off the books, phone tap on Taylor; not reported up the line, up the chain of command. In order to install an authorized phone tap, I sanitized, destroyed and deleted all data pertaining to the earlier, undocumented phone tap."

"What the hell?"

"Rest easy. We don't want IG trouble. I have been down that road, sir."

"Screw the Inspector General."

"I had a decision to make. Since last night's recording between Taylor and her father was pursuant to the undocumented tap, I destroyed all evidence of that phone call."

"Today is Thursday. The earliest we can initiate new surveillance on the Taylor residence in West Springfield is Monday. I'll give you a further report Friday noon."

A composed Mitch replied, "So you have a little bad news for me. Shit happens. Life is imperfect, what the hell; a couple of days are not going to make that much difference. I want to nail the bitch. It's important to me that our surveillance devices be up and running by Monday noon. Do you understand?"

"Yes sir, I do."

"Good. Recall that I work out of the Norfolk area. Tomorrow I'll provide you the name of a local DC contact to coordinate surveillance activities on my behalf regarding Natalie Taylor. I rambled when I gave you instructions; did I make myself clear?"

"Yes sir; you did. I got it. Tomorrow you provide me a new contact. All future surveillance to be conducted under normal surveillance reporting procedures."

"Right you are. Give me a report by secure email at close of business on Monday and every day thereafter. Goodbye for now."

Natalie and her father had a telephone conference. The bitch is up to something. I'll check her father out.

21

WEST SPRINGFIELD
Daddy to the Rescue

Today is Thursday, January 28th. Jet will fly 831 miles from Hamilton, Bermuda to Ronald Reagan Washington National Airport, near downtown Washington, DC, in the Sabreliner, an ancient charity owned twin engine business jet aircraft. Jet logged a few hours in the US Military version of the Sabreliner, the Air Force T-39, while he was a Major in the Virginia Air National Guard at Richmond, Virginia.

As usual, Jet will fly the Sabreliner hands-on from the captain's left seat. The de-jure captain along for the ride is Ewe Schweglewski, a retired officer from the German Air Force, the Luftwaffe. Ewe is a former fighter pilot; the only kind of pilot Jet will have anything to do with.

According to Jet, if you ain't a fighter pilot, you ain't shit. Everyone else is barely tolerated, definitely not professionally respected. Jet has his own two-tiered caste system: fighter pilots alone in tier one; the rest of the world in tier two. Stony, Natalie and Estill are the only exceptions. Navy SEALs and Army DELTA troops merit honorable mention.

*

After breakfast, Helen and Amanda each kissed goodbye to the man they know as William Pennington; a sisterly goodbye kiss on the cheek. After Jet departed, each girl proceeded to her private over-sized cubicle.

The girls attend college full time, each having earned a four-year charity sponsored college scholarship. Weekday mornings, Helen and Amanda engage in three hours of college level internet study. Helen, a sophomore, earned scholarship #5. Amanda, a freshman, earned scholarship #6, the final scholarship to be awarded.

Afternoons are reserved for four hours of paid ($20 per hour) internship activity at different divisions within the charity, the bank and the insurance company. Helen is in charity advertising and Amanda is in insurance accounting for this term. Six internships per year per student; 12 total internships for each student during the first two calendar years of the scholarship.

An important scholarship feature during years one and two of study is one-week field trips to both profit and not-for-profit corporations throughout the world, such as Volkswagen, Rolls Royce and Seagrams; four field trips per year for each girl. The freshman summer is dedicated to internships at the mansion and two field trips. After completing the sophomore year in June, each student enrolls in summer school at Utah State University in Logan, Utah. Two years later she graduates from Utah State University with a BA or a BS degree. Graduate school is an option.

Jet is accompanied today by Stony Randolph, recently promoted hierarchy CEO. Early on, Stony doubled as Jet's personal body-guard, in addition to his normal junior executive responsibilities. He is trained in the martial arts, is a small arms marksman and is proficient with knives and nunchakus, also known as Karate sticks. Among other vocational skills, Stony is an assassin, a highly compe-tent hired–gun, killing machine.

When Jet recruited Stony from Gulfstream in 2012 and appointed Stony as an executive trainee, he required Stony to adopt an alias, Michael "Mike" Hill. Stony has no US government record other than his 'real name' green card address in Savannah, Georgia; no additional indicia of United States presence or activity; no IRS forms 1040, no driver's license, no US credit cards, no bank accounts.

Jet and Stony walked to the mansion garage where they were greeted by one of the charity's three licensed chauffeurs. They were driven from the mansion to Bermuda's Wade International Airport in one of the charity's two bulletproof limousines.

The United States maintains customs clearing facilities at airports in Aruba, Bahamas, Bermuda, Canada, Ireland, and United Arab Emirates. Not a time saver, but a method whereby foreign source aircraft can land at smaller US airports which do not have US customs clearance facilities. Reagan National Airport, located near downtown Washington DC, does not have a United States customs clearance facility.

After clearing US customs in Bermuda, Jet and Stony walked with their carry-on luggage to general aviation facilities at Wade International Airport. The Sabreliner was chocked and waiting outside. The two men were met by Ewe, who had earlier filed an ICAO instrument flight plan for the Sabreliner to fly to Reagan National Airport.

"We're ready and waiting, boss," smiled Ewe. After Jet smiled back, he and Stony fell into tandem trail behind Ewe, who climbed the metal folding ladder connected to the Sabreliner entrance/exit, on the left side of the aircraft. Ewe eased into the co-pilot's right cockpit seat; Jet claimed the captain's cockpit seat on the left, which relegated Stony to command of the six seat cabin.

One hour and 50 minutes later, Jet landed the Sabreliner at Reagan National Airport at 9:35 am EST, then taxied pursuant to ground control authority to a reserved spot on the tarmac in front of FBO (fixed based operator - aviation fuel and other essentials) servicing facilities. Jet shut both engines down, turned responsibility for the aircraft over to Ewe and told Ewe he did not know when he would return, but to be ready as early as midafternoon. Ewe and Jet confirmed each other's cell phone numbers by making a test call to one another.

Since Jet and Stony cleared US customs and immigration in Bermuda, they proceeded directly from the Sabreliner to a nearby neatly aligned row of taxis for hire. Accepting the offer of a $50 tip, the yellow cab driver tactically exceeded speed limits and selectively violated a few red lights, arriving at Natalie's RyeGate townhome in West Springfield, Virginia at 10:35 am.

Natalie was glued to the window in the townhome family room, anxiously awaiting the end of a three-year absence from her father. She was elated when Jet's taxi pulled up. The presence of another man was mildly disturbing.

A cold front recently pushed through. Temperature outside is 35 degrees. Even so, a coatless Natalie met her father half way down the paved entrance walkway, reached up, gave him a big kiss on the cheek and walked hand-in-hand with him into her townhome, beaming but ambivalently eyeing Stony.

Comfortably inside the townhome, the three settled down at the kitchen table. Natalie said, "Daddy, Don is in his room, on detention. May I have an introduction?" then, "What is your pleasure, gentlemen; coffee, tea, juice, you name it."

"Natalie, this is Stony Randolph. He is management. Stony is with me on this trip to become acquainted with some of the ins and outs of our aircraft and commercial equipment brokerage business. Stony, please say hello to my daughter, Natalie Taylor."

Puzzled by the presence of a woman with a prominent black eye on the left side of an otherwise beautiful face, Stony muttered, "Pleased to meet you, ma'am."

Lightning strikes in the strangest places. *What is the name of the chemical which appears in or is created by men's bodies pursuant to human sexual/physical attraction? Pheromones, yes, pheromones.* Natalie is attracted to the "Italian Stallion" her father fostered upon her. *I need to watch my step with this one, he is trouble. He resembles a taller and handsomer Sylvester Stallone.*

"Stony likes coffee, black. Do you have any sparkling bottled water?" asked Jet.

"Yes, Daddy, coming up; Perrier. The coffee is on, from this morning," spoke the deputy director of the FBI as she carefully sized up the not yet welcome intruder. *Stony, a name for a street fighter. He looks more like a bareknuckle brawler than an executive broker trainee. The jury is out on this Stony Randolph, if that's his real name.*

"As for the bottled water, regular glass, half full of ice; that ought to do it," Jet trying to lighten up an uneasy atmosphere. A Perrier brand of bottled water and a glass half filled with ice appeared seamlessly. Stoney's steamy black coffee tasted great, an aromatic mocha blend provided by a local coffee house.

"Daddy, Pete's body is at the--"

Jet interrupted Natalie, "Nats, can we discuss this at a different room in the house? Stony understands that you and I have personal business. He can remain here in the kitchen while we go somewhere else; is that okay?" asked Jet.

With understanding and approval, Natalie replied, "Yes, let's use my bedroom. We can talk there. Please follow me up one floor. We'll have privacy," said Natalie as she and Jet proceeded toward the stairs accessing upper townhome floors.

During the interim Stony retrieved surveillance detection equipment from his oversized 'Canadian style' man bag, a large purse really, and commenced a sweep of the town home. He started in the basement. The first thing that caught his eye was the crypt resting at an odd angle in the backseat of the Audi.

He tried the doors of the Audi. They were locked. He accessed his automobile window intrusion device, approached the Audi and flicked the device in and out and up and down a few times. Like clockwork, the left front door window of the Audi invited Stony inside. Accepting the invitation, Stony checked out the Audi's front passenger area, then turned his attention to the large cardboard box in the Audi's back seat.

He examined all surfaces of the box, turning it completely over.

The only way he could access the interior of the box was to risk violation of the integrity of the box, tearing and rupturing the cardboard beyond repair.

This Stony was unwilling to do. He exited the automobile after raising the left front door window and relocking all four doors. *Jet is certain to be interested in an unusual aroma emanating from the back seat of the German sedan, the smell of one-to-two days old, spoiled dead meat.*

Stony knows the smell of human dead flesh. That very same odor is emanating from the Audi's back seat. Natalie has a dead body in her garage! Stony reckoned the body is two days old. The body's clothing and shoes are contained in a hotel laundry bag in the trunk of the Audi. *Jet hob knobs with some strange people. That's no understatement.*

Now 33 years old, Stony is originally from a small town in southeastern Ontario, Canada. After graduating from Syracuse University with a degree in electrical engineering he obtained a USA immigration green card. Because he was a permanent US resident with an engineering degree, he was quickly hired on by General Dynamics in their Gulfstream division at Savannah, Georgia. Jet met Stony ten years ago when the charity purchased a Gulfstream jet aircraft, a G550, since outgrown and traded in.

If it says electronics, Stony probably redesigned it or rejected it. Among his specialties are bugging and debugging all kinds of electronic devices, computer hacking and electronic security. Stony never married. Close once, but not close enough.

Finished with the basement, after Stony climbed the stairs to the first floor of the townhome he commenced a systematic checkout of land line telephones in the kitchen and the family room. Natalie's kitchen telephone and family room telephone are clean.

Six weeks ago, Stony detected unidentified bugs on both of Natalie's pair of telephone land lines. As of today, those bugs are no longer active. Stony does not know when the unidentified bugs were deactivated.

Two weeks ago, Stony remotely took down, terminated surveillance devices which he installed in Natalie's home shortly after Pete's accident four years ago. Stony is comfortable that his bugs were not detected by the unknown bug installer.

22

NATALIE
Straight from the Shoulder

Upstairs, Jet and Natalie engaged in their first get together in over three years, "Daddy, I have only one chair in my bedroom. Take it, please. I'll sit at the foot of the bed."

Jet acquiesced. It's Natalie's show. He wonders what her problem is. *It must not be as important as she suggested on the telephone. She's cool, calm and collected, as if on a Sunday afternoon stroll. Maybe so, maybe not. Time will tell.*

Natalie commenced, "Like I was saying, Pete's body will be cremated. His funeral service is scheduled for Tuesday at 9:30 am, a private service at a local funeral home here in West Springfield. Today is an off day for Betsy Ann, our nurse/housekeeper."

"Your grandson, Donald, is in his bedroom on the third floor, on detention. I'll explain why when the time comes. There's something more important I need to address, the main reason I asked you to come here under, and I hate to admit it, under emergency conditions. I really do have an emergency, Daddy."

"I don't know how to say this any other way, Daddy. Today is Thursday. I killed a man Tuesday night, actually early Wednesday morning. You heard me right, Daddy. Yes, I killed a man yesterday. The body is in the back seat of my Audi, parked downstairs in my basement garage. His clothing is in a laundry bag in the trunk of the car. Nobody knows about this except you and me, Daddy."

Changing subjects, Natalie asked, "Daddy, who is this Stony Randolph guy? He looks more like an enforcer than somebody actively involved in the sales and marketing of commercial jet airplanes, don't you think?"

Reluctantly recognizing that he could not hoodwink Natalie, Jet more or less came clean, "He's one of my executives. He is also a bodyguard, my bodyguard. He's very, very good at his job; highly recommended, superb CV, endorsements out the kazoo and on a positive note, somewhat personable."

"He's been with me for nearly eight years. He's a genius, a Canadian from the Niagara Falls area educated as an electrical engineer at Syracuse University. He has amazing instincts for business. I would trust him with my life. Let me rephrase that. I trust him with my life, Nats."

"My business has expanded and is doing really well. Nevertheless, good fortune is more often than not accompanied by collateral problems. Although I have not made any enemies, there's more than one entity out there jealous and covetous enough that, over time, it's conceivable I could be exposed to risk of bodily harm. I'm not trying to scare you. This is error on the precautionary side for the most part. Am I understandable?"

"No, no you aren't. Definitely not, Daddy. But if it's good enough for you, it's good enough for me. I can live with it. Let's get back to the cadaver, Daddy," Just like her father, Natalie was never one to beat around the bush.

"Nats," (Jet always uses Natalie's childhood nickname, with which she has a love-hate relationship) although a cadaver in your garage is quite a stretch, I suppose the two of us together can handle it. Please embellish before I retort," Natalie always admired her father's vocabulary.

"I screwed up, Daddy. I won't spin the story. As a matter of fact, no pun intended, about screwing that is. Two days ago, I intentionally killed a man named Jethro Armstrong. His body is downstairs in the backseat of my Audi, propped up at an angle, enclosed in a cardboard box. I busted his larynx and neck bones, a fatal blow, with a right foot kick at about 6:30 am Wednesday morning, yesterday."

"I didn't plan to tell it to you this way, but chronologically it's important for you to know that I brought the body back here from a hotel room in Arlington, arriving here at my townhome at about 9:30 am. My goodness, I should have initiated my recollection of this bizarre event by telling you I killed the guy in self-defense. Daddy, apparently my cognitive skills have deserted me or they are all shot to hell."

"Anyway, when I got home yesterday the first thing I did after parking the cadaver laden Audi in my garage was call my secretary. To my surprise she let me know I was scheduled for a solo oval office visit with Bill Wilson, our president, at 1:00 pm, a notice of only three hours and change."

"So as the cookie crumbles, the same day the president summoned me to the king's court on about three hours' notice, I had both a fresh black eye and a cadaver in my garage to account for."

"How about that, Daddy? Hollywood couldn't have scripted it better. A plot from hell for me; a blockbuster for the fictionists. It appears that your li'l darling has arrived, does it not? As you always told me, things happen fast in the fast lane."

"Anyway, today is Thursday. I planned to take Wednesday off and dispose of the body, but that wasn't in the cards considering the importance of my appointment with the president. I had no meaningful idea what the meeting was about, except I knew I was being considered for a highly classified new FBI job assignment."

Removing her sunglasses, Natalie showed Jet her black left eye. The skin surrounding the eye was multicolored, brown, blue, orange and yellow; ugly, indeed ugly.

"What a beautiful shiner you have there, daughter. Normally

one would ask what happened to the other guy. That's not necessary, is it?" Jet hadn't seen it all, but he had seen enough in his lifetime to accept Natalie's rendition of the disparate event. Natalie did not answer so Jet continued, "I know that's not the end of it; how close are you to the punchline?"

"Another three to five minutes, Daddy. For openers, during the past two years I strayed significantly from the straight and narrow. On the contrary, Daddy –"

Natalie cut herself short, hushed for two or three seconds, then said, "I'm telling you this the wrong way, Daddy. I don't want to beat around the bush. I'm going to shoot straight from the shoulder, like you always do; no ambiguities, no half-truths, down and dirty."

"For openers, two years ago, out of frustration I let myself get picked up by a friend of an acquaintance during an after work gathering at a DC bar. It was a one night stand. I had sex with a complete stranger who pronged me like the common tramp I am. I never laid eyes on the guy again. I think he was from out of town. It gets worse."

"We had sex all night long; regular sex, oral sex, kinky sex; the first time for me in over two years. In the morning, I hated myself and I loved myself. Weird. All my life I've been taught, you taught me, Mom taught me, to be a good girl. I used to be a good girl. Matter of fact I was better than good. I was the best girl in the world, until Pete's accident."

"The accident killed me; it murdered me; it decimated me; it suffocated me, it destroyed me; one moment, on top of the world, the next moment in the depths of the most despicable despair anyone could ever imagine. Hell could be no worse. That's where I've been the past four years, in hell."

"That's where I am today; right here, right now, in hell. I function at work solely on the momentum of my youth. I have no interest in my job. I am experienced and competent enough that I'm able to fake it, Daddy. Regardless of anything else I've said or implied today, I have no interest in anything or anybody other than you and my son."

"Daddy, for whatsoever reason, misery, self-pity, funkiness, desperation, despair, you name it, for whatsoever reason I commenced and established for two years a senseless pattern of behavior whereby I would pick up and screw an absolute stranger for half the night, one new stranger each month, never a repeat. I'm not proud and I'm not ashamed. I've been with little ones, big ones, fat ones, skinny ones, young ones, old ones, wild ones, tame ones, you name it."

"I know more about sexual activity in America than Masters and Johnson. Havelock Ellis has nothing on me. I could write a book on 21st century sexual practices and procedures in the United States. It might embarrass you but I guarantee it would be a New York Times bestseller."

"Two days ago, while still a married woman I screwed my brains out with a complete stranger, exhibiting absolutely no concern for job, family, morals or anything else. We humped each other mercilessly. I loved it. Later I hated myself."

"It's ironic, weird that Pete died yesterday, his death more or less sanctioning and exonerating me for my lewd, lascivious behavior during the past two years."

"Daddy, I'm a widow now. I'm single, but I can't say with any degree of certainty how I feel about my personal life. Two days ago, I didn't give one single damn about my personal life. Fortunately, the drug thing with Don, I'll get into that later; along with the new job, has triggered both my maternal instincts and my vocational instincts. I'm back in the groove, Daddy. At least, I think I'm back in the groove. At any rate I have convinced myself that I'm more than superficially back in the groove."

"Pete's dead. It hasn't sunk in yet but I really do know and understand that I'm single, Daddy, for the first time in almost 17 years. I loved Pete more than anything in the world and he's gone, absolutely gone. I know he's gone. I know he's not coming back. It's a blessing, Daddy. It's similar to a criminal conviction, Daddy. I feel like I deserve it. I feel like I don't deserve it. I feel like living. I feel like dying. No matter, Pete's dead."

"Back to my confessional. Two days ago, I picked up this guy at the Pentagon City Hotel in Arlington near the Metro stop. He seemed nice enough, a little hickish, clean-cut, well-dressed and all that malarkey. We made it up to his room and fornicated for one or two hours; then I began dressing to go home."

"Oh, yes. I forgot. Part way through the session, I took a drink of water from what I thought was a sealed water bottle. He had laced the water with a date rape drug, a Roofie. Fortunately for me I had only one drink of water, a small one at that."

"He drugged you?" asked Jet.

"Yes, he drugged me. Once the guy saw me dressing to leave, he asked me where I was going. I told him I had to be at work tomorrow. He didn't appreciate that. He walked across the room toward me and before I had a chance to do anything about it, he hammered me with a closed fist. He was fast and strong, took me by surprise."

"Had I downed more of the drug laden water, I'm certain you would have a dead daughter on your hands as well as a dead son-in-law. Luck of the draw, I guess."

"You may have heard about a serial killer tormenting DC for the past three years. I killed him. His body is downstairs about 50 feet from you as the crow flies. I woke up from the limited effects of the drug at about 4:45 am Wednesday morning. I didn't know where I was but I had most of my wits about me."

Jet acknowledged that he knew about the DC serial killer by nodding his head.

"When I checked out the injury to my left temple, I noticed for the first time I was restrained by a pair of plastic handcuffs, fortunately in the front and not in the back. The only weapon available to me to defend myself from the DC serial killer was my feet. As it turns out my right foot was enough."

"The SOB didn't plan to kill me on site. He intended to pack me into a large cardboard box and carry me off via a hotel luggage carrier to the trunk of his car. I figured it out. When he leaned over me in the bed, thinking that I was still drugged out, I planted a hooking right foot kick on the center of his throat, killing him with one blow."

"It took some doing, but I got my handcuffs off, sterilized the room, stuffed the killer into his cardboard crypt and wheeled his dead body out to my car. I made it home with three hours to spare. The rest is history. I have a concern that the body may have bled out through the cardboard box. There may be some blood on the Audi back seat upholstery. I haven't checked yet."

"If you don't mind, Daddy, I'd like to discuss two less important matters. One is family; the other is something which may affect my future."

Jet is nothing if not pragmatic. A normal father listening to Natalie's story would have been overwhelmed with anguish. Not Jet. During Natalie's soliloquy, he analyzed and evaluated a range of plausible solutions to the cadaver problem.

There's a big difference between normal fathers and fathers who are world-class international criminals. Jet is a world-class international criminal, white-collar, of course; big money, of course; extreme risk, of course, but a criminal nevertheless.

Jet understands that if he is a criminal, he is a criminal only according to the definition of criminality in the Western World. In Jet's view, the Western world does not have personal jurisdiction over him. He is comfortable in his belief that, for whatsoever reason, he is above and beyond Western Law, untouchable and unassailable. That may very well be true.

"Have at it, Nats," said Jet.

"The family matter regards your grandson, Daddy. Partly by accident, partly by curiosity and partly by observation of aberrational behavior, about three months ago I suspected Don might be on drugs. I hired a private investigator. He confirmed my suspicions."

"Tuesday afternoon, two days ago, I pulled Don out of his elite DC private high school and put him on detention, grounded him at home, no automobile, no cell phone, no friends, etc. I'm working on a transfer for Don to MMI. You know, the secondary school,

Millersburg Military Institute in the town of Millersburg, Kentucky, central Kentucky. Good reputation; landed gentry students and all that. I'm trying right now to save his credits for the second semester of his junior year."

"I told him he has to finish high school at MMI. If there is college in his future, it will be at a military oriented school such as VMI or the Citadel with a major in accounting. From the looks of it, Don's not too enchanted with his educational prospects."

"Last subject, Daddy, concerning my future. I don't have proof positive but I do have circumstantial evidence and over the top premonitions that I'm being tailed, personally stalked and observed, by either the Secret Service or the CIA. Recall, two days ago your daughter was selected by President Wilson to head an important new, highly classified, joint task force. I think that's the reason for the tail."

"The task force is more confidential and undercover than top secret. The job is so important that even I don't know yet what the assignment entails. I haven't received a mission briefing. I'm sure the job involves super-duper clandestine stuff, but I don't know for sure."

"Today is Thursday. I'm on two day bereavement leave. I report to President Wilson's Chief of Staff at 8:00 am Monday morning. The new job requires me to relocate to Langley Air Force Base, down at Norfolk, for the time being, which could be two to four to six months, maybe more."

"When I showed up at the oval office with my black eye, Bill Wilson gave me more than a once over. He has a reputation for being a suspicious man, extremely cautious. Never took a chance in his entire life. Doesn't gamble unless he's an odds on favorite to win. I don't think he's completely sold on me."

"One last thing. You may be wondering why I didn't simply call 911 since I killed the guy in self-defense. Believe you me, I know this town. On the facts, the media and the people who have a grudge against the FBI would have buried me as an offering to the Gods of their agendas. Absolutely no doubt about that."

"Were I to have called 911 and vented my spleen, bared my soul to the Arlington police, at a minimum I would have lost my job, been fired, embarrassed, reputation in the tank, out on the street, no income, and no prospects. End of story. Even the slightest vocational vulnerability can be fatal in Washington, DC. The media and both political parties are opportunistic and vicious, with a capital O and a capital V."

"Wait, one last thing. A presumed missing persons investigation regarding the dead body downstairs is almost certain to reveal my assailant booked and paid for a room at the Pentagon Center Hotel via credit card under the name William Marlette. He probably parked his car there."

Reaching into her purse, Natalie retrieved Jethro's car keys and wallet. "With these keys the car can be identified by flashing lights. You know what I mean, Daddy. I have no use for the wallet."

"You have it all, Daddy. My job is to get Don all squared away in his new school. Your job, and I hate to have to ask you, Daddy, is to help me, show me, whatever, how to dispose of the cadaver and to resolve the parked car problem. Easy as pie," whispered Natalie through pursed lips.

Well before Natalie intoned her prayer for relief, Jet evaluated and chose his solutions to Natalie's problems. He handed her a folded item and said, "Nats, please deposit this check for $250,000 into your personal bank account today or for certain by close of bank business tomorrow, Friday. The proceeds will tide you over during your period of mourning and loneliness."

"From what I know about banking, you should close any and all joint accounts you had with Pete and open your own bank account, exclusively for your personal use."

"I reiterate, tomorrow you should open your own bank account with you being the only signature on the account, and deposit this check in it."

"One purpose of the $250,000 is to replace your Audi, if necessary. I don't know about you but I fancy Lexus in that price range."

"Regarding the cadaver, it will be removed from your home

before 5:00 pm today. A tow truck will back into position with its rear end facing the garage. Using a cable, the tow truck operator will place a hook on the frame, enabling the truck to tow the vehicle up and out of your garage, and then to a location known to me but unknown to you."

"It's possible, but not necessarily probable, that the body bled out, soaking the cardboard box; the blood leaching into your Audi's upholstery. If so, resulting DNA evidence could, and probably would, associate you with the deceased at or about the time of his death. That won't do you or me any good. I'm going have your car destroyed, but if and only if your upholstery is bloodstained."

"If the Audi is bloodstained and ultimately destroyed, you are not in such event to report your car to the police as missing. You will not, repeat not, notify your automobile insurance company that you sustained a theft or otherwise loss of your vehicle."

"If you don't get your car back by close of business tomorrow, assume it has been destroyed. If you do get your car back, it's business as usual. After I leave today, remove all documents and such from the Audi's glove compartment and leave both sets of car keys in the Audi's glove compartment; wiped down, no prints. Please open your garage door at 4:00 pm."

"As for the cadaver's automobile, I'll have that checked out today. By the way, how's it going to work, you arriving in Norfolk on Monday afternoon and the funeral in West Springfield scheduled for Tuesday morning? That's a hell of a way to start a new job, a new and important job; two interruptions in the first five days."

"FBI helicopter, I suppose. I agree, it's absolutely essential that I get off on the right foot with this new job, Daddy."

"Let's move along to the bad guy's vehicle. I have the keys and wallet. Did you wipe them down?" Natalie nodded yes.

"Good. You no longer have to be concerned about the cadaver, his vehicle and his personal effects." Natalie's internal sigh of relief went unnoticed.

"Regarding Don, I understand what you have in mind. Please let me handle it. A man to man, mano y mano, face-up is best for me and best for Don. I promise you no problems with Don, no school problem, no college problem and no drug problem. No problems with Don, period."

"Nats, you may think I'm crazy or that I don't understand your situation or something else along that line, but of the problems you described to me, in my view the most serious is the possibility that you're being tailed."

"With your permission, I'm going to electronically sweep your entire house and garage up and down with anti-surveillance gadgets. I need to look at your computer so that – No. No, I have no expertise in that area."

"Backtracking, I'll have a computer expert come over tomorrow and determine if your computer has been hacked. He will install a state-of-the-art firewall on your desktop and do whatever else he deems necessary for you to have first class computer security at home. Both the tow truck driver and a computer technician will call you before coming. They will tell you that they were hired by your father to do a job for you at your home."

"Nats, I'm sorry but I'm not going to make the funeral. I'm up to my ass in alligators and the swamp is rising. Actually, I have challenging, difficult problems at work, which occurs from time to time. I'm on top of things. One problem which nags at me is that I don't get to spend much time with you. With that in mind, I'd like to see a lot more of you. Is that possible? I hope so."

Natalie was amazed. Her father didn't question her one iota. *I just told him that I committed a murder, self-defense, but nevertheless committed a murder, and asked him to cover it up by permanently disposing of both the cadaver and the cadaver's automobile, plus possibly disposing of my own automobile.*

He absorbed it as if I told him I had stopped going to Sunday school or taken up tango dancing lessons. 'Unfucking believable,' and I never use that word, almost never. He said he would handle Don. What does my dad know about drugs, about teenage drug use? So far as I know, he doesn't know a damn thing about disappearing cadavers, destruction of automobiles, suppression of evidence and teenage drug use. I'm looking, hoping is more like it, for a novice high schooler to solve a PhD problem, that's for sure. With nobody competent to help me, I'm going down, I'm going down soon!

Natalie answered Jet, "I hope so too, Daddy. Question for you, I tell you an impossible to believe story about murder, conspiracy, politics, drugs, intrigue – and you don't lift an eyebrow, don't criticize me one single bit, don't ask me one question. Why not, daddy, why not?"

"Easy as pie, pretty girl. You're my daughter. You can do no wrong. Let's get on with this thing."

Shaking her head in wonder, Natalie said, "Daddy, I don't know what to say. I'm speechless. I believe you can pull this off. I don't know how you'll be able to, but you're my Daddy and I trust you 100%. Yes, I'd like to see a lot more of you, Daddy, a lot more."

"How are you fixed for cash, daughter?"

"Oh, I forgot to tell you. Eight years back, a really competent salesman convinced us to insure Pete's life by acquiring a new and larger term policy of life insurance. Personal finance wise, it was the smartest move we ever made. Pete took a qualifying physical exam, and we canceled his other life policies. As owner, I bought a one million dollar life insurance policy on Pete's life, which proceeds will be paid to me in the next few weeks.

"Good," said Jet. "Is it all right if I talk to Donald now?" Natalie nodded in the affirmative, bemused as to how her father could possibly affect the behavior of a known drug addict. Stranger things have happened.

23
DON BRANSON
Druggie Dress Down

At 12:30 pm Jet alerted Ewe for departure within three hours, back to Bermuda. Stony completed his sweeps and was watching TV.

"Nats, let me have a cup of coffee. I'll be on my way after talking with Donald. Do you have a taxi number handy?"

"Coffee coming up, Daddy. I'll call a cab. Does Stony want anything to drink or a snack? I have a full pantry and refrigerator," said Natalie.

"No, thank you Ma'am," said Stony. "I'm all right."

Natalie was attracted by the resonance in Stony's voice, the authority and the confidence he exuded. *Apparently Stony is a real man. I don't need this. The timing is gross. Cross your legs, Natalie.*

"Nats, please tell the taxi to pick us up 30 minutes from now, destination Reagan National Airport. I'm going to share a few words with Donald," said Jet.

"Yes, OK, Daddy," Natalie complied again. Jet said quietly to Stony, "You're driving the kid from here to Millersburg Military Institute, located at Millersburg, Kentucky, rural central Kentucky.

First leg, I-64 westbound, nine hour drive. Spend tonight in a motel close to Millersburg. 'MMI' is the moniker for the high school."

"Order a car from the nearest rental agency. Pick up here today and drop off at Louisville, Kentucky tomorrow. Louisville is about 100 miles west of Millersburg, back roads. Fly commercial tomorrow from Louisville to Bermuda, ASAP."

"Yes, sir," responded Stony. *I haven't told Jet about the stiff in the garage.*

"Donald, it's your grandfather," said Jet as he knocked on Don's bedroom door.

"Come in, grandpa, come on in, the door's open," replied Don disinterestedly.

The kid is a piece of work. This is the boy Natalie described to me downstairs, the one with a silver spoon in his mouth who is pissing in his own soup. He must think there's a free lunch. We shall see about that.

"Donald (Jet always calls him Donald, not 'Don'), I understand you and your mom are at an impasse and she dressed you down. She told me her side of the story. Would you like to tell me your side of the story?"

"No, sir, if you don't mind sir, I'm just not up to it," still lackadaisical.

"I can understand, Donald, I surely can. Please listen to me. I'm your grandfather. Your father is at the funeral home. His body will be cremated Tuesday. According to the way I grew up, you are now male head of household in the Branson family."

Don perked up. *I wonder what my grandfather is up to. The man doesn't appear to be angry. His tone of voice is almost friendly and his body language is at least neutral. Everything he has said up to now has been, at least, reasonable. Maybe this will be OK.*

"Donald, I don't have a lot of time. By chance work has piled up on me. So I will be brief and to the point. Listen to me carefully young man. If you use any more drugs, I will kill you; kill you dead."

"In case you didn't understand me the first time around, I said,

'I'm going to kill you,' arrange to have you killed if you continue to use drugs."

Don was shocked. *I can't believe my grandfather just told me he is going to kill me. I must have heard him wrong. I had to have heard him wrong.*

Jet continued, "If I ever discover you have used drugs again, I will arrange for you to be killed. I have eyes and ears all over the world. It's not going to be a problem for me to monitor your progress, or lack thereof, at the military school in Millersburg, Kentucky."

"Your mother's my firstborn. She's the apple of my eye. She's the best daughter any man could have. I never gave my mother any problems. Your mother never gave me any problems. I will not allow your drug use to give your mother any problems, any more problems, that is, than the problems you have already given her."

Firstborn? I thought my mom was his only born! What gives?

"As you slovenly sit there, sucking on your thumb, feeling sorry for yourself, you make me so Goddamn sick I could throw up all over your room. We both know I won't vomit, don't we?"

Not anticipating an answer, Jet continued, "But you can be sure, you can be certain, you can take it to the bank, you can know without a doubt that if you ever again consume any drugs, you won't be around to give your mother any trouble. You will be in that cold black hole in the ground, just like your father."

"It's no big deal to me, kid, but at this point in time, if your mother were so inclined, you would have driven her to drink. You would have turned her into the worst bag lady alcoholic known to womankind. Your mother is worried to death about you, you worthless little bastard. I took you off her hands. You have experienced an epiphany, haven't you?"

"Can you define epiphany, you sorry ass excuse for a human being?"

Only silence emanates from Don. The pale faced salamander squirms perceptibly.

"I thought not. An epiphany is when you are born again, when you have a new birth, a new understanding, a new plan, a new life, that's you, isn't it, Donald?" Jet drove the words into Don's heart and soul, piercing the remnants of whatever shield remains in his defensive reserve.

"Look, this is relatively simple. You're a druggie. Your mother is upset because you're a druggie. Your mother being upset upsets me. Your mother is a woman. She loves you like only a mother can love her firstborn son. I am your mother's father. I love her. I don't give a damn now and never did give a damn about you. People have to earn my respect, and you are way out in left field on that score."

"Donald, you are representative of what's wrong with the United States of America. An entire generation, your generation, the me-now generation, impersonating real people. I am aware the only words you know how to spell are reefer, hit, downer, high, bong; all those drug culture words which I'm certain you are more familiar with than anybody in this household. Well, kiss all that bullshit goodbye, permanently."

"You are part of the youth of this country, which youth is systematically destroying itself pursuant to implementation of the objectives of your progressive society. 'What's in it for me, now?' and 'Everybody lies, cheats and steals, why not me?' along with 'Where are my food stamps?' plus 'Where is my Supplemental Social Security?' and 'Where is my free cell phone?' including 'How much money do I get back from the IRS under the earned income credit scheme?' and finally 'Where is my daily diet of drugs?' Where, when, how? Ad infinitum, ad nauseam."

"It makes me sick to my stomach to think about how Goddamn young people like you have raped our wonderful country. You, you little bastard, are on your way to joining the sons of bitches that are standing in line for a free lunch. But not on my fucking nickel and not on your mother's nickel."

"Not if I have anything to do with it, to say about it, and you can bet your bottom dollar, if you have one, I'm going to have a hell of a lot to say about what happens to you from now until the time you are 25 or 30 years old, if you live that long, Mr. drug user."

"Ground rules. Your detention is terminated, now."

Don's ears perked up. He wonders what is coming next. He is totally confused. *First friendship, next a double, triple, quadruple dose of ridicule, followed by friendship again. My grandfather must be crazy. He simply doesn't understand how this country has changed and how out of touch with reality he is. And he said he's gonna kill me. Nah, I don't think so. Fat chance. No chance.*

"I know what you're thinking, you little son of a bitch. I've got you totally pegged. You think you can weasel your way out of the mess you got yourself in. Think again, you sorry ass. Listen to me carefully, very carefully."

"Like your mother told you, you are going to MMI. You're going to be an honor roll student. You're going to be an athlete. You're going to be demerit free. You'll graduate from MMI and attend college. You'll go to a military college. You'll major in accounting. If you don't do these things, I promise I will kill you."

"I want to indelibly impress on your limited mind something of importance, extreme importance. You were on your mother's probation list. I just let you off. Now you are on my shit list. Probation is harmless to a druggie like you in terms of longevity; conversely, my shit list can and will be fatal for you, fatal when you violate the drug use terms and conditions I am imposing upon you here and now. If you do not immediately straighten your little white ass out, I will kill you."

"Do you understand what I just said to you, you slimy son of a bitch? Others might cut a druggie some slack. Those worthless liberal feel good-do good welfare socialist types are in tune with the drug culture, or so they say. It's a disease, they say."

"The hell it's a disease. It's a Goddamned self-induced habit, and you know it. It's not your fault, is it, Donny Boy? Bullshit. I say bullshit to you and every Goddamned liberal who ever did, or ever will, cut slack for a drug user. Rehabilitation. That's it, rehab. That'll do it. No Goddamned way you'll ever see the inside of a Rehab center. No Goddamned way. Rehab sucks."

"Look at my side of this conundrum. I don't give a good God-damn what you do. I don't care if you're dead or alive. You screw around with your mother and you're dead, dead as a doornail. Do you understand that? Do you really understand that? I'm not even looking for an answer from you, you sorry ass bastard."

"I don't believe in drying out. I don't believe in treatment. The only thing I believe in is cold turkey. Get off it. Let the games begin young man, good luck to you, not that I believe in luck or not that I believe you will live very long. Look over your shoulder. I'll be right there. You fuck up and you won't have a shoulder to look over."

"I'm gone. I'm outta here. I'm gone but not forgotten. The day you forget me and forget the message that I am laying on you is the day you commence to die. I'll be seeing you, hopefully not in all those old familiar places."

"About a year from now we will have a face to face, provided you're clean. If you are not clean, I will appear at your funeral, as a pallbearer for the wayward grandson. That would be just peachy, wouldn't it?" Jet quietly left Don's bedroom, closing the door behind him.

Surreal. I just experienced the most realistic dream I ever muddled through. I'm not on detention, great. I can call Sam and Bill.

Two minutes later Jet reentered Don's bedroom and said calmly, "Donald, if you like, I can kill you right here and now; put you out of your misery. Do I have your permission to kill you right here and now, Donald?"

"No, I thought not. If you're wondering why I came back to deliver an epilogue, you should understand that I know what is going through your pitiful little mind in terms of detention. You can party with your buddies, right? Wrong, you worthless son of a bitch. I'll kill you today if I have to."

As Jet left Donald's bedroom for the last time, he passed Stony coming up the stairs. "Sweep?" questioned Jet.

"Clean with mixed results," responded Stony. "Be advised there's a dead body in the basement."

"I know. Automobile?"

"Reserved, your taxi and my rental. I'm ready to roll, to Kentucky."

"Good, see you back downstairs," Jet said, more pissed off and angry than he has been in a long, long time. Stony noticed but said nothing.

Jet continued down to the kitchen where Natalie was preparing a snack for the three males. Stony did not knock on Don's bedroom door. He opened the door and walked in unannounced.

"Hi, my name's Stony; I work for your grandfather. I don't know the entire story or anything like that. What I do know is enough for me to disagree almost totally with your grandfather. I don't have a lot of influence, but since I'm younger than him, I don't share the same feelings he has about the ways of the world."

"Your grandfather told me to have you pack your clothes. You and I are leaving for Kentucky in one hour in a rental car. We will drive straight through." Don looked at Stony with a quizzical facial expression of both amazement and disbelief.

"You and I are leaving by automobile in one hour, Interstate I-64, arriving in Kentucky about nine hours later." Don shook his head no.

"We will make it to Millersburg, Kentucky by around midnight; spend the night in a local motel and check-in with MMI at 9:00 am Friday, tomorrow. After check-in there will be two or three hours of administrative details, registration, uniform issue, textbooks and similar things. You will be in class tomorrow afternoon at Millersburg Military Institute. No loss of credits." Don still shaking his head no, firmer than before.

"Please pay attention, I'm the good guy. I'm on your side, Don. I don't know why but your grandfather appears to despise the ground you walk on. I don't. The old folks grew up a certain way. Not me. I believe everybody deserves at least one chance, regardless." Don retreats toward the hallway, ready to leave the bedroom and get away from Stony.

"I apologize for this but your grandfather expects me to be hard on you. I don't want to be hard on you but somebody has to, because you need protection. You need a friend. Show me your chin. Your grandfather expects me to be hard on you. If I'm not hard on you, he'll send some really mean ass to do a number on you. You might not survive. From the way I see it, Don, it's either cooperate with me or anticipate, I don't know any other way to say it, anticipate instant death." Don starting to cry.

"I kid you not, Don. You are truly between a rock and a hard place. The way I see it, you and I have no other recourse." After finishing the sentence Stony took Don down via an advanced martial arts move.

Stony is 6'4" tall and weighs 230 pounds of rock hard muscle. Don is 6'1" tall and weighs 155 pounds. No match. Within three seconds, Stony had knuckle punched Don twice near his left rib cage and had open hand slapped his face hard enough to cause a moderate bruise. Don slowly sunk into plush bedroom carpet.

In the recent past, Don stopped paying attention to words. Words are cheap. Words are for old people. Words mean nothing. The only things important are drugs, money and girls. As of this afternoon, Don now believes violence matters, a lot. In one marital arts move, Don was rudely introduced to the world of violence. In his own way Don recognized his mortality, recognized the situation he was in, and recognized he was outmanned, outmaneuvered and outgunned.

A quick study like his mother, Don knows the only way he will live to see another day is to pull in his horns and wait until he puts some age on his bones. *For absolute certain, there will come a time in the future when I will kill my grandfather, sneak up on him, the same way Stony snuck up on me, and kill him dead, absolutely dead. The number one item on my bucket list is to kill my grandfather.*

Bottom line, whatever Stony wants, Stony gets. If you beat the shit out of a kid he will probably do what you want him to do; if you talk to a kid there's little if any chance the kid will do what you want him to do.

Times change. Contemporary kids do not think the way adults think. They don't care like adults care. They don't live like adults live. They don't love like adults love. They don't work like adults work. They do hardly anything the way adults do. As far as it goes, the younger generation might as well speak Arabic, Chinese or Japanese. Contemporary American adults and kids simply don't understand each other.

*

Jet worked everything out with Natalie. She was amazed. In a two hour visit her father had somehow resolved all her outstanding problems. *How in the world did he do that? Don't look a gift horse in the mouth, Natalie. Don't do it.*

Today is Thursday. I have to show up at the white house at 8:00 am on Monday to see Tom Redding. Depart for Norfolk at noon Monday. Tuesday is the funeral.

Wait a minute, sister! It makes no sense whatsoever to arrive at Norfolk at two or three in the afternoon on Monday and have to be back at West Springfield (175 miles) on Tuesday morning. No sense whatsoever. I don't think Redding will have any trouble granting me an additional two days of bereavement leave. Any decision to the contrary is nonsensical. Yes, a two day bereavement extension is appropriate. I'll talk to Redding by telephone tomorrow, Friday. I can gin up my task force tomorrow. Good.

Let's review what I have on the table.

Number one – Place Audi keys in glove box.

Number two – Audi (with cadaver) departs my house prior to 5:00 pm today.

Number three - Daddy will handle Jethro's car, as necessary.

Number four - Don registers at MMI tomorrow morning, a miracle.

Number five - Electronically, clean my home. Technicians at work tomorrow.

Number six – New desktop computer tomorrow. (Coordinate 5 & 6 - Betsy Ann)

*

Everything resolved. How can my Daddy be so competent? Everything we have done and now plan to do is so far removed from his area of expertise. How can that be?

24
APPALACHIAN MOUNTAINS
The Orphan

"Daddy, while we're at it, if you have time, would you please tell me that story again about your mom and your stepfather. I know it's a dreadful story. You told me the story when I was 16 or 17 years old. Back then I didn't understand the nature of and the significance of the problems you, your mother and your sister had with stepfather. I remember he died, but that's it. I'm an adult now. I can handle the truth, bad though I suspect it is."

"Why in the world would you want to rehash that old story, Nats?"

"If you're willing to tell me the story again, it will be easier for me to understand how you made it, your transition, from penniless orphan at Country Day School in Jefferson County, Kentucky, to become one of the best airplane brokers in the world. I'm really proud of you, Daddy. All those accomplishments solely by means of your own bootstraps, no help from anybody; completely, and I mean completely, on your own."

"True enough, so far as it goes."

"From my memory, you didn't have financial aid from anybody from the time you turned 18. Considering the important jobs you worked at over the years, you didn't know anyone with whom you could talk and from whom you could ask or receive advices about the vagaries of business life. You grew up all by yourself. You did it, Daddy, you did it completely on your own. I am so proud to have you for a father, to be your daughter, so proud."

"Don't lay it on too thick."

"In one of my philosophy classes at Vanderbilt, I recall the writings of an English philosopher whose name I have forgotten, perhaps John Stuart Mill, but I'm not certain. The philosopher hit upon a truism about England during 1800 - 1850. I remember the moral of the story was that, similar to the caste system in India, in 19th century England it was extremely difficult, if not impossible, to transcend social strata."

"The philosopher implied that one collateral effect the cast system in England imposed at that time was to assure only the brightest young men, and essentially none of the women, could rise above their upbringing, could transcend social strata. A peasant is a peasant, always was a peasant and always will be a peasant, with rare exception. I believe the story was true then and I believe it's true now.

"In today's world, nobody can move up like you did. Tell me how you did it, Daddy, tell me how you got it done, from orphan to out of sight successful businessman, please."

Jet didn't want to tell Natalie the story. He didn't want to tell anybody the story. Old wounds are better left unopened. On the other hand, the story didn't bother him as much now as it did long ago.

"OK, Nats, listen up. I was born in 1958. I have one sister, Margaret. She was five years older than me. She was born in 1953. We lived in a hollow, a gap in the mountains caused by eons of running water, pronounced "holler," near the eastern Kentucky – Virginia state line, on the Kentucky side."

"As the crow flies, I lived about 30 miles southwest from Black Mountain, the tallest mountain in Kentucky, elevation 4,145 feet above sea level. I lived 13 miles south southeast from the county seat,

Harlan, Kentucky, and about three miles East of Cawood, Kentucky, near the hamlet of Cranks, Kentucky. Some years back I checked Google for population numbers of those thriving metropolises as of 2010. I was astonished by the results, which I'm certain have not changed very much.

Harlan, Kentucky 2010 population 1693

Caywood, Kentucky 2010 population 731

Cranks, Kentucky 2010 population 522"

"I grew up about midway between Caywood and Cranks, half way up a holler, the name of which I don't remember. No car, no TV, no hot water, no refrigerator, one pair of denims, two shirts, two undershirts, two drawers, one pair of shoes, two pair of socks, all either from a second hand store or 'grown out of hand-me-downs' from what few friends we had."

"Margaret was a girl. She needed more clothes, but had only a very few more. We lived a meager, survival existence at best. Hardly anybody ever filed a tax return. No cars, no refrigerators, no washing machines. No nothing, to speak of. Earned income credits were unheard of for another 40 years. No food stamps or free cell phones either."

"My real father was a coal miner. His father and his father before him were both coal miners. Air in the mines often was not the best, sometimes downright unhealthy. My real father died of black lung disease when I was six years old, in 1964. Later I looked up the definition of black lung disease in an encyclopedia. It was not pleasant reading. I memorized the definition, word for word."

'Black lung disease is caused by inhaling coal dust. It's called black lung disease because lungs having the disease look black instead of pink. Black lung disease is a form of pneumoconiosis named coal worker's pneumoconiosis (CWP), of which there are two forms, simple and complicated. The complicated form involves progressive massive fibrosis (PMF).'"

"Bad stuff, but indigenous to mountainous eastern Kentucky. It used to pain me to revisit Cranks, Kentucky in my head, to recall abject poverty pervading practically all of Appalachia, including the homes in our little holler, including with rare exception, everybody in those hollers, to a person, all destitute. My father, my mother, gone long before their time. Tragic. No money, no opportunity, no nothing. Such is life."

"Mama remarried in 1966, a year and a half after my real father died. At first, things were okay so far as I knew. But little by little, month by month, both my mother and sister, Margaret, started to mope around the house, seemed unhappy all the time, even sad. Our new life was nothing like it was when my real father was alive. Dad was kind and gentle, reasonable, fair-minded, a perfect father for me, at least that's the way I remember it."

"Leslie Johnson, to my childhood understanding, had what I as an adult identify as 'no redeeming social values.' The short answer is he was a real bastard, hard-working on-the-job, but meaner than hell at home with my mother, my sister Margaret and myself. I sensed problems. I was eight years old. What could I do? What could I say? Hopelessly, nothing. Nothing at all. Innocent as hell, a child unable to identify, unable to discern, and unable to avoid disaster. Nats, this subject is difficult for me to revisit, even now."

"I'm sorry, Daddy, but please continue. It's my heritage and my pain too, Daddy."

"OK, then. My mother had a job cleaning houses. She was a stoic, hard-working, responsible woman. I never knew her to say a curse word. I never knew her to complain. Sixth grade education and I never knew her to misspell a word. She was our rock of Gibraltar, protecting Margaret and me."

"When my father died, my mother became solely responsible for two children. There was no money, no money whatsoever, from the time he died until she married Leslie 18 months later. Leslie had a job in the mines."

"I sensed there was something wrong. I couldn't put my finger on it, but there was something wrong, bad wrong. I started paying more attention to things around the house. Remember, I was eight years old and Margaret was 13 years old. More often than not, when my mother had to work cleaning houses, or some other odd job, Leslie would backtrack to our house. Sometimes I would be there; sometimes I wouldn't be there. Margaret was almost always in the house. Early on, she was a recluse."

"If I was to be in the house when Leslie was sniffing around after Margaret, Leslie would lock me in the back room and tell me "Jet, if you don't keep your mouth shut, I will tan your hide!" or words to that effect.

"I'm certain Leslie would have killed me with a beating if I had spoken out against him to his face. His weapon of choice was a big leather belt with a huge brass buckle which left marks and indentations on my back and on my buttocks when he beat me. I still carry reminders of those days on my body; 54 year old scars, evidence of a family gone wrong, unmistakable signs of childhood abuse."

"I was scared of Leslie. I was scared he would beat me to death. So I cowardly kept my knowledge to myself. I hated myself for my entire life for not ratting Leslie out to somebody. Of course, there was nobody within shouting distance to rat Leslie out to."

"If there had been, and if it had been a man, the man probably would have joined Leslie in a dual incestuous rape; eastern Kentucky mountain lifestyle. On each and every occasion I just described, Leslie would have his way with my 13-year-old sister, a young girl barely into her teens, serially raped by her stepfather; not an uncommon occurrence in mountainous Eastern Kentucky during those days."

"People who lived in the Appalachian Mountains of eastern Kentucky often viewed incest as no more than a hobby, something to perhaps snobbishly look down upon, but, all things considered, no big deal. Old enough to bleed, old enough to butcher, the way it often was for those folks, in those days."

"Yes, Nats, I said: 'Old enough to bleed; old enough to butcher.'

In some venues, the comment is meant to be a joke. In the eastern Kentucky mountains, for my sister and mother, the joke was real, calamitously real."

"The 'upper crust,' and I use the term loosely, citizens living in our county seat, Harlan, Kentucky would say 'No, incest is not happening in eastern Kentucky. Incest is not happening here,' knowing full well the young girls in the hollers as near as ten miles distant were screaming on deaf ears as their hymens were ruptured by sex crazed irresponsible middle-aged men, more often than not, blood relatives. For the most part, nobody could do anything about it. It was part of the 'code of the hills,' or something closely akin."

"My mother knew what Leslie was doing to Margaret. Nobody had to tell her. She just knew. She also knew there was nothing she could do about it. From Leslie's viewpoint, Leslie was having his way with his stepdaughter two or three times a week. No big deal. From my mother's viewpoint, Leslie was having his way with her daughter two or three times a week. Big deal! Big fucking deal! Perspective is a marvelous thing."

"My mother was a good woman. Her father and mother were good people. My mother didn't deserve what Leslie was doing to Margaret. She knew there was nobody could help; there's nothing nobody could or would do, except for my mother."

"On a Monday morning in September, I shall never forget the day, at about 6:00 am in the morning she commenced heating water. It took about 45 minutes to boil the water in the family bathtub, a wash tub really. She heated the water on the only stove we had in our hovel; the stove for cooking our food and for keeping us warm on cold Appalachian winter days."

"At first boil, my mother placed four wash rags on the two metal handles of the washtub and carried the tub full of boiling water into their bedroom. So as not to wake Leslie by stumbling, she put just enough water in the tub she thought would do the job. She noiselessly crept the 25 or 30 feet from the stove to the side of the bed where Leslie was sound asleep, tub leading the way."

"With malice aforethought, with conviction and without remorse, my mother intentionally scalded Leslie Johnson to death on that Monday morning. From a hiding place I watched her do it. He died a horrible death."

"Alive and in misery with third-degree burns over his entire upper body, including his face, Leslie lasted for 10 or 12 hours before the Lord put him out of his misery late in the afternoon. My mother didn't call for help. She didn't offer help. She didn't assist Leslie or attempt to assuage his pain. She let the miserable son of a bitch suffer, just like he deserved to suffer."

"After Leslie died, somewhere around 6:00 pm, it was not dark yet; my mother walked the hundred or so yards to the Jones house. The Jones' had a telephone. Mr. Jones called the sheriff and the undertaker."

"Leslie was buried behind our house, on top of a 30 degree slope, out of sight. My mother was never again the same. The local authorities decided not to prosecute since they knew very well what the circumstances were. The County of Harlan paid for Leslie's funeral. My mother was, I guess incarcerated is the word, taken to what amounted to be an insane asylum, Madison State Asylum, near Madison, Indiana, 35 miles upriver from Louisville, Kentucky on the north side of the Ohio River."

"Mother never recovered. She died eight years later, in 1972, age 37. Nobody told me about her death. She married when she was 15 years old and delivered Margaret at age 16. The legal age of marriage in Kentucky in those days for girls was 14 years old with parental consent and 16 years old with consent not required. For boys, the ages were 16 years and 18 years, respectively. Mountain folks struck while the iron was hot. That's the way it was back then. For all I know, it might still be that way. I escaped."

"Margaret and I were shipped without our permission, nobody asked us, to Country Day School in Louisville, Jefferson County, Kentucky. We had no kinfolk. We had no guardian. We were owned by the state of Kentucky, lock stock and barrel. I adapted. I lived better than I had ever lived in the mountains. Everybody but me complained. They didn't like the rooms; they didn't like the beds; they didn't like the food; they didn't like the school; they didn't like anything. I liked everything."

"I loved the place. Eight years old. It was as if a dream had come true for me to live at Country Day School, rather than to live in the mountains. The food was great. Playgrounds were great. The schoolbooks were great. The teachers were great. A new life began for me, for which I'm grateful to Jefferson County, Kentucky, and will be grateful for the rest of my days."

"I made it from third grade all the way to 12th grade at Country Day. Neither Margaret nor I were adopted. An old couple named Hayes took an interest in Country Day boys and girls who made good grades in high school and tested well on achievement tests. They set me up with a second shift job at an appliance factory, told me to apply for college entry at the University of Louisville but to lie and say I did not work. They let me use their address for the application."

"Mr. Hayes cosigned my loan application for my first car, a six-year-old 1970 four-door Toyota Corolla. Wheels were essential. No car-no job; no job-no college. Simple as that."

"I lied. The University of Louisville accepted me. I enrolled in ROTC. I worked second shift full time at the appliance factory for four years, bought a car, drank beer, chased girls, got married early, an all-American boy. I attended college full time. I made straight B's, sprinkled in a few A's; majored in government and politics. Graduated on time after four years, went to United States Air Force pilot training the following November."

"I never lived in Kentucky again. Margaret and I see each other every few years; she is 67 years old, never married; lives in an ACLF, an adult congregate living facility, in Richmond, Kentucky, just south of Lexington."

"Seven years in the Air Force on active duty, followed by seven years as a weekend warrior with the Air National Guard in Richmond, Virginia. When I resigned my regular Air Force commission at the seven-year point, I signed on with my now deceased partner and commenced working full time as an inexperienced used aircraft salesman. I parlayed that job into ownership of the most successful used commercial aircraft brokerage firm in the world. That's it. End of story, Nats."

Natalie did not understand the Appalachian Mountains incest story when she was 16 years old. Try as she might she still cannot comprehend or understand, much less accept, the incestuous society that spawned her father.

Who in the world could ever, under any circumstances, condone devious incestuous behavior by grown men, forcing themselves upon innocent early teen and preteen females? Perhaps the existentialists are correct. Perhaps life really is absurd. That small slice of life certainly was.

25
WASHINGTON, DC
Birth of USTF-18

Natalie arrived at her FBI headquarters corner office at 9:00 am on Friday morning, January 29th. She has been a widow for two days. Her mind is made up. She is not going to work in a make-shift CIA facility 175 miles from Washington DC. No way. *Screw Mitch Donahue and Tom Redding. Screw them both.*

At 9:04 am Natalie called the telephone number President Bill Wilson provided to her. When a secretary answered, Natalie said, "This is Natalie Taylor, Deputy Director of the FBI. I'm calling at the suggestion of President Wilson. Please have the president call me at FBI headquarters at his earliest convenience. The subject is confidential and urgent. There is no emergency." Natalie gave the secretary her private number.

"I'll tell the president right away, Ms. Taylor," was the curt response. All business.

During the initial hour of Friday's workday, Natalie raided the national security branch for the first three of her five supervisory billets. She commandeered the supervisors of the divisions of counterterrorism and counter intelligence, along with the supervisor of the weapons of mass destruction directorate, all three senior supervisors of the national security branch of the FBI.

For the final two supervisory billets, Natalie selected the executive assistant director for the intelligence branch of the FBI and the executive assistant director for the information and technology branch of the FBI. Natalie knows FBI director Jim Burns will have a shit hissy when he learns about his loss of valuable supervisory personnel, especially from the FBI's national security branch.

Natalie's five supervisors are authorized to select their own assistants, two each. All supervisors shall understand that information technology will be strongly represented, along with counterterrorism, counterintelligence and weapons of mass destruction.

Natalie opened her personal Farley File and turned to the CIA. Every important person with whom Natalie ever came into contact is an entry in Natalie's Farley File. Each file contains important positive and negative personal information. The files are sensitive to deviations from the norm, and always contain information regarding family, awards and commendations. Mitch Donahue's entry comprises two single spaced pages. The average entry contains a bit more than a quarter page. She read Mitch's entry twice.

At 10:17 am Dina buzzed Natalie on intercom, "The President is on line two."

Un-cradling her Government Issue landline telephone, Natalie said, "This is Natalie Taylor, Mr. President. Thank you for promptly responding to my call, sir."

"Not at all, Natalie, what can I do for you today? Aren't you on bereavement leave until Monday?"

Natalie commenced, "Yes, sir, I am. But I was able to clean up all my problems in one day. I'm needed here at work, Mr. President. Switching gears with you, sir; regarding the location of my task force assignment, I know it was not your decision to posture all task force personnel in CIA facilities at Langley Air Force Base. It must've been Tom Redding's idea. Mr. President, I can work at any facility, anywhere in the world. One caveat; regardless of where I'm working, the actual physical location, it is essential for adequate FBI personnel and equipment support to be reasonably available. The farther I am away from home, the more difficult it is to satisfy the adequate support requirement."

"Mr. President, the only acceptable place to locate FBI domestic USTF-18 personnel is at our DC headquarters, where the best of the best ply their trade every day, the best support facilities, the best personnel and the best equipment and supplies for an exceptionally broad range of mission requirements, including the requirements of our joint task force mission. CIA joint staff operatives should be domiciled at CIA headquarters, Langley AFB, Virginia, as they are."

"If you buy my premise, hopefully you will agree that the only remaining decision is where to locate task force supervisors one and two, myself and Mitch Donahue. Frankly, it makes little difference where the two head knockers are located, what with modern day communications capabilities."

The president interrupted, "Argument accepted. You and your folks stay in DC. Donahue operates from Norfolk with his folks. Are you sure you should be at work? Do you have anything else?"

"I should be where I am, sir, right here at work. Yes, I do have one another issue. Before I get to that, since both Mitch Donahue and I will be at different locations, I will coordinate with him to provide you with daily morning status reports. I recommend Donahue and I personally attend weekly face-to-face meetings here in DC with you and Tom Redding, along with others nominated by the two of you, if any. 15 minutes should suffice. Friday afternoon or Monday mornings or afternoons are recommended; your choice." *Screw Mitch Donahue.*

"I'll let you know, Natalie."

"In closing, I request a personal conference with you at your earliest convenience, the two of us alone, no others at the meeting or aware of the meeting unless absolutely necessary. Will you accommodate me, Mr. President? I hope so."

The President was mystified by a request from a middle

management executive with only two days on the job, breaching all protocol in the book; bypassing all superiors in her chain of command, right to the top. Normally the President would have been insulted. Not so with this wild ass but effective Goddamned split tail.

Bill Wilson recognizes there is more to Natalie Taylor than meets the eye. No report yet from Donahue on her personal surveillance, which is to commence in three days, on Monday. "Approved, Natalie. My secretary will call you with appointment date and time. Don't disappoint me, my dear," soothed the misogynist.

"Natalie, my previous response was ambiguous. I am sorry. Your personal conference with me is approved and as well your request to domicile FBI task force personnel in DC is approved."

"Thank you, Mr. President. Thank you very much. My FBI team won't let you down."

"I am sure you won't, let me down that is. Natalie, I see why you were nominated for this job. You are gutsy. You make sense. I like your style."

"Pay attention now. You know task force directors generate a lot of paperwork, especially in the areas of mission, procedure, schedules, etc. Make the sole subject of your first written directive the bifurcation of FBI/CIA task force physical locations."

"Listen closely. Tell Tom Redding both the idea and the decision to domicile FBI task force personnel in DC were mine and mine alone. I do not want you and Tom butting heads over an administrative detail which has little relevance to your overall task force mission. Do you understand me?"

"Yes, sir."

"Young lady, do you really understand me?"

"Yes, sir." *He's treating me like a child, the way I handle Don!*

"Get it done, Natalie. Daily written reports to Tom Redding on his desk no later than 9:00 am the following day. Do you have anything else, Natalie?"

"No, sir." *Hang up, you misogynistic bastard!*

"I understand your husband died unexpectedly a few days ago. Please accept my sincere condolences."

"Thank you, sir. Thank you very much." *Bullshit Political Correctness. Will it never cease? Crude, thoughtless handling of my bereavement. Par for the course.*

"Call my secretary and have her remind me to set a personal appointment with you at my first available opportunity, 20 minutes maximum. May God be with us," the President hung up.

Condescending son of a bitch. On the other hand, what else do you expect from a trust baby who has had a spoon in his mouth from day one? His lifelong vocation: dabbling in politics with his pappy's money. Y'all come back, now.

My country, right or wrong; maybe. My president, right or wrong; definitely wrong, because Wilson is a weak-kneed, talk first, retreat later, take no chances, retain your political appointment or elected position, kinda guy.

Worthless as hell and visible only after real men have spilled their blood and guts in paving the way for mediocre, nefarious performers like President William Woodrow Wilson to proliferate like cockroaches. Regardless of the moniker, Bill Wilson is not the second coming of former President Woodrow Wilson.

*

"Dina, take a letter to; Correction. Send a secure Email to Tom Redding."

"QUOTE Dear Mr. Redding: By order of the President, USTF-18 physical locations for the CIA and the FBI shall be bifurcated. CIA shall conduct task force business from their Langley Air Force Base location. FBI shall conduct task force business from FBI headquarters in Washington DC. Enclosed please find the USTF-18 initial written directive. It outlines the task force mission and responsibilities of task force personnel; the bifurcation issue is addressed in the written directive. UNQUOTE"

"Dina, make sure this email is sent to Tom Redding at precisely 11:00 am on Monday." Dina nodded in acknowledgment.

Natalie mused. *Screw Tom Redding and Mitch Donahue. Screw the President. I'm the boss of this here railroad. I'm the director of USTF-18. I've got more balls than most of the men in this world put together. Talk is cheap. I call the shots. Make it happen, girl.*

*

For Friday lunch Natalie chowed down on five fat FBI personnel files, one for each of her five supervisory designees. If they knew what they were facing in their afternoon half hour interview, they might all call in sick.

When will our task force get its first valid lead, when, when, when? Right away, if Natalie has anything to do with it, which she surely has. Woe be it upon the slacker who faces the wrath of the Director of USTF-18. All aboard that's going aboard. Natalie's task force is leaving the station. 'Full speed ahead. Damn the Torpedoes,' as Admiral Farragut is reputed to have aggressively commanded.

Natalie has in mind a method to accomplish all major task force objectives within the week, to find the perp without delay. She knows the shit will hit the fan when Tom Redding learns she bypassed him in springing upon the president a proposed new, bold and different course of action for his consideration.

*

Meanwhile, Jet resolved all but one of Natalie's cadaver related problems by close of business on Friday. Yet unresolved is Natalie's bugs and tails problem, surveillance on her home and on her person.

However, Jet negated one problem his daughter did not tell him about. Friday morning one of Jet's men approached the Pentagon Metro Hotel's housekeeping department and asked if lost and found recovered any items from Room 381, after checkout on Wednesday morning.

"Yes, Sir, we do have an item, a lady's black winter coat."

"How do I go about claiming the item," flashing a $100 bill?

"I have the coat right here, sir."

"Thank you very much for your trouble. Please don't spread any word of this because the lady is married, if you know what I mean," producing another $100 bill and handing $200 to the housekeeping matron.

"I won't say nothing. You can depend on that, sir," said the housekeeping lady as she slipped the $200 under her bosom cover and handed Natalie's coat to Jet's man. The coat was shredded and burned to ashes on Friday afternoon.

*

Betsy Ann provided home access to Jet's computer technician. Natalie now has a brand new desk top computer, virus free, equipped with high end anti-hacking software. In addition to malware-proofing her device, the technician transferred all applications and all data from her old computer hard drive to both of her two-new solid state one trig SSD hard drives. He then performed a permanent deletion procedure on her old hard drive, making it essentially impossible to recover data from that drive. Afterwards, he shredded the old hard drive.

Her new computer has a stand alone, external hard drive; independent of the other two solid state hard drives. Triple data entry; double back up.

Overkill, but one can never be too careful where, when and why computer information is stored and deleted. Don't forget to ask Hilary Clinton what can happen when a Federal Government employee stores classified information on a home based computer. She knows.

*

The cardboard crypt enclosing Jethro Armstrong's body was delivered via truck southbound on I-95 from West Springfield, Virginia to a Pompano Beach, Florida, corporation which owns a 45 foot sport-fish yacht. Within hours the yacht transported the crypt to the Bahama Islands for an at-sea rendezvous and crypt transfer to an inflatable seagoing vessel owned and operated by Sam Turner, the Bahamian national who rescued Jet when his Gulfstream G650 was shot down over the Atlantic Ocean.

After transfer of the crypt, the Florida yacht turned tail for home. Solo Sam navigated his inflatable to the center of the Tongue of the Ocean. While drifting in choppy Atlantic Ocean waters, he securely wrapped 50 feet of chain-link iron around the crypt; then firmly attached a 75 pound anchor to the chain.

Sam Turner buried the body of Jethro Armstrong 7,000 feet below the surface of the Atlantic Ocean. No final rights for the monster. Gone and forgotten; antithesis of the Unknown Soldier resting in his tomb at Arlington National Cemetery.

No receipt/delivery documents were exchanged between the parties. Neither Sam nor anyone associated with the assignment was aware of the contents of the crypt. They all knew their job was to do as they were told and to keep their mouths shut. Everybody received a cash bonus of $10,000. Sam paid off his home mortgage with $1,488 left over. Bless the lord and bless the old man. Cuban rum and Cuban cigars tonight.

*

Both Natalie's Audi and Jethro's Chevrolet were shredded by state of the art automobile destruction devices. The vehicles were cut into little pieces too small to be identified. Two different companies performed vehicle shredding at two different locations. No record of vehicle destruction exists. The earth swallowed both cars.

*

I wonder if I will ever hear from Stony Randolph again, Natalie mused on a cold winter's day. Little did she know that Jet had assigned Stony responsibility for electronically sweeping her RyeGate townhome for bugs, commencing in one week.

26
ROMEO & JULIET
Act 1

On Friday, January 29, at 9:00 am, Stony Randolph and Don Branson walked up the steps at Millersburg Military Institute. Don didn't give Stony any trouble. Even so Stony was not enchanted with the results of the assignment.

All things considered, the druggie is safely locked down for now, confined to his quasi-military jail without bars for the next 18 months. Jet handled everything overnight; tuition payment, fees, transfer documents, grades; everything required to register Don in military secondary school. Money talks. All Stony had to do was deliver the kid in one piece to his new warden at MMI.

The last thing Stony said to Donald Branson was, "Don, hopefully you'll take heed. Hopefully you'll believe me. If you don't stay off drugs, if you go back on drugs, your grandfather will kill you. For absolute certain he will kill you, Don. I'm satisfied this is your last warning, I wish you luck, because you're going to need it."

Don's response was a shrug of his shoulders and a view of his backside as he walked away. Stony knows from experience Don Branson will jump ship at MMI within three months.

At 2:00 pm Stony dropped off his rental Chrysler 300 at Louisville International Airport. Against specific instructions Stony returned to Washington, DC via the next available Delta coach flight to Reagan National Airport, paying the extra $40 dollars to avoid Baltimore - Washington Airport.

Although Stony is six years younger than Natalie, he is absolutely certain he did not mistake the body language and eye contact he and Natalie shared yesterday. Stony learned from his father that if something is worth doing, it is worth doing now. Stony is not one to hesitate. He will never be mistaken for a nerd.

In for the night at the Hampton Inn & Suites hotel located in Virginia near Reagan National Airport, Stony called ahead in an attempt to set an appointment with Natalie for Saturday morning at 10:00 am at her RyeGate townhome. No answer; his call was diverted to voice mail. *I hope Natalie received my message.*

*

With two telephone instruments in hand, on Saturday morning, January 30th, Stony rang the Branson family doorbell at 10:00 am. He prayed Natalie was home, even if the housekeeper/caregiver was there. Donahue's surveillance is not yet 'hot.'

"Please come in, Stony," half-smiled Natalie, glistening straight teeth, fresh lipstick and mascara, a beautiful woman in her prime, even considering the residue of a huge shiner on her still less than glamorous left eye.

Damn, what a knockout. "Thank you, Natalie. Can we sit somewhere and talk about what might be a surveillance problem with your townhome?"

"Sure. My housekeeper, Betsy Ann, is off for the day. We have complete privacy anywhere in the house. How about some fresh coffee at the kitchen table?"

"Great," said Stony as the male and female leads in a modern-day Romeo & Juliet reenactment commence feeling each other out as championship prizefighters do in the early rounds. Boy meets girl. Life is good.

As Natalie set the brewing process in motion Stony said, "Natalie, here are two throw away cell phones. Please do not make any more telephone calls to Jet on the number you used yesterday. Please use one of these cell phones to call your father as necessary and then throw away, destroy the used cell phone after one call."

"Please make any such call to your father from at least three miles away from RyeGate. The telephone number to call is on this piece of paper," Stony handing the paper to Natalie. "Please destroy the paper when you no longer have any use for the telephone number. This precaution is necessary because of a possible bug put on you by person or persons unknown."

"OK, I understand," Natalie said as she examined the two throw away cell phones, curious about the cloak and dagger goings-on.

Acknowledging Natalie's understanding with an affirmative nod, Stony sat at the kitchen table and commenced his carefully scripted spiel. He opened with surveillance and not with a play by play recapitulation of Donald Branson's enrollment at MMI yesterday.

"Natalie, right now your home is clean of all bugs and surveillance devices. There is no assurance there won't be a change in the future. With your permission, I'm going to give your place a weekly once over, preferably on Saturday or Sunday. The schedule might be a little tricky seeing as how you will be working out of the Norfolk area for an indeterminate period of time."

Natalie is ambidextrous. Holding up her left hand, she said to Stony, "Interruption, Stony. The Norfolk thing is off. I won't be leaving DC, won't be leaving my RyeGate home in the foreseeable future."

His game plan inadvertently modified, Stony hesitatingly responded "OK, well, OK. Changes my surveillance plans a little, but nothing fatal. OK, Good. Today is Saturday; how's about we make an appointment for next Saturday here at your home at, say, noon. Does that work for you?" *She's available now, right now. Damn.*

"I don't see why not," Natalie offering more than a half-smile;

initiating a hint of body language to smoke Stony out. A little leg here, a little cleavage there, that sort of thing; teasingly enticing, intentionally enchanting.

This is too good. Damn, she's truly table grade. If only I had met you a long time ago, girl. My life would have been considerately different. Take what's there with a smile, Stony; with a smile.

Stony abandoned musing and bore down, "Ms. Taylor, I was taught by my parents to be respectful to females, all females. Natalie, respectfully, I'm interested in getting to know you better, on a personal basis. My intentions are honorable. I want to get to know you better, Natalie," Stony muttered redundantly. *Pitiful. My courtship will never get off the ground at this rate. Pick it up, Stony.*

Regaining composure, "I know you have been a widow for only three days. I realize my approach can be interpreted as crass and discourteous. I have tried to respectfully share with you an understanding of where you stand with me. That's good enough for me, for now. I don't anticipate an answer or response, Natalie."

"Unless you tell me different I'll be leaving and be back here at noon in one week, Saturday. Here's my business card," Stony placing a card on the kitchen table containing his name and telephone number in Savannah, Georgia, nothing else. Never before had Stony provided his US private telephone number to anyone.

I screwed this one up royally, Romeo thought to himself.

Juliet took pity. "Well, Stony, at least you can share a cup of West Springfield's best mocha before you beat it out my front door. It gets lonely, don't you know? As of today, I commence a significant personal transition. I'm living alone for the first time in my life. I don't especially look forward to living alone."

"I'm 39 years old with a dead husband. My druggie son is in what amounts to a rehab jail posing as an education facility. My decimated personal life is imbued with a promising vocational career. Do you want to bite into that, Stony?"

"Would I be a cougar? You're obviously younger."

"33 years old," said Stony, encouraged.

"Six years difference. That means you were finishing 6th grade when I graduated high school. You were still a wet behind the ears 22 year old recent college graduate by the time I had completed both law school and two years clerking at the US Supreme Court and was an FBI agent new hire with one year's experience under my belt. You had not yet drawn your first paycheck, Junior." Stony smiled. *Progress, thankfully. Look at those boobs, that body, that cute little ass. Perfect. Damn. This one is a keeper for somebody. Why not me? Who knows?*

Juliet asked "Have you ever spent any quality time with a woman your equal, perhaps even more than equal to you in both intellect and vocational development?"

The more Stony looked, the more he liked. The more he listened, the more he heard. *I need to begin touching; I would like very much to touch more and more. Dream on, Stony.*

"Would it disturb you to bed down a woman who could buy and sell you to the highest bidder, controlling both your body and your soul? Are you up to it? Do you want anything to do with that can of worms?"

No, I would not be disturbed. Yes, I'm up to it. If it's your can of worms, I want 'everything' to do with it.

"How macho are you? Do you have misogynist tendencies or traits? Why haven't you ever married? What are your work prospects? Are you scared of me, Stony?" Natalie paused for effect.

Stony took his time framing a response. He knew better than to tell Natalie about his 12 million dollar annual salary at the charity and his 20 million dollars on deposit at the hierarchy bank, increasing at the rate of one million dollars a month; not counting Harvey's trust money, which now belongs to Stony, whose net worth is now 178 million dollars. *My vocational prospects are good, thank you, madam.*

The pair stared one another down. Intense gazing. Kitchen temperature increased by the second, or so it seemed. Although both are in heat, neither is willing to surrender to instinct. These things more often than not proceed according to Hoyle, according to custom, according to reason, yet pursuant to inherited, anciently imbued instinct, which instinct unconditionally demands procreation and mandates sexual activity.

End result: hot pants versus societally imposed medieval Puritan dogma. Round one. Watch the fur fly!

Thinking it over, an impetuous Stony decided, *Fuck it; let's get it on; here I go, off the deep end. Sink or Swim, Stony.*

"Natalie, I'm game if you are," Stony said carefully.

With gazes still locked Natalie rose, smiled, walked over to Stony, took him by the hand, abandoned two hot cups of coffee and led Stony upstairs to the bedroom which has not witnessed an act of love (coition or coitus if you are erudite, copulation if you are somewhat open minded, sexual intercourse if you are straight laced; fucking if you are a redneck) in over four years.

The spirit was willing and the flesh was weak. It was love at first sight. Is family approval in the future? No one knows. Romeo and Juliet will soon discover the hard way how lovers with starkly divergent pedigrees often skate on thin ice. Collateral damage looms. Suicide anyone?

FYI, Stony is a redneck at heart; Natalie is erudite. The sex was great. Differences attract. Life is good.

*

Stony left for Bermuda three hours later accompanied by the fondest memory of his 33 years. He has more reason to live today than ever before. He understands and appreciates life differently, in a way he never before understood, much less appreciated. All previous females in his life were mere girls. Natalie is the first real woman Stony has ever known in the Biblical sense; perhaps the last. *I am besotted, smitten beyond reprieve.*

Stony recalled listening to a TV documentary a few years back featuring a then 'in vogue' female psychologist who minted a theory regarding love. *First and foremost, love is self-centered. You are in love when being in the company of someone you believe you are in love with inclines you to feel better about yourself. If you always feel better about yourself when and after being in the immediate presence of a certain person, always; then you are probably in love with that person.*

Sensible, perhaps valid. Who knows? Then again, who cares? I care, that's who. I care about Natalie and I feel better about myself when I'm with her. It's a start. Let's see how it goes from here. Who cares if she's a cougar? I don't. I don't think she does either. I have everything. She's the equivalent of a whore in the bedroom and certainly a grande dame in the living room. Damn! Every man's dream and my reality.

Checking his cell phone messages, the only one he opened was a text from Jet. 'Where are you?' Trouble, but the afternoon was more than worth it. Stony has a new lease on life. He has a 'keeper' in his life. He is not certain he can match her blow-by-blow, tit-for-tat, but he is sure as hell going to try. Time will tell.

*

At 3:00 pm Saturday afternoon Betsy Ann Mathers received three month's severance pay. She won't be back. With Don's Power of Attorney, Natalie conveyed the RAV4 to Betsy Ann as a parting gift. She was sad to leave but grateful. On her way home Betsy Ann drove Natalie to the Enterprise Auto Rental store at 6536 Backlick Road in Springfield, Virginia.

From there Natalie drove her rented Chevrolet sedan to the Porsche dealership at 3100 Jefferson Davis Hwy, in Arlington, Virginia, where she paid cash for a new 2021 English racing green Porsche 911 Carrera S Coupe with all the bells and whistles. MSRP was over $130,000; subject to a small discount, plus Virginia combined sales tax of 6%.

After arranging for the dealership to promptly return the Chevrolet to Enterprise, Natalie drove the Porsche 911 home to RyeGate. Yesterday she deposited Jet's $250,000 check in her personal checking account, the account she used to pay life insurance premiums. She also closed her joint bank account with Pete.

27
NATALIE
USTF-18, Day One

I t's Sunday — duty calls. Settled in after completion of mundane household chores, Natalie concentrated on her impending search for an unidentified perpetrator/s attempting to purchase a nuclear bomb on the nuclear weapons market.

If anyone can catch the SOB, I can. He's mine, all mine; in the bag. Conviction is beyond my pay grade, not my gig. The Department of Justice (ever since Attorney General Holder, known as the Department of 'Injustice') is responsible for trials and convictions.

Natalie harbors no guilt about having had sex with Stony. She is at peace with God. Her sexual interlude with Stony did not violate wedlock, so her delightful exploits with Stony did not displease God. Not a single unpleasant afterthought crossed Ms. Natalie's mind on that subject, her first non-regretful pairing in two years.

Stony, a child perhaps, but with potential. He will return Saturday next, six days from today. Let's see how my mule team, the joint staff, reacts to bullwhips. I can't wait to spring my latest brainstorm on weak-kneed Bill Wilson. Monday, here I come.

*

Her personal shadow, a CIA tail, began trailing Natalie at 6:00 am on Monday, February 1st, as she drove away from RyeGate in her new Porsche 911, headed for FBI headquarters. Her future comings and goings will be observed 24/7 by Secret Service agents, reported daily in writing to Mitch Donahue,

After Natalie left home for work, a CIA agent effortlessly broke into her RyeGate townhome, bugged her land line telephones and placed clandestine video and audio recording devices in her kitchen, living room and second floor bedrooms.

Cameras and recording devices can be viewed and listened to off premises in real time. Accumulated audio and video data is permanently recorded. All things considered, Natalie is screwed, blued and tattooed. Fortunately, she swore off trolling pursuant to agreement with God.

Half an hour after arriving at work, and after leaving instructions for Dina to register the Porsche with FBI administration, Natalie took a government limousine from FBI headquarters to the white house for a 7:45 am task force 'full' briefing by Tom Redding. She should have been the one dishing out the skinny. Redding should have been the one listening and learning. His briefing was pitiful.

Stripped of unnecessary drivel and incidentals, Tom Redding told Natalie it is her job to identify and neutralize (euphemism for 'kill') the individual/s attempting to purchase one or more nuclear weapons from a nation which is known to have perfected and stockpiled nuclear weapons.

No ground rules; just get the job done. No mention of support, logistics, budget, travel, rules of engagement; nothing. As for the topics addressed, one minute was required, two minutes at most. Redding slow danced through thirty minutes of absolute misery, spewing one Government Speak word after another, all minutia, all rumor and all old hat. Tragic.

After Tom Redding completed his hapless presentation Natalie asked, "Tom, when are you going to get around to providing me with the name, rank and last known address of the CIA operative who first learned about the alleged nuclear weapons purchase?"

Embarrassed, Redding responded, "I'll send it to you right away, probably by way of secure email. Are you prepared to leave for Langley AFB at noon?"

Natalie condescendingly replied, "Of course, Tom," as she whirred past the President's Chief of Staff like a speeding bullet. Next stop, FBI heaven. The hostess of the first briefing of the USTF-18 team of FBI'ers is in the saddle and is hell bent for leather, ready to ride herd on her staffers. *Screw Tom Redding and Mitch Donahue, both Peter Principal prototypes.*

One hour later, Dina greeted Natalie at FBI headquarters, FBI auto tag sticker in hand. Together they fashioned Natalie's schedule for three months, February, March and April of 2021.

At 11:30 am Natalie met with her FBI task force staff of 15 players in room 209 of the FBI headquarters building, five executives and ten middle management types. She opened the meeting with encouragement.

"Gentlemen, welcome to one of the most simple but important assignments you will ever have in your professional career. The hooker is if we fail, the entire country might just go down the tubes."

"The 16 of us, along with 16 similarly situated CIA folks down in Norfolk, have been tasked with the responsibility of identifying, then capturing or killing one or more perpetrators who are alleged to be engaged in the purchase of weapons of mass destruction, presumably nuclear weapons, from a rogue state/s willing to sell nuclear weapons to a party or parties anxious to use nuclear weapons to destroy a target/s within the contiguous United States."

"You now know as much as I know about our mission. From here on, we learn together, mostly by OJT, on the job training. There is no template available to help us with this mission. We are navigating uncharted waters. Welcome to stratospheric level, federal government confusion, obfuscation and disconcertion."

"First, some ground rules. I am the boss. What I say goes. I have an open mind. I do not tolerate yes men. I abhor speculation, half-truths and gossip. If you have something to say, say it. Don't hide anything from your associates or from me."

"This is a team effort. You and I both know I will get all the credit should we prevail, but that's the way it goes. If you are good and if you are lucky, your turn may come. Otherwise suck it up, do your job and posture yourself and this team for optimum performance. Hope is never an option."

"To the best of my ability, if you make an effort of either commission or omission which turns out to be frowned upon, I'll cover for you. Later you may have hell to pay as relates to me but I won't let others crucify you, as often occurs in this town when high profile missions such as ours go south. Nobody in this room is ever going to throw anybody else in this room under the bus."

"Don't expect CIA to play fair. To the extent possible, ignore CIA. They have their job and we have ours. When it is necessary to work with CIA, directly or indirectly, hedge your bets whenever possible. Have a fall back, emergency position, if possible."

"No comment, I repeat, no comment related to our mission in any way is to be made to anyone outside this room absent my approval. No comment to the press. No comment to family and friends. No comment to co-workers not a member of this task force. No comment to any person in government employ, including VIP's such as Chief of Staff Tom Redding and members of congress, elective or otherwise. No comment, period."

"Specifically, no comment to any CIA personnel other than the asking of a question or responding to a question, both of which question and answer is essential to our mission. I know this instruction is vague but it is the best I can do under the circumstances."

"Everything you say can be used against you in this world, remember that. Finally, in the event you feel compelled to discuss anything with any CIA personnel, you must have authority from me or Fred Price. No exceptions."

"Our mission is and must remain the most secretive operation any division of government ever engaged in, including the invention and manufacturing of the first atom bomb back in 1945."

"In the event of my absence for whatsoever reason, Fred Price steps up, assumes control of our task force. Be aware I am responsible not only for FBI task force operations but also for CIA task force operations. Fred Price shall assume control of all FBI and CIA task force responsibilities in the event of my absence. CIA shall never exercise command or control over our task force. Be respectful to all CIA personnel with whom you have task force business."

Natalie nodded to Fred Price, soliciting acknowledgment of his task force responsibilities. Fred nodded back affirmatively, confirming his understanding and acknowledgment. Time is money. Sign language is alive and well at USTF–18.

"We now break into two groups. Group 1, our five main men, remain in this room. Fred Price is in charge of Group 1. Tommy Pearsall is in charge of ten man Group 2, which meets in room 215 within ten minutes. Remember, room 215."

"Gentlemen, both groups have the same objective, the same responsibility. The 16 of us are going to do something no one in the past has ever done, catch a nuclear weapons poacher. Today each group will create, produce a plan (phase 1) to catch the poacher. With 16 of the best minds in the world at work, surely we can detect, discover, identify, find out, chance upon one or more methods to catch this sucker."

"During phase 2 we shall produce an 'implementation document' describing in detail the duties of each of us during the next three months. The plan, along with the implementation document is your new Bible."

Natalie's cell phone rang. Tom Redding. *He must have received my Email. Good old Tom.* She diverted the call to voice mail.

"Are there any questions?" asked Natalie. One minute delay. There being no questions, Natalie closed the meeting, "Good hunting, gentlemen. I have confidence in you, one and all. Dismissed for now."

Two hours later Natalie said via secure voice telephone, "Tom, sorry I missed your call. What can I do for you?"

Tom Redding ranted, he raved, he sobbed, he moaned. In the end he capitulated, specifically because Natalie told him she has a personal appointment with President Wilson in the oval office at 1:00 pm tomorrow. Knowledge of Natalie's second presidential meeting in the oval office shut Tom up. Permanently, she hopes.

Both Tom Redding and Natalie know that Tom Redding is not up to the job. He is a political hack who was promoted way far above his level of expertise. Tom knows he will eventually be found out, called out. He is surprised it hasn't already happened. He wonders how Natalie will handle her newly discovered leverage. Time will tell.

28

WASHINGTON, DC
the Bounty

At close of business on Monday, Natalie called Mitch Donahue. He was cordial as he and Natalie compared notes on the first day of task force operations. They coordinated proposed activities, discussed oral and documentary administrative reports, and shared substantive theories about how to catch the perpetrator.

Early on Tuesday Mitch received the first written shadow report. Bugs and tails are operational. No suspicious behavior by Natalie during the observation period.

All efforts to locate Natalie's father failed. From government records Mitch learned her mother, Sarah Taylor, is dead. Her father's name is James Edward Taylor. He served on active duty in the United States Air Force as a fighter pilot for 6 ½ years and for an additional seven years in the Virginia Air National Guard base at Richmond, Virginia. His highest attained rank was 0-4, Major.

There the trail dries up like invisible ink. No IRS forms 1040 on record. No state personal income tax forms on record. No real estate transactions on record. No credit card transactions or accounts on record. No driver's license on record. No record on record. The man apparently does not exist, except perhaps as an ex-patriot. A spy, maybe. James Edward Taylor is not going to be easy to find.

I always get my man. I never fail. I'll show the bitch. I'll show Tom Redding. I'll show the president. This assignment is my showcase, the tool I am going to use to ensure my promotion to CIA director. Nothing and nobody, especially Natalie Taylor, is going to stop me from getting full and sole credit for terminating the nuclear weapons perp and closing this file. I'll get the bitch, too. I'll destroy her, the worthless cunt. Mark my words!

*

No tears were shed at Pete's Tuesday funeral. The spate of sadness during the past four years more than made up for the absence of tears at the respectful Christian commemoration of the life of Peter Branson. In the recent past Natalie made peace with God and with Pete's memory.

FBI Director Jim Burns and personal secretary Dina Watters scored points with Natalie by funeral service appearance, attesting to Natalie their respect for the lifetime achievements of her late husband. Betsy Ann Mathers was the sole additional attendee.

I wonder why Mr. and Mrs. Branson canceled out. It's strange for parents to no-show at the funeral of their only son. On the other hand, attendance at funerals is similar to cutting teeth, more often than not, intolerable. At least Jim Burns and Dina are here.

In at 9:30 and out at 9:50, dreadful funereal efficiency. Why was Pete horribly maimed and his life cut short by an alien, an illegal immigrant? Why? Why on earth? What the hell is the meaning of life, anyway? No one has ever answered that question satisfactorily.

A dead husband, a druggie son and a new Canadian squeeze; what am I doing, where am I going? I used to be in control of everything. Now I control nothing. I used to act. Now all I do is react. Oh, well, I'll stay on autopilot until I run out of gas, all by myself, in my new Porsche 911. Woe is me.

Pick it up, girl. You're profiled for a stumble, a recipe for disaster. More often than not, mistakes in your trade are fatal. You're a supervisor. Although FBI supervisors seldom get killed, at this rate you're going to be responsible for the death of subordinates. Enough said.

*

On the afternoon of Pete's funeral, Natalie was escorted into the oval office for the second time at a rescheduled hour, 2:35 pm. President Wilson sat behind his desk. Natalie asked permission to 'approach the bench,' which was granted. Natalie toted her chair over to the front of the President's desk and perched four feet away from the leader of the free world.

This gal has character, if nothing else.

"Mr. President, thank you very much for sharing your valuable time with me. I'll get right to the point."

"I know you are out of your element as relates to our nuclear perpetrator mission. I know you graduated law school but never practiced law, instead running for local office at age 26. After election as a justice of the peace, you never looked back, never lost an election, never was involved in a scandal. An American success story if there ever was one. I congratulate you and commend you on your record."

President Wilson commenced rubbing his chin when Natalie remarked that he is out of his element.

"This is not condescending. In the 20 minutes allotted, I am bringing to your attention the fact that you are a highly successful politician."

"Your long suit is politics. Your long suit is not administration. You have surrounded yourself with what you believe to be the very best administrators obtainable by and through prestige and political influence."

The president rubbed his chin harder.

"My point is that you have little if any personal experience and/ or personal ability in chasing down and killing nuclear perpetrators, little or no experience in selecting and appointing subordinates with such ability. More importantly you have absolutely no experience or ability in realizing and discerning whether or not your 'nuke perp' appointees are doing their job to the best of their ability or are attempting to bullshit you as they have always bullshitted others."

Moderate presidential chin rubbing.

"Sir, you and I both know you have no clue who's doing what, why they're doing what they're doing and what's probably going to happen. Don't look so unhappy, Mr. President. That's normal. Nobody can know everything about everything. That's why you hire good people; people you can trust, people you can depend upon to do right by you and to do right by the country."

Nearly severe presidential chin rubbing.

"Cutting to the chase, you appear to be unaware that you are being shortchanged. No never mind. I will provide you one clue as to how your staff, to the last man, has screwed up, has fucked you over in regards to our nuke perp mission. Here's your clue. How was Saddam Hussein captured?"

Violent presidential chin rubbing.

No complete dummy, President Wilson knows Saddam and his sons were captured because they were 'ratted out' in return for bounty payment in excess of 40 million dollars; a Bush II example of presidential incompetence, paying 40 million smackaroonies to capture an alleged perpetrator who was innocent of all charges, since there were NO WEAPONS OF MASS DESTRUCTION in Iraq, ever. Chin rubbing tones down.

Damn. Of course, a bounty. Why didn't I think of that? Why didn't anybody think of that? If they did think of it, why didn't they mention it to me? The only person I talked to about this project is Tom Redding, and this split tail isn't fingering Tom. Why not? What does she know that I don't know? Chin rubbing terminates.

"You made your point, Natalie. Bounty. You want me to authorize a bounty. How much do you recommend?"

"250 million dollars."

"That much?"

"That much."

"Approved."

"Do I have your permission and authority to contact Secretaries of State and Treasury to coordinate the offer and payment pursuant to the 1984 Act to Combat International Terrorism, Public Law 98-533?"

"Is that the bounty statute?"

"Yes, sir. It is."

"Permission granted."

"Thank you, Mr. President. My presentation is concluded. Do you have any questions, sir?"

"No."

"In parting, please agree to a memorialization of our mutual postures via a classified executive order, TOP SECRET – IAR, sir."

"Draft the document and send it to the personal attention of my secretary."

"On your desk before the end of the day, Mr. President."

Maybe I ought to nominate you as my replacement. Man or woman, I never met anybody with the savvy, gumption and intellect of the bitch standing in front of me. What's her name? Natalie Taylor. I'll never forget that name as long as I live.

"Thank you, Mr. President. I know my way out. Paperwork to follow, sir." *The son of a bitch Wilson is bypassing Chief of Staff Redding without me even mentioning Tom's name. Good work, Natalie. Mitch Donahue is next.*

As Natalie departed the oval office she smiled over her shoulder at a middle-aged man contemplating his naval.

*

After the meeting Natalie coordinated with the Secretary of State and the Secretary of the Treasury. On Wednesday, the president executed an executive order adopted word for word as presented by Natalie to the President's secretary at 5:00 pm on Tuesday afternoon.

The President's proof reader/fact checker recommended no

changes to Natalie's proposed executive order. Natalie's understanding of the English language, American law and federal government bureaucratic processes is remarkable. The operative text of the executive order recites, in part:

'.....such person providing such information shall be entitled to a payment of not more than $250 million in the event the perpetrator identified is found by a court of law to be guilty of the offense of treason against the United States of America, or is killed by agents of the United States of America, pursuant to investigation and attempted arrest or incarceration.'

With the executive order in hand, on Wednesday afternoon Natalie published the bounty offer to a number of FBI field sources and a few selected others. Both Tom Redding and Mitch Donahue were astonished by receipt of the executive order.

President Wilson has never been exposed to staff work of Natalie's caliber. He knows from experience that if his personal entourage had worked on the document for two weeks, it still would not be in presentable form. Never in the past has a proposed document made it past president Wilson's fact checker unscathed. Remarkable!

This gal needs to be promoted. She needs a faster track to run on. Perhaps deputy secretary of state; perhaps deputy Attorney General; perhaps deputy Secretary of Defense. What the hell, perhaps presidential chief of staff. Stranger things have happened. I got elected, didn't I?

*

Tom Redding realized he had come within a hair of losing the only job he had for the last thirty years, head gofer for Bill Wilson of the "Texas Oil" Wilsons. *I cannot afford to lose my collateral benefits.*

Although Mitch Donahue was busy tracing the whereabouts and identity of Natalie's 'Daddy,' he dropped everything and circulated the bounty offer among CIA field agents, including the agent who brought the existence of the nuke perp to Mitch and Tom Redding's attention. 'Daddy' will have to play second fiddle for a while.

With a recently created 'final form' USTF-18 task force plan in hand, Natalie reviewed the proposed implementation document at 5:00 pm on Tuesday afternoon. After a scrutinous review, a 'final form' implementation document was adopted at 9:00 pm, four hours of non-compensatory overtime for 16 FBI employees

Content of both the basic plan and the implementation document was comprised of content recommended and adopted according to the following approximate percentages, 45% by Group 1, 25% by Group 2 and 30% by Natalie's editing.

The implementation document contains an in depth, item-by-item description of procedures task force personnel shall use to catch the nuclear poacher/s. There is the right way, the wrong way and the FBI way. Natalie coaxed and cajoled her task force into doing things the FBI way.

Implementation activities were initiated on Wednesday morning. Duty schedules were distributed. Field work commenced. Natalie makes her big play on Thursday.

29
NSA
People Finders

On Thursday afternoon, Natalie traveled 30 miles from FBI Headquarters to Fort Meade, Maryland to meet with National Security Agency (NSA) Director Seth Bennison.

"Director Bennison, thank you very much for meeting with me."

"You're welcome, Deputy Director Taylor. What can I do for you, ma'am?"

"Director Bennison, as you know I am the newly appointed director of USTF-18, the ultra-special task force created pursuant to a meeting in the oval office at which you were an attendee."

"True enough."

"Director ----"

"Move it along, Natalie. My name is Seth. What do you want? I am busy, very busy," the NSA bigwig interrupted in a fatherly tone.

"Yes, sir, Seth it is."

"Seth, I don't understand why FBI was selected to head a task force whose sole responsibility is to locate and detain a foreign national living and operating outside the United States, except we are not military and are one of the few civilian entities which has arrest authority."

Director Bennison said, "Strange you should open with such a statement because nobody in their right mind could fail to understand or appreciate that NSA is uniquely postured to provide invaluable aid and assistance to your joint task force."

"Natalie, please bear with an old man as I digress. You have a sterling reputation. You have everything going for you except maturity and experience. Your performance to date has more than made up for those shortcomings."

"I'm going to give you a primer on intelligence as intelligence is practiced by the present United States government. In the first place, there are over 75,000 personnel working full-time for the United States government whose primary concern and responsibility is intelligence, emphasizing international intelligence."

"For reasons known only to the administration, the definition of intelligence, as we knew it up until about 15 years ago, has changed significantly. In the past, intelligence gatherers regularly gleaned the world for important bits and pieces of information which the gatherers mustered and organized into meaningful facts, which facts often supported conclusions, which conclusions were normally taken into consideration by the administration in determining various and sundry courses of action."

"Sometimes the courses of action were outcome determinative. Sometimes conclusions were incorrect. Sometimes conclusions were not acted upon. Intelligence had its place. In general, the better the intelligence, the more valid the conclusions and in most instances the safer the nation."

"Everything has changed. Intelligence has been politicized, much to my chagrin and the chagrin of professionals like me."

"Here's how it works now. As from time immemorial, American intelligence personnel still gather facts and draw conclusions. However now, if the facts and/or conclusions are inconsistent with the agenda of the political party in control of the administration, the intelligence sources are strongly motivated (some say strong-armed) to reevaluate the facts and redraw the conclusions so as to be consistent with the political objectives of the party controlling the administration."

"This is even more grossly the case in the event pertinent facts and conclusions bear on and relate to a forthcoming election."

"Our country no longer relies upon functional intelligence. Intelligence provided to our nation is under the sole control of the President of the United States of America, come rain or come shine, like it or not."

"Be advised the administration of the United States of America has no idea, no clue, how to use intelligence sources efficiently and effectively. My sad story is exacerbated by an over four year scourge of rampant serial leaks of classified information, including top secret leaks reasonably well known to have been made by career intelligence bureaucrats and others similarly situated, which leaks appear to have been systematically released and planned to embarrass the administration, especially the Trump administration. I have never seen anything like it. Shameless, simply shameless."

"I appreciate you listening to my sad story; please proceed, Natalie."

"Thank you, Seth. I more or less suspected what you just told me is true. The difference is now I have heard it from the horse's mouth."

"Seth, I'm old school. All I want to do is nab the guy I'm after and go back to my job at the FBI. I need your help. Please reassign your most qualified NSA people finder to my task force. If you're having trouble with budget, I'll eat his expenses."

"I'm asking you to temporarily assign to me the most qualified person you have in terms of finding foreign perpetrators. I'll take any and all heat associated with the assignment. What say you, Seth?"

"I'll be damned. I could not have cut to the chase any better. Whoever taught you did a hell of a job. I'll help you out, Natalie. Your man is Wilson Patterson, one-of-a-kind. If anybody can find the guy you are looking for, it's Wilson."

"Please give me a moment, Natalie."

"Grace Ann, page Wilson Patterson and have him come to my office; If he's not available let me know right away."

"I'm on it, Mr. Bennison."

"Natalie, the way I envision this going down is Wilson will first analyze your requirements. If you two are compatible, he will recommend a course of action for your consideration. Wilson has the authority to cause NSA to conduct probing activities in a manner consistent with optimum probability of locating your perp. If Wilson can do it, I'll authorize him to do it, with top priority in the entire NSA workload queue."

"I'm dumbfounded, Seth, totally impressed. There aren't many of us around. Perhaps we're both lucky. Anyway, thank you. Thank you so very much."

"Director Bennison, you rang, sir?" said Wilson Patterson, heir apparent to 'nerd of the year.'

"Wilson, you have a new gig. I am assigning you to temporary duty, working with the smartest lady in Washington DC. Say hello to the Deputy Director of the FBI, Natalie Taylor."

"Hello, Ms. Taylor."

"Hello yourself, Wilson. You come highly recommended. DC is 30 miles away, a 40 minute drive except during rush hour, then well over an hour. I anticipate the duration of your assignment to be at least one month."

"I would appreciate it if you will temporarily relocate to the DC area, at my expense of course. My secretary, Dina Watters, will arrange accommodations. Here's my business card. Do you have any questions, Wilson?"

"Only one question, ma'am. Today is Thursday. I am on your job as of right now. I will delegate my present workload to qualified associates. Is it okay if I show up for work a week from Monday morning at 9:00 am, or earlier? That's the 15th of the month."

"In order for me to gin up for your job, equipped and primed with devices and operators, I need to be armed with a custom built, search parameter software application, which requires at least one week to create. From you I need foundational information (who, what, where, when and how, as applicable) which I am sure you will send to me by private top secret courier tomorrow. We promise to work harder than Egyptian pyramid day laborers, both while creating your search software and while actively searching for your perpetrator."

"I'm impressed, Wilson, yes. Yes, regarding delayed reporting to DC. Yes, regarding NSA parameters. Background information and statistics delivered to you tomorrow. I look forward to working with you."

After Wilson Patterson left director Bennison's office, Natalie said, "Seth, when my joint task force job is over, would you consider hiring me on at NSA?"

"Normally I would, Natalie. But in your case I'm afraid you would Shanghai my job within six months." They both smiled as Natalie shook hands, kissed Seth lightly on the cheek and departed for RyeGate.

*

On Friday morning Mitch Donahue's CIA task force team created a CIA task force plan with implementation features. FBI and CIA plans are not exact duplicates but are close enough for government work.

On Friday afternoon Natalie approved Mitch Donahue's CIA task force personnel. There were no derogatory Farley File entries on any of Mitch's 15 CIA agents. Mitch signed off on Natalie's FBI agents on Saturday. CIA is also working weekends. The task force Command Post was manned on Friday at 5:00 pm.

Natalie scheduled herself for down time from Friday at 5:00 pm to Sunday at 5:00 pm. A believer she should never assign a job to someone which she would not personally perform, Natalie scheduled herself to man the overnight task force duty desk (how can a woman MAN a desk?) from Sunday, February 7th at 5:00 pm to

Monday at 9:00 am. Natalie and FBI task force members shall be available via cell phone 24/7 for as long as the task force is active.

Stony is due at RyeGate at noon Saturday. I am committed 24/7 to my task force. Although it's nice being the boss, I have subordinated my personal priorities to my vocational obligations for 13 years, from day number one as a government employee. Not once did my needs come first, not once.

I now know that nothing is forever etched in stone. My troops do not need me to stand guard over them every minute of every day and night. They will do very well in my absence during the next 48 hours. I'm going to be there for Stony and that's that.

Every waking minute a haunting impression looms over me. I sense being followed, being watched, being listened in on. Weird. Let's see what Stony's townhome sweep turns up. Nothing, I hope. God, I already miss Stony. He fills a void in more ways than one.

30
ROMEO & JULIET
Act 2

Light snowflakes cover the DC Metropolitan Area; icy roads for the next few days. No problem. The sun is shining somewhere and Stony is headed this winter Saturday morning for what is now his all-time preferred destination, RyeGate and its precious feminine inhabitant. Man does not live by food and tax shelter alone.

Driving well within the speed limits from the Reagan National Airport Hampton Inn where he spent Friday night, Stony's mid-sized Chevrolet motored by a late model dark blue Ford sedan parked 100 yards from Natalie's townhome, on the route Natalie drives from RyeGate to FBI headquarters. Perhaps a tail; perhaps not.

Ringing the doorbell at noon precisely, Stony was anything but disappointed. The woman is all smiles and beautiful, stunningly beautiful. Imagination does not do Natalie justice. She is infinitely more attractive in the flesh than in Stony's memory banks. She presents better in jeans than most women present in gowns. Only a trace of the shiner is visible. Stony is hot to trot, evidence of masculine instinctiveness proudly on display.

"Hello, sweetheart, what's doing?"

"Come in out of the cold, Romeo. I have just the right thing to warm you up. Coffee, tea or me; or hot toddy; or coffee Royale; or hot buttered rum, a house specialty; custom orders cheerfully accommodated. Gentlemen's choice, on or off the menu. À la carte available. Steak tartare recommended. Order now; inventory limited to only a few prime selections. Satisfaction guaranteed. No samples. No discounts."

"I missed you, Stony," a yielding invitational smile welcomed her chosen one.

"I missed you too, Natalie," Stony yearning, hungry, needfully deprived.

It was not meant to be; later, perhaps. Ever alert, an inconsistency captured Stony's attention. Producing a notepad and ball point pen from his right coat pocket, he guardedly touched the first finger of his right hand to his lips vertically, signaling Natalie to keep quiet. Stony scribbled a few lines.

'We have company. Room bugged; video & audio. I'm going to ask you to have brunch with me. You say ok, get house keys. Leave with me. Shake head up & down if you understand, small shakes.'

Natalie read the note. She re-read the note, then shook her head up and down, small shakes.

"Natalie, I'm famished. I didn't have breakfast. Do you mind sharing brunch with me, out?"

"Not at all. Great for me, Stony. No dishes. I need a coat," Natalie said as she retrieved her favorite winter week-end Navy style pea coat and house keys. *Coat, damn!! I left my black dress coat in room 381. I can't believe I was so dumb. It must've been the Roofies. Well, what's done is done. I have to live with it. What a humongous boo-boo.*

With sign language, Stony asked Natalie to maintain silence as he drove 15 miles south on interstate highway I-95 to the Waffle House in Dumfries, Virginia. Observing the dark blue Ford settle in a respectable trailing distance behind his rented Chevrolet, Stony reckoned that the Ford's interest in Natalie is, for now, limited to reconnaissance. *Hopefully, violence will stay off the table.*

The two government voyeurs remained in the parking lot after Stony and Natalie parked their Chevrolet and entered the fast food restaurant. The spies elected not to idle the Ford's engine, rather to practice freezing in their unheated vehicle, now a refrigerator on wheels.

Stony ordered waffles, sausage patties, black coffee and water with lemon wedge. Natalie ordered hot tea with lemon. "Natalie, your home is bugged, an audio microphone and a video camera in the kitchen, state of the art devices. Where there's smoke, there's often fire. Anticipate your land lines and cell phones to be tapped; living rooms and both TV's to be bugged. Perhaps your automobile and garage also. By the way, sweetheart, what are you driving these days?"

Embarrassed, Natalie whispered, "A 2021 Porsche 911, English racing green."

"Impressive, madam. My kind of woman," bantered Stony. "On my drive to RyeGate I fantasized all kinds of amorous activity but not now, what with the bugs and tails. Your house is off limits for the time being. While in your townhome, did you say anything or do anything even remotely actionable at law?"

"No, of course not."

"I thought not, but I had to ask."

"Thank you for thinking of my welfare."

"You're welcome. This thing is not going down at all like I planned. Please help me out, Ms. Policewoman, I'm stumped."

"Before you answer that, I see you brought your cell phone with you and it's hot. You must be on FBI call."

"Yes"

"I understand. What does that do to our plans for today, if anything?"

"Nothing, unless the phone rings."

"Do you expect it to ring?"

"No."

"Damnation, I have never experienced anything like this. It's as if I have another family, or a dog, or an Amway salesman, on my back, in my knickers or riding herd some other way. How do you handle this, Natalie?"

"It comes with the territory, big guy."

"Can I disregard it and be myself?"

"I don't know, can you?"

"I'll give it a try."

"Progress at last."

"You are the damndest woman I ever met."

"Apparently you never met many women, certainly not an active cougar like me."

"Don't go there, Natalie."

"Touchy, big man, touchy, touchy."

"I'll show you touchy," said Stony as he dropped a twenty dollar bill on the table and escorted Natalie from the fast food franchise with a firm grip on her right arm.

"Where are we going?"

"My hotel."

"My, my, how romantic! At 2:00 in the afternoon. Refreshing. Do we christen our second meet-up with an exchange of body fluids?"

"Yes."

"You just got my attention. Perhaps you're a keeper after all."

"Courtesan rules?"

"Yes."

"Are you always this agreeable, woman?"

"Hardly."

"I thought not."

It's a half hour drive from the Waffle House on I-95 to the Hampton Inn near Reagan International Airport. The Ford trailed a healthy distance behind the Chevrolet.

The second round of sex was better than the first. Natalie knew sex with Stony would sell like hot cakes if only she could bottle it.

She learned that youth really is wasted on the young. Natalie wasn't having fun; she was basking in emotionally induced prurient pleasure. Enormous difference; all the difference in the world.

Stony didn't complain that Natalie knew more about sex; more positions, more variations, more techniques and more sexually oriented psychological mood conditioning methods than he could ever have experienced in a lifetime with an ordinary woman. He knows he is one lucky guy.

She smiles. She laughs. She giggles. She teases. She pouts. She tantalizes. She mesmerizes. She strips. She dances. She flouts. She flaunts. She skips. She hops. She dances. She sings. She bedazzles. She palpates. She bumps. She grinds. She kisses. She licks. She sucks. She twerks. She fucks. Wow! *Damn! Sum Bitch! I love it; I love it so. Out of sight! Sign me up; long term contract, exclusive access!*

She's a snapper. Natalie has strong vaginal muscles which when contracted squeeze and release, squeeze and release, inducing a phallic sensation impossible to duplicate by a nominal female or by an adult toy.

On an occasion when Stony slowed down the intensity and frequency of his pelvic thrusts and rested for a few seconds, Natalie assumed control of activities and showed Stony a thing or two about grabbers (her terminology for 'snappers'). Stony is hooked for life. Not only is Natalie a genius and an accomplished executive, she is Geisha Girl and courtesan material of the highest caliber. At an earlier time and place, she would have easily qualified as a 1,000-horse woman, worth several fortunes to a placated caliph.

In short, Natalie can do things to and for a man which other women or sexual devices cannot do. If you have had sex with Natalie, if you have physically pair-bonded with Natalie, you have experienced the best life has to offer, now or at any time in the past or future. She is irresistible and irreplaceable.

Natalie consumed Stony. She took everything he had, digested it all; then shamelessly demanded more. Lovemaking with Natalie postured Stony on the brink of space/time, life/death; infinity, neither here nor there; simultaneously everywhere and nowhere. With Natalie, Stony has his cake and eats it too. She's that good.

He soared as closely as possible to heaven and survived with his body relatively intact. His mind, unquestionably a different matter. It will never be the same. *"Once in love with Amy, always in love with Amy," comes to mind.*

She will be the death of me yet. Death from sugar and spice and everything nice, Indeed. There will never be another Natalie, never. How sweet it is. Life is so good. May we live happily ever after.

Damnation, this is more than an ordinary man can handle. How does she do it? How does she know exactly what turns me on? What can I say? I give up.

*

"You do know of course, we were tailed from RyeGate to the Waffle House and from the Waffle House to my hotel?"

"No, I don't know that at all. What's up with you? What do you know that I don't know?" asked Natalie.

"I know one thing. As an investigator, you appear to be a very good dog handler. A dark blue recent model Ford was parked about a half block from your townhome when I arrived. At first I didn't pay much attention. Later the Ford followed us for over 14 miles; all the while maintaining a respectable trailing distance behind during our drive from RyeGate to the Waffle House. An excellent driver, the tail managed to maintain optimum trailing position even when interstate traffic clogged him up for a while."

"The Ford remained in the Waffle House parking lot during the 45 minutes we had, or for that matter only I had, breakfast. Departing the Waffle House on the way to my hotel, a distance of about 25 miles, the Ford continued to shadow us."

"Unless they're idling the motor or hunkered down in the hotel waiting room or bar, the driver and his mate must be shivering in their knickers. It's about 27 degrees outside. Fortunately, it appears they are in reconnaissance mode only, no aggression."

"Natalie, here's what I suggest. Let's dress, leave here for your townhome and see if they follow us. Do you know of any reason why your home is being bugged and you have a professional tail on your ass?"

"No, I don't. Wait. A few days ago, I told my dad I have premonitions about being watched. No evidence, only a sense of uneasiness. I was recently appointed by the president of the United States to head up an important joint task force with a classified mission. My number two guy hates my guts. I don't trust him, even half an inch. I'm certain he is out to get me, just as I'm out to get him."

"Maybe I'm being bugged and tailed because the CIA or the Secret Service wants to learn what bent nose activity I'm involved in. I don't know of any other reason."

"Okay, let's assume it's either the CIA or the Federal Gestapo. What course of action is best?"

"I hate to tell you, Stony, but this is beyond your pay grade, beyond your authority. I'll take care of it on Monday. Meanwhile, how much difficulty is it----belay that."

"What I was going to ask you is whether or not you can debug my home. I don't want that. I do not want you to be involved with my vocation in any way, shape or form. Not you, not anybody. I don't want anyone in the US government to know anything about you other than that I'm seeing you and you're a Canadian citizen with a green card and a clean record in both countries."

"OK. So far, so good. Let's go back to the townhome, have a couple of drinks, participate in domestic dialogue and in general imply by word and deed that we're both good citizens."

"Hopefully the CIA or the Secret Service, or both, will come to the conclusion that there is nothing here, that bugging and tailing you is not only unreasonable, but is also overly expensive in terms of recovery of solid intelligence which can be used against you for government purposes."

"Stony, my lover, where and when did you acquire your legalese jargon? Whence cometh thou first to stand in the house of justice and spar with an esteemed barrister? There appears to be more to the man than meets the eye." Teasing, Natalie asked, "Is my observation valid?"

Stony replied, "You surprise me not. How do I love thee? I love thee in more ways than thou can possibly know. When I was blind, thou caused me to see. When I was deaf, thou caused me to hear. When I met thee, I was essentially dead. Now I am more alive than I have ever been. I'm living proof that love at first site is a valid proposition, Natalie."

Visibly moved by words from the mouth of her lover, Natalie responded, "Take me home. Be respectful. Stay 15 minutes. Trust me. I will resolve this problem. You spoil me. On what date and time will you once again bless me with your presence as we continue our merry-go-round of life, Act 3?" smiled the most beautiful woman Stony has ever known.

"Saturday next at noon, my love, the 13th, and every Saturday thereafter; subject to a deluge of important job-related tasks I must attend to. Don't call me. I'll call you. Anticipate voice mail. I don't need your confirmation of my travel. When I show up on a Saturday noon and you don't answer your doorbell, I'll know you're vocationally engaged. Your rain checks are good; I'll be back one week later, same time, same station."

"As you Yanks are famous for saying, 'You're the cat's meow, Natalie.' Officially, I am besotted and beholden, madam. It appears I am yours until death do us part, which hopefully will be a very long time from now."

Mitch Donahue has other plans.

31
ROMEO & JULIET
Act 3

Today is Saturday, February 13, 2021. Jet departed for Pakistan in the new Gulfstream this morning. As usual Stony spent Friday night in the Hampton Inn at Reagan National Airport. *Rendezvous number three with Natalie in one hour.*

The recently anointed rich man upgraded his choice of rental automobiles. At noon Stony parked a 2021 black Lincoln town car in his usual spot in front of Natalie's RyeGate townhome. *I see no tail automobile in the vicinity.*

Stony is never disappointed when Natalie answers her doorbell. Informed in advance that Stony was taking her shopping at Tyson's Corner boutiques, Natalie dolled up lavishly. At first sight, the self-appointed paramour was beside himself with admiration, joy, lust and a dozen other off the chart emotional responses. Stony loves the woman.

Speechless, Stony smiled. Natalie handed him her version of hot buttered rum. Really cold winter weather outside; the home-made drink hit the spot. Natalie brushed her body against Stony as she kissed him softly on the right cheek. Stony lit up like a Las Vegas marquee. She has that effect.

After conducting sweeps and confirming the townhome to be free of bugs and other surveillance devices, an out-of-comfort zone Stony said, "Come here, you."

Ever resistant to male control, Natalie impishly snapped, "No!"

"No, did you say no?"

"What is there about N-O that you do not understand, my man?"

"You're not interested in your present?"

"I didn't say that."

"Then come here to me."

"Yes, sir."

"That's better."

Stony gave Natalie a big hug. She nuzzled closely and hugged back. Life is good.

"Natalie, first, I apologize for ordering you to do something. I will never do that again, darling woman." Demurely, Natalie smiled.

"I have something for you. I know it's been only three weeks, but believe me, this is the proper thing to do, what I need to do."

Masking nervousness while recovering a small gift-wrapped package from his coat pocket Stony said softly, "This is for you, Natalie, especially for you."

The demure smile widened, "Stony, you shouldn't have." Natalie is coy. She is never coy, at least not in this lifetime. *Out of character, gal. Way out of character.*

"Please open it, Natalie."

"Yes, sir," said Natalie as she commenced removing the wrappings.

"It's so beautiful!" gasped the astonished figment of Stony's imagination.

He acquired the ring from an internationally reputed diamond brokerage business with offices in the Diamond Quarter in Antwerp, Belgium. The Diamond Quarter does more than 13 billion dollars in the polished diamond business every year.

Stony knows a friend who knows a friend who got Stony a good deal on the ring, which is described thusly: Multi-Stone Diamond Ring; large stone 7.04 carats, VS1, F color, perfect cut; smaller stones: 2 side mounted baguettes, each 1 carat trillion; ring size 7, 18 carat yellow gold mounting. Retail Price: $595,000 US. Stony's price: $430,000 US.

Natalie knows jewelry, "Holy Cow, Stony! Did you hit the lottery?"

"Damn near, I got promoted. By the way, is that a yes?"

"You really know how to sweep a girl off her feet, don't you, Mr. Canadian?"

Chuckled Stony, "Only if she has round heels. That's levity, not for public consumption."

"Natalie, a major factor for me is how long it takes to find a woman like you in case you and I don't work out. You are a 20 year woman. I reckon that if today I started searching for your equivalent, it would take me 20 years to find you, on average."

"Shut up. Yes, I'll marry you, Frederick Stone Randolph."

"How – "

Natalie cut him off, "I'm FBI, that's how. The 'I' stands for investigation. You were born at Niagara on the Lake, Ontario. You don't have a criminal record, Canada or US. Clean green card record." Under her breath Natalie thought *You also file no IRS form 1040 tax returns, have no driver's license in any US state, have no US credit cards and otherwise exist under the radar.*

"Magna Cum Laude at Syracuse University; you didn't tell me that. Is there anything else you would like to know about yourself, Mr. Canadian?"

"No, not now. No. You do understand, don't you, that in some circles a lady is not considered engaged unless she has a ring plus a marriage date? How do you feel about that, Miss Policewoman?"

"Today is February 13th. Our wedding date is July 13th. Why postpone the inevitable? However, I have one condition."

"July 13, 2021, it is, madam. What's the condition?"

"I don't intend to mingle in public with a half million dollar rock on my left hand, a target for every pickpocket and mugger in DC. Please get me a moissanite duplicate stone, similar to my beautiful engagement ring."

"Done. Shopping, now or later?" asked Stony with a big, loving smile.

Whereupon Natalie clasped hands with Stony and led him upstairs to the bedroom where they first made love 14 days ago. It's a two week romance, not three weeks. Three sexual interludes, not three weeks. Whatever? Nature and romance work in wondrous ways.

The lovers did not make it to Tyson's Corner. They surfaced to breathe, barely. The third round of sex was better than the first two rounds combined. This round shall be memorialized forever and a day as the betrothal mating.

Later, over a cup of his now favorite coffee, Stony invited Natalie to travel to Canada and meet his parents. She agreed, providing the trip does not interfere with her current FBI assignment.

Stony's handsome appearance, dynamic persona and imposing magnetism notwithstanding, the joint task force is the most important thing in Natalie's life, now and for the foreseeable future. *Somehow or some way I will fit Stony in. I have to fit him in. I know I have to fit him in. Never again will I ever say no to Stony. He is too important to me. I cannot antagonize him in any way. I'll get this done, or my name is not Natalie Taylor.*

32
BERMUDA
New Management

Back at the mansion and full of piss and vinegar, on Monday, February 15th, Stony stirred the corporate pot. Asserting himself as senior executive in the hierarchy and seeing as how Mr. Big was off premises until Thursday, Stony instigated a heap of activity at the charity's internal logistics division, the entity responsible for mansion maintenance, upkeep and repair.

After housekeeping moved all furniture and fixtures not nailed down in Harvey Pryor's office to a vacant office, Stony inspected the mess. All documents were shredded. All furniture and removable fixtures, including art work, were donated to charity, specifically to Big Brothers Big Sisters of Bermuda.

Stony did his own interior design. Harvey's old office walls were repainted in beige. The carpet was removed and replaced in a wool and polyester beige blend. On Tuesday, new furniture arrived from England via air cargo. The tab was over $190,000 to furnish one office. New artwork was purchased and mounted, mostly still life and ocean scenes. Additional setback: $82,000.

Stony promoted Sidney Wilson, former CEO of the Insurance

Company, to the number two hierarchy executive position, equivalent to Executive Vice President of the hierarchy, Stony's old job. Sidney was replaced by his number two guy at the insurance company, and so on down the line. Sidney was provided a generous cash allowance to refurbish Stony's old office, now clean as a whistle. Sidney's salary was increased to $2 million per year.

Stony promoted the charity's logistics and supply executive to Harvey's hierarchy maintenance and supply position at a salary of 500 thousand dollars per year. Amelia Drew is sure to attract Jet's attention, being a female and all. Amelia is now the number four guy in the Taylor Hierarchy. Only Jet and Stony know from whence the majority of the hierarchy's profits emanate. *I need to discuss this topic with Jet, soon.*

Stony knows Jet is reluctant to relinquish his luxury office because he does not like change and because he has two beautiful young women on premises to take care of. Jet will no doubt ultimately relinquish his personal office, but not yet.

How in hell am I going to handle this job when Jet gets killed and the hierarchy and I are still standing. A hundred billion dollar estate subject to neither will, trust nor probate. Damnation. If anyone broaches the subject, it will be Jet and not Stony.

*

Stony and the mansion limousine awaited Jet's Wednesday, February 17th, near midnight return from Pakistan. The alternate mansion limousine accommodated Ewe and two bodyguards.

"Welcome home, boss," said Stony. "Yea or nay?"

"On a scale of one to 10, I give it a nine, not quite a 10. I'm tired. We'll discuss this first thing tomorrow, OK?"

"Of course, boss."

"How is my daughter?"

"Never better."

"The store?"

"Some changes, which I trust will meet with your approval. As your schedule permits, I'll bring you up to date on everything."

"The girls?"

"Awaiting your arrival, boss, with beer on ice, steak in the oven and Malbec ready to be decanted."

"Watch yourself; you might get promoted if you keep this up."

"How soon we forget, boss; how soon we forget."

After a midnight steak dinner with the girls, Jet and Helen left Amanda to clean up the few dishes and utensils. The mood at dinner was endearing. Jet was glad to be home. The girls were pleased that Jet was glad. Nineteen year old sophomore Helen conceived that night. Life is good.

*

At 8:00 am on Thursday, perfectionist Jet inspected new office arrangements, which reluctantly met his with his approval. Jet is not into change.

Sidney Wilson is an unknown commodity because his professional experience is limited to the insurance business. Banking and Charity are somewhat related, but obviously distinguishable from insurance.

The jury is out on Amelia Drew. For one thing, it's not clear that she will ever be trusted; privy to the primary source of Taylor Hierarchy income, the money laundered criminal cash. Amelia has the highest rank and the highest salary of any woman who ever worked for Jet. She requires observation.

Jet is pleased that Stony made timely administrative personnel decisions and did not sit on his responsibilities. *That's good. I'll have my powwow with Stony in Harvey's old office, for one thing to see if and how Stony has adopted psychologically to the hierarchy's executive control changes.*

*

"Where would you like to start, Boss?"

"My daughter."

"OK, Boss. Good news mostly. I visited with your daughter last Saturday afternoon and conducted a complete sweep of her townhome. No more tails. No more bugs and surveillance devices at Rye-Gate, for now."

"Interesting."

"Natalie anticipates a White House response to her bugs & tails complaint up through channels. She handled the matter herself. The bad guys apparently respect her. It's impressive for her to have taken on both the CIA and Secret Service simultaneously and still be standing after all shots have been fired."

"Schedule permitting I'll see her again on Saturday, five days from now, the 20th of February." Stony neglected to tell Jet that he and Natalie have already shacked up on three occasions and are engaged to marry. Discretion is the better part of valor. One does not want to be on the wrong side of Jet Taylor. *Everything will get done in its own time, I hope.*

"How goes it with the Muslims who are running Pakistan? How far up the chain of command did you infiltrate the sub-continent Islamics?" asked Stony.

"Good question. First an interesting fact; of all countries where English is spoken, Pakistan is third largest. Pakistan's number two guy chaired our meetings. The office of president is ceremonial. The CEO of Pakistan is the Prime Minister. In the event of his death, he is succeeded by the Chairman of the Senate of Pakistan. The current Senate Chairman's name is Omar Shamasthrustra, a mouthful."

"Omar and I got along well, not fabulously, but well. Apparently he had or has a personal relationship with the Pakistani who is credited with development of Pakistan nukes, a chap named A Q Khan. Mr. Khan is the revered father of the Pakistani nuclear weapons program."

"Regardless, I cut a deal with Chairman Shamasthrustra. I stressed that since he and I are both Islamists and are both interested in the establishment of a worldwide caliphate, it is in the best interests of Pakistan to assist those who engage in acts which substantially promote the probability of establishing a worldwide caliphate. It worked."

"As for price and terms of payment, it appears I pulled off a coup. After a lot of horse trading, we agreed to the following. I guarantee to destroy Washington, DC with the detonation of a nuclear weapon provided to me by Pakistan. I agree to buy four nuclear weapons from Pakistan at a cost of 250 million dollars per weapon, $1 billion in all."

"In the event I destroy Washington, DC with a nuclear weapon within 90 days, I do not have to pay the billion dollars. This has the effect of Pakistan entering into a bailment agreement with me as relates to the weapons. I rent the weapons with a conditional agreement to pay for them. If I cause one of the weapons to detonate at the right place at the right time, the four weapons cost me nothing. In the event I do not comply, I pay Pakistan one billion dollars."

"My promise to pay is guaranteed by an irrevocable letter of credit issued by our bank, payable in the event that I do not comply by blowing up a US city with their atom bomb within 90 days. Thereby Pakistan takes down the letter of credit. If I timely blow up a US city, the letter of credit is worthless. Bottom line, we got the bombs free and clear, Stony."

"I'll be damned, boss."

"Better yet, two more items; listen to this: number one, we are going to fleece the government of the United States of America out of 250 million dollars in ransom money. I stashed the frozen cadaver of an Enrique Echeverria look-alike in a refrigerator in a bungalow on a small cay in the Bahamas."

"The idea is to convince the Feds that at the end of the day they caused the death of Mr. Echeverria. He kills himself with C4 explosives in a suicide bombing act of terror. Number two, I intend to nuke Karachi with one on their own bombs if possible."

"Wow," said Stony.

"I agreed to pay Cuba a 10% commission on the billion dollars.

It will take two to four weeks to get the deal down on paper and executed by Pakistan, Cuba and myself, who the Pakistanis and Cubans know as Enrique Echeverria, a nuke buyer. I will negotiate Cuba's 10% down. We don't have to deposit the good faith billion dollars. The transaction bank, our bank, will issue a billion-dollar letter of credit in exchange for my billion-dollar IOU. After this all occurs, our bank will 'back in' a compliance-proof, bank-examiner conforming audit trail, proving the deal went down according to our edited version. End result - we are not a penny out-of-pocket."

"Damnation, Jet, how in hell can we get away with this?"

"Stony, you read the Goddamn money and banking book. You have had a firsthand look at how I handle banking for the past three years. Hopefully you now know that it's a bigger crime to open a bank than to rob one. At this level, international bankers do what they damn well please; the hell with everybody and everything else. Remember that, young man. Remember it well."

"Moving right along, our plan, subject to change, is on or before March 24th to accept shipment of four nuclear weapons FOB Matanzas, Cuba for transshipment along with illegal drugs to a US southern border site to be selected. Date of arrival in the US is on or about March 28th."

"I forgot what FOB means, Jet."

"It's an acronym for Freight On Board. FOB is important in long-distance business settings wherein casualty insurance coverage is an issue. The term FOB informs the parties and the world (casualty insurance companies) of the place and time where ownership of the insured product is transferred from the seller to the buyer. The owner is normally the insured, so you can see that when shipment involves transshipment and ownership shifts at the transshipment point, the goods will have been owned by, covered by, two different owners and two different insurance companies during the transaction."

"Jet, if you have any strong suits, none of them are stronger than your ability to translate complex, obscure thoughts and phrases into plain, understandable English. Bless you."

"Thanks for the compliments my man. Flattery will get you anywhere, except with me. Back to business. We acquire four nuclear weapons. We agree to babysit three Pakistan technicians who will keep tabs on us. The technicians will validate our claim of dud weapons, if any. More importantly, the technicians will validate the destruction of our target city."

"Regarding you and your priorities, young man, I see you as primary hierarchy executive and my number one backup as relates to 'Fresh Start.' Assuming we are successful in overthrowing the government of the United States, martial law will be established and we will operate and control the US government through two retired four star US Army Generals whose overall philosophy is similar to ours."

"Within the next two weeks you and I will determine what happens to the Taylor Hierarchy, who runs the store, when and if you and I are both dedicating our attention to running 'America,' our new wholly owned country."

"Along those lines, my investment company, the one that stashes Colombian drug profits, has liquidated all United States denominated investments; Facebook Stock, corporate bonds, US Treasuries, that sort of thing. The entire account is worth the equivalent of over 1.5 trillion US dollars and more importantly has no US currency risk."

"I want you to do the same thing for our bank. Set an appointment for us with new bank president Gerard Wainscot, earliest. I want it perfectly clear to Gerard that you are running the show pursuant to his steering committee. No misunderstandings; no ambiguities. Gerard is to take your orders, be responsible to you and you alone."

"Your first two directives to Gerard are for our bank to commence orderly trading to dump all US denominated assets no later than March 15, then to commence short selling of both actual dollars and calls on the dollar, along with put buying of the dollar, so as to short US currency by two trillion dollars in total, with positions established no later than April 1st. Gerard does not need to know why we are shorting the dollar."

"Between you and me, I have a gut feeling the US Dollar will trade at 90 cents on April 6th, will trade for about 50 cents on April 15th, and will trade at less than a penny, with no bids, on or about May 1st. Our bank stands to earn two trillion dollars net or thereabouts in the next three or so months. We pre-sell the US Dollar for 99 Cents and buy it back for less than one Cent; two trillion dollars' worth."

"No shit, Jet, two trillion dollars?"

"No shit, two trillion dollars. I anticipate bank and brokerage reneges. We will cross that bridge when we come to it."

"New subject. I am working with three 'Fresh Start' flag rank candidates. One of the generals will soon be eliminated from consideration. The remaining two generals will have near co-equal, independent domestic and international military authority in our revolutionary martial law army. The four-star generals are Ben Tate, Tommy Thompson and Bull Flanagan."

"All three generals know guns. None of the three generals has any expertise to speak of regarding butter. The generals depend upon us to review and reorganize, as we deem appropriate, every aspect of American life other than traditional military functions. We are on the same page with the generals."

"When we take over the USA, the appointed generals will be responsible for our Army, Navy, Marines, Air Force and Coast Guard, nothing else. Every other aspect of American life will be controlled by us; by me while I am alive; by you and your successor/s thereafter. A big job, but somebody's gotta do it."

"My death squads are poised to terminate any general in the event he strays from the company line. Three moles are postured in strategic positions in each general's chain of command. Each independent mole reports on his general once a month."

"I am moving the reports up to every 5 days, then to every second day, as of one week prior to T-day; thereafter daily until further notice. 'T' stands for takeover. Takeover day is T-day. My best estimate of when T-day will occur is on or about April 5, 2021. The date is subject to change."

"Our single nuke target is Washington, DC. I saw the grimace. Yes, we need to get Natalie out of there, somewhere else, anywhere else. Fear not, it's doable."

"I'm meeting with one general, four star General Ben Tate, US Army, Retired, on Friday, February 19th, at Boise, Idaho. Ewe and I are taking the Gulfstream VI. Afterwards I'll spend eight days at the Farm in Logan, returning to Bermuda within nine days of departure. How is your bookwork coming along, Stony?"

"Okay for now boss, but a lot to learn. As you pointed out a couple of minutes ago, of more importance is what happens to the store here in Bermuda in the event you are 'down' and I must step up as lead player on our 'Fresh Start' team. We are short a man now that Harvey is no longer with us. We glossed over the subject earlier. Comment solicited."

"I'm thinking about your Miami PI as a new hierarchy executive, possibly at the top. Importing an outside executive for Bermuda has always been a last resort for me. Even so, with me working 'Fresh Start' exclusively, it's clumsy for us to have only one other person, you, in the entire hierarchy who is aware of our source of Colombian funds. Think about it. Give me your recommendations by the end of the week."

"Wilco, boss. First, the PI. His name is Tony Preston. By chance, Tony shows up for a mansion interview on Tuesday next, February 23rd. Our new terminator is on board. He's a former US Army Cobra attack helicopter pilot, fixed wing reciprocating engine qualified. 28 years old; mean bastard, tough as nails, six confirmed kills on his resume."

"That's good, both topics. Stony, are you fucking my daughter?"
Damn. "How did you know, Jet?"

"Easy as pie. West Springfield is about halfway between Louisville and Bermuda. I tasked you to commence weekly sweeps of

RyeGate the week after you met Natalie. You have not missed a day's work in eight years. You were one day late to work, returning from Millersburg to the mansion on Sunday instead of Saturday. It defies logic to suggest that you did not spend Friday night and part of Saturday in the DC area, playing footsie with my daughter."

"You have my blessing, Stony. One piece of advice, do not allow your gonads to interfere with your cognitive responsibilities. Mind over matter. More than one good man has gone down the tubes attempting to simultaneously juggle vocational obligations and basic instincts. I plead guilty on that score. Take it from me, you can't live with 'em and you can't live without em."

Stony shook his head and smiled at his future father-in-law.

In the recent past Stony heard stories about General Bull Flanagan, ranging from controversial to disastrous. He doesn't know anything about the other two generals, Ben Tate and Tommy Thompson.

Stony is uneasy about Natalie but more uneasy about Bull Flanagan. It is not a good idea to take over the USA by force and then hand the country over to a wild ass retired U.S. Army general with an ego bigger than Donald Trump and Muhammed Ali combined.

I need to know more about Ben Tate and Tommy Thompson. I know enough about Bull Flanagan. Our Alexander the Great versus their combination of the Louisville Lip and Raging Bull. Quite a match. I don't like it. Root for Ben Tate or Tommy Thompson. Jet's instincts are amazing. Tony Preston is as close to an acceptable executive augment candidate as we will ever come across.

33
NSA
the First Lead

On Wednesday February 17th, NSA technician par excellence Wilson Patterson showed up at FBI Headquarters at 9:00 am sharp. Natalie knew he would be on time. Nerds always are.

"Come in, Wilson. Welcome to the FBI. Privately I am on a first name basis with all my important employees. Please call me Natalie when we are alone. Otherwise I'm Director Taylor or Ms. Taylor. Fair enough?"

"Fair enough, boss."

Natalie smiled at the nerd's subliminal resistance to authority, "Wilson, please fill me in, a brief NSA description."

"OK. First, Natalie, I apologize to you for being two days late. I'll make it up to you. Now the cook's tour. National Security Agency headquarters is located on an Army post, Fort Meade, Maryland, 30 miles northeast of downtown Washington DC. Although the number of NSA employees is officially classified, there are at least 40,000 military and civilian employees at Fort Meade; speculating, NSA has as many as 75,000 to 100,000 employees worldwide."

"NSA is not people oriented. NSA is electronic intelligence oriented. NSA functions in the areas of both foreign intelligence and foreign counterintelligence. 'Signals Intelligence' is NSA nomenclature associated with global monitoring, collection and processing of information and data."

"Although NSA is responsible for protecting our communications and information systems from penetration and network warfare, that's not applicable to us. You and I are concerned with passive electronic data collection throughout the world, clandestinely snooping and listening to cell phone and telephone conversations, among other things."

"NSA is authorized to use clandestine methods of intelligence data collection. Clandestine methods may involve bugging and use of subversive software. As you know we are located in a large number of countries throughout the world. We have been accused of burglary, wiretapping, and breaking & entering."

"Interesting, Wilson. Be that as it may, our job, your job, is not complex and is easy to understand. Your job is to search for and find the individual/s attempting to purchase nuclear weapons from a nation which is willing to sell nuclear weapons. Finding a potential seller is relatively easy. Eliminate those countries with nuclear weapons friendly to the United States. The remainder of nuclear capable nations constitutes the short list of possible sellers. That list is comprised of Iran, Pakistan, North Korea, Russia, China, and India. It appears to me that NSA activities should be limited to those six countries. Do you agree?"

"Not necessarily, Natalie. Other unfriendly but nonnuclear countries may be used for communications purposes by a country offering nukes for sale."

"Ah-ha, I see."

Wilson continued, "On the other hand it is mission plausible to have NSA prioritize clandestine observation of the prospective six nuclear selling nations along with nations friendly to the political purposes of the six nuclear selling nations. That's what we have been doing for the last two weeks."

"In review, Natalie, you're perfectly correct. Our task is simple. An infinite number of possible buyers is the major hurdle, but the overall mission is nevertheless simple. We are on top of it. Now let me share with you what may very well be a stroke of good fortune."

"I'm not going to tell you how we obtained the following information. Yesterday NSA learned about a recent Pakistan meeting related to an earlier Cuban meeting, the combination of which two meetings provides us a plausible early lead:

a. a meeting in Havana, Cuba six weeks ago involving nuclear weapons occurred on Tuesday, January 5, 2021. The sellers are North Korea, Iran and Pakistan. We don't know the ID of the buyer; and

b. meetings in Karachi, Pakistan on February 15th and 16th, involving the second ranking officer in the Pakistani government and a British citizen, principal of the largest charity in the world, which charity provides valuable services to developing countries including Pakistan and Cuba."

"Regarding Havana, according to our sources no American passport holders traveled to or from Cuba by way of public or private air transport at times material. A number of non-Cuban foreign nationals traversed Havana during those times but each traveler had a legitimate business purpose in Havana. Although we gathered half a lead, the sellers, we were nevertheless dead ended early on. We had no buyer lead."

"'We don't give up easily. We meticulously and continuously crosscheck every bit and bite of data in our system. Yesterday one of our electronic surveillance geeks discovered what might be a harmless continuity, but could be a big break for us."

"A British national by the name of William Pennington is apparently an unnamed principal of the largest international charity in the world, One New World Ltd, a Liechtenstein trust with home office in Hamilton, Bermuda. The charity provides more assistance to Cuban citizens than any entity in the world. Mr. Pennington lives in Bermuda. He travels to and from Havana, Cuba regularly."

"His January 4th arrival in Havana from Nassau and his January 5th departure from Havana back to Nassau, then home to Windsor, Bermuda on the same day, are routine events in the ordinary course of business for Mr. Pennington, as far as our intruding security probes are concerned. Mr. Pennington traveled to and from Cuba via an aircraft owned by Lyons Air, a licensed Bahamian nonscheduled air carrier for hire."

"This aspect of my story does not end there. Of possible importance is the fact that a Gulfstream G650 aircraft owned by the charity was apparently shot down on January 4th by a heat seeking shoulder mounted missile at noon EST just after takeoff from Lynden Pindling International Airport at Nassau."

"Our National Transportation Safety Board (NTSB) is assisting Bahamian aircraft investigators in determining how and why the aircraft was downed. Best guess from our guys - it was an assassination hit by a person or persons unknown. One fatality occurred, James 'Bubba' Jasper, American citizen, licensed commercial pilot in the US and Bermuda, in command of the Gulfstream G650 at the time of the incident. William Pennington was copilot on the fatal flight."

Regarding Karachi, not only did William Pennington show up in Havana on the same day as the Bahamas aircraft loss, which was the eve of the Havana four party nuclear weapons purchase and sales conference (with Pakistan in attendance); by chance Mr. Pennington reappeared in Karachi, Pakistan (a presumed nuke seller) on February 15th and 16th, ostensibly on business for the charity."

"That charity, One New World, Ltd, does a lot of good work in Pakistan as well as in Cuba. They distribute more goods, services and cash throughout Pakistan than any other charitable entity. Mind you, since the charity does a boatload of really positive things throughout the world we need to be extremely cautious not to tread on them if they are clean."

"Natalie, on balance it is possible; I cannot say with any degree of certainty that it is probable; it is possible that William Pennington is our nuke buyer."

"Bottom line: William Pennington is our best lead to date. We are concentrating on him but not to the exclusion of other ongoing surveillance."

"Wilson, as usual the FBI accomplished nothing to date and you accomplished everything. I owe you, man."

"All in a day's work; a pleasure toiling for the brightest woman in Washington DC," smiled Wilson Patterson.

Natalie returned the smile with one of her own, a rare occurrence these days.

*

Both Jet and Stony know from high level federal mole reports that Natalie is director of a federal task force named USTF-18. A present mission of the task force is to apprehend and/or kill a man named Enrique Echeverria, a Venezuelan passport holder who resides in the Berry Islands area of the Bahamas.

Natalie does not know she is tracking the whereabouts of her father. She does not know the man she intends to apprehend and/or kill is her father. She knows nothing of the Taylor Hierarchy. She intends to use the bounty money to flesh out Enrique Echeverria.

Jet and Stony know everything except how to react to what they know. Natalie knows nothing now but will know what to do when she learns something, which event is certain to occur in the near future. Will she kill her father in the line of duty? She has motive. One day soon she will have opportunity. In the grand scheme of things, Stony may ultimately have no role other than self-aggrandized spectator. Time will tell.

34
GENERAL BEN TATE
Treasonist

On Friday, February 19, 2021 Ewe and Jet lifted the new replacement Gulfstream G650 off the runway at Wade International Airport, Hamilton, Bermuda, at 6:00 am local time, headed for Salt Lake City, Utah, 2,649 miles to the west. The flight consumes a tad over four and one-half hours. Since Salt Lake City is three times zones west of Bermuda, Jet lands one and one-half hours after he takes off.

At 7:30 am MST, Ewe transmitted on frequency 121.9 MHz, "Salt Lake Ground Control, this is VQ-CBJ. Request detailed taxi instructions to TAC Air – SLC for tie down and refueling, over."

"VQ-CBJ, turn right at end of runway, 180 degree turn at first taxiway, continue straight ahead. TAC Air is on the SE perimeter of the airport. Follow detailed taxi instructions," said Salt Lake Ground Control to Ewe.

"VQ-CBJ, Roger, wilco," said Ewe.

Five minutes later, the tires of the Gulfstream G650 were chocked in front of the FBO, TAC Air – SLC. Jet said, "Ewe, you are on your own for up to eight days. Your rental car keys and hotel accommodations information are waiting for you at the desk clerk station inside the FBO building.

We have a daily cell phone check at noon. You are on three hours' notice for departure; otherwise this Mormon town is yours for the taking. A $250 daily per diem should have been advanced to you by finance yesterday. Your hotel is prepaid. Did you get your $2,000 cash?"

"Yes, boss."

"Any questions?"

No, boss."

"Well then, have a pleasant week. Keep your cell phone charged and live."

"Will do, Thank you for everything, boss."

Jet walked from the FBO premises to the Hertz rental car counter at the main airport building. "Good morning, my name is Robert Farnsworth. I reserved a Ford Super Club Wagon for nine days. Please look me up on your computer."

"Oh, yes, Mr. Farnsworth. Your vehicle is ready. Charles, here, will accompany you to the vehicle via our people mover. Will there be anything else, sir?"

"I am prepaid, correct?"

Yes, sir. The only paperwork you need is right here. May I see a photo ID, Mr. Farnsworth?"

"Certainly," answered Jet as he provided his fake Robert Farnsworth Utah driver's license.

"Everything is in order, Mr. Farnsworth. Have a great February week here in Salt Lake City."

Charles, the modified golf cart operator, drove Jet the one-half mile from the front desk to the muster area where Hertz rental cars await to be driven away to who knows where by who knows whom.

Next stop, a luxury rental home in a high-end complex in a prestigious district of Salt Lake City, six bedrooms, sleeps twenty. *The girls ought to like this* thought Jet as he toured his four-night pad with the rental agent. "Will that be all, Mr. Farnsworth?"

"It surely will," countered Jet as the smartly dressed Draper Company female real estate agent departed Jet's rental premises near downtown Salt Lake City, leaving Jet with a key in his right hand and a saggy open mouth savoring possibilities which will never come to pass.

*

At 9:00 am Jet's contract Learjet took off from Salt Lake International Airport for a 340 mile flight to Boise, Idaho and a meeting with General Benjamin Tate, US Army, Retired. Appointments for Bull Flanagan and Tommy Thompson were rescheduled. Jet has big time problems with General Tate.

Arriving in Boise at 9:50 am Jet rang General Tate on his throw away cell phone, "General, this is Philip Jackson. How are you this morning?"

"Fine, Mr. Jackson, quite fine. Thank you."

"Our meeting is on for 10:30 am, 40 minutes from now, in the conference center of the Grove Hotel at 245 South Capitol Boulevard in downtown Boise. Don't be late. Please read back for confirmation."

"Roger that, Grove Hotel, 245 South Capitol Boulevard at 10:30 am. I'll be there."

A month ago, each of the three generals was provided a different April kickoff date for T-day. The dates were April 12th, 19th and 28th. Ben Tate's date was April 28th.

Yesterday Jet's primary federal mole reported that the US Government is in possession of proof positive evidence that T-day is April 28, 2021. Today Jet's job is to determine, to the extent possible, whether or not Ben Tate is a counter spy for the Federal Government, a turncoat attempting to treasonably finger Jet to the feds.

Jet paid cash for a taxi from Boise Airport to downtown Boise, Idaho, arriving at the Grove Hotel at 10:25 am. The cabbie double parked two blocks away with the engine running. He demanded a $300 waiting fee in advance, fare to and from the hotel included.

Disguised in a beard, sunglasses and a San Francisco Giants baseball cap, Jet exited the taxi and briskly walked to the hotel. He ambled from the main entrance to the vicinity of the ground floor conference room, where four, maybe five government security types were assembled, most clandestinely posted, one milling around outside the entrance to the hotel's conference center. Obvious government agents. Obviously waiting for Jet to show his face.

Jet did a slow 180 degree turn and leisurely departed the Grove Hotel, walking in a normal gait toward the awaiting taxi, engine up and running. The driver was cautioned to motor within the speed limit on return to the Boise Airport. Ground time in Idaho was less than an hour. Jet was back in Salt Lake City by noon.

Jet saw more than he needed to see in Boise. On three separate occasions he told General Tate that all meetings between Jet and the general were to be one-on-one. General Tate knows if other personnel try to "crash" a Jet/Tate conference, he is to immediately abort the conference via cell phone, for later rescheduling. The sole conclusion: General Tate is a traitor to the hierarchy and must suffer pre-ordained consequences, death to both he and his family.

Bypassing his newly commissioned 'Army General' Death Squads, Jet speed dialed number nine on his international cell phone. "Customer service," answered the cell phone in Spanish. "How may we help you today, sir?"

Jet replied in Spanish, "This is Beaver 1. Implement plan CXL 27, read back."

"Roger, Beaver 1, we have instructions to implement plan CXL 27, numero Dos Siete. Please provide the password."

"La contraseña es 'Tres Amigos', (The password is 'Three Friends')" replied Jet.

"Roger, 'Tres Amigos'. Muchas gracias, Señor," once again stoically replied the death squad employee. "Estado informe manana." *We are doing a lot of business lately* thought the death squad administrative handler.

Ben Tate, his wife, his two sons and their families were all dead three days later. Philip Jackson's passport and other ID documents died the same day, swallowed by a Fellowes paper and plastic shredder, emitted as ¼ by ¼ inch flakes of papyrus and plastic.

35
LOGAN, UTAH
The Farm

Early Friday afternoon Jet departed the Salt Lake airport temporary parking lot, easing an unwieldy 20 passenger Ford van into traffic eastbound toward the North/South Interstate Highway servicing Salt Lake City. Turning north on I-15, Logan, Utah and the farm are on the nose, 89 miles ahead; one hour and 30 minutes of leisure driving, half of the journey via sparsely traveled interstate.

Just short of Brigham City, Jet turned right onto US highway 89/91, a road shared by two US routes for 50 miles or so. US highway 91 separates Logan, Utah on its way to Idaho Falls, Idaho.

After driving for one hour and 35 minutes, Jet parked the oversized Ford in front of the farm, a 7,500 square feet, 8 bedroom, 8.5 bath ranch home situated on 2 acres of land at the end of a cul de sac off another dead-end spur, a few miles southeast of Hyde Park and Logan-Cache airport.

It is 2:00 pm MST in the Robert Farnsworth family home. A reunion of sorts is underway, uniting Jet Taylor, alias Robert Farnsworth, and his four wives: Wilma, age 24, Joyce, age 22, Diana, age

21 and Beatrice, age 20, along with Jet's children, 2 by Wilma, a boy age 3 and a girl age 2; 1 by Joyce, a boy age 2, a girl by Diana, age 1 and a girl by Beatrice, age 3 months.

The "sisters" (wives) are elated to see Jet. The two and three-year-old children recognize their father and compete for his attention. First things first, small gifts for the two and three-year old's, then elegant jewelry for each of the four wives, a gold necklace for Wilma, a gold bracelet for Joyce, clip on gold earrings for Diana and a gold ankle bracelet for Beatrice. Wives and children were all delighted with the presents.

55-year-old widow, housekeeper/den mother Yvonne Smith appeared and announced, "Mr. Farnsworth, you must be famished. I know you are not fed well when you are off working. Soup's on ladies. Dinner is served."

Yvonne carried, strolled and led the five children to the den for a snack. Watching all five carefully, Yvonne transferred Jet's lovely tiger lily flower arrangement to a compatible vase. She sprinkled a preservative into the vase water. The flowers were as beautiful the day Jet departed as they were the day he arrived.

Diana and Beatrice served a late lunch. Jet occupied the end of an elegant twelve setting, plate glass & granite dining table with Wilma and Joyce on either side, Wilma on Jet's more important right side.

"How was your journey, my husband?" queried Wilma.

"Just fine, Wilma. But I'm glad it's over and I'm home with you."

"Robert, you always say the nicest things," replied Wilma as she familiarly stroked the top of Jet's right thigh.

"And you, Joyce?"

"I am fine as always, Robert, waiting for you to light up my life."

"My pleasure, Joyce, ever my pleasure. Your children, ladies?"

Joyce deferred to Wilma, who has seniority over the other 'sisters.' Wilma said, "Our boy, Hubert, is a handful; into anything and everything; very curious. Yvonne and I have to watch him like a hawk. Our girl, Wilhelmina, is turning into quite a domestic; she enjoys dabbling at setting tables and washing dishes."

"We'll see about that, and you, Joyce?"

"Robert, Bobby junior is a complete joy. He looks more like you every day. I see mannerisms in him which substantially emulate you. It's almost like me looking into your eyes when I look into Bobby's eyes. Weird. Pleasant, but spooky. Motherhood has made a complete woman out of me, Robert."

"School?"

Wilma said, "The more I get into it the more I understand I made the correct decision by choosing elementary education as my major.

I graduated from Utah State University in Elementary Education almost two years ago. I taught 4th grade for the past 19 months and will complete my required two years of elementary school teaching in the next two months, when school recesses for the summer."

"I am on track for re-admission to Utah State in September. My application is to the Eccles School in their three year PhD program in education. Cross your fingers. My grades and Graduate Record Examination ("GRE") scores are competitive."

"Marvelous, Wilma, Goodonya," said Jet. "And you, Joyce?"

"Robert, I'm in a pickle, a quandary. I want to stay here, to live here forever. Logan is a paradise. It's a perfect place to raise children. I love the four seasons. I love the mountains. I love the inter-mountain region."

"Robert, I love you. I love my sisters; all your wives. We love each other. I love our lifestyle. The thing is, I also love knowledge, learning, and books. As you know this is my second semester of a master's program in Physics at Utah State. Lamentably the Utah State physics faculty has no 'heavies,' no professors with a national reputation for excellence in the field of physics."

"Three of my professors and advisors have convinced me I can get into, most probably be accepted by, either Cal Tech or MIT; two world class universities. My graduate record exam numbers and my near 4.0 GPA make me competitive in terms of admittance. My course of study would be for four or five years, a PhD in physics, emphasizing theoretical physics, the same discipline as Ash Carter, Obama's Secretary of Defense."

"There are two kinds of physics, theoretical and applied. For instance, knowledge of higher mathematics related to magnetism might be used by theoretical physicists to conduct experiments about how magnetism works by and through certain different atoms, such as hydrogen, which could lead to engineers and applied physicists creating machines which can come up with images based on magnetism, an MRI scanner in this hypothetical. Without the theoretical physicist, applied physicists would have no project to perfect. I can do it, Robert. I can become a theoretical physicist, able to help all humanity lead better lives."

"Then go for it, sweetheart. We'll work it out. You have the makings of a wonderful career in front of you. California Institute of Technology is closer; located in the LA area, Pasadena, I think. Massachusetts Institute of Technology is located in or near Boston. I like MIT's reputation better; six of one, a half dozen of the other. Both schools are rated in the top 10 universities in the world. Go for it. You have the support of the entire family."

Joyce was certain Jet would say no. She is overwhelmed with elation, "Oh, Robert, thank you. Thank you so very much. This is the most wonderful day of my life, Robert. I have everything, thanks to you. I am somebody, thanks to you. Bless the day I met you, Robert Farnsworth. Bless the day. Robert, please take me to bed, right now, please. I know I am out of order, but this is such a special occasion I cannot wait to properly thank you."

Wilma said softly, "Service your wife, Robert, service her right now."

"Yes, ma'am," said Jet as he followed Joyce up the stairs. Once inside Joyce's private bedroom Jet said forcefully, "On your knees, bitch, now. You know how I like it, woman. You're my favorite bitch; my only bitch, you know that don't you?"

"Yes, master," replied Joyce, on her knees, busily engaged in fellatio. She anticipates being tied up, gagged and blindfolded by Jet after he climaxes, then to be violently fornicated under extreme conditions in varied and unusual positions. Pure vanilla S&M.

"Remember I own you, Joyce. Remember, I will kill you if you ever look at another man. Remember, you are inferior; you must earn the right to be fucked by me, for you to fellate me. Remember, I am your master. I will always be your master. You will always be my love slave, mine to use and abuse as I see fit."

"Yes, master, I am ever mindful. I beg of you, please get off so you can handcuff me, gag me and take me. I beg you, master, please fuck me, now. I need it, I love it, master. I have worked so hard at school. I have provided you such a bright, healthy child."

"That was then, bitch. What have you done for me lately? What have you done to deserve me fucking you? I'll answer that. Nothing, nothing at all. However, I shall give you a mercy fuck, this one time; but you shall be punished first, ten hard spanks. A hot bottom paired with a hot special place is what you need, bitch."

"Yes, master, yes."

Jet ejaculated pursuant to fellatio. He then handcuffed, gagged and blindfolded Joyce. He spanked her hard with his open hand, eleven repetitions. The spanks bruised her buttocks. As was their custom, she uttered "thank you, master," after each painful, burning spank. After the last 'thank you,' Jet proceeded for 45 minutes to manhandle Joyce in the fashion she required and adored. One more ejaculation for Jet and two climaxes for Joyce.

"Thank you, master. Thank you for everything. You are a real man. You are a wonderful man, the most wonderful man in the world. You are my darling, Robert."

"You are most welcome, my favorite bitch. Joyce, you are my darling, too. I love you, Joyce. Let's join your sisters." Jet squeezed Joyce's hand, intimately. She squeezed back.

*

Earlier Beatrice asked, "Where are Robert and Joyce?" She suspects

Joyce is participating with Robert Farnsworth (Jet) in bouts of sadism and masochism but is not yet certain.

"Indisposed, returning shortly," said Wilma. Along with the den mother, every sister knows 'indisposed' is the family euphemism for sexual activity, one of Jet's long suits. During the eight days he is in Logan, he will service each 'wife' four times, sixteen sexual interludes; comprised of union with two different sisters per day for eight days, one in the early am before breakfast and one in the late evening after supper. Jet is a stud.

Wilma is pregnant with her third child. Diana is pregnant with her second child. In Bermuda, Helen is pregnant with her first child. She is not yet married in the church. The rooster works overtime.

Diana is in her senior year at Utah State studying government and politics. She is considering a Doctorate in Public Administration at the University of Southern California, ultimately to work as a city manager, an airport manager or a hospital manager in the Logan, Utah area, or perhaps to teach at university level.

Beatrice is a second semester junior at Utah State majoring in accounting. She is leaning towards becoming an accountant or an attorney, like Alan Dershowitz. Beatrice is the brightest of the sisters and the one with her feet most solidly on the ground. Beatrice is also the most emotional sister of the bunch. As with all the sisters, she idolizes the ground Robert Farnsworth walks on.

Eight years ago Jet's personal life was going nowhere. He consulted a Zurich, Switzerland leading edge psychiatrist and submitted to psychoanalysis. As a result, Dr. Zwiffen introduced Jet to 'Solomon therapy.'

In the past Jet was willing to give away the kitchen sink to each of his then current squeezes, only to crash and burn in despair when the squeeze turned out to be temporary in nature. As a result Dr. Zwiffen suggested to Jet that he change his approach to feminine companionship.

Dr. Zwiffen advised Jet to consider polygamy; to abandon serial monogamy; to give polygamy a try, but only in a jurisdiction where polygamy is legal.

Jet allowed as how the USA was then (2013) essentially polygamistic. Unmarried men and women cohabited in large numbers throughout the nation. Nobody cared whether or not those pairs were married. Nobody except old fashioned Jet, who does not like change.

Creative thinker that he is, Jet opted for polygamy. He gave it a try. He advertised four year scholarships to 17/18 year old exceptionally bright, beautiful, curious, ambitious young females, one scholarship per year. The scholarship is full ride, providing tuition, books, fees, room & board, travel and related incidentals. Paid internships augment the value of the scholarship.

The first two school years are in Bermuda, co-op, part internet college curriculum study, part internship. Years three and four are purely academic, at Utah State University in Logan, Utah, about 100 miles north of Salt Lake City.

The first scholarship was earned by Wilma. By halfway through her third semester Jet imposed his will upon Wilma so profoundly that she accepted Jet as her self-appointed idol. She allowed and encouraged him to do anything with her mind and body, trusting him to do right by her. Which Jet did; which he continues to do. She remains his first, his favorite, and his only legal wife.

Jet convinced Wilma he could 'clone' her five times; six Wilma's is the optimum number. Wilma helped Jet seduce Joyce and so on and so forth. The rest is history.

In the summer prior to the start of the third year of the polygamy experiment Jet bought a two acre lot in Logan, Utah. On the lot he built an eight bedroom ranch home for Wilma and enrolled her at Utah State University, visiting her once every two months, four day visits. It worked for Wilma and worked for Jet.

With Wilma in Utah, Joyce helped Jet seduce Diana. In the third year of the Utah experiment Joyce joined Wilma in Logan, establishing an unparalleled 'dual perfecta' sex saga; two wives in Utah and two maidens in training in Bermuda.

The marriage 'thing' for second wife ('sister') Joyce and subsequent sisters was tricky; one ground rule, no bigamy, no law-breaking. Joyce and Jet settled on a marriage ceremony conducted by a cooperative LDS (Church of Jesus Christ of Latter Day Saints, the original American polygamists) minister, but without memorialization of the church 'marriage ceremony' by a notary public or equivalent; no marriage document filed in the Utah state capital at Salt Lake City, so as to avoid bigamy.

Only Wilma is married to Jet, in the view of the state of Utah. All sisters kept their own names. All children have two last names, i.e. Farnsworth/Brown; Farnsworth/Suggs, etc. All 'wives' are treated equally, without exception. No 'wife' is more important than another 'wife,' for any reason, at any time.

Last but not least, a generous retirement/legal separation document was signed by Jet and each of his 'wives,' a funded and legally binding agreement. If a sister wants 'out,' she is free to leave at any time, taking 1 million tax free dollars with her, plus an initial payment of $200,000 per child, along with an extra $100,000 annual payment per child, per year, until the child is 18, or if a student, until the final year of school is completed, so long as progress is made towards an advanced degree. If the sisters outlive Jet, each current 'wife' shall inherit $15 million, in addition to the 'continuation payments' in the event children are involved. All contract amounts are irrevocably funded, guaranteeing the sisters true lifetime financial security.

Each sister in Utah receives free room and board, free tuition, books and college fees, travel allowance and an annual stipend of $5,000 tax free per month wire transfer deposited into her personal bank account. Each year the stipend increases by $1,000. As of today, Wilma receives $8,000 per month, Joyce receives $7,000 per month, Diana receives $6,000 per month and Beatrice receives $5,000 per month. There is a $10,000 lid on monthly stipends, subject to CPI adjustment. There are five vehicles at the farm, one for each 'sister' and one for den mother, Yvonne.

As Dr. Zwiffen predicted, Jet and his wives never argue. The wives always have their way, however unusual their idiosyncrasies. They get away with murder. No drugs, no booze and no tobacco in the house, as per LDS tenets. No swearing, just pure and plain unadulterated good living, by good people. Unusual people, but nevertheless, good people. If it was good enough for Solomon, it's good enough for Jet. The Bible says so. The Bible cannot be wrong.

On the afternoon of day one, the entire family, including Yvonne, packed into the 20 passenger Ford and motored down to Salt Lake City, the family together for the first time away from the Farm. During the next four days, they visited the Mormon taber-nacle, the state capitol and Great Salt Lake, among other tourist des-tinations. TV and sex filled their nights.

On day five the family returned to the Farm. Yvonne took care of all the children almost all the time. For eight days, the sisters had a ball, the children had a ball and Jet had a ball. Life is good.

During the eight days, the family talked and laughed; they vis-ited museums, restaurants and tourist traps in Salt Lake City; at home in Logan, they made love; they watched TV; they played trivial pursuit and chess. They watched the children grow up before their very eyes, with love all around. An ideal life in the intermountain (American Rocky Mountains) region of Utah.

*

Jet leaves for Bermuda tomorrow, Saturday, February 27th. "Wilma, I want you to come down to the basement with me."

"Yes, Robert."

"The paper I am giving to you should be kept in a safe place known only to you. It contains the combination to a safe," as Jet showed Wilma how to remove a basement wall panel and expose the face of a combination lock.

"In the beginning, you must turn the pointer to the left four times past zero; continuing on to the left, stop at the four combination numbers in turn, 60, 13, 87, 49. After stopping on 60, turn back to the right to 13, then back to the left to 87, then back to the right to 49."

"When turning to numbers three, four and five, pass the number once, past zero, then stop the second time by. After stopping on 49, turn left to zero. Then activate the door handle, opening the door to the safe. Please give it a try."

Wilma opened the lock on first try. Jet was not surprised. "Wilma, please examine the contents of the safe."

"I prefer not to, Robert."

"I understand, Wilma. Be advised there is $5 million in the safe, $4 million in gold and $1 million US equivalent in Canadian cash. This money is in addition to your 'contractual right' money as per our agreement. The money is for emergency. I trust you to do the right thing if you are confronted with an emergency."

"Robert, are you ill? Are you going to die soon?"

"No, silly goose. This is nothing more than estate planning for my wonderful family."

"All right then. Could we make love right here, in the basement, like we used to do when you first courted me?"

"Of course we can, Wilma. You're my favorite. Anything for you, dear woman."

Wilma closed the safe cover, spun the dial twice, closed the access panel and looked Jet straight in the eye. "Fuck me, Robert. Fuck me now, like the old days. I stashed a blanket and a pillow down here, for my ass, not for my head. Do me, Robert, like you used to do me. You know I love to touch you, Robert," said Wilma as she commenced a slow circular motion with her right hand on Jet's groin.

"I will, Wilma, right now. You are the best of the bunch and the only legal wife of the bunch. You and our children will always be special. I love you for everything you have done for me, Wilma, and always will."

Jet 'did' Wilma on the basement floor. She was happy. Jet was happy. Life is good. The conjugal schedule is skewed. It is day number seven. He serviced Joyce before breakfast and is scheduled with Diana after supper; three rounds today.

Maybe Diana can get along with a double dose of oral sex. Tomorrow is a half day. Jet will do Beatrice before breakfast and Wilma again after breakfast. The stud is slipping a bit, backsliding toward normalcy. *A normal sex life. That would be tragic.*

*

After Jet left the Farm at noon on Saturday, Wilma pondered. *Robert does not lie, so he is not unhealthy. Something about his business activities is dangerous for him. I pray to God he gets through this calamity unscathed. Robert is the love of my life.*

*

Duty calls. Jet's future is totally dependent upon the failure/success of project 'Fresh Start.' The bomb may be a dud. Not all presidential line of succession personnel may be killed in the nuclear destruction of Washington, DC. Jet's chosen presidential successor/s may develop cold feet, or for any reason refuse to cooperate with Jet. The generals may turn on Jet. Jet may be assassinated by his own cadre of revolutionaries, or by his drug business cronies. His 'Fresh Start' martial law project may fail on day one. Many loose ends. At least the Farm residents are taken care of. Helen and Amanda are open items.

*

After a positive interview at the Mansion, Stony hired Tony Preston on as probational executive vice president of the hierarchy, at a salary of $80,000 per month. Tony Preston will not meet Jet nor be made aware of Jet's existence during his six months probationary period. Neither will Tony Preston be privy to money laundering during the probationary period. Stony will bird-dog Tony Preston on a very short leash.

36
TURKS & CAICOS ISLANDS
Love & War

Jet announced to Helen and Amanda at breakfast, "Ladies, get your swimsuits and flip-flops packed. We are spending the next three days and nights at a beach front vacation villa in the Turks and Caicos Islands, a British overseas territory in the Caribbean Sea close to Cuba and Hispaniola. Today is Monday, March 1st. We return home on Thursday, March 4th," said Jet.

Both girls giggled and said "I don't have anything to wear."

Jet was prepared, "Jeans and flip-flops on the airplane; boutique splurge in the Grace Bay area of the islands. We are staying at the Tuscany facility in Grace Bay, which has beachfront accommodations with pool, sunset views, terraces, home theater, garden, dining and gymnasium. A short walk to the beach. We'll be together all the time except for a two hour meeting on Thursday."

"Booooo," said both girls, referring to Jet's meeting. "Thank you, Mr. Pennington, thank you very much," said Amanda.

Helen chimed in, "Yes, Mr. Pennington thank you very much. What time do we leave, sir?"

"It's 8:00 am now. We board the Gulfstream at 9:30. Bring your passports, toiletries and sun screen lotion. I'll take care of everything else. Don't forget tooth brushes."

"Imogene, confirm with Ewe my departure on the Gulfstream at 10:00 am, destination Turks and Caicos, with Helen and Amanda as passengers. Return in three days. Confirm also with Estill Barnes."

"Yes, Mr. Pennington, right away, sir."

*

Jet and the girls settled in on Monday afternoon at the Tuscany complex, splurged at three different boutiques in Grace Bay, had dinner at a tourist seafood restaurant, and arrived back at the hotel by 7:30 pm. Jet is anxious to confirm that his January 5th soirée with Amanda was not a onetime proposition.

"Ladies, on the schedule for tonight is Amanda. Tomorrow night, Helen, and for the third night either a three-way or the two of you flip a coin for me. Ladies choice." Both girls blushed. Amanda offered her hand to Jet. The couple disappeared into Jet's master bedroom.

"Amanda, I want to thank you for committing to me the last time we were alone together, January 5th, two months ago. If you don't mind doing so, will you please share with me the reason or reasons for your decision?"

"Sure, Mr. Pennington. I'm glad to share with you. Please don't think ill of me when I tell you that it boils down to lifetime financial security. You are an old man, a very nice old man I might say. You have decades of memorable events and accomplishments in your personal resume. At age 18, 19 next month, I'm barely a woman. My parents are middle-class. I'm exceptionally bright. Some say I'm pretty. At 5'8" tall and 130 pounds, I have what most people refer to as a good figure."

"Otherwise I don't know what you see in me, sir. Whatever you do see in me pleases me immensely. For me it isn't why I committed to you; it's why you committed to me. I know you're a family man and don't sleep around."

"You can have any young woman you want. The fact that you want me, the way I see it, gives me more self-confidence and belief in myself than you can imagine."

"As far as the sex is concerned and you taking my cherry, every young woman knows it's eventually going to happen. I'm just glad it happened with you; proud also. I believe I have a lot to offer you because I'm young, bright, attractive, ambitious, adventurous and honest.

"I want you to teach me everything you know about life, about sex. I want you to share with me everything you know about sex. I want to experience sex with you in as many different positions, and at as many different times and places as you have ever had sex before, in the morning, at noon and at night. I want our sex to be memorable."

"I want to be the only woman you think of when you are hungry for sex; when you masturbate, if ever. As I understand the term, I want to be both your courtesan and your wife; especially your courtesan."

"I'm competitive, Mr. Pennington, always have been. You bit off a lot when you chose me as your 2020 scholarship winner. I may not be more than you can chew, but I'm more than a handful. I know you selected me personally."

"Bottom line, I want you to fuck me every day, day and night, until I conceive, until you knock me up. I'm a single-minded, goal oriented girl. Screw me, Mr. Pennington. Fuck me on your bed, on the floor, in the pool, in the limousine, on the grass; on your office desk; fuck me anywhere you please Mr. Pennington, anytime you are hungry for sex. I will always drop everything I'm doing, including my panties, to please you. I'll be your whore in the bedroom and your princess in the boardroom. I will never let you down. I promise."

Flabbergasted, Jet could not believe what his ears were telling him. *She's exactly what I would be like if I were female; a man-killer in the making if I ever saw one.*

Drawing near to Jet, Amanda continued, "Yes, Mr. Pennington, you deflowered me. I was a virgin. I won't lie to you. In the past boys fondled my tits and fondled me down below. Boys have titillated my clitoris, gotten me off, but only a few times. No big deal. No emotional interest. Teenage experimentation with my body. I was neither satisfied nor disgusted. I knew it would get better. I just didn't know how soon and with whom."

Standing five feet in front of Jet, Amanda commenced disrobing, blouse first. Jet subconsciously licked his lips in anticipation of 'hanging out' with the nymph teasing him mercilessly, flaunting explicit, varied burlesque poses, one after delicious another.

"Helen helped me by explaining her unusual relationship with you and your unusual relationships at the Farm. I have read a lot about sex and eroticism, and have theoretical knowledge but no experience. I am game for fellatio, cunnilingus, bondage, mild S & M, ménage a trois, and a three-way with Helen," said Amanda as her unzipped short shorts fell to the floor. Jet shook his head left and right in disbelief.

"I don't know if Helen is into three-ways. I don't know if you're into three-ways. Nothing anal, please, sir. One request, please suck my tits for at least five minutes each. They love it, Mr. Pennington."

On that note, Amanda deftly flicked her brassiere at Jet's face. He caught the garment in midair, tossed it on the bed, picked up Amanda with one arm, grabbed the crotch of Amanda's panties with his free hand and savagely ripped them off her behind.

"Are you satisfied, Amanda?" rasped Jet.

"I believe I am, Mr. Pennington. I believe I am," whispered the siren in a tone of voice exuding wisdom beyond her age, suggesting the possession of consummate seductive characteristics, randomly but sparingly bestowed, then only upon truly fortunate young women.

Amanda, one in a thousand; belonging to Jet, the final addition to his six mare stable. *You have come a long way, baby.*

Amanda has no idea what's to become of her when she grows

up. A hint perhaps, but no real idea. Jet has more than an idea. The lothario knows what is going to become of Amanda; he means to play a major role in Amanda's future, starting tonight.

"Take me now, Mr. Pennington. Have your way with me. Show me. Tell me what to do. Tell me what you like. You won't be sorry, Mr. Pennington. I guarantee you won't be sorry," teased Amanda, her self-fondled breasts standing at attention, taut nipples taking dead aim at Jet, now gaping in anticipatory awe.

"Yes, ma'am." Jet took her. He suckled each nipple for five minutes, the left one first. He had his way with her. He showed her what to do. He told her what he liked. There was no chance he would be sorry.

The couple locked loins for two straight hours. Two climaxes for Jet and three for Amanda, above and beyond the call of duty. Fellatio and cunnilingus were featured. Both parties achieved precisely their objective; Jet was blessed with a unique birthday present, the sexual companionship of a promising apprenticeship courtesan; Amanda was blessed with a leg up on both lifetime financial security and sexual emancipation/self-actualization. They each slept soundly.

After the Amanda workout, Tuesday night with Helen was tame. Wednesday night was new and different for everyone. The girls resolved to venture a three way, a triple, a two-on-one, with Jet. Since none of the three had participated in a ménage a trois, everybody was edgy and unsettled until Amanda said to Jet, "Mr. Pennington, please help me undress Helen."

All hell broke loose. The first scene of the episode commenced with Jet lying on his back in the king size bed. Amanda rode Jet in the female superior position facing Helen, who unabashedly relished cunnilingus. The girls could not stop giggling and smiling at one another. Everyone was in seventh heaven. Since imagination knows no bounds, you can predict how the script played out for the remainder of Wednesday night. Kinky is the word.

Jet senses he is getting younger. The girls know they are growing older and wiser. This proves girls and boys are different. Nineteen year old Helen is pregnant. Eighteen year old Amanda is working on it. Life is good.

*

Early Thursday morning Jet met with Estill Barnes in New Providence, the business district of the Turks & Caicos Islands. Estill booked into the Amanyara Resort at Providenciales. The resort features contemporary Caribbean Island settings with villas scattered among small ponds and indigenous vegetation. Rugged stone outcroppings abound. A fine sand alabaster beach is in close walking distance. The resort is a private, exclusive out-of-the way executive vacation spot.

"Estill, how much money did I pay you for this gig?"

"You know damn well you paid me one lump sum in advance, $100,000 per month for 30 months; no discount for early payment. The check cleared in November, 2018, three million smackers. Our contract terminates on T-Day. We have not negotiated terms and conditions for my two year extension."

"$5 million total for the two year extension, Estill. Two payments, each payment one year in advance - $2.5 million, commencing on T-day, $3 million for the option year."

"Done. Half in euros, half in Canadian."

"Agreed."

"To date, what did I get for my money, Estill?"

"There are many ways to answer the question, Jet. Let me begin by telling you I'm uncomfortable if I don't get things done early and come in under budget and you are uncomfortable if you get things done early and do not come in over budget."

"Our target date is April 5, 2021. Today is March 4th. I am 100% finished with my responsibilities; T-Day approaches; four weeks away. I came in one month early and 10 billion dollars under budget. You authorized me to spend 40 billion dollars. I spent 30 billion dollars."

"I'm impressed. Where do we go from here?"

"First, I'm not responsible for nuclear weapons. Second, I'm here for final review of our T- Day Schedule of Events document. Since I haven't received any gripes from you regarding the document, I can only assume you have no objection to the projected activities of our military commanders and their commissioned subalterns."

"You assume correctly. Nobody could have done it any better. The section on post T-Day anticipated problems and corrective action to be taken when and if we confront such problems, is pure genius. We revised the ten T-Day activities. Review those with me."

"If there is no first day nuke strike, a number of agenda items compete for next event down the pike on T-Day, including but not limited to:

1. Emergency and Medical Care for T-Day survivors;

2. Our Charity mobilizes to assist T-Day survivors;

3. Close all banks; a bank holiday for seven calendar days; ATM - $400/day;

4. Close the Federal Reserve Bank permanently;

5. Close the IRS permanently;

6. Close Islamic mosques; deport all imams; illegalize Islam in the USA."

7. Shut down all TV and radio stations, emergency transmissions only;

8. Establish national 8:00 pm curfew;

9. Withdraw from the United Nations, kick the UN out of our country;

10. Terminate (i) personal income taxes; and (ii) Social Security taxes. No withholding for either tax. Wage earners keep all they earn.

"Question for you, Estill. In your brainstorming did you come across facts which at that time were not important enough to bring to my attention? What, if anything, did you omit from your T-Day document?"

"Nothing, Jet. I left everything on the playing field. My life's work, my reputation, my legacy, is in that document; depends upon the validity of that document. If our militia Army executes as anticipated, we remain projected to achieve control of the majority of American Society no later than April 12 2021. I'm pleased to announce that we are on track, precisely on schedule."

"Solemn statement, Estill, solemn. Fair enough; four weeks away from owning and controlling the United States of America. I'll be damned. Thank you, Estill. Three days notice for our next meeting. Good luck to us all."

Four weeks and counting. Time to tie up every loose end as though I will not be alive after April 5, 2021. Never fail to address a repugnant contingency.

37
THE GENERALS
Reluctant Necessity

Upon return to Bermuda, Jet created his personal schedule from early March to Monday, April 5th, commencing with a General Tommy Thompson interview on Monday, March 8th in Cincinnati Ohio; followed by interview with General Bull Flanagan on Tuesday, March 9th, in Salt Lake City, Utah at 9:00 am MST; later that same day with Estill; time, open.

Since Jet had a positive experience with the girls in the Turks & Caicos Islands, he invited them on the excursion to Cincinnati/Salt Lake. They both enthusiastically accepted.

The Gulfstream G650 departed Bermuda for Cincinnati/Northern Kentucky International Airport at noon on Monday, flying 1,208 miles and arriving in Hebron, Kentucky at 2:42 pm EST. Jet checked in at the Courtyard by Marriot in Erlanger, Kentucky. At 4:00 pm, he is scheduled to powwow with four star General Tommy Thompson, eight miles away in a meeting room of the Wingate/Erlanger Hotel.

The Marriott hotel suite has a living room, a bathroom and a bedroom with two king size beds, which Jet reckons will satisfy requirements for a weekday tryst. The girls are on their own; free to watch TV and gossip among themselves until 5:30 pm. Ewe is at a different hotel. He is preparing a flight plan to depart the Cincinnati area tomorrow, Tuesday, at 7:00 am, for Salt Lake City, Utah.

Prior to General Tommy Thompson's arrival, Jet took a taxi to the nearby Wingate hotel and cased the conference room for 30 minutes, the cab driver waiting ½ mile away, on customer hold for up to two hours. As usual, the general was five minutes early for his 4:00 pm appointment, his fourth meeting with Jet.

Jet, alias Bernard Scudder, said, "Good afternoon, General Thompson. It's good to see you again, sir. We ought to be able to cover everything I have in mind within a half hour. For openers, I'm reluctant to share with you what I'm going to say; but you would find out about it by the grapevine anyway so here goes."

"It's tough enough to take on an adversary like the United States Military. It's even more difficult when compatriots and associates you depend upon turn out to be treasonous turncoats. As I told you earlier, three retired Army generals with identical credentials are under consideration for selection as joint commanding generals of all military forces for a new American government to be formed within the next two months."

"General Benjamin Tate was executed last week, along with his wife and his sons, their wives and their children, because General Tate cooperated with the current United States government by attempting to arrange for my capture and for my execution."

"My remedy was swift. Death to traitors against our revolt. Death to their families. It gives me no great pleasure to tell you this but I'm really serious about what I'm doing. I presume we are on the same page."

General Thompson nods his head affirmatively.

"Enough of depressing news. Our forces are postured on three days' notice to take over the current United States government. T-Day is Wednesday, April 14th. Remember that date, it is critically important."

"Yes, Mr. Scudder."

"General, are you ready willing and able to take command of our revolutionary forces within the next five weeks?"

"Yes, sir, Mr. Scudder, I am."

"In the event you are not selected, are you ready, willing and able to serve as my number two man totally independent of the general in command and be my alternate in the event the general in command is for whatsoever reason unable or unwilling to serve?"

"Yes, sir, Mr. Scudder, I am."

"What is your salary, General Thompson?"

"$10,000 a month plus expenses, Mr. Scudder."

"I'm raising your salary to $20,000 a month backdated to January 1, 2021, increasing to $40,000 a month as of T-day. Acceptable to you, general?"

"Yes, sir, Mr. Scudder; acceptable."

"Assuming we all have reservations about many things, what reservations do you have about this duty assignment, General?"

"I would think I have the same reservations as anybody in the same boat, Mr. Scudder. I'm a traitor to the United States of America. I have deep-seated pain about that. On the other hand, the government of the USA is currently run by scoundrels, traitors and otherwise worthless sons of bitches who should be burned at the stake. Is that sufficient, Mr. Scudder?"

"On the button, General Thompson. My feelings precisely. Remember, T-Day has been selected, Wednesday April 14, 2021. Please confirm the date for me, General."

"Wednesday, April 14th. "

"Thank you, General Thompson. It's a pleasure working with you. If you move or change cell phones, please keep yourself available. Can you handle that, General?"

"Yes, I can, Mr. Scudder. You will always be able to locate me."

"OK, General, within two weeks you will be provided day by day schedules for the first week of operations post T-Day. Thank you, sir, and good day," said Jet.

Both parties left the conference room. General Thompson drove his late model Buick back to his retirement home in Hamilton, Ohio, 25 miles north northwest of Cincinnati. Jet returned via taxi to his soon to be putative wives for the first of two three-way orgies on this trip. Life is good.

*

Jet and Ewe flew the Gulfstream G650 from Cincinnati to Salt Lake City, Utah on Tuesday morning, a distance of 1,652 miles. Departing at 7:00 am EST, they landed at Salt Lake City at 8:15 am MST, gaining two hours.

Jet has a 9:30 am meeting with General Bull Flanagan at a hotel near the Salt Lake airport, as well as an 11:00 am meeting with Estill Barnes in a different hotel in downtown Salt Lake City.

"Ewe, we are on the ground here in Salt Lake City for about five hours. I want you to rent a car, share brunch with the girls and give them a brief automobile tour of the city. Take the girls along with you to flight operations and show them how to prepare and file an IFR flight plan to our next destination, New York City, LaGuardia. Return to the aircraft in time for a 1:15 pm departure."

"Yes, boss."

At 9:30 am, General Bull Flanagan received the same pitch provided to General Tommy Thompson, except Bull Flanagan was told that T-Day is Thursday, April 22nd. Jet is testing the generals for treason. Idle tongues can be life threatening in treasonous situations. World War II version: 'Loose lips sink ships.'

Next Jet met with Estill Barnes in a Salt Lake City Holiday Inn Express at 11:00 am for discussion and review of the 300 page Schedule of Events document.

"Estill, I'm comfortable with the entire document except for how we handle local, even national, uprisings by military and civilians who are unhappy, for whatsoever reason, with our initial martial law activities."

"With good reason, Jet," said Estill. "The way I see it, the primary problem is convincing active duty military generals and admirals that we have legitimate control over the United States military. Toward that end I have targeted every Goddamn active duty general and admiral in a command position. They will all be systematically arrested, cashiered out of the service and incarcerated for a minimum of six months, then retired."

"This reduces the probability of initial and follow-on military interference with our martial law activities. Additionally, an adequate number of qualified patriot troops have been assigned the responsibility of neutralizing any bellicose resistance by either lower ranking military personnel or civilians. We will ruthlessly kill any and all individuals resisting martial law activities; after reasonable warning."

"Impressive, Estill."

"A program of cashiering out, retiring, all other active-duty generals and admirals will commence on T–Day +8 days. Six months after T-Day, there won't be any holdover active duty generals or admirals; all gone and forgotten."

"Civilian police, federal marshals, and National Guard and reserve troops will be handled in a similar manner."

"When all else fails I have established the equivalent of a Praetorian Guard, that elite bodyguard of troops protecting Roman Emperors. These men are our most trusted, most valuable, most capable militia men, primarily prior service Special Forces, Rangers and Seals. Hired guns, killers one and all. I anticipate no one standing in their way. Deployed in units. I named the six units the 'Responders,' Responder Group 1, Responder Group 2, etc. These guys are intended to plug the dikes when unusual difficulties are encountered."

"Enough, Estill. I am sure as hell thankful you and I were assigned to the same squadron when we were first lieutenants."

"Careful what you're thankful for, Jet."

"That's excellent advice, partner," said Jet as the pair of revolutionaries departed the hotel separately.

*

The Gulfstream G650 took off from Salt Lake International Airport at 1:30 pm MST with an ETA of 8:05 pm to LaGuardia airport, a distance of 1,979 miles, losing two hours (MST to EST). After climbing to cruising altitude of 30,000 feet, Jet invited the girls to occupy Ewe's co-pilot seat, one at a time, 30 minutes each, Helen first, Amanda second.

One hour later Ewe opened the cockpit access door to reclaim the co-pilot seat. "Ewe, take the Captain's seat," said Jet.

"Amanda, Ewe is going to explain to you how some of the instruments work. Meanwhile Helen and I are going to join the mile-high club."

Ewe smiled and shook his head in mock disbelief. Since Amanda does not know what the mile-high club is, she figures she will ask Jet later about that organization. Jet closed the cockpit door and entered the passenger cabin where Helen was reading a magazine and drinking bottled water with fresh lemon wedge.

"Helen, drop your drawers. I am initiating you into the mile-high club."

"What's that, Mr. Pennington?" asked Helen.

"You'll see, my dear."

A variation on a theme, Helen saw, Helen came and Helen conquered. "Do I get a membership card, Mr. Pennington?"

Jet smiled, "Yes, you do Helen, in due time."

Twenty minutes later Helen tapped Amanda on the shoulder, whispered into her ear and switched seats with Amanda, who headed for the cabin. When the cockpit door closed behind her Amanda disrobed and appeared before Jet in her birthday suit, ready for initiation.

"I'll be damned. The pair of you are way ahead of me. I need to go back to school to keep up with you two."

"Remember, I am your courtesan, Mr. Pennington. I take it and I dish it out. Come here, Mr. Pennington, I have something for you, up or down, your choice."

"How about sideways?"

"I am not Chinese."

"Touche, wench. I'm impressed. I admit it. You are 18 years old and a quicker study than I'll ever be. You don't need any instructions; you are already journeyman qualified. You are courtesan material, young lady," smiled the lecher.

Thirty minutes of silence, interrupted by grunts, groans, and squeals. The mile-high club dual initiation was heavenly.

The girls were elated. Their man is a pilot. He knows everything about cockpit dials, gadgets, switches and controls. He is a genius. Both Helen and Amanda deplaned in New York City with newfound respect for Jet. They loved him even more than ever.

For the uninitiated, the mile-high club is exclusively reserved for those persons, male and female, who have engaged in fornication at more than 5,280 feet above ground level ("AGL"). Established by pilots in the propeller age, the club is open to crew members and passengers as well. There are no honorary memberships in the mile-high club.

The trio of lovers settled in Tuesday night at the Hampton Inn at 102-40 Ditmars Boulevard, East Elmhurst, New York. Ewe bedded down at a nearby hotel. Jet scheduled their departure from New York City to Bermuda at 5:00 pm tomorrow, Wednesday.

The girls were full of it, enraptured. They couldn't stop talking about 'flying the airplane,' up so high and 'moving so fast,' in such a beautiful, giant machine. They both wanted to know where and how Jet learned to fly and if they could learn to fly.

Jet said in the Air Force, and yes, if they wanted to learn to fly, they could learn when they moved to Utah. Neither girl forgot that promise. Neither girl asked about the mile-high club.

*

Up early on Wednesday, Jet took the girls to the New York City garment district and later to the New York City Diamond Center. Each girl was allotted $10,000 to spend on garments and another $10,000 to spend on jewelry. They both went crazy.

As Jet anticipated, Helen was conservative and Amanda was way far out aggressive. *She would have tattoos if I allowed it.*

The garment district is smaller than one square mile and runs from 5th avenue to 9th avenue and from 34th Street to 42nd Street in Manhattan. With 15 billion dollars in annual sales, New York City is the global fashion center for the USA. Major fashion labels such as Oscar de la Renta, Calvin Klein and Liz Claiborne have showrooms and production facilities in the garment district.

Non-stop shopping from 10:00 am to 3:00 pm, no lunch. No interference by Jet as the girls looked at, tried on and selected one expensive garment after another to their heart's delight. Jet remained low-profile, flashing a credit card from time to time. He vicariously enjoyed the girl's youthful enthusiasm. Hopefully they won't ever change.

Both teenagers preferred the garment district. They shamelessly implored Jet to change their allowance to $15,000 in garments and $5,000 in jewelry. Jet capitulated. He changed the allowances to $20,000 for garments and $5,000 for jewelry. No one within 20 feet could hear over the squeals.

The garment boxes more than filled the Gulfstream cabin. Back home, two limousines could not accommodate the haul. Ewe had to stay behind and safekeep the extra garments as one of the limousines made a repeat trip to the mansion to tote the excess feminine loot to the mansion.

Helen and Amanda are no longer loose ends. How is my daughter handling the tails and bugs, or is it bugs and tails? I never can remember.

*

Back on Monday, January 18th, Natalie reported to the FBI through routine administrative channels that she was being illegally tailed and that illegal surveillance devices had been recently planted in her townhome.

The next day FBI techies fine tooth combed her townhome. They discovered bugs and surveillance cameras. The techies dismantled and deactivated the bugs and video devices the same day. As well, the technicians reported to FBI internal security the identification, existence, location and target of the surveillance devices, along with the date the devices were dismantled and the disposition of the devices.

On Wednesday, January 20, 2021, FBI internal security: (i) reported the personal tails violation to the Secret Service; and (ii) reported the townhome surveillance violations to the CIA.

Thereafter, as is so often the case in government investigations, the clock ceased ticking on activity related to Natalie's bugs and tails complaint. Leisurely, the Secret Service and the CIA conducted a slow motion, time-consuming investigation. Much later the Secret Service coordinated with the FBI and the CIA.

Even later still, on March 3, 2021 the Secret Service issued a report to Chief of Staff Tom Redding regarding both the tails and the surveillance devices. Only the shadow knows who sat on the report, FBI, Secret Service or Tom Redding. Who cares who sat on the report? At least action was taken, which is unusual in similar situations, a la Presidents Obama and Wilson.

The CIA admitted they planted the surveillance devices, the bugs. The Secret Service admitted they were responsible for shadowing Natalie, the tails. The FBI was notified that the tails were terminated by the Secret Service upon receipt by the Secret Service of the FBI's notice that the tails were occurring. Nobody made any excuses because nobody cared. No corrective action, No reprimands, no punishment. Business as usual in the Washington DC bureaucracy.

No attention to detail; no sense of urgency, ever. No notice to the FBI by the CIA regarding bugs. Interesting.

*

"Mitch, this is Tom Redding. Drop everything you're doing; take the CIA stand-by helicopter to the White house landing pad and report to my office at once."

"Yes, sir."

Mitch knew he screwed up something awful. Within 15 minutes, as lone passenger he boarded a 150 mph Marine helicopter headed from Langley AFB to the White House, 175 miles away.

At 1:30 pm on March 5, 2021, Tom's secretary showed Mitch into Tom Redding's office. Tom pointed to the chair in front of his oversized mahogany desk, indicating for Mitch to sit down, "Read this, Mitch."

Two lines into the first paragraph of a documentary report on the penetration, incursion and invasion of the personal home of an important US government employee, Mitch knew Natalie had discovered Mitch's surveillance gadgets and reported the 'find' up through the ranks rather than petulantly bawl to Tom or the President. *Wise lady.*

"I got caught with my pants down, Tom. I won't bother to say I'm sorry. I know how this makes me look, how it makes CIA and the Secret Service look. It won't happen again."

"Strike one, Mitch. Perfection is an ideal, not an absolute requirement, but you don't get a second strike," said Tom Redding. "Make sure that the record of your surveillance, if any, is eradicated in total, destroyed, removed, disappears from all places of any kind or sort, however remote, forever, not to be recovered, ever. Is that clear, perfectly clear?" reprimanded Tom Redding to the non-promotable Deputy Director of the CIA.

"Yes, sir," responded a resigned Mitch Donahue, on his way to the Marine helicopter with his tail in a stationary position between his legs.

38
OVAL OFFICE
Mitch Drawn & Quartered

Natalie invited Supreme Court Justice Andrew Thompson, the jurist she clerked for at the US Supreme Court 15 years ago, to the Monday, March 8, USTF-18 weekly 9:15 am live briefing for the president and Tom Redding by Natalie and Mitch Donahue.

"Mr. President, do I have your permission to tape this briefing?"

"Yes, you do," said the president, mildly concerned.

Neither the President, Tom Redding nor Mitch Donahue knew what to expect. "Justice Thompson, please swear the witness, Mr. Mitchell Donahue," said Natalie.

"Do you. Mitchell Donahue, swear to tell the truth, the whole truth and nothing but the truth, so help you God?" Justice Thompson asked Mitch, intentionally including the reference to God which former president Obama so diligently attempted to eliminate.

"Objection," Donahue stoically responded.

"Overruled," said the Justice. "State yes or no." The president shook his head yes.

"Yes," said Mitch Donahue.

Natalie asked, "Did there ever come a time when you caused, directly or indirectly, or had anything to do, directly or indirectly, with surveillance bugs or any other monitoring equipment, audio, video or otherwise, being installed in the personal dwelling of Natalie Taylor and hence monitored?"

"Yes."

Tom Redding knows this is his Waterloo, the day he loses it all. Mitch is confused and nervous. He is used to asking questions, not answering them. He does not understand that he is flailing around in the mouth of a shark, soon to be devoured.

"Same question, but directed to a 'tail,' someone who follows someone else. Did there ever come a time when you directly or indirectly caused a 'tail' to be put on me, Natalie Taylor, or had anything to do, directly or indirectly with any other party putting a 'tail' on me?"

"Yes."

"Regarding surveillance and bugs, who or which party installed surveillance, audio or video or other, in my personal dwelling?"

"The CIA, by and through an installer/monitor officer. I don't recall his name."

"At whose order did the 'installer/monitor' install such equipment?"

"At my order."

"Who, if anyone, ordered or authorized you to have such equipment installed?"

"Tom Redding."

"Did Tom Redding order you or authorize you to have such equipment installed?"

"Order."

The jig is up, the presence of Justice Thompson precludes a presidential pass for me on this one, thought Tom Redding. Mitch Donahue still does not know what is happening to him.

"Was there probable cause for the surveillance devices and the bugs to be installed in my personal dwelling?"

"No."

"Same line of questions, but regarding the tails."

"At Tom Redding's order, I had the Secret Service tail Natalie Taylor, 24/7."

I'm history, down for the count, KO'ed by a female; I had a good run, Chief of Staff and all that. My lucrative part time job is also terminated, that's for sure.

"Was there probable cause for a tail to be assigned to follow and track me?"

"No."

"I have no further questions, Mr. Donahue. Justice Thompson, you are excused, sir," said Natalie as she switched off her recording device. Justice Thompson departed the oval office. Remaining behind were President Wilson, Chief of Staff Redding, Mitch Donahue and Natalie.

"Mr. President, I respectfully demand that you publish an order disqualifying Mr. Donahue from any US government job which requires a federal security clearance."

"I respectfully demand that by executive order you cancel Mr. Mitchell Donahue's security clearance and terminate his employment with the United States Government; either as a direct government employee, or as an employee with any entity which has any agreement and provides services to the US Government. Also to terminate any right the same Mitchell Donahue has to government benefits, including pension, to the extent permitted by law."

"Your demands are granted, Ms. Taylor. Draft the document."

"On your desk before the end of the day, Mr. President."

Switching her recorder back on, Natalie surprised the president by addressing the Deputy Director of the CIA, "Mitchell Donahue, I hereby place you under arrest pursuant to Federal Law as relates to violation of personal privacy, misuse of government property and personnel, and other offenses as determined after further investigation. You have the right to an attorney. If you cannot afford an attorney, one will be appointed to defend you. Anything you say can be used against you in a court of law. Do you understand your rights, Mr. Donahue?"

"Yes."

After turning her recorder off, Natalie restrained Mitch Donahue with handcuffs. He commenced crying. He sobbed violently as he was led from the oval office by Natalie. She transferred custody of the prisoner to Federal Marshall Timothy Jones, who on a hunch Natalie arranged to stand by for the arrest of Mitch Donahue. Natalie plans ahead.

Marshall Jones accompanied the handcuffed ex-Deputy Director of the CIA to the Washington, DC Central Detention Facility (CDF/DC Jail), a booking facility located in Southeast Washington DC at 1901 D Street, SE. Mitch's CIA career is finished. His detention was the first arrest ever made in the Oval Office.

"Mr. President, the important government office Mr. Thomas Redding holds and his 30 year relationship with you prohibit me from making any recommendation or comment regarding allegations by Mitch Donahue against the interests of Mr. Redding. I defer to your better judgment, sir."

"Thank you, Natalie; we shall proceed after a five minute recess. I have a matter which I must timely attend to."

The President and Tom Redding stepped outside the oval office. "Goddamn it, Tom. Find Donahue; thank him for taking the fall for both of us. Assure him we will take care of him financially, for life. Make sure he personally continues to shadow Natalie pursuant to any leads he has uncovered to date, his activities to be conducted off government premises and absent government records, recordings or videos, but with clandestine CIA support."

"Right away, Mr. President; consider it done," said Tom Redding.

Bullshit is what you are, Tom Redding, bullshit; and I am mucking it up.

*

Tom Redding did not accompany the president back to the oval office after the five minute break. Continuing once again one-on-one with the president in the oval office Natalie said, "Mr. President, we have a lead."

"The name of the alleged nuclear buyer is Enrique Echeverria, a Venezuelan national residing on Bird Cay, a small 247 acre privately owned island on the southern edge of the Berry Islands area of the Bahamas, about midway between Nassau and Freeport; closer to, and 37 miles from, Nassau. The cay is accessible only by boat."

"Bird Cay is owned by a Panamanian trust, whose trustee is a licensed Panamanian lawyer. The lawyer won't talk to us, citing attorney-client privilege. Although Mr. Echeverria was born in Caracas, Venezuela, we are proceeding under the assumption he is a radicalized Islamist."

"The Bahamian government has granted to us the authority to arrest Mr. Echeverria. We are permitted to use force if necessary to ensure a successful arrest. We have coordinated with the Navy and the Coast Guard, both of which have provided to us assets and cooperation necessary to make a personal arrest in a foreign nation."

"Mr. Echeverria is not presently in the Berry Islands. The Coast Guard is on station and performing surveillance of Mr. Echeverria's Bird Cay bungalow."

"In response to our quarter billion dollar bounty offer, a high ranking Pakistani government official ratted out Mr. Echeverria, maintaining that for two days within the last six weeks Mr. Echeverria personally visited the second ranking government official in the Pakistani government, in Karachi, Pakistan. The purpose of the visit was to discuss the purchase and sale of nuclear weapons."

"Allegedly the Pakistan government agreed to sell Mr. Echeverria four nuclear weapons. Delivery date is pending, to occur in the near future. We have no information regarding weapons selling price. We have not yet confirmed this allegation by other intelligence sources but are working hard to do so."

"We entered into a written agreement with the Pakistani national, Nouri Mohal and deposited 250 million dollars into an escrow account at a reputable international bank, pending proof positive Mr. Echeverria is our man. Be advised we will continue our task force investigation until and unless Mr. Echeverria is proven to be culpable."

"The name of the bank is All World Commercial Bank, NA, a Cayman Islands Corporation with home office in George Town, Cayman Islands and branches in Zurich, Switzerland, London, England, Hamilton, Bermuda and Hong Kong, China. The bank has gross assets of 135 billion dollars and a net worth of 24 billion dollars."

"There is no need to replace Mitch Donahue on our joint task force. I know and get along well with the number 2 and number 3 guys from CIA who are assigned to the task force."

"Very well, Natalie."

"Today's business is complete. I'll keep you advised, Mr. President."

"You are excused and commended for a job well done, Natalie."

Donahue, you son of a bitch, I buried you. Will the president bury Tom Redding? Probably not. Southerners are true blue to one another. Enrique Echeverria versus William Pennington, is there a connection there?

*

That afternoon Tom Redding visited the oval office. "Redding, what do you have for me? It had better be good?"

"Mr. President, I ran this by Justice. After I explained the delicate nature of our situation, Attorney General Patricia Samuelson recommended a Presidential pardon for Mitchell Donahue, along with termination of his federal civil service employment for cause, simultaneous with his normal retirement. Since Mitch is 57 years old with 32 years of government service, he is eligible for immediate civil service retirement."

"I bought off on her recommendations. Please sign this pardon document," said Tom Redding as he handed the paper work for Mitch's pardon to the president.

"Tom, am I going to have trouble with this? The Taylor bitch is smart as a whip. If she gets wind of our shenanigans there will be hell to pay, I assure you."

"I have us covered, boss. CIA will cooperate with us. They are none too keen on Natalie Taylor since she sliced and diced one of their own with no warning."

"Mitch was booked a half hour ago. When his pardon hits the booking agency he will be released on his own recognizance. His CIA office in Norfolk has been closed, his personal staff reassigned, and his classified responsibilities transferred to other agents."

"His personal effects and the original entire file on Natalie Taylor will be delivered to Mitch tomorrow. He will never again set foot on CIA premises at Langley AFB, Virginia. As of today, the CIA has no record of any investigation of any kind or sort regarding any aspect of Natalie Taylor's past performance or behavior."

"An offshore CIA slush fund entity will enter into a written agreement with an offshore Cayman Islands corporation to pay the corporation $10,000 per month for five years. Mitch will own the corporation. He walks with non-taxable entitlement to $600,000 over the next five years, supplemented by his normal CIA retirement annuity."

"Mitch will be a party to a clandestine contact with a CIA designee. The designee will coordinate with Mitch regarding the surveillance of Natalie Taylor, her father and her new Canadian fiancé. I reiterate, Mitch will never again set foot on CIA premises."

"That's it, Mr. President. Wrapped up and ready for delivery, any questions, sir?"

"I suppose not, Tom. We can do no better, given what we have to work with," said Bill Wilson as he reluctantly executed Mitch Donahue's pardon document.

*

Later, Stony received a telephone call from MMI. "Mr. Randolph, this is Dean Philip West at MMI."

"Yes, I recall meeting you, Dean West; what do you have for me, sir?"

"Please understand this is highly irregular because we have regulations prohibiting dissemination of any oral or written comment regarding our cadets to anyone other than parents. However, I recall the special circumstances under which Donald Branson enrolled with us six weeks ago."

"As a courtesy, I am informing you that Donald's grandmother, a Mrs. Branson of Nashville, Tennessee, picked up Donald Branson yesterday. Donald told us he is not coming back to MMI. His father is dead and he is going to reside in the future with his paternal grandparents. I am sorry to be providing this news to you, sir."

"Think nothing of it, Dean West. Thank you for the heads up. You may close your file on Don Branson. Please attempt to obtain a grade of withdrew passing for his permanent records."

"Consider it done, Mr. Randolph."

Jet is not going to like this at all. Don Branson is as good as dead. Damn it all to hell. Don Branson is my fiancé's son. Since Don is living with his grandmother, I'm going to give the kid a break. I'll hold off fingering him to Jet and hope for the best. Preston & Associates have a babysitting assignment in their future.

*

Even later, primary federal mole Tom Redding informed his contact at the mansion that President Wilson, the FBI, the CIA, the NSA and USTF-18 have all been briefed that T-day has been adjusted to and is set for Thursday, April 22, 2021. Of all people, Bull Flanagan turned out to be a traitor. He, his wife, his divorced daughter and her two children were 'taken out' on Wednesday, March 10th. Jet is down to one general. A good soldier makes do with the assets he has, not the assets he would like to have. Jet is a good soldier.

39
BAHAMAS ASSAULT
Seal Team 2

On Thursday March 11, the Atlantic Area Commander, three star Admiral Anthony Obermyer, greeted Natalie Taylor, "Director Taylor, welcome to Portsmouth, Virginia and the Atlantic Area of the United States Coast Guard."

"Admiral Paul Tsonga, Commandant of the Coast Guard, directed me to provide to you anything and everything you require, which is within our operational capability to provide. It's a first of its kind order, the first one I ever received or ever heard of anyone else receiving. You must be working on a hell of an important issue, Director Taylor. Rest assured I'll help you any way I can."

"Thank you, Admiral Obermyer. My mission is of extreme importance to the United States of America. To my understanding your organization is the one I can count on to get the job done."

"We believe a radical Islamic terrorist is holed up on a small private island in the Bahamas, specifically 247 acre Bird Cay in the Berry Islands, 37 miles northwest of Nassau. The 37 miles is all open ocean."

"The FBI is authorized by the government of the Bahamas to

arrest a man named Enrique Echeverria, a Venezuelan citizen residing on Bird Cay. We do not have the wherewithal to navigate the Atlantic Ocean, posture manpower and assets, then make an arrest. We understand you are experienced and prepared for missions such as ours and are ready, willing and able to help us."

"True, Director Taylor. We received word from Admiral Tsonga describing your mission and your request for assistance. We created a plan which we believe will meet with your approval. Please wait for Commander Charlie Owens to join us."

Admiral Obermyer hit the hot button on his intercom and said, "Send Commander Owens in."

Ten seconds later Commander Owens saluted the Admiral and said, "Commander Owens reporting as ordered, Admiral."

"Stand at ease, Commander. Please meet Director Natalie Taylor of Special Joint Task Force–18. Director Taylor is working directly for the President of the United States."

"My pleasure, Director Taylor."

"Same here, Commander. You have the floor, sir."

Mildly taken aback by having been referred to as sir, Commander Owens commenced, "Director Taylor, I command a National Security Cutter (NSC) named the "Hamilton" (WMSL 753), one of sister ships which are the largest and most sophisticated in the United States Coast Guard, 403' in length."

"Each NSC is an on-site operational-level headquarters for law enforcement, for defense and national security missions involving Coast Guard and for any other government entity. In addition to size, speed and on-station duration time, special features of NSCs include, without limitation: (i) advanced communication capabilities; (ii) sophisticated surveillance equipment: (iii) an on board helicopter; and (iv) two small attack boats."

"For armament we have one Mk 110 57-mm naval gun system, one Phalanx 20-mm close-in weapon system, four .50-caliber machine guns and two M240B 7.62-mm machine guns."

"We control the arrest phase of your mission. Navy Seals make the physical arrest. We selected Seal Team 2 from Little Creek, Virginia to penetrate the Bird Cay dwelling and capture your alleged perpetrator. The perp will be delivered by us to your custody at the location on Admiral Obermyer's delivery order to us. You are invited to observe arrest activities from our ship, if you so desire."

"Yes, commander, I would like to observe your work. How soon do you begin?"

"The schedule is yours, ma'am. We can commence tomorrow if you give the go-ahead. The Hamilton is on station within ten miles of your target. To get there from here takes four hours by fixed wing transport to Jacksonville and by helicopter on to Bird Cay. It's noon here in Virginia. We can be on station in the Bahamas by 4:00 PM local time, EST."

"On second thought my presence might interfere with your operation, Commander. You fly to the Hamilton today and commence your mission as early as first light tomorrow. I suppose you will surround the building with Seals. You might position the seals prior to dawn and assault the building at dawn."

"We will take that into consideration, ma'am. Please be advised a U.S. Navy Seal Team commander has final say on all Seal operations and tactics."

"I understand, Commander. Admiral Obermyer, please arrange to have the perp flown by helicopter to Florida, then by military jet aircraft to Washington, DC. Admiral, I believe we are in good hands with 'All State,' wouldn't you say so, sir?"

"Indeed I would, Director."

Jet does not agree. Jet is ready for the best the Navy and Coast Guard can bring to the table; Seals and their press clippings be damned.

*

A Seal Team is commanded by a Navy Commander (O-5) and is composed of a Headquarters element and eight 16-man Seal Platoons. The platoons can be deployed as 8-man Squads, 4-man Fire Teams or 2-man Sniper/Reconnaissance Teams.

A Seal Platoon is composed of two junior officers and 14 enlisted men. The platoon commander is normally a Navy Lieutenant (O-3). More often than not Seals function as 8-man Squads or 4-man Fire Teams. Every Seal is dive, parachute and demolitions trained.

An 8-man squad from first Platoon of Seal Team 2 is assigned to Natalie's Bird Cay mission. Commander Charlie Owens handpicked platoon commander Lieutenant Elmer Amundson to lead the assault. Lieutenant Amundson selected 13 of the ship's best Seals for the mission, his 8-man squad and five specialists, one each sniper, communicator, medic, heavy weapons operator and technical surveillance specialist, a total of 14 professionally trained maritime killers, including the platoon commander.

"Elmer, review your assault tactics with me," said Commander Owens.

"Commander, assuming no 'unusual unknowns,' this mission is routine. We open with flash/bangs, battering ram for the side door, then reconnaissance of the premises with capture of the lone perpetrator as the sole objective."

"Our tactics are to bang and flash the building with stun grenades, simultaneously to breach a side door, to enter the building, and within 20 seconds or less, to conduct a room by room search, locating and neutralizing the perpetrator."

"Lethal force is authorized for self-protection. Four Seals to enter the building, point man David Thomas, along with Smith, Armstrong and Villalobos."

"OK. Allowances for unusual unknowns?"

"First and foremost, mines and booby traps. Yesterday's advance patrol tested clean for mines, both visible claymores and buried devices. Electronic sweeps of the building were negative, but you and I know those sweeps are not always reliable."

"Our sensors observed activity inside the dwelling, talking, as in telephone use, TV and cooking. One person only. To our understanding we were undetected. No other comment. Our point man is one of the best; highly experienced and competent. We depend upon him to sniff trouble out. Business as usual for Seal Team 2."

*

A stun grenade, sometimes referred to as a flash grenade, flash bang or sound bomb, temporarily disorients the senses of sight and sound. Although deaths have occurred, stun grenades are normally nonlethal.

A stun grenade produces an extreme flash of light and noise of approximately 170 decibels. Loud banging impairs hearing temporarily and causes loss of balance because fluid in the middle ear is disturbed.

A target's vision is diminished for about five seconds after a flash; thereafter relatively normal eyesight resumes. After images diminish the ability to aim and fire rifles and hand guns. Stun grenades were first used by the British in the 1970s.

Prior to first light on Friday, March 12th, the 14 Seals surrounded Enrique Echeverria's bungalow on Bird Cay. Each of the four home entry invaders carries an HK 416, a German assault rifle designed by Heckler & Koch, the weapon which killed Osama bin Laden. Each man is also equipped with the favorite pistol of Navy Seals and a host of other handgun aficionados, a Sig Sauer P226.

As the sun breached the Eastern horizon at 7:19 am, Lieutenant Amundson gave the signal to commence attack. In seconds the side door crumbled under battering ram force. Simultaneously, stun grenades were cast into the house through the now open door and through three smashed windows in the four room Bahamian bungalow.

Point man Dave Thomas rushed past the doorway and continued straight ahead, searching in the smoke-filled living room for the perpetrator. Close behind three Seals fanned out across the room, each headed for his assigned search sector. Villalobos heard the recording first, in an Arabic accented loud but slightly garbled male voice: "Allah Akbar; Allah Akbar; Allah Akbar; Allah Akbar."

"Abort! Abort! Abort!"

"Ambush! Ambush! Ambush!"

"Get outta here! Abort! Abort! Abort!"

Villalobos turned tail and ran for the side door. He did not make it.

Fifty pounds of booby-trapped Composition C-4 high explosive material does much more than extensive damage. In the flash of an eye the bungalow disappeared, along with four Seals and a planted cadaver for good measure. The only thing remaining on the foundation site other than smoke and super-fine debris was a concrete enclosed safe containing a passport, a driver's license and credit cards in the name of Enrique Echeverria. There will be no caskets on display at the four funerals.

Seven of the exterior assigned Seals were also killed by the C-4 explosion. Their bodies will be displayed in sealed caskets at seven individual military funerals. The three survivors sustained permanent injuries. None of the three will ever again serve on military active duty.

Commander Charlie Owens assembled an EOD ('Explosive Ordnance Demolition') investigating team, perimeter defense personnel, medical dispensary personnel and Shore Patrol personnel; all of whom were transported by the Hamilton's helicopter the two miles from the ship's anchored position to the site of the C-4 detonation, now nothing more than a bare concrete slab.

Lieutenant Commander (O-4) Wilbur Sheridan, the Hamilton's XO (Executive Officer - 2nd in command) supervised the blast scene investigation.

"Wilbur, what the hell happened?" asked Commander Owens.

"We don't know yet, Skipper. The only evidence we have is 11 dead and three critically wounded Seals, along with a bare ass foundation of what used to be a Bahamian cottage, plus a digital voice recording of all transmissions of our crew from commencement of assault on the dwelling until the detonation, then nothing more."

"Absolutely nothing except for one thing; surviving the explosion was a piece of metal, apparently a home safe, for money and important papers. Although mangled, the safe is intact. We handed it over to higher qualified EOD personnel for opening."

"I didn't hear you mention body parts, Wilbur."

"There were none, Skipper; none as relates to our four Seals inside the bungalow at the time of C-4 detonation."

"No smears, no bits and pieces?"

"There were smears, but no bits and pieces. We used swabs and bottles to collect the smears, perhaps 200 or so, nothing more."

"Any sign of a perpetrator?"

"None, post detonation. Pre-detonation we have telephone transmissions and indications of internal dwelling activity, both detected by our sensors, along with a pre-detonation voice transmission in Arabic to the tune of Allah Akbar, four times."

"Damn, if that's all we have, that's all we have. Headquarters requires a full report, yesterday. You know how they are, demanding instant access to data and evidence when politically oriented assignments go sour. Heads will roll on this one. Be sure to address the issue of whether or not a perp was on premises at the time of our attack. Argue both possibilities, yea and nay."

"Yes, sir. It's 9:00 am. I'll get my final report to you by 11:00, Skipper."

*

"Stony, our moles tell us the feds sustained 11 dead and three seriously wounded last week during an abortive assault on a private home in the Bahamas. I hear tell Enrique Echeverria turned suicide bomber and took a lot of Seals along with him."

"Could be, boss. Yesterday our bank exchanged 250 million US dollars for equivalent funds in Euros, Canadian dollars and Swiss francs. We have no US dollar exposure."

"Good," replied Jet.

40
FINAL PREPARATION
Estill & General Thompson

"Estill, today is April 1st. It's ironic to engage in a 'Fresh Start' dress rehearsal on April Fools' Day. Be that as it may, I evaluated your documents. As usual they are as close to perfection as possible. I don't have any questions. Hopefully our troops can decipher your hieroglyphics."

"Yes, hopefully." Estill knows Jet well. He is pleased with a complement most others would interpret as criticism. He beamed with delight.

"Your command post is in the St. Louis area, Clayton, Missouri. As I told you, our lone remaining commanding general is Tommy Thompson, retired and living in Hamilton, Ohio, a suburb of Cincinnati. He is due to set up military housekeeping at Fort Bragg, North Carolina, the Army's Special Operations Center and Airborne Center. His personal travel and the relocation of 10,000 of his militia troops has been coordinated. My command post is in the Fort Knox vicinity."

Estill smiled. He knows Jet is anxious to audit the federal gold repository at Fort Knox, Kentucky.

Jet continued, "Two nuclear weapons, small atomic bombs in the

20–40 Megaton range, are postured and awaiting detonation fusing. For redundancy purposes, a second weapon is located near downtown Washington DC; a third weapon is postured on the outskirts of Fort Bragg. Weapon four is in reserve at a warehouse in Dayton, Ohio."

"Although our A-bombs are Stone Age equivalents in comparison to contemporary nuclear weapons, nevertheless the Pakistani produced plutonium atomic weapons are suitable for our intended purpose, the destruction of Washington, DC. We are not employing hydrogen bombs. We are employing small atomic bombs."

"Estill, our final radio check is scheduled for 9:00 am EST on Sunday, April 4, 2021. That's 8:00 am your time. How is your old friend, General Henry "Speedy" Oswald doing? You know, the Army Adjutant General from South Carolina. I may need him."

"I haven't talked to Speedy for some time, but he is standing by to help us any way he can. Are you sure about him?"

"We need him, Estill. Alert him. Let him know."

"Will do, Jet."

On April 4, 2021 @ 9:00 am EST, T-Day eve (Armageddon Tomorrow) Jet said, "Bird Dog, commo check."

"Panther, Loud and Clear, Bird Dog," replied Estill Barnes.

"Bimbo, Loud and Clear, Bird Dog," said General Tommy Thompson.

"Bird Dog, out," said Jet as he terminated telephone contact with Estill and General Thompson, the two men absolutely essential to the success of his revolt.

*

It was a short drive south along the Niagara River from Niagara on the Lake, Ontario to Niagara Falls, Ontario. Lounging high above horseshoe falls in the Hilton Hotel, Natalie said, "Stony, our visit with your parents was great. I regret we had only one day and a night's layover, but it was well worth the trip. What time is tomorrow's flight home?"

"Air-time an hour and change, 350 miles. Arrive at the airport at 7:30 am; take-off at 9:30 am and land at Washington Dulles International Airport at 10:45 am, via WestJet, the Southwest Airlines of Canada, my love."

"The view of Niagara Falls is so beautiful from up here," said Natalie as she enchantedly observed river mist rising from the Niagara River in wave after mesmerizing wave. No *wonder this is the favorite honeymoon destination of North America. That reminds me:*

"Stony, for sure, we must honeymoon in Niagara Falls, Canada side. This is the most beautiful place I have ever been in my life. Only three more months. I love this place. I love you, Stony. I love you so much."

Stony basked.

Natalie is three months pregnant. Two and only two men are the possible father, Stony Randolph and Jethro Armstrong, deceased. OB/GYN physicians tell Natalie that although it is physically possible to determine paternity identification pre-delivery, there is some risk considering Natalie's uterus is irregular to an extent that invasion by any means is not advisable unless absolutely necessary.

Natalie decided to forgo the paternity ID test, and have the baby; not to abort. The chance Natalie's unborn child belongs to Stony is 50/50. Delivery - early October, 2021.

*

Jet considered relocating Helen and Amanda to the farm but decided against it. The four sisters would not appreciate young intruders who have not paid their dues. The new girls do not have the benefit of two full years of internship in Bermuda. Helen confirmed her pregnancy to Jet. He was pleased. Amanda bombed out. Jet was either shooting blanks or the 87% rhythm method failed this time around.

I'm relieved Stony was able to convince Natalie to spend a couple of days in the Niagara Falls area. There is a problem with his availability on and after T-Day, but we can handle that.

41
T-DAY
April 5, 2021, 10:00 am

A WestJet Airlines Boeing 737 headed for Dulles International Airport took off from Toronto Pearson International Airport at 9:30 am with Stony and Natalie on board.

*

In a rare turn of events, Wilson Patterson is in possession of internal leak information (not signals intelligence) from an NSA operative in Bermuda, which suggests William Pennington is associated in some way with Enrique Echeverria and that her fiancé, William Stone Randolph, is associated in some way with William Pennington.

"Wilson Patterson here calling Director Natalie Taylor."

Dina Watters answered the 9:40 am telephone call, "Mr. Patterson, she is expected to arrive at her office before noon. I will have her return your call."

"Thank you, Dina. As calls go, this one is quite important."

"I won't let her forget, Mr. Patterson."

*

At 9:45 am, Mitch Donahue met Tom Redding at the McDonald's restaurant at 911 "E" Street NW, Washington DC.

"What do you have for me, Mitch?"

"Something big, perhaps very big, Tom. Natalie Taylor's fiancé is a Canadian green card holder named Frederick Stone Randolph. He has a façade address in Savannah, Georgia. He is never there. He lives and works in Bermuda."

"Natalie's father, James Edward Taylor, lives and works in Bermuda also. There is no record of a James Edward Taylor, as such, living in Bermuda. He is using an alias. James Taylor's alias in Bermuda is apparently William Pennington, which William Pennington is undisclosed CEO of the largest charity in the world."

"I am not much into coincidences. Someway, somehow James Edward Taylor and Frederick Stone Randolph are associated. I don't yet have a connection or an association of Natalie Taylor with the business activities of either James Taylor or Frederick Randolph, but I'm busy working on it."

"Great, Mitch, great. Stay with it. I have an appointment so I have to cut our visit short. Damn fine work, Mitch," said Tom Redding as he left the coffee tab on the table for Mitch to cover.

This development is bizarre, quite strange and unusual thought Tom as he opened the door to his new Cadillac at 10:00 am. He did not make it to the first stop light.

*

Nikita Khrushchev had it half right when he said 'We do not have to invade the United States, we will destroy you from within.' The Russians did not destroy America from within. America commenced literal destruction of itself from within on April 5, 2021, when Jet annihilated Washington, DC with an atomic weapon at 10:00 am EST.

Washington, DC metropolitan area population on T-day was slightly more than 6,500,000. City population was approximately 680,000. The Pakistani atomic bomb which exploded at ground level in downtown Washington, DC killed upwards of 1,500,000 victims. Another 500,000 more died within a week. Yet another 1,000,000 casualties sustained permanent injuries associated with shock, burns and radiation, ranging from moderate to severe. Additionally, 1,000,000 residents sustained minor injuries. Summing up, over 4,000,000 casualties.

Among the decedents were the President, Vice President, Speaker of the House, president pro tem of the Senate, 92 senators, 412 representatives, all nine Supreme Court justices and the five four-star generals and admirals assigned to the joint staff.

Two individuals in the presidential line of succession survived, the Secretary of Labor and the Secretary of Transportation. Both men were absent from the capital on business. All other cabinet members died in the atomic blast.

Secretary of Labor Wayne Ganley was sworn in as president of the United States at 10:15 am CST on April 5, 2021 in Minneapolis, Minnesota by Judge Sam Williston.

President Ganley declared Martial law at 11:20 am CST. Pursuant to a declaration of martial law, General Thomas Thompson was appointed commanding general of all United States military personnel. His first act was to order three nuclear missile attacks, on Iran, North Korea and Pakistan. Within five hours Tehran, Pyongyang, and Islamabad were attacked by state-of-the-art, ICBM delivered atomic weapons. The three cities were destroyed and rendered uninhabitable for years to come.

Nuclear capable nations were timely informed of the three attacks and were advised that no further nuclear attacks are to be conducted by the United States of America; further that the United States of America will defend itself and its allies in an appropriate manner in the event of attack against the United States or its allies by a nuclear capable nation.

*

The WestJet Boeing 737 carrying Stony and Natalie was overhead

Boston when all airborne aircraft in the United States were ordered to land at the nearest available airfield as a result of 'an enemy attack upon the United States of America.' The 737 diverted to and landed at Boston Logan International Airport.

Cell phone usage was not authorized on the aircraft. After the pair deplaned at the arrival gate, Natalie called her office. No answer, diverted to voice mail. She experienced the same result on six different follow-up Washington, DC telephone calls to separate government offices. Dread and understanding replaced fear.

"FBI," replied the telephonic Boston area FBI robot.

Natalie repeatedly dialed zero. On depression number eleven, a live administrative assistant answered, "How may I direct your call?"

Natalie said," This is Natalie Taylor, the assistant director of the FBI. Please put your senior agent on the line."

"Yes, ma'am."

Fifteen seconds later Timothy O'Neill answered, "Ms. Taylor, Tim O'Neill here. How may I be of assistance?"

"What the hell is happening, Tim? I just landed at Logan airport and don't have a clue. Nobody in DC is answering their phones."

"DC does not exist anymore, Director Taylor. We have it on good authority that a terrorist atomic weapon destroyed the city."

Natalie calmly replied, "I see. After a ten second delay, Natalie said, "Tim, I am now in charge of the FBI. I will arrive at your office via taxi within twenty minutes. Prepare a private office for my use. Assign one assistant to the office, do you understand?"

"Yes, ma'am."

"Can you handle that?"

"Yes, ma'am."

Natalie closed the cell phone call. "Stony, you're on your own. Sorry. I'm needed at work. Apparently, Washington, DC has been obliterated, probably by Islamic terrorists."

Stony was amazed. Natalie responded to the loss of her capitol city and presumed millions of casualties, as if a physician had just diagnosed her with common cold complications. This one has her emotions completely under control. *Damn, I have never seen anything like Natalie's reaction to disaster. Amazing.*

*

Jet, Estill and Tommy Thompson implemented T-Day scheduled activities. All civilian and military medical facilities within 750 miles of Washington, DC provided emergency first aid and medical care to surviving nuclear casualties. Washington, DC was quarantined from ground zero outwards to a circumference established by a 25 mile radius, an area of approximately 2000 square miles. The only personnel allowed in the area of quarantine were medical personnel protected by radiation resistant attire.

Additionally:

1. All banks in America were closed for one week. ATM - $400 limit/day;

2. All TV and radio stations were shut down, emergency transmissions only;

3. All aircraft were grounded until further notice;

4. 8:00 pm curfew was established in all cities and towns;

5. Military was placed on full alert; all leaves canceled;

6. IRS was closed;

7. All Islamic Mosques were seized and closed;

8. All Islamic Imams were arrested and taken into custody;

9. No foreigners were authorized to enter America until further notice. The only exception was for current green card holders.

10. The US renounced UN membership & closed all UN facilities in New York.

*

With 'Fresh Start' underway, Jet has 2,000,000 deaths and 4,000,000 casualties on his conscience, a psychological collateral problem.

When the theoretical health, safety and welfare of a country's future billions of citizens in perpetuity is measured against the value of the lives of 4% of that country's population, a secular pragmatist has little if any difficulty in opting for the greatest good for the greatest number of persons living now and certain to be alive in the future.

Liberals will bust a gut to save one useless life while exposing an entire nation to certain severe risk of harm in perpetuity. For Jet, the problem is simple; if we do nothing, take no action, an important city, perhaps New York City, is guaranteed to be destroyed by an Islamist atomic weapon attack within less than five years; as early as tomorrow, so far as we know.

Due to fiscal insanity, the USA is certain to deteriorate and die in the long run, day by day, sooner rather than later. Over time the Grim Reaper is certain to obliterate and destroy arguably the greatest nation in the history of the world. He will systematically mow down the American population, young and old, rich and poor, healthy and sick, essentially every man, woman and child. The few survivors, all physically and mentally maimed, will exist dismally in squalor the likes of which has never before been confronted by any inhabitant of North America.

Such event will never happen on Jet's watch. For that reason, among others, all of Washington, DC is now an expanded Arlington National Cemetery.

*

Stay tuned for "Epiphany," Book Two of the 'Fresh Start' series, the beginning of American life under Jet's benevolent dictatorship, to be published in the spring of 2018.

www.ingramcontent.com/pod-product-compliance
Lightning Source LLC
Chambersburg PA
CBHW021946170626
46808CB00001B/41